The Swan Knights

STEFAN SCHEUERMANN

"The Swan Knights," by Stefan Scheuermann.

ISBN 978-1-947532-02-1 (softcover); 978-1-947532-03-8 (hardcover); 978-1-947532-04-5 (eBook).

Published 2018 by Virtualbookworm.com Publishing Inc., P.O. Box 9949, College Station, TX 77842, US. ©2018, Stefan Scheuermann.

TABLE OF CONTENTS

Centerfold of Rudolf's Map

Prologue

THE FOLLOWING PAGES are the narrative of Verena Elisabeth Kessler, looking back from adulthood to her adolescence, recalling and documenting the events that stitched her to an ancient enterprise and the legendary figures who shared it with her. The story begins in 2005, when Verena is eleven years old and entering a new school in the sixth grade. She lives in Centennial, Colorado, in the U.S.A., a growing, middle-class suburb of Denver.

Verena's father is of German heritage. His family came to America from Bavaria into the port of New Orleans, Louisiana in 1848. They settled into the German section of New Orleans, called "Little Saxony". In the German section of the city, it was easy to maintain the culture and language. As the five generations between the immigrants and Verena's father passed, the Kessler family clung to their German-ness as much as they could, memorizing the family tree, passing forward the stories, the recipes, and the language. As expected, a slow and subtle dilution occurred. By the time Verena's father moved to Colorado with his parents, in 1984, more German pride than German culture remained. But they still spoke the language — and the language was their greatest source of pride. They spoke and they studied.

1

They read and they spoke. Their German was exquisite. Verena's father passed the language painstakingly to his children, often force-feeding them when their appetite for study was not there.

Verena's father diligently investigated his geneology. He wanted a complete family tree to be his legacy, his gift to his descendants. He succeeded in passing the line of men, the line that carried the Kessler name, all the way back to the 1560s. But the women of the family were harder to track. It is from their side of the family that a very special strain of German blood ran through the generations since before they came to America. It is this strain of blood that seized Verena's destiny and made her life extraordinary — the product of some long forgotten marriage, in some obscure Bavarian town, between a Kessler man and a woman with no idea of the sacred magic inside of her.

CHAPTER 1

Dawn of an Obsession

ON THE FIRST DAY, we had to choose our names. Every student of first year German chose a German name. That was the name they would use in class for the whole year. It was meant to create an authentic, foreign immersion atmosphere, to make us feel like we were in Germany, which it eventually did to a mild degree, after the weeks of chaos while students forgot their chosen names or changed them each time they came to class. Most of the students looked forward to this ritual, their eyes tasting each morsel on the a la carte menu of German names printed and handed out to each of us. I used the list of names differently. I eyed the list for names of my relatives and ancestors from the expansive family tree that I had set to memory as soon as I learned to read.

I didn't need to choose a German name. I already had one. I had been answering to "Verena Beth" my whole life and saw no good reason to change that now. My name *was* on the list. One girl in my class tried to choose it as her class name — until I evil-eyed her into a change of mind. I think the students liked choosing a new name because it allowed them to escape themselves, to take on a new identity. I had no need or desire to do so. As the class took on their German identities and began to learn the language and culture, I felt like a host, welcoming them to my world.

Now, I am only about half German, but I grew up speaking the language with my father. He spoke it with his parents. It served not only as a point of bonding, but also as a code for secrets we wished to speak out loud. My parents pressed the school to allow me to skip sixth-grade German and begin in German III with the eighth-graders. They were denied, so I drudged through the first year, counting to ten, writing the days of the week and the months of the year, and drilling the conjugations of the basic verbs. I took solace in knowing that I was good for Herr Fischer's sanity. Herr Fischer, the school's only German teacher, was a young man, maybe twenty-six or twenty-seven. He was much older in sensibilities than in years. He was an American of German descent, much like me. He was the philosophical type, and an old soul. I can easily imagine him as a young boy, hidden away in some dusty corner of his public library, reading old, yellowed pages of German poetry.

Herr Fischer loved the German language. He tried to dispel the stereotypes and teach the beauty of German by passionately reading passages from Goethe and Schiller. As he read the words, his face grew blissful, as if he had stepped outside and savored the sweetest spring air in a long and thoughtful inhale. He also betrayed his irritation — with wincing of the eyes and twitching of the mouth — each time a student made fun of the language by reciting the spoken assignments with forced and exaggerated hacking in the throat, or by simply putting "Das" in front of an English word. I tried to soothe his irritation by researching elegant passages on my own, setting them to memory, and reciting them when they seemed most needed. He clearly shared my frustration with the repetitive drilling of the most rudimentary building blocks of the language. From time to time, he would erupt in a blast of conversation aimed directly at me. We fed each other's excitement as I answered with an equal and obvious fervor. We lived in Centennial, Colorado. It was not a hub of international travel. Opportunities to converse in a foreign language were scarce, especially for an eleven-year-old girl.

My father was so excited that I was finally taking German in school, he often forgot that I learned nothing from the given assignments and was only improving my German through the brief, passing conversations and in-class quips I shared with Herr Fischer. But even those were enough to expand my well of expressions and my father delighted in my use of them at home. He started cooking our favorite German dishes more often and playing his old German records almost daily. We found ourselves more often repeating those same dreamy talks of a visit to Germany. None in our family had returned since the original immigration in 1848. My father swore we would be the first. He talked endlessly about how we would hold hands and walk down the same streets our ancestors had walked. My little brother was still too young to be affected by such dreamy, sentimental talk, but Karl was learning the language too and I was dubbed an official steward to his education.

As German became a point of bonding between my brother and me, I gained a slight glimpse into my father's heart, being reminded so often with flashing memories of when I was that age and my father taught me. My experiences in sixth grade German prepared me well to preside over my little lessons with Karl. The lessons increased my pity for Herr Fischer, as I realized how much more difficult was his job. Not only was Karl's

German more advanced than that of my classmates, his seven-year-old brain was not filled with the hormone storm of a middle-school student. His German progressed nicely and I took great pride in my contribution.

I became increasingly interested in German culture and history. There was an inexplicable draw, deep in my gut, toward all things German. Although I was taking class in school, teaching my brother, and subjected constantly to my father's extreme and almost ridiculous pride in his heritage, the pull at my heart seemed to be coming through all of that, not from it. It felt disconnected from anything near me. The source of the draw was distant and foreign. My obsession felt higher and more ancient than the sometimes clownish parade of diluted German culture on display at home, a display of culture that felt sickeningly unauthentic, leaving me hungrier, not more satisfied, after its consumption. Unable to express or even understand the phenomenon, I continued to grasp at what *was* within my reach.

In the second semester, the school celebrated "Multi-Cultural Week". The different foreign language classes were assigned different facets of culture to highlight and share with the school, from music and dance, to art, history, and food. My class was chosen to prepare and present German food. I hoped that a full embrace of this assignment would help satiate the bizarre and sometimes aching, inexplicably German pull at my soul. With my parents' help, I prepared soft pretzels and sample strips of Wiener schnitzel with onions. I printed up fake menus with instructions on how to place an order in German. Students and teachers from across the school took their best stab at ordering schnitzel and pretzels in German. I had a wonderful time and my preparations and performance were lauded by faculty and students alike. At the end of the day, once I was home, sitting at my bedroom desk, the high feelings of the day turned rapidly rancid, and the thirst for an authentic experience of Germany seized me by the throat.

As the year progressed, this sensation continued to grow stronger. It seemed connected to the past somehow. I taught myself to read the old German script and old German penmanship. I scoured the internet for examples of handwritten correspondence from the giants of German literary history. I bought old books. The more I read, the more I desired to read, like an itch that grows in intensity the more you scratch it. I began to sense that the direction of my studies was not guided by me, but by some phantom tutor leading me along to a destination that only he knew. My fascination began to focus on the time surrounding German unification in 1871. I sailed through the rest of German I, fantasizing about what delicious challenges that German II & III might give. Toward the end of the school year, rumors sprang up about the initiation of an annual eighth-grade trip to Germany. This ignited my imagination with scenarios and images that would steal my consciousness during every mundane moment of the summer after sixth grade.

I fantasized about everything from casual conversations with passers-by to slipping away from my class and backpacking around Germany. The legalities and logistics of the latter were no concern of mine. After all, these were just wild fantasies. My studies that summer fueled my imagination, which in turn gave fervor to my studies. My father couldn't have been more delighted with me. But he didn't know how unsatisfying this imported culture and long distance study was for me, or how it suffocated me despite my desperate desire to consume it. As the summer progressed and I followed the dictates of my phantom tutor, researching and studying incessantly, I began to sense that some revelation was near at hand. But the summer ended and my free hours were ravaged by the mandates of a new school year's schedule. My private studies fell off and I was too distracted with the chaos of life to really mourn it. Still, somewhere in the back of my mind, tapping gently with one finger on the inside of my skull, was the thought of my eighth-grade trip to Germany. And in that little chamber of my brain, new fantasies were being born and new adventures being played out.

Seventh-grade German began slower and well behind the end of sixth-grade German. Being young and immature, I didn't realize that this was a temporary condition, and my frustration was boldly expressed at home and only thinly veiled in class. But the lessons quickly began to progress and short, simple conversations broke up the monotony of conjugation drills. By October, the hushed rumors of an eighth-grade trip became open and loud discussions. No word of corroboration had come from the school, but Herr Fischer entertained the occasional tangent from the lesson plan of the day to muse as a group over the possibilities. The class was giddy with the notion. But I was not giddy. By this point, the idea of it — the necessity of it was rooted so deeply to my soul that the conversations did not elicit lightness of mood but awakened a desperation that had just begun to soundly hibernate inside of me.

By the middle of seventh grade, a few of my more apt classmates had brought their German along nicely. The girl I evil-eyed for trying to steal my identity became one of my good friends and an excellent release valve for the German conversations that were building up inside of my mouth. She had taken the name "Birgit". Sadly comical, I knew her only as "Birgit" until months into our friendship, when I called her house and had to ask for her by name.

I asked her mother, "Is Bir, Birg … Is your daughter home?" Even after learning her real name was Hope, I continued to call her Birgit, and she embraced the name as her own.

Birgit's locker was eleven lockers from mine. When the halls were crowded and bustling, and locker doors were opening and slamming shut, she thrilled in shouting to me in German across the many ears between us, or leaving notes for me on my locker, for all to see. I think she was drawn by the earnestness of my connection to the language. There was a stark and obvious contrast between the frivolity with which the other students — even the good ones — approached their study and use of German, and the rooted necessity of mine. Their German, like their chosen names for class, were put on and taken off like a sweater. Mine was sewn to my very flesh. I believe that Birgit found such a focused devotion alluring. I also believe that she picked up on the underlying hunger that usually hid itself effectively beneath my smile. I have come to recognize that hunger in others, peeking out from the soul, shyly and stealthily through the depth of the eyes.

So gripping was Birgit's growing fascination with Germany, and her affection for me, that she began to wear boldly that which was the primary chord of connection between us. In March of seventh grade, she celebrated her birthday at our town's only German restaurant. She didn't want an encore of the light and frivolous "German-ness" of class. So she only invited my family, assuming that we all shared the same intensity. That thought was shattered when my father wore his "Made in America with German Parts" t-shirt. The authenticity that our imaginations tried to construct in that quaint little German restaurant fell to dust with each glance at my father's touristy t-shirt. That XL cotton piece of counterfeit culture was endearing on him, but forbade us from maintaining our suspended disbelief.

Dad made up for it though, by injecting many interesting historical and cultural facts into the experiences of the night. He also spoke strictly in German when the waiter was at the table, and delighted the birthday girl by directing a few comical comments in her direction in what he knew would be simple enough German for her to understand. Looking back, I am proud of my father's behavior that evening. He was always a unique blend of the admirable and the ridiculous. I grow melancholy as I write this, missing him and knowing how he would have loved to share my many experiences since I was pulled away. But that is a much later part of this story.

In April, the school announced the initiation of the annual eighth-grade foreign language immersion trip to take place the following spring. My class was to inaugurate the program. Permission slips went out for the next year's trip to Germany for all eighth-grade German students. As this long-time dream materialized before my eyes, I felt as if every wish I had ever made was granted simultaneously. I half expected to be able to open the classroom window and fly across the ocean on my own. Never had human civilization known such a sacred document as that permission form. I refused to fold it or put it in my backpack. I carried it home with the care and reverence of an ancient and historical piece of precious parchment. I shed a few tears between the school and my house — and I didn't care who noticed. I was going to Germany. I gave no thought of ever coming back. In fact, I felt at the time a rather prophetic permanence concerning the trip. I knew it was only a visit, but it felt as if I was moving there. I didn't know yet that I would never return home, but my heart prognosticated the finality of the voyage in its refusal to envision a conclusion in its dreamy fantasies.

My parents were expectedly excited for me. But a distinct jealousy oozed through my father's pores. It's not that he wanted to go instead of me. He wanted to go with me. He held tightly to our shared dream of tracing the steps of our ancestors together. He was elated that I was going to Germany. But he had to mourn the death of a fantasy he had nursed and developed for many years. Certainly, we could still make that trip someday, but we would not be sharing our first visit to Germany together. Dad was never good at veiling his emotions, try as he did to put on a happy face for my sake.

My mother had the point of a pen on the permission form, about to apply her signature, when my father stopped her. He insisted upon signing it. My mother yielded it to him with the grin of a parent who sees more than what appears to the eye. My father had never placed his signature so fastidiously, as if he was etching it to a document to be revered by posterity. The next morning, I carried the form and attached deposit check back to school with me.

As I entered the school grounds, I looked at hands. I looked for permission forms with attached checks. Who would be branded to my memory as permanent figures in this masterpiece experience? Birgit stood outside of the front door to the school, both hands behind her back and rocking from heel to toe. I did not need to see the paper she held behind her. Her smirk revealed all. Her excitement fought to break through her attempt to wear a solemn face. The plan she had hatched and rehearsed early that morning, to try to convince me that she could not go, only to reveal the permission form and scream "Wir reisen zusammen", was foiled by the facial convulsions that punched and kicked their way from her heart to her skin. The plan was scrapped and replaced with a ritualistic-looking dance we broke into together. To the lookers-on, it must have seemed choreographed, with mirrored steps and the sudden eruption of a chant performed in perfect unison.

German class bore a distinctly different aroma for the last six weeks of the school year. The posters that were meant to make us feel like we were in Germany, the fake names, the poor grammar and pronunciation of my classmates, even the childish exaggerated accents of the circle of obnoxious boys in the corner ceased to agitate me. It was all beautiful to me now. I think back with a slight degree of mortification at how silly Birgit and I acted together. For the rest of the school year, we must have appeared intoxicated, especially in German class. But when I got home, my silliness morphed into intensely fervent study. I tried to imagine everything that could possibly be said to me while I was in Germany. I wanted to have a flawless, however canned, response. I walked my imagination from the first blink of my opening eyes in the morning, through the fall into nightly sleep, scripting and rehearsing every possible encounter. Again prophetically, my imagination failed to include Birgit in its musings, a fact that did not strike me until pondering it years later. The scenes in my head were a conversation between me and the phantom tutor that loomed in varying degrees of prominence over every moment of my life, haunting me in alternating cycles of twisting, pinching pain and cradled nurturing.

A great deal of attention, conversation, and money were poured into the preparations for my trip. It dominated all other household concerns. My parents bought every tour book, devise, article of clothing, and everything else they thought I might need. They even bought things for Birgit that they thought might not be provided by her parents. These preparations began the day I returned the permission form. When seventh grade came to an end, for the first time I found myself wishing away the summer. To help me survive it, I made a chart of daily duties, studies, and preparations. Almost every word I exchanged with my father that summer was in German. As he gradually resigned himself to my going without him, his excitement grew to match mine.

That summer, I had Birgit over several times. Each was a plunge into my father's earnestly intended, endearing, but grossly unauthentic attempts to provide a real German experience in the home. One evening, when Birgit was visiting, my father had his old German music playing during dinner. Once we cleared the table, and the old, scratchy record ended, I played some more current German music. My father loved it, but I had to translate some of the slang expressions in the lyrics. He took them to heart and set them to memory. He danced giddily to my music and forced the use his new vocabulary whenever the opportunity arose. I often think of my father, but never so tenderly as when I recall that evening. He was so silly, so alive, so … my father. I miss him terribly.

I realize that I have written little about my mother. That is not because we weren't close. But Mom took care of the mundane — the logistics of life, and Dad was the dreamer. She was earth and he was sky. The time of my life relayed in these pages relate more to the sky. My memories of it are dreamy and surreal. That and the obvious German connection with my father draws him more intimately into this narrative. But my mother was wonderfully supportive through all of this. And my dreams would have had no logistical foundation without her diligence. I often think of her too. I think of my father when I want him. I think of my mother when I need her. And I need her often.

The aching draw in my gut that had me firmly in its grip since sixth grade intensified as summer drew to a close and eighth grade approached. Only, it had become more lifting than pulling. By German III, the students who had made it to that level were serious and by that point impressively proficient. Most of them were unable to go on the trip, so we tried not to occupy much class time with the topic. Class consisted mostly of selected readings, conversations (scripted and unscripted), cultural lessons, and history. I loved it all, but while the others lightened me, German history gripped me. As each era was covered, I tried to imagine my ancestors reacting to the events we studied. What was daily life like for a girl my age? I applied such ponderings across each of the eras and events.

We dedicated a week to a quick review of Bavarian history. This interested me because I knew my family came from Bavaria. When Herr Fischer began to speak of the Wittelsbach Dynasty, the Bavarian royal family until 1918, I caught myself holding my breath unintentionally. When he mentioned King Ludwig II, I believe my heart jumped. I could not understand my emotional and physical response to the subject, to a king who lived so long ago. But an addiction was formed, one that could not be satiated. Study of Ludwig II and his magnificent castles consumed my thoughts and time, often at the cost of my other studies and activities. Each book, each documentary, seemed to apply weight to my rib cage, restricting my breath, yet I continued to pile it on myself as quickly as I could.

"Crazy King Ludwig" they called him, declared insane and stripped of his throne in 1886, found dead the next day in Lake Starnberg (then called the Würmsee in German) with his psychiatrist — Ludwig, the builder of magnificent castles, who sank himself into the romanticism of ancient Germanic lore. His death, and most of his life, has remained a mystery to the world. My fascination with Ludwig II was not only intense and inexplicable. It was spiritual and Providential — and remained just out of my reach to grasp, like scooting something with your outstretched fingertips, unable to pull it toward you. I wanted to grab this phenomenon with both hands and consume it directly to my hungry heart. But all I did was scoot it around with the fingertips of my mind.

I felt such a connection to Ludwig that I was caught on occasion staring at images of the king, locked and utterly fixated on him, unaware of the world around me. I was pulled in by those dark and mysterious eyes. I felt that they were trying to communicate with me. Several times, while staring at them, my eyes darted from his eyes to his lips, as I swear I saw them slightly part, as if wanting to whisper something to me. These experiences always cudgeled me in the chest, jolting my heart, seizing my breath and leaving me with a haunting but intoxicating sense of dread. The dread gave way to an irresistible level of curiosity, drawing me persistently back to his photographs and paintings. I gazed fixedly at his face, shifting from his eyes to his lips, hoping, begging him to communicate with me. My entreaties apparently leapt from my mind to my mouth. On a few occasions, I had to create some explanation for talking to a photograph of a long-dead king. These momentary embarrassments did not long detour my attempts to see beyond the photographs. I would quickly dive back into the world of Ludwig. When I stared at his eyes, I thought his lips moved. When I stared at his lips, I thought his eyes moved, creating frantic and frustrating tail-chasing sessions that often ended with a scream and a headache.

CHAPTER 2
A Personal Invitation

ONE DAY, Herr Fischer brought in a poster-sized image of Ludwig. He began a biographical lecture, but after the first several words, his voice faded into a swirling, windy sound. I stared at Ludwig's eyes until I thought I saw his mouth move. I snapped my gaze to his lips. They continued to move! Herr Fischer's voice and the sounds of the room faded until they disappeared beneath a slow and low whispering that correlated to the moving lips on Ludwig's image. The whispering was at a volume between what I could hear and what I could understand. I stood from my chair and walked slowly toward the portrait. I was terrified! I finally had before me what I had so desperately sought, and it frightened me out of my own breath. Waves of chills started small at the center of my chest, and grew into violent shakes at my extremities. Still, I continued to walk toward the image. The lips continued to move and the sound of whispering continued to sail at me in pulsating cycles, growing louder and quieter, building and crashing like waves on a beach.

I continued to walk toward it until I stood inches from the image. I remember asking the image a question, though I don't remember what I asked. The sharp lines of the portrait began to wobble. I felt as if Ludwig was about to reach out and touch me. I could not tear my cemented eyes from the lips that continued the subtle movements of a whisper. The image grew fuzzy and distorted. Then the room grew darker until completely black. I awoke on my back with Herr Fischer and a few students huddled over me. I awoke with the memory of a dream that was vivid and colorful in my mind then, but has since evaporated into obscurity. I have spent many hours trying to lasso that dream and pull it within view of my memory. I wonder now what my classmates thought of my behavior as I stood shaking and gasping, right against the portrait of Ludwig, until dropping flat on my back. Clearly nobody else experienced any of what I went through, not the movement of Ludwig's lips, nor the low whisper from the photograph. Once back on my feet, I momentarily considered that it must have been some hallucination brought on by my sleep deprivation or low blood sugar, coupled with my recent obsession. I quickly ejected the notion for one far more romantic. Ludwig had something to say to me and I would somehow, someday discover what it was.

The incident with the poster quickly passed from the minds of my classmates, peculiar as my behavior seemed to them — all except Birgit. Herr Fischer apparently was not overly surprised by the spectacle. He viewed it simply as an extreme eccentricity, not entirely incongruent with what he had witnessed in me for two years. Birgit found the experience hauntingly intriguing. It got under her skin and itched and irritated. She was half-delighted, half-disturbed. For days, she tried to bring up the topic gently, laying it just beneath the surface of more casual and mundane comments. I knew what she was asking. I pitied her discomfort, as she skirted around the subject, never flatly addressing it. I would have loved to rescue her from her agitation, but I frankly did not know how to explain what had happened to me. If I told her the truth exactly as I saw it, it would sound insane. If I diluted it to an explanation more easily consumed, it would be dishonest — and I would not be dishonest. So, I ignored her daily (sometimes hourly) struggles to gently introduce the subject. I needed more answers, more research, more experiences with this phenomenon. I needed to grasp it more firmly before I dared try to explain it. At least from Birgit's perspective that day, it must have born a distinct air of the mystical to have seized her so zealously. Her reaction strengthened my faith in my own mystical interpretation. To her, this was not some outburst of eccentricity. Something profound happened to me that day. Birgit witnessed that from her seat across the room. And it haunted her almost as much as it haunted me.

Despite my self-assurance that she saw something arcane, something unearthly in my experience with the image of Ludwig, and despite my confidence that sharing it with her could do me good, my uneasiness in discussing it kept a relentless hold of me. Every time I tried to slip through its fingers, it squeezed me harder, almost taking my breath. The experience was so intensely personal, so internal, so completely my own that translating it accurately into the common paradigm of my classmates, friends, teachers, or even my family seemed utterly futile. So I kept it under my skin, where it filled every inch of me and seasoned with its flavor every thought that entered my head.

Few details about the class trip had reached our starving ears. We did not yet know where in Germany we would be going or what sort of activities would be planned for us. All of my fantasies had put us in Bavaria, studying history and visiting historical sights. It hadn't occurred to me that we would see any of the many other wonders of Germany. One morning, just a few minutes before my alarm was to wake me, I arose with a start, with the notion of traveling to Germany and not being able to pursue my obsession. I tried to reconcile myself to the idea. The realization that our schedule on this trip would be strictly regimented, not at all allowing the pursuit of independent fancies, no matter how academic in nature, shook me awake with violence. I got out of bed desperate for details of the trip. Each school day that passed without word lacerated my spirits.

October came with no word on the trip — no word of any kind. This began to worry my parents. They contacted the school. They were told that a parent meeting would be held on Friday evening of the following week for an important update. "At last", I thought. I would finally know where we were going and what we would be doing. I resolved not to fantasize about the trip until after the meeting. It was the most trying test of my self-control. But I trusted in the profound sense of destiny planted inside of me by my expeience with the portrait. Every time I closed my eyes, I saw Ludwig's lips moving. I saw the expressiveness of his eyes. During my tired, weakened hours, when my mind wandered without my control, I indulged its fancies and bent my fading, half-conscious thoughts around the poster of Ludwig. It was only in this state that my memory of the experience regained full clarity, in this state that I tried to read the moving lips and interpret Ludwig's low whisper.

As the reasonable and the fanciful competed in their tug-of-war with my mind, I swayed dramatically between belief and disbelief. In my lucid and logical state, I pondered the academic value of a real immersion experience and I tried not to care where in Germany we went or what activities were mandated upon us. In my more fanciful state of mind, I was drawn irresistibly to southern Bavaria and could allow no musings outside of my desire to yield to the cryptic call of Ludwig. I spent the days and nights before the meeting teetering between those two polar worlds.

Before my parents came home from the meeting, before they had a chance to tell me themselves, Birgit called me. The annual trip to Germany was canceled that year. The program was delayed until the following year. In other words, it was too late for us. The next year's eighth-graders would inaugurate the program. Birgit and I both resorted to our own natural inclinations in such circumstances. She whined and cried, listing all the things we would not be doing on our long anticipated, thoroughly fantasized trip to Germany together. I made a list of the enemies of our happiness, from the school board members to the state of education in America, sharply and bitterly chastising every figure to whom I could attach some blame. My parents came home as this nonsensical teenage tirade continued. They saw me on the phone with Birgit. They saw the anger in my face. I told Birgit that my parents were home and I promised I would call her back. Before my parents could open their mouths, I made a seamless transfer of audience, continuing my complaints exactly where I left off with Birgit.

My mother shushed me with such calmness, such confident nurturing that I was immediately silenced and captivated by curiosity. She told me that they knew how much the trip meant to me. She told me that the cancellation was a blessing in disguise. She said that this is an experience we were meant to have as a family. In the drive from the school to our home, my parents decided to take us all to Germany — as a family. My mother told me to think about where I wanted to go and what I wanted to see. In an instant, all of my dreams became as real, as present, and as tangible as the shirt on my back. The tug-of-war was over. The reasonable and fanciful shared a common ground and could now walk hand in hand toward the same destination. I looked at my parents as they watched my reaction. I saw in their eyes a level of love and devotion that I would not truly understand for many years. Then, at the zenith of my elation, my thoughts turned to Birgit. I could not call her back without sharing the news and I could not bring myself to share the news — not yet.

I expected to be more heart-broken for Birgit. My strongest feelings were not of compassion, but of guilt for not feeling compassion. I loved Birgit, but my obsession with Germany and Ludwig was always internal and highly personal. The loss we both felt at the cancelation of the school trip was not an equal loss. What had been robbed of me was infinitely more valuable than what was robbed of her. I obviously did not know her as well as I thought. I expected jealousy, anger, even a sense of betrayal in her reaction when I told her about our family vacation. I dreaded telling her but knew that it was a task that required attention, as soon as possible.

I called her the next morning and delivered the news, first by eulogizing the lost school trip, then most hesitatingly relaying my parents' idea. Birgit proved to be a better person than I had given anyone credit for being. She confessed that her lamentations on the phone were in mourning for my loss, not hers. She was sincerely delighted for me. And other than a short list of demanded souvenirs, she talked nothing of her own feelings, of her own dashed hopes, and spoke entirely of my excitement and the glorious opportunities that awaited me. For many years now, I have wished for an opportunity to praise her for her goodness. Had I only said it when I could.

Planning our travels was easy. Aside from the long dreamed stroll with my father down the streets of our ancestral town, on the banks of the Main River, in northern Bavaria, I would be plunging headlong into the world of Ludwig II. My mother found a package tour of Ludwig's castles, Hohenschwangau, Linderhof, and Neuschwanstein. This excited me exceedingly. The tours were inclusive of every amenity and every necessity we could think of. We booked the tour for late June of the coming summer. My mother, true to her nature, secured every facet of planning and booking the trip. It was done. It was secure. This paved a solid road down which my imagination could travel. Brochures with vivid photographs and detailing particulars about the tour served as the launching docks from which many fantasies embarked over the months that followed.

Although my classmates were disappointed by the cancelled trip, they were not broken by it. Their desires quickly found another focus. They were not embittered by my effusions of excitement over my planned family vacation. Most enjoyed my daily torrent of particulars about the tour. My passion was clear, abundant, and seductive. I found myself presiding over large swaths of class time, with detailed lessons about Ludwig II and his castles, Munich, the region, the history, and of course the language. The question and answer sessions often consumed a greater part of the hour than the lectures. Herr Fischer sat back and readily yielded his time to me. The lessons I gave were primarily in German, with English sprinkled in where my excitement ran faster than my ability to translate. I smile now, as I think about how little I understood about the history. History is written by the effusive, the communicative. The truth of the past dies behind the silent lips of the secretive. I thank God that those silent lips have spoken to me. But I will get to that later.

The comfort provided to me by the secured logistics of our trip liberated me to portion out my attention to other parts of my life, other studies. My grades improved in my other classes. My friendships tightened. My mood was generally jovial. But on my own, in the silence of my own thoughts, I was still obsessed. I began to dream in German, dreams of Bavaria, magical dreams with strange creatures surrounded by ancient forest. I often woke still thinking in German. I would occasionally and inadvertently address people in German, and I struggled to quickly provide the English equivalent. I have no doubt that this annoyed some, but most found it endearing as it drew them more intimately into my excitement. Another avenue unblocked by my mother's diligence was my long overdue explanation to Birgit concerning my experience with the Ludwig portrait. She had stopped her ginger attempts to raise the subject. My introduction of it caught her by surprise. I saw the hairs of her forearm rise as I sat her down and initiated the topic with a soft and grave vocal tone. I had no fear of her rejection or doubt. My fear was that I would be unable to do justice to the depth and reach of the experience.

I stuttered as I tried to articulate the more intangible sensations. I tried to speak to her in German, as had become by this point our general practice, but stalled in frustration when the concepts left the sphere of my vocabulary. I bounced back and forth from German to English, patching together what must have been a bizarre linguistic quilt. Nevertheless, Birgit's mind snuggled up to mine underneath it. By the time I exhausted every way to explain the entire scope of the phenomenon, Birgit was as thirsty for answers as I, and she understood both the absolute necessity of my upcoming journey of discovery and the often-enigmatic behavior I had displayed for the majority of our friendship. She looked at me with an expression in her eyes that displayed understanding.

A small bubble of sadness broke the surface as she said pensively, "I wish I could go with you."

The comment pinched my heart and I expressed that pain involuntarily. Not wishing to dilute my excitement with any selfish feelings of hers, Birgit changed the subject quickly and excitedly, probing for details on how and where I intended to pursue my answers while on a guided and regimented tour.

The truth is, Birgit had brought up a serious question. I did not feel that I could return home without some profound, life-changing discovery, but feared that I would find myself on a plane back to America with nothing in my experience that would jolt me out of this frenzied state of confused wonder. Or worse yet, I feared that a fruitless journey would strip me of *all* wonder and rob me of my passion. Those fears were thoughts, from my head, not feelings from my heart. Deep inside, I knew that a destiny, either profound or subtle, awaited me in Germany.

The summer felt like a million years away. So I spent the time priming my palate to most piquantly savor the experience. I read and I pondered. I stared at pictures and allowed my imagination to dive into them. Support came from all corners of my relations. My father even perfected the spätzle recipe he had been comically botching for years. I felt good. I felt hopeful. I keenly heard the call of destiny. And having finally shared the mystical nature of my obsession with Birgit, my deepest, most personal ambitions were authenticated. Her acceptance and faith legitimized my own. Her wisdom and encouragement ring in my ears, my mind, and my heart to this day.

All of my other thoughts and actions during the rest of eighth grade are so dwarfed by the events that followed, that I struggle to recall much to relay to you. At the time, the interval between booking the tour and leaving home felt eternal, but my memory of that time fits into a few quick thoughts. I wish I could recall that time more vividly. For most of the people in my life, it was the last time I ever spent with them. I am saddened that my ignorance of the coming events precluded me from savoring their company as I now wish I had. I was focused, and I failed to delight in the mundane moments of life. I failed to adhere them to my memory. I will not accentuate this failure by trying to document the vague and foggy months leading to our departure. The end of eighth grade not only signified a graduation into high school, but the beginning of the most anticipated summer of my life. The searing hot frenzy of excitement and preparation branded itself to my memory. I will continue from that point.

The last day of school was only a half day. We got out before lunch. Each class was held, but was only half an hour. Half an hour was too much time in most of my classes. The final details were wrapped up in a few minutes and the rest of the time was spent trying to talk over the fifteen simultaneous conversations. Half an hour was not nearly long enough for German III. Herr Fischer had so much to tell me. I knew I had been good for his sanity over the three years. But I had no idea how firmly I had affixed myself to his affections. He spent about three minutes with the year's closing logistics. He spent the rest of the time talking to me and about me. We spoke about my upcoming trip, about my final project in his class, but mostly about sixth grade. Herr Fischer reminisced with great tenderness about the many shared moments that helped us both through that year.

The class didn't seem to mind foregoing the usual last-day prattle to sit quietly and listen to Herr Fischer speak of me and my trip. Aside from having tutored much of my class through the last three years, I had become something of a celebrity, through my quirky and apparently fascinating behavior. Most of them were excited about my trip and forced promises of stories and souvenirs upon my return. I have often wondered what they were told about me when I didn't come home, when I didn't show up at school the following August.

The half day of school ended and we all began our summer with the assumption that we would see each other again. My farewell to Herr Fischer was emotional for both parties. I was to go to high school the next year and was unlikely to see much of him even if I had returned from Germany. Of all the people in my life, he was the only one to whom I said a proper good-bye.

The weeks between the end of school and the trip flew quickly. Indeed, I wished them away. Now I would like to have them back, to live over again. I would take advantage of those weeks to set firmly the precious memories that are now fading from focus — my father's smile, my brother's laugh, and the smell of my mother's pillow. I wish daily for the spectacles that would bring these fading memories into clear focus, to be honored and mourned as they should be. I will forego trying to relay those weeks in this account because of the inability of my memory to do them justice.

CHAPTER 3

The Trip

PACKING BEFORE THE TRIP was exciting, but driving down the driveway, embarking for the airport, was thrilling. We were on our way, and I knew I would not return before seeing Ludwig's magnificent palaces, Neuschwanstein, Hohenschwangau, and Linderhof. I wanted to see the palace at Herrenchiemsee, but we put that off for another visit. After the tour of the castles, we planned a trip north, to the Main River and the Kessler family ancestral home. This is what drove my father — as much as King Ludwig II's castles drove me. We rode away from my house and out of my neighborhood, each rotation of the tires carrying me closer to a dream.

My thoughts were ahead of me, not behind, not of the bedroom desk I would never sit at again, not of the dining room where I would never eat another meal, or of the living room where I would never decorate another Christmas tree. I gave no thought of the house that disappeared behind me, and no thought of the friends and neighbors I left behind. In fact, I gave little thought of the road ahead of me, or the flight. My mind was already hiking up the hill to Neuschwanstein, running the halls of the castle, admiring the art and the furnishings, and opening my heart to be spoken to by my dear Ludwig Otto Friedrich Wilhelm of Wittelsbach, King of Bavaria.

From leaving home to landing at the airport in Munich, Germany was a blur to me. It was a long, frantic run of images and imaginings, shaken and jumbled together into one long, surreal day. I struggle now to extract the facts from the fantasies, the experiences from the free wanderings of my mind. We boarded a bus from Munich to Füssen, where our hotel was located. The drive took us through beautiful landscape, dreamy hills, and dark, ancient woods. I gazed out of the window of the bus, imagining myself riding a swift horse on the way to visit Ludwig. As conscious thought released its grip and shared a smaller portion of my musings, I became the horse, and then a unicorn, running through the forest around me, darting between trees on some secret and magical errand. The woods on my side of the bus opened into a green field, just outside of the village of Schwangau. The disappearance of the woods snapped me from my fantasies and allowed me to soak in the quaint, red-roofed town. We crossed a river into Füssen.

My mother, thinking of me and my obsession, booked us into a hotel named after my Ludwig. The street was everything I had imagined. The quaint, stone, pedestrian street was framed by wide sidewalks and patio tables with large umbrellas. The front of the hotel had a picture of King Ludwig II high on the outside wall, above the entrance, facing the street, painted directly onto the facade. There, in gigantic form, was the image of my Ludwig, staring down at me from the wall of my hotel, welcoming me to my fate — or so it felt. Walking into the hotel could not have felt more right. From the images consumed to that point by my hungry eyes, I imagined the hotel room to be more "Old-World". It was a very modern room. I was surprised, but not disappointed. I suppose I had placed my welfare in the hands of my phantom tutor by that point and trusted that everything that happened to me was exactly as it was meant to be.

I jumped on my modern bed, with its bright red blanket and tried to go to sleep in the clothes I had worn all day. My mother pulled my pajamas from my bag and threw them at my face. I pulled the pajamas off of my head and stared at my mother, who had already taken her attention elsewhere. Only then did I realize that I held my night-wear in my hand and should probably change. By the time I fell asleep that night, I had stuffed the entire day into a mental file to be recalled and sorted at some later date. As he tucked me in, my father spoke of the cuisine and conversations that awaited us at sunrise. But my mind was on Ludwig, and whether actual or imagined, my connection to him felt stronger than ever, as a fever of anticipation boiled my blood.

I did not sleep well. All night, I rode the waves from consciousness to shallow, dreamy sleep. The experience branded itself into my memory because of the nature of the dreams and because of my frustration. I just wanted to sleep soundly and wake in the morning, ready for the tours that were planned for the day. I laid down and tried to coax myself to sleep by piecing together the images I had seen of Hohenschwangau Castle, one of Ludwig's childhood homes. I gave myself a virtual tour until I finally drifted off. I dreamed that I was at a dining table in Hohenschwangau Castle. Dining with me were the young Prince Ludwig and his brother Otto, my mother and father, Herr Fischer and a few students from German class. Birgit was not there. There was an empty seat beside me that was reserved for her. Everyone at the table was angry with me for holding up dinner until Birgit arrived. She never came, and just as it became intolerably awkward, I surfaced into a weak and dull consciousness, only to slip into a new dream.

In this dream, I had the keys to Neuschwanstein. I stood at the gate, in charge of the castle's security. Birgit came to me and asked to be let in. I wasn't supposed to let anybody in, but I caved under the pressure of my friend. Birgit ran through the castle, tearing paintings off the walls and smashing artifacts. She was arrested inside the castle and sentenced to remain there for the rest of her life. I begged for her freedom, which she was granted. She left the castle and I walked through it, room by room, smiting my poor spirits with guilt at every destroyed item I beheld. When I returned to the castle gate, Birgit was there with hundreds of rowdy, school-aged kids, banging on the castle gate, demanding to be let in. I awoke from that dream in severe agitation. To soothe myself, I tried to walk my mind through my house, starting at my own bed, through each room, and out the front door. By the time my mind stood outside my house, I had crossed a seamless transition from conscious thought to another dream.

In this dream, my house was on fire. Karl and I stood in the lawn watching it burn, knowing that my parents were inside. We both started to cry. As we did, I became aware of a host of strange creatures surrounding us, strange flat creatures that looked like hairy flounders with four legs — and thin, stick-like creatures with no faces. I was startled by them, but not frightened. As strange as they were to me, I felt the warmth of compassion from them. When my attention went back to my brother and our burning home, I heard the creatures crying around me, mourning my parents, whom they seemed to know, and pitying my despair with familial sympathy. As we cried together, springs of water burst from the ground around us and shot several feet into the air. They did not move to extinguish the flames, as I wished them to do, but continued to spray upward where they stood, joining their light, whispering cries to ours.

I awoke violently from this dream. I sat up and held my breath until I could soundly identify the breathing of my mother and father. I laid down again, but in vain. My heart was still heavy from the emotions of the dream and I continued to listen for signs of life from my parents for at least an hour. I do not know when I fell back asleep, but I awoke exhausted from a deep, dreamless slumber. By the time I was out of bed, I had shaken the effects of the dreams. In fact, my recollections of them seemed absurd to me. I silently shamed myself for losing sleep over them. My excitement about the day's events was the perfect tonic for my sleep-deprived exhaustion. I am not sure what fuel my body was burning, but by the time I was out of my pajamas, I was as energetic as I recall ever being.

After a leisure breakfast, we boarded a bus for Hohenschwangau village. The area around Hohenschwangau boasts two of the most magnificent sights in the world, within view of each other, Neuschwanstein Castle and Hohenschwangau Castle. Hohenschwangau Castle was renovated by Ludwig's father, when he was still a crown prince. Ludwig and his younger brother Otto spent much of their childhood there. The area on the east shore of the Alpsee had long held the name Hohenschwangau (High Swan Country). Neuschwanstein Castle was built by Ludwig, begun not long after he became king. I knew enough about the castles to strengthen my emphatic draw to experience them more intimately, but remained ignorant enough to delight in the joy of surprise.

Just on the other side of the river from Füssen, themes from Tchaikovsky rolled through my head as the bus driver pointed out the Schwansee (Swan Lake) on the right side of the bus. I stared, expecting to see ballerinas on the lake. My expection of a magical experience was so primed that I doubt I would have been astonished if I had seen ballerinas on the lake. The lake gave way to a thick bunch of trees and the driver announced Hohenschwangau Castle on the right. My heart skipped. I had no idea it was so close to Füssen. From the hotel to Hohenschwangau was a blink, and my consciousness reeled in the fantasies of the short drive and tucked it away for later use.

I scanned the tops of the hills to the right side of the road and there it was, Hohenschwangau Castle, Ludwig's childhood home. I easily spied the yellow walls and red trim poking out above the trees that lined the road. Before my imagination could place me at the castle a hundred fifty years ago, we parked in a very normal, perfectly modern parking lot, with normal modern cars and tour buses around us.

We saw Neuschwanstein first. The castle is difficult to approach. The bus let us off at the foot of a steep hill, atop which sits the castle. The hike to the gatehouse was not taxing. The whole family took it with zeal. As we approached the proscenium of the gate, I had a vivid flashback of my dream, so vivid in fact, that I turned quickly back expecting to see Birgit begging me to let her in the castle. My gasp and sudden jerk of my head caught my mother's attention. My panic and dismay must have been quite apparent. She grabbed me by the shoulder and asked me what was wrong. I bumbled through the introductions of some half-baked excuses.

"I thought I saw... I was afraid I forgot... There was a..."

My mother had seen enough in my recovery to satisfy her maternal concerns. She relinquished her grip on my shoulder and replaced it with a couple of reassuring pats. She grinned at me and beckoned me onward with a subtle nod of her head.

No amount of study or imaginative anticipation could have prepared me for the overwhelming sense of awe and holy reverence I felt as I walked through the gatehouse and into the courtyard. My spirits stood between two towering experiences. On one side, my eyes took in beauty on a scale I could not have imagined before. On the other, a sacredness blessed the very floor beneath me. The scene bustled with visitors. Several languages were being spoken. But I felt alone. I felt like the castle stood for my sake, like it had extended a special, private invitation for me to enjoy an intimate encounter. For my mother's sake, we joined a tour being given in English.

The guide had much to say before we entered the castle, but I heard none of it. My mind very effectively cleared away the crowds, the noises, the bustle of the scene. I closed my eyes and cordially invited the alpine air into my welcoming lungs. I curled my toes inside of my shoes, as if to hug the ground beneath me with my feet. I opened my eyes, turning them upward to see the greenish-grey roof of a tall tower contrast against the clear, pure blue sky. I closed my eyes again and begged for a spiritual audience with Ludwig. I felt a mystical connection, but not with Ludwig, at least not like I had in the classroom that day. He didn't feel home to me. He didn't feel present. The hallowed stones around me lost none of their sublimely consecrated influence. But I felt no nearer the answers I sought and I could not wait to go inside the castle.

The castle interior showed no sign of vanity in its decor. Oh, it was extravagant in the extreme. But every ornate sculpture, every embroidered piece of furniture, every painting smacked of dutiful homage. To say that the image of the swan was a dominant feature would be a gross understatement. The swan image was squeezed into every nook and cranny. It was carved into the walls. One might guess that the sovereign king who built the castle *was* a swan, or he built it *for* a swan with whom he was deeply in love and devoutly committed. Lively scenes of medieval German lore decorated many of the walls. Life-size knights and maidens, kings and saints stood high on the walls, in murals that covered most of the wall space, looking down on the dozens of visitors who stood beneath them at any given time. One of the most captivating themes was the Holy Grail. It was a symbol of obvious significance to Ludwig. In the paintings that featured it, the Grail shone with radiant power.

The Salon on the third floor encased my attention. The Grail and swan motifs saturated the room. Although I had seen those motifs in other rooms, in the Salon, they possessed me. On the crown molding, dozens of swans sit in pairs, facing each other like bookends. Between each pair is a shield, protruding out from the molding. Above the swans, are the names of figures from the Grail legends — Arthur, Percival, Guinevere, and others, painted in brilliant gold. There are many paintings on the walls, but one in particular drew me in. My eyes were first caught by the central image, the Holy Grail, large and radiant, resting atop an altar. Facing the Grail is a knight, with long, beautiful hair, flowing from under a helmet. Atop the helmet is the image of a swan.

In the Salon, there are upholstered chairs and sofas, and tables with matching coverings, all riddled with swans. The floorboards rise almost waist-high to me. Carved into it are dozens of swans. I could have spent an entire day in that room, piecing together what seemed to me to be clues to a great mystery, answers, perhaps, to the many mysteries of Ludwig's life and death. I felt my mind trying to force the pieces of the puzzle together. Just as I felt like an image was coming to me, out of the many puzzle pieces, the tour moved on and I left the room.

The rest of the castle offered similar mental exercises, intriguing to the brain, but not the spiritual experience I had primed myself to have. I studied the ornate furnishings, the murals, the artwork, all with a very academic approach. As I passed through the castle, I came to know more about Ludwig, even to understand him better, but I felt no tighter connection to him. His spirit seemed to pass through me as I walked through his possessions, through a world of his creation, but it did not grab me — and I could not grab it. I enjoyed the tour of Neuschwanstein. To say otherwise would be a lie. I savored every mental morsel. But I left hungry. A second and third course to this spiritual meal awaited me. It would have to be in Hohenschwangau Castle or Linderhof Palace that my answers must be found, that my connection to Ludwig would reveal its secrets and embrace me openly.

We planned lunch after leaving Neuschwanstein, before touring Hohenschwangau Castle. I expected to be impatient, but surprised myself. I enjoyed the meal just as my family did. During that meal, I was simply on vacation. I thrilled in talking to the other guests and the waitress, in joking with my brother, laughing with my mother, and relishing the joy in my father's face as he was living a long-time dream of his. My father compared every bite of his lunch to his mother's and grandmother's recipes. He broke into a lecture on the geographical cuisine of Germany. None but I paid attention to him, and I only halfway. It didn't matter to him. He was in heaven. My memory holds a few visual snapshots of that meal. I treasure them.

Ludwig spent little time at Neuschwanstein Castle. And the tours were crowded and rushed. So I was not so surprised that I did not connect deeply with him there. Hohenschwangau Castle was a childhood home of his and a place he loved. The next stop on our tour was certain to provide me with an experience nearer the secret purpose of the trip. Like the tour of Neuschwanstein, the Hohenschwangau tour moved more quickly than I would have liked. The pace of the tour ripped me out of dreams just as I began them. I begged to remain in any one room long enough to listen for the message that Ludwig began telling me in that haunting whisper, through the paper lips of that poster image in the classroom that day. If he could speak to me so loudly through a poster in Centennial, Colorado, how much louder should I hear him as I wander through the halls of his childhood? Some guests scanned the rooms quickly and were ready to move on. For them the tour moved too slowly. Others stood in awe of the rich splendor, studying each contour, each brush stroke. I spent much of the time with my eyes closed, trying to wish myself back in time, often whispering solicitations to Ludwig.

Just under my breath, I reminded him, "It was *you* who reached out to *me*. Now I have come all the way from America. Say what you need to say. I am listening."

I repeated this as a mantra, in every part of every room I was allowed to see. I neither heard nor felt any answer until I stood in a passageway, beneath a painting of Lohengrin, the Swan Knight. Lohengrin stood regally in his little boat, pulled by a swan. The painting reached to me somehow, much more deeply than the images of Lohengrin in Neuschwanstein. I stopped dead in my tracks and sat down. I felt my father's hand touch my shoulder. He knelt down behind me and spoke softly into my ear, regaling me with the story of Lohengrin from the Wagner opera. My father loved Wagner, so much that he wanted it played at his funeral, as it was at his father's funeral.

I didn't understand what it was about that particular moment, with my father touching my shoulder and telling me the story of Lohengrin, on the floor in a hallway of Hohenschwangau Castle, but I was hit with a flash of warmth, not one sensed by my flesh, but one that encompassed my spirit. I felt taken back in time, not to Lohengrin, but to Ludwig. I clearly envisioned those deep, hungry eyes as my father spoke to me. I felt a powerful sense of déjà vu. We fell behind the tour. In fact, they left us behind entirely. I turned to face my father. He grabbed me by the armpits and lifted me up, even though I was not much shorter than he was. I wrapped my legs around his waist and he carried me, like he did when I was six years old, back to the tour where he put me down, ruffled my hair as he always did, then took my hand and pulled me onward.

The warmth and connection I felt from Ludwig in the passageway remained with me. We went into his childhood bedroom. I saw his writing desk and his bed. I lingered, imagining that this might be the place to hear his voice again. I felt him. I truly felt him, but did not hear him.

My interest in his bedroom faded quickly and I felt a pull to move on, as if Ludwig stood right in front of me saying, "This is a place of my past. Come. I have more important things to show you."

I took a moment to enjoy the beauty of the room and to briefly contemplate its historical significance, and then I skipped on, deeply believing that some profound transcendence waited just around the corner. Each step in the rest of the tour of Hohenschwangau Castle charged me with greater anticipation.

While Neuschwanstein Castle appears more as an extravagant gift or offering, manicured and opulent, Hohenschwangau Castle looks more like a home, built for knights and kings to roam, eat, sleep, learn, and live, not built to enshrine the image of the swan and the Holy Grail. Although it is wonderfully ornate, it is not so gilded. It is dominated by earth tones, with a very masculine amount of wood, large and stately. Hohenschwangau may have been Ludwig's childhood home, but it was his father's creation. Ludwig II's father, King Maximilian II, was a practical man. The farthest flight of his fancy was into the paintings of Germanic heroes adorning the walls of Hohenschwangau.

Unlike at Neuschwanstein, I could easily picture royal life occurring in the rooms I visited. I could picture Ludwig's life. I felt his spirit around me, running, swirling out of reach. I felt him around me, but not in me.

The tour ended, and although I felt like I was held in Ludwig's embrace, I heard nothing from him. I felt more agitated than I did after seeing Neuschwanstein, like I was forced to stop one step away from my destination and stand there with my hands at my side when a simple reach forward would put it in my grasp.

I wanted to go immediately to Linderhof. But Linderhof was far away and the tour of that palace was the next day. Linderhof was the last tour. After that, we were to travel north to our ancestral town to fulfill the often-discussed dream of walking those streets. As we wrapped up the tour of Hohenschwangau, I began tallying the benefits of the trip to that point, convincing myself of its worth, preparing myself to head north after seeing Linderhof Palace, no nearer my destiny than when we rolled down our driveway in Colorado. I prepared myself to amputate the dreamy connection to Ludwig and savor what remained of the Germany trip with my family.

We returned to the bus, which took us back to Füssen and the bed that held my restless mind and body the night before. The previous night, the flight, departing home, all seemed like years ago. The restlessness of the night before was far behind me. I slept well that night. I fell asleep thinking about Lohengrin and the swan that pulled his boat. I did dream that second night in Füssen. I remember that I dreamed. But I don't remember the dreams. I remember that they were related to the experiences of the day. And I remember that they warmed me and held me, suckling me like an infant, and providing the nutrition that my soul needed to recover from the high agitation of the day, enough to rest soundly.

Of the three palaces in the tour package, Linderhof was the one that interested me the least. I had been certain that my answer waited for me at Neuschwanstein and Hohenschwangau. But now it was down to Linderhof. I reminded myself that Ludwig spent much time there and it was dear to him. I had done much less reading about Linderhof than about the others. I was less familiar with the grounds and the layout of the palace. I was keen to see the Venus Grotto, an artificial cave that Ludwig built as a personal sanctuary. It was one of the first places in Bavaria to be lit with electric lights. The images I had seen of it were breathtaking and thought provoking. Knowing that Ludwig wiled away many hours on a small boat, on a small, artificial pond inside the cave baited me seductively. I awoke, dressed, and ate much more calmly that day. I was quiet, but the serenity in my face allayed any concerns that my silence may have aroused in my parents. The morning was pleasant and I was patient, just beginning to resign myself to the fate of any obsessed tourist.

The long bus ride to Linderhof was not a stage for imagined horse rides. My eyes may have faced the bus window, but my thoughts were inward, deep and distant, and intensely contemplative. As we entered the valley of Linderhof, and my attention turned to my surroundings, my breath was frozen in an experience reminiscent of my experience with the poster portrait. I felt my extremities shaking. Although unfamiliar to my eyes, to my heart the valley and surrounding hills felt as familiar as my own bedroom, but like a reminder of intimacy, like when you come home after a long absence and see the things that were once a daily part of life but had been forgotten, or like hearing a song that you memorized as a child but hadn't heard in years. My heart hummed along with the tune, but remained one count behind the lyrics, remembering them only as I heard them. Every little contour of the surrounding mountains, every gap in the trees, even the way the low clouds rested in the sky, were all words in that familiar song. The shaking of my hands and the jigging of my legs wiggled free a few bursting giggles, which sneaked their way to my throat and only announced themselves as they rushed unexpectedly from my smiling face.

We parked the bus and walked toward the palace. All of my preparations for disappointment flew away.

Each breath of air seemed to shout to me, "This is it! Here it comes!"

I braced my spirits for the profound revelation that I anticipated with each step. The palace beckoned me, but so did the surrounding hills and the lush valley. Everything around me, every tree, every rock, was home — my home — Ludwig's home. I felt firmly in the grasp of destiny, like with the portrait in the classroom, one thousand times over. I caught my parents staring at me as we walked toward the palace, with a surprised wonder and adoration, like when a parent hears a child speak its first word. Even Karl looked around the area, marveling at everything, as if he had never seen trees before, gawking in astonishment at their very normal branches. Perhaps he felt something too, something similar to me.

We toured the park before entering the palace. I saw fountains and statues and stone gazeboes. Everything was heavenly. Unlike with Neuschwanstein and Hohenschwangau, I felt no pull to enter the palace. I would have been content to stroll around the park and explore the many beauties it boasted. The one thing I really wanted to see, the Venus Grotto, was closed for repairs. The tingling thrill in the air stole my mind quickly from the disappointment. When we walked into the palace, as inviting as its magnificent façade was, I felt like

I was being torn from the surrounding park. This was a strange sensation. There was much inside the palace I wanted to see, yet crossing its threshold felt wrong somehow. I tried to bury the feeling and open myself to what the palace could offer.

The strange feelings subsided, or were simply buried beneath the beautiful wonders of the palace interior. Every inch was sumptuously ornate. The feeling of destiny wrapped its powerful fingers around me again and pulled me from one deliciously lavish sight to the next. My sweeping, wondering, indefatigable eyes froze in a sudden halt as they encountered a portrait of Ludwig. I could not look away, despite the tantalizing spectacles all around me. I don't remember walking forward to the portrait, yet in a moment I stood directly under it, as if I had been lifted and carried to it.

The sounds of the crowds around me began to muffle, then went silent, exactly as they did in the classroom that day. The movement of Ludwig's lips did not surprise me this time. I expected it. I invited it. I begged for it. They moved as the same whispering sound reached my ear, but with much more sharpness and clarity than in the classroom.

I heard the portrait tell me, "Geh...geh...geh" (Go...go...go). The voice became more desperate as it repeated, "Geh jetzt" (Go now).

My breath was taken when Ludwig's eyes became angry. His eyebrows turned downward at the top of the nose.

The whisper became vocalized as he loudly yelled, "Geh jetzt!"

There was a desperate cruelty in the voice and expression that terrified me. I turned away, then looked around to see if anyone else had heard the voice or seen the changes in the image. There was nobody. The hall was empty — completely empty. The muffled voices of the crowds of tourists returned, but nobody was there. I could not understand what they were saying, but they spoke casually and in concert, as they were before. The sound remained muffled, like the conversations of a pool party when you dunk your head under the water. I frantically scanned the area and saw nobody. I glanced back to the portrait of Ludwig. It maintained the fierce scowl it was giving me when I turned away from it. This was in disturbing contrast to the warm welcome I expected from the man over whom I had obsessed.

I panicked and ran down the hall, yelling for my mother and father. The voices of people were all around me, but still muffled and indistinct. As I ran through halls and rooms, I felt myself brush against people, but I still saw nobody. I still could not distinguish one mumbling, muffled voice from another. I called desperately for my parents until I found my way to the palace entrance and ran into the sunlight as if running into my mother's arms. As soon as the sunlight touched my face, the voices stopped. The terror stopped. The desperation gave way to a warm sense of well-being. I turned and looked back into the palace. I thought about those scowling eyes of Ludwig. I thought about my family and furiously wished to find them. I ran all over the palace grounds calling for them. It seemed like an hour to me, an hour of running up the slope away from the palace, through the trees, and back to the palace. I stopped for breath and realized that the only place I did not check was the Venus Grotto. I sprinted to the grotto and found the stone door entrance open.

There was no sound coming from within, no sound around me, not even the lively sounds of nature that made the park so dulcet when I strolled it before entering the palace. I am not sure what I expected to find in the grotto, or why I felt that each step across its threshold was so profoundly Providential to me. But I walked gingerly and tentatively, as if afraid to crush something precious beneath my feet. The grotto was lit, just as I had seen it in photographs. Nothing about the grotto was visually unexpected, except that the photographs did not capture its beauty or the sacredness in the air. Still, I found myself unable to breathe deeply, terrified of breaking the silence with my inhales and exhales.

The pond inside the grotto was as green as an emerald. There was a precious richness to the water. My eyes drifted slowly from the water to the large mural, highlighted by the warm lights that illuminated it. The image of Venus in the mural seemed to put off its own light. The figure of Tannhäuser, reclined at Venus' feet, wrapped me in a film of pensive compassion for him. A small stage thrusted into the lake, just beneath the mural. Stalactites hung from the ceiling, seeming to reach for my face and gently turn my attention back to the mural. My eyes took in every inch of the mural, then drifted to the boat on the water. It was held out of the water by four legs so that it hovered just inches above the emerald liquid. The boat appeared slightly larger than it did in the photos. As I stared at it, it appeared to move toward me, or I toward it, though I did not step and it remained fixed to the legs that held it above the water.

On the seat of the boat sat a book, the very corner of which I could barely see over the rim. The minute image of the corner of the book despotically imprisoned my mind. All other thoughts, all other concerns were obliterated as I was drawn by an irresistible imperative to see it closer. Before I knew it, I was standing in the water, pressed against the side of the boat, fixedly staring at an old, leather-bound book, tied shut with a thin leather strap.

There was writing on the cover that read, "Das Journal von Ludwig II".

I read it out loud, breaking the silence I had so painstakingly maintained since I entered the room in awe of the spectacle before me. My words echoed off the walls — my words, but not *my* voice. The words came back to me in identical inflection and tone, but in a voice that was strange to me, soft, feminine, almost like one voice in harmony with itself, a lonely voice, striking me instantly but briefly with haunting and unsettling sadness. This sensation was buried quickly by a wave of wonder at the curious splendor that surrounded me. A strange sense of familiarity and comfort momentarily subdued the book's tyrannical clutch as my eyes scanned the cave. But my attention was quickly snapped back to the book.

Entirely unaware and without control of my physical actions, I found myself sitting in the boat, holding the book with both hands reverently beneath it like a sacred altar. I stared at it, unable to disengage my eyes until my lungs instinctively and violently responded to my long held breath with a gasp of desperately needed air, breaking the rigid cord of connection that linked the book with my very inner being. I took several moments to slow the desperation of my gasping lungs and assure them that the air would keep coming. Once they accepted my assurance, my attention went back to the book.

"The Journal of Ludwig II"? Could this be? I held the book to my nose and inhaled deeply, as if I could have authenticated it by some signature smell. I held that breath awkwardly long, waiting for it to speak to me. That action having provided no answers, I drew the book slowly from my face until it pressed gently on my lap. I untied the leather strap slowly and fearfully, as if expecting to be caught doing something forbidden, or as if expecting to trigger some trap that would do me in. The leather bow unknotted easily, at the end of a nervous and shaking pull on one strap. I opened the book and found a piece of thick parchment, folded, tucked inside of the front cover, pressed firmly against the binding. I pulled it from the book and unfolded it. It was a map. It was drawn with amazing detail, with writing in the most exquisite, antiquated penmanship. I was grateful to have studied old German handwriting.

At the top of the map it read, "The Sweeter Realm". At the bottom was a signature. It was sloppier, as if the writer attempted to make the signature over-stylized. It read, "Rudolf". The map was divided into sections. I recognized parts of the words, but had never seen these word combinations anywhere in my study of German — words like, "Eulesänger, Zweigwesen, Brunnen, and Wühlenvogel". I recognized the word "Einhörner", the German word for unicorns. Aside from the exquisite penmanship, the map had some immaturities, clearly not the work of a professional cartographer, from any era. I assumed that it was a pretend map that Ludwig made as a child. I folded it and wedged it back where I found it.

I turned the first page and saw, in writing that seemed rushed and emotional, a penmanship that soothed my nervousness with a keen sense of familiarity. But the sense of familiarity did not have my studies to thank. There was something deeper, warmer, and almost motherly in the way the writing made me feel, before I translated the first word. By the dim but colorful lights of the grotto, I began to read the book. I will translate it now. Before I do, you must know that this is a current translation, colored by the experiences I have had since finding the book all those years ago. I was ignorant then. Now, I have read the book countless times, studied it. I am intimately familiar with it now and understand every fantastic phrase and description. My experience as I read it for the first time, sitting in that boat, in the Venus Grotto of Linderhof, was different — more excited, more naive, more mysterious, fresher and more nervous.

This is how the book reads.

CHAPTER 4

The Ancient One

9 June 1886

I MUST SOON FACE MY ENEMY, for my sake, the sake of my dear friends, for my family and for my kingdom. It is unlikely I will prevail, unlikely I will survive. However this battle ends, the last page will be turned in an ancient story, one with many heroes, a story that began with a holy quest and must end soon with me. I must preserve the story in this, the only written account, for if I fail, none who could recount it will live. The glorious wonders and heroic adventures of the Swan Knights would sink beneath the rising waters of time to dissolve into obscurity and oblivion. Because the only voice still capable of singing our song may soon be silenced, I appoint my pen as the bard of a fantastic history, one whose survival I strongly desire.

Where do I begin? I begin with me. I first entered my kingdom on 25 August 1845, on the feast day of Saint Ludwig, patron saint of Bavaria. I was named Otto, a name I would not keep long. I was born on the fifty-ninth birthday of my grandfather, King Ludwig I of Bavaria. My grandfather, deeply steeped in tradition and rooted tightly to a superstitious and eccentric family legacy, insisted that I carry the name Ludwig. My parents did not protest and at only a few days old, I became Price Ludwig of Bavaria, a name I have worn both as a talisman of fortune and as a beacon for disaster.

In 1848, revolts erupted all over Europe. As king of Bavaria, my grandfather bore his share of the burden. I was not yet three years old. I did not understand the affairs of state. I did understand that my grandfather spent much of his time wandering the forest, to the neglect of his official concerns. There was nothing in his behavior peculiar to me. But the people began to accuse him of insanity, as they had of so many in my family. So often did I hear the word "crazy" in reference to my family that I did not understand the meaning of the word until I was much older.

In March of 1848, my grandfather gave up his throne to my father. This created quite a stir in the family and beyond. I heard servants and tradesmen blame the revolts. Others spoke of Lola, the Irish dancer who stole my grandfather's heart. But my grandfather spoke very differently to me. He sat me down and told me that I was crown prince, that my father was now king. He told me that he was following the advice of "The Ancient One" and attending to a burden that would someday be mine. In the following years, when he spoke to me of his abdication, he spoke of "The Laws of Ermenrich" and of King Rupert. None of those names meant anything to me at the time. Although I was very young, there are things I remember about those conversations. Grandfather told me that his concerns were no longer for the Bavarian people. He told me that he is a Swan Knight. As a Swan Knight, he had concerns that I could not yet understand.

The drama around my grandfather was quickly dispelled by another family event. One month after he yielded his throne to my father, my brother Otto was born. He bore the name that was first given to me. At my young age, this fact connected him supernaturally to me. I felt like he was a younger part of me. I tried never to be very far from him, for fear that the distance might sever a connection that would cause me true damage, true pain. My brother's company became dear to me. As my father, then Maximilian II, King of Bavaria, already a cold and distant father, assumed the duties of state, Otto and I became an even smaller part of his life. My grandfather was warm and nurturing. He delighted in the things and people around him. My father's thoughts were always lofty and removed from the daily needs, desires, and thoughts of young children. My father always said that had he not been king, he would have been a university professor. I do believe that such a life would have suited him well. He had a dry, academic relationship with every subject to cross his mind, even his own children. As much as he tried to shield himself from his Wittelsbach heritage, there was still a tug at his heart. The part of my father never seen in government showed splendidly at the family home in Hohenschwangau, in the castle he rebuilt and adorned as a young man and crown prince.

Otto and I spent much of our time in and near Munich, in Nymphenberg Palace, where I was born, and the Royal Residence. But we loved the time spent at Hohenschwangau, seventy miles southwest from Munich. The castle there had fallen into ruins until my father chose it as the country retreat for the royal family. When he was just twenty-one, and Crown Prince of Bavaria, he fell in love with the ruins of the old crumbled castle. It had a storied past with an intimate connection to my family. In the old ruins, my father found the one place where he felt the ancient, romantic pull that had taken full control of his father. He renovated the castle in an effort propelled and navigated by his heart, rather than by his usually dominant mind. It was only in discussions about the castle that my father's warmth could be felt by those around him.

It is a beautiful place, with serene lakes and majestic hills seen from every window. The old ruins of another castle rested on the unapproachable precipice across the valley. As a child, I could see the old ruins from the eastern windows of Hohenschwangau. They always stirred my imagination. My mind took the legendary figures of Germanic lore and placed them among the ruins. Once I was old enough to explore the ruins, I spent many childhood hours there, in a constant state of fanciful musings, with knights walking past me and magical creatures running around my feet and flying over my head. The servants of Hohenschwangau referred to the old ruins as Vorderhohenschwangau. But my family called it "Brunhilde's Castle" or "The Swan's Old Castle". Those names piqued my imagination from an early age.

The entire area surrounding my father's renovated castle harkened my family back to its early roots and the legends associated with our dynasty. But I spent most of my time looking at the castle interior. My father had it lavishly decorated with reminders of Wittelsbach lore. Murals of knights and swans covered the walls. There was nowhere in the castle to escape the mystic tales of German heroes. One day, when I was six, as I stared at a painting of the knight Lohengrin, in his brilliant armor, being pulled in a boat by a swan, my father knelt down behind me. He placed his hand on my shoulder, in a rare moment of tenderness, and he told me that Lohengrin himself had inhabited this very castle, that Lohengrin's great-grandson was born in a room mere steps from where I stood. He told me that Grail Blood had occupied our home and that it finally occupies it again. There was such earnestness in his voice, such mysterious depth in his expression as he knelt beside me and stared into the same painting, informing me — or rather instructing me — on the origins of the castle, weaving the legend of Lohengrin into the castle's history in a warm and fanciful tone of voice, and squeezing me as if his stories had intimate relevance to me.

My father was always serious, and too academic to allow fanciful wanderings of the mind. He criticized me early for the wild flights my mind would take. When he spoke to me, with his usual earnestness, about the Grail and Lohengrin, his words seemed to join me in my dream world. But his address was sober and austere, as if his stories were the subjects of academia, not the playground of fancy. These subjects, the stories of my fantacies, were a strange topic of exchange between us, but they were the only place our minds would meet. I wanted to ask him to tell me more. I wanted to uncork my curiosity. But I had been burnt too many times by his harshness, and fear kept the cork of my inhibitions firmly in place. Nevertheless, my father spoke that day with such unexpected and impassioned sincerity that his words possessed me. They further fueled my imagination and unchecked passions. From that point, the murals of Hohenschwangau Castle did not just entertain my imagination. They seemed to grasp at my destiny, each time I walked by them. I was simultaneously disturbed and invigorated by their grip on me.

I did not know a moment of boredom in Hohenschwangau. Often, when sent to be alone as punishment for some breach of expectations, the walls would speak to me. The paintings came to life, or at least they appeared to in the mind of a young prince fascinated with his mystical connection to his surroundings. "Grail Blood occupies this castle again." My mind went savage trying to connect my surroundings with the mysterious words of my father. I would lose myself for hours, yielding the navigation of my imagination to the paintings on the walls and to the walls themselves, which seemed to cradle me when I needed cradling and prod me when I needed prodding. Long after my punishment was over, I sat in captivated thought, staring at the walls in front of me.

Tutors and servants tried to entertain me, but I did not want to be entertained. I did not want to be distracted from my thoughts. The house was all the company I needed. It was rooted to me somehow, or I to it. When my focus steered toward the outdoors, it was usually in my dreamy and imaginative fascination with the old ruins atop the opposite hill. In conversation, my family paid a holy reverence to the place. It held some ancient and revered meaning, though the specifics of which were never told to me by family or tutors. I came to understand that reverence in the same way I came to learn who I am, not from my parents or Fräulein Meilhaus, my governess. My most profound and pertinent knowledge came from a teacher I had not yet met — a teacher and a most cherished friend.

With each passing year, my intolerance for the city increased. I had to be in the country. In the city, I felt disconnected, anchored to nothing, floating at the whim of any random breeze. In the country, I felt my feet on the ground. In those days, there was only a humble hunting lodge at Linderhof, on the site where I built my palace. This was a common retreat for the inner circle of my relations. It was a sacred retreat and visits there were planned meticulously and spoken of reverently. Only my immediate family went there. The bustle of the preparations for a trip to Linderhof felt more like the preparations of business than hunting. The lodge at Linderhof stood in particular contrast against the Royal Residence in Munich. Not only were there so few people there, only my nearest family, but I saw amazing things when I walked the woods and valley.

One section of the forest, behind the lodge, was off limits to me. This sparked a curiosity in me that would have been overwhelming if not for the wonders in the other parts of the valley and surrounding woods. They were quite a distraction from the seductive call of the forbidden. I saw animals there at Linderhof that I never saw in my strolls around Hohenschwangau. My favorites were the Unicorns. They were tall goats, a little taller than a horse, with cloven hooves and a hairy mane that ran down to fully cover the chest. Long hair ran from the side of the head, down to the chin where it hung like a beard. They were broad at the chest, like a horse, but narrow at the hips. Their backs sloped downward from shoulder to tail. Some were white, some black, some brown. But most of them were some shade of grey. They stood, walked, and ran majestically. But the most wonderful part of the Unicorn was the tall, spiraling, brilliantly white horn. Some had hints of blue or purple in the recesses of the spirals. The horns seemed to catch the sunlight even when there was no direct sunlight upon them, as if they created their own light.

I spoke often of the Unicorns. But I was so isolated as a child, almost always restricted to the company of family, servants, and my governess Sibylle Meilhaus. On the rare occasion that I spoke of the Unicorns to strangers, the topic was laughed off as another outburst of eccentricity, a trait of mine for which I was already notorious. At that age, and in my state of isolation, I did not think them fantastical, or particularly peculiar. All I knew was that I only saw them around Linderhof and even then, only rarely. I often caught glimpses of other creatures around Linderhof that I never saw elsewhere. But I never gained a close enough perspective or they did not linger long enough for me to make a proper study of them. Even they added to my love of the old lodge. Everything about Linderhof, from the behavior of my family to the peculiar things I saw there, stood in sharp relief against the normality and bustle of Munich — and even Hohenschwangau.

In 1854, when I was only nine years old, my beloved governess was taken from me. My father told me that she was getting married. She did marry, but that was not the reason for the timing of her departure. I should say that when I turned nine she was finally able to marry, because a new tutor awaited me, one who had been waiting since my birth for his pupil to come of age. This new tutor was off the royal payroll and entirely off the record. An official teacher had to be assigned to me. For this position, my family chose Major General Theodor Basselet de la Rosée. Otto also lost the services of Fräulein Meilhaus. He too was handed over to de la Rosée, but Otto was not in line for the throne. His needs always fell to mine. Fräulein Meilhaus left when I was of age to move on, regardless of what was best for Otto. In exchange, he was free as an adult to do things, to commit to things that I could not. I have kept in touch with Sibylle Meilhaus, sharing with her some of my most intimate secrets, including some that should never have escaped my lips. I trust her unreservedly. Otherwise, I would have lost much sleep over the escape of such precious secrets.

To a nine-year-old prince, Sibylle's marriage was not a good reason to rip her from my life. I was devastated. De la Rosée was no teacher. He had no idea why he was handed this new post, a peculiar one for a man of his nature. He had lofty notions of royalty. He taught me to be above the people and not to associate with anyone beneath me. As a military man, his sense of rank was firm and unfaltering, and in his eyes, only my father outranked me. I thank God for the balancing effect of my next teacher. The Major General taught, but he did not inspire. He fulfilled his duties to the best of his abilities. I would soon realize that he was just a figure to satisfy the public's expectation of a royal tutor. Upon that realization, I portioned my dedication and loyalty to him accordingly. The poor man never received affection from me. He propped me upon an altar. He revered me for my position. He tried to prepare me for the burdens of state that would someday be mine. I wish now that I had paid him more attention.

I had no reason to imagine that my father would leave his throne as my grandfather had. The burdens of state seemed so very far away. I did not pay de la Rosée the obedience he deserved. As a result, I was ill-prepared for kingship when it came. I remember with some mortification the coldness with which I treated him. At first, it was because he replaced my beloved Sibylle. Afterward, I associated him with concerns that were distant from my heart. I was still distracted and perturbed by the loss of Fräulein Meilhaus. I was not left in the dark over my governess' departure and the assignment of de la Rosée for very long. There was much bustle around the royal residences in those weeks and most of it seemed to involve me in some way that was kept secret from me.

Still unrecovered from the loss of my governess, I packed for a trip to the hunting lodge at Linderhof. There was to be nobody there but the Royal Family, my father and mother, my grandfather, my Aunt Alexandra, Otto, and I. Otto was not so broken up by Sibylle Meilhaus' departure as I was. The orders to prepare for the trip came to me with such sympathetic tones that I was certain the expedition was intended to distract me from my mourning. The attention of my parents was on me as we left Hohenschwangau and remained on me as we arrived and settled into the lodge. We were certainly there on my account. I thought it all a bit much just to cheer me out of my sadness. Still, the area is beautiful and was always a place I found peace. As I settled in for the night, I appreciated being there, and I appreciated all of the effort and attention lavished upon me that whole day.

As I was lying flat on my back, staring upward with my arms crossed over my chest, too agitated to sleep, my thoughts were not on Fräulein Meilhaus. They were on the morning forest to which I would soon wake. They were on the rich sense of mystic adventure those woods always elicited in my young mind. As my eyes closed and allowed the rare mixture of dream and lucid thought, those images only half-controlled by the mind, I saw myself riding on a swan. I was clad in the armor of Lohengrin, from the paintings at Hohenschwangau. I rode on the swan across a foggy and eerily placid lake toward the Holy Grail, which seemed to tease me, allowing me to approach it only to drift farther away.

I awoke refreshed and eager to embark on whatever excursion was planned for the day. There, beside my bed was a set of hunting clothes. It was a new outfit, but in an old and traditional style. As I put it on, the mirror whisked my imagination away to the past, a trip that needed little encouragement. My mother would often dress Otto and me in common clothes for our walks around Hohenschwangau. But there was something special in the way that this outfit was left for me while I slept. The hose were of beautiful, deep-brown leather. The shirt was intensely dazzling white. There was a hat with a long greyish-brown goose feather. I ran into the main hall and saw my father, only my father sitting and waiting for me. I asked him where my mother and brother were.

He said, "Today is for us, my son. After today, you and I will never run out of things to talk about."

I scanned everything within range of my eyes from where I stood. The silence was broken only by my father's breathing, long, slowly drawn inhales followed by quick, bursting exhales, as if he was trying to muster the courage to perform something difficult. I could not stand the sound of it. It felt like an omen of something dreadful. I interrupted it by asking him if we were finally going to hunt together. I had long awaited the day when his excursions from the lodge, away from the family and into the woods would include me. My draw was not particularly toward hunting. I despised hunting. But upon his return from his jaunts into the forest, the King always wore an expression of deep thoughtfulness, sometimes more jovial and sometimes stricken with a deep sadness, but always profoundly altered.

He did not answer my question about hunting. He had no gun, no knife. As he stared at me — or though me — in what was obvious deep contemplation, I began to doubt that I would be hunting that day with my father. The King stood, took me by the hand and led me out of the lodge with nothing for the day but the clothes we wore. We walked together toward the hill behind the lodge, to the forbidden sloped woods that had long taken my curiosity where my eyes could not follow. We walked hand-in-hand for a good distance behind the lodge, until we reached the edge of a more densely wooded area. There, my father let go of my hand and allowed me to take a few steps more before ordering me to stop.

He stood behind me and took me tightly by the shoulders. He made a few small adjustments to the direction I faced, as if aiming me for a precise target. I felt the immense importance of the moment through the grip of his hands. As I felt his pulse, I sensed for the first time the thick connection of blood with my father that I had long felt with my grandfather. The King reminisced aloud, but not to me, about his father holding him just as he now held me. Any childish defiance that may have erupted from my spoiled little mouth was silenced by the flow of energy from my father's hands into my body. For the first time, my position as Crown Prince ceased to be a possession to be flaunted and hoarded. It rooted me to my father and mother and to the little brother whose nose I had rubbed in my royal title since he was old enough to understand it. My father gave me a quick series of four or five squeezes, then nudged me forward one step and let go of me. I continued to move forward, like a small paper boat set into a brook on its inaugural voyage. I stepped gingerly, hesitatingly, judging by the sober austerity of the prelude to this journey that each step could change my life forever.

I had no expectation of being horrified. But I did expect to be startled. I suffered neither. I became aware of a quickly growing sound, one that irritated the ears while beckoning with an imperative seduction on my soul. It grew to full loudness within a few more steps. I stared into the forest in front of me, where the sound seemed to come from. I stopped walking, leaned my head forward and watched as a small circle of the hill and forest in front of me seemed to disappear — or become covered by a circle of nothingness. I stared at this circle for a few moments, then slowly stepped backward in confused wonder until it disappeared, and in its place stood a large swan of the purest white. The swan stood nose high to me. Its beak glowed deep orange, as if it had been polished for the occasion. It had remarkable expression in its face as it tilted and gently waved its head, at the end of a long and slender neck. I had been bitten by swans before, while feeding them at Hohenschwangau. A swan this size could snap off my entire hand. But I had no fear of it. There was such peace and wisdom in its expressions and such tenderness in the gentle tilt and sway of its head.

I had almost forgotten about my father standing behind me. I broke my hardened gaze toward the swan and began turning my head to my father. Before I could scan my eyes over my own shoulder, I was recalled to the swan by a voice — the swan's voice. With a sound both ruggedly masculine and nurturing the swan spoke to me.

"Ludwig" it said, "a name both familiar and dear to me. You are much like your grandfather, and much like many of your ancestors."

"Who are you?" I asked.

The swan introduced himself by a name, or more of a sound that I do not think the human mouth can make. I spent much of the next few years trying to reproduce it. My attempt to repeat it back to the swan that day spawned a laugh from behind me, which reminded me again that my father stood near. The swan's expression brightened at my failed attempt to pronounce his name. He interrupted my second attempt to tell me that he has been referred to as The Ancient One. I remembered my grandfather's words all of those years ago, "I am following the advice of The Ancient One." The swan stared at me so directly and so supportively that I felt like I was being lifted and cradled by his sympathetic gaze, as I repeated back to him, "The... Ancient... One."

The swan stretched his long neck and turned his head to the left, catching the morning light across his noble face. At that moment, I recollected the many images of the swan riddled throughout my childhood residences, and was struck with familiarity and the a very distinct notion that all of those images were depictions of this very swan. This was not an idea that crawls into the head and awaits verification before boldly pronouncing itself. This was a realization, the very certainty of which was absolute the moment it entered my mind. I felt destiny take me by the hand, interlace its fingers with mine, and invite me to run with it headlong into my future.

My father's voice brought me back to the situation at hand. I turned to him as he said, "This is your teacher. He taught me. He taught your grandfather. He has taught all of us."

I looked back to The Ancient One. The light off his pure white feathers seemed to sing. My eyes took in rich, glimmering visual harmonies as he swayed back and forth, allowing the sun to reveal complexities in the radiant whiteness. Each feather seemed to throw at me the entire spectrum of colors, all while remaining undeniably and brilliantly white. The Ancient One was not like the Unicorns or other creatures around Linderhof. Although they were rare and beautiful, they never appeared as magical to me. Sheltered as I was, I knew there was something special and mystical about this swan. Perhaps it was the manner in which he appeared to me, through the crackling hole in the air. Had he flown to me from the sky and not spoken a word to me, his physical appearance alone would not have signified his uniqueness beyond that of the other Linderhof creatures. But he did speak, and with such a tone of wisdom — of legend, that as I stood near him, I felt as if someone had painted me alongside Lohengrin in one of my favorite Hohenschwangau murals. I soon found out exactly how fitting that feeling was.

I was drawn again from my fantasies by my father, this time by the rustling of the ground beneath him as he turned toward the lodge and walked away. I looked back to the swan, who nodded gently to me. Without instruction, I walked toward him. The crackling sound and the hole in the air returned. I felt their connection to me. I realized that I caused them.

By my father's departure and the lingering of The Ancient One, I assumed my lessons were to begin immediately. I stood near enough for him to have wrapped his long neck around me two times. With reverent politeness, he asked me to sit on the ground beside him. My body obeyed before my mind had the opportunity to consider the request.

To the accompaniment of the crackling hole, The Ancient One said to me, "You can apply no lesson to your life until you know who you are. You cannot adorn a wall until you know what the wall is and where the wall is. Listen, young knight, and I will connect you to me, to your blood, and to your burden."

His brilliant figure against the dark depth of the forest behind him forbade any deviation of my attention. The addition of his voice, as he spoke, secured my focus with tyrannical force. I felt paralized in my attention to him, as if under a spell. Only, this was a spell that I, in my amazement, curiosity, and admiration, had cast upon myself. I had long sensed my connection to the figures of Germanic lore, placing my own face atop their images as I sat, staring at the art of Hohenschwangau. I suspected that an ancient, arcane truth would soon explain the sensation. The Ancient One validated the childish imaginings of a foolish young prince, as he relayed to me the history of my blood. The Ancient One told me a sacred and viciously guarded secret. He told me the history of my family.

CHAPTER 5

The Swan Knights

IN THE YEAR 515, the knight Parsifal was in possession of the Holy Grail, the cup that Jesus used at the Last Supper, the vessel that held the first consecration of wine into the Blood of Christ. Parsifal was bound by an oath to God to keep the Grail safe and out of evil hands. An ambitious king called Klingsor had grown as powerful as he was wicked, and he began a campaign to acquire the Grail. Parsifal knew he could not defend the Grail against Klingsor. He protected it in the only way he could. He fled his home with the Grail, in search of a safe place to keep and protect it. He was prepared to wander the world as long as he must to keep the Grail safe.

He carried only a bag with the Holy Grail and some personal items, a pouch with some silver and gold, and his sword and armor. Parsifal knew that he had to take the Grail far away, putting as many barriers as possible between Klingsor and the power of Christ's sacred cup. He traveled far, over seas and mountains, in search of a secure home for the Grail. He resigned himself to a life of endless travel, if that was what it would take to keep the Grail hidden. Klingsor was bent on possessing the Grail. Only with the Grail could he reach the height of his ambitions. He sent hundreds of his servants in search of Parsifal.

In the Bavarian Alps, Parsifal encountered one of Klingsor's servants, disguised as a flowermaiden. It was in the late spring. The valley was lush, adorned with colorful flowers, and crowned with the high, sharp peaks of the surrounding mountains. The flowermaiden appeared as in a dream. Her skin glowed in the spring sun. Her long hair appeared to dance in the Bavarian breeze to the nature song of the valley. There, in the most beautiful place he had ever seen, the flowermaiden bewitched Parsifal, seducing him into a kiss. In the depth of the kiss, she stabbed him in his side with a poisoned blade. Parsifal felt the blade pierce through his body and into his soul. He fell to the ground, landing on his bag and squeezing it tightly to his chest with all of his quickly fading strength.

The flowermaiden struggled to move Parsifal and dislodge the bag from beneath him so she could retrieve the Grail and return it to her master. She rolled Parsifal onto his back. Just as his strength was about to yield to the fight of the desperate flowermaiden, a young woman skipped down the hill, out of the thick forest, and into the valley where Parsifal fell. She stumbled upon them and screamed in fear. The shrill and piercing scream echoed across the valley, frightening the enchanted flowermaiden away.

The woman ran to Parsifal's assistance. Parsifal felt himself fading and feared for the fate of the Grail if he should die. With the last of his energy, he asked the woman to take the Grail from his bag, fill it with water, and return it to him. When she returned, she stopped and stared in horror. Parsifal appeared to be dead. She called to him in a voice half crying, half scolding. He did not respond. Mortified by the sight of Parsifal's pale, sunken face, she defeated her instinct to run away, took one deep breath, and knelt down beside Parsifal. The woman propped the knight upon her knee. She felt the cold, clammy skin of the back of his neck against the warm and youthfully vibrant flesh of her forearm. She held the Grail to Parsifal's lips. The touch of the Grail revived him enough to sip the water.

Just as soon as the water cleared his throat, his face regained its color. The young woman felt the warmth of life return to his body. His wound began to close. Before it did, a drop of Parsifal's Grail enchanted blood fell from his wound and hit the ground. The immediate rise of a terrifying crackling sound frightened Parsifal and the woman. With the woman's help, Parsifal rolled away from the sound. A large hole appeared in the air, at the very spot where Parsifal's blood hit the earth. Parsifal, frightened for the Grail, got to his feet, and with the help of the woman, moved as quickly from the hole as his weaken body would allow. As they moved away from the hole, the crackling sound muted. They both turned to see that the scene had returned to normal. There was no sound and no sight but the forest and the hill, as it had always been.

The woman brought Parsifal to her home. By the time they arrived, he had regained his strength and could discern no effects of the wound, nor any sign that a wound had ever been inflicted. Parsifal's quest to protect the Grail from Klingsor still dominated his thoughts. But his fear that the flowermaiden would return put him in fear of the kind woman's safety. He remained with her, her father, and her sisters, intending to continue on his quest once he felt assured of their safety. Parsifal and the young woman grew attached. The attachment blossomed into a powerful love. Parsifal proposed marriage but told his love that they could not marry until he fulfilled his quest. He fiercely guarded the secret of his quest. He did not tell her of the Grail, or Klingsor, or the reason for the flowermaiden's attack. But the woman had seen the powerful effects of the Grail. She watched Parsifal's wound close. She saw him revive from near death to full strength, right before her eyes. She saw the magical hole appear in the thin, crisp mountain air. She knew that he held a magical secret but she was too proper, too modest and unassuming to demand answers.

The ring that Parsifal was to offer her had been among the items in his bag. He searched the bag but could not find it. Convinced that it had fallen from the bag when he fell to the ground after being stabbed, Parsifal returned to the site of the attack. As he approached the place where he fell, the crackling sound returned, followed shortly by the hole in the air. Startled at first, he jumped back. He turned his body away from the hole, but could not tear his eyes from it. Frozen in this twisted position, Parsifal stared at the hole until his fear subsided. He remembered first seeing the hole, as he lay weakened, in his most desperate moment. A thought crossed his mind, one that warmed him, that caressed him. When his life was in danger, the Lord sent the young woman. When his fear for the safety of the Grail was at its most desperate, the Lord sent the hole, which opened when he drank from the Grail and his blood hit the earth. And now, it opens again for him, as he approaches the same spot. Surely it was the work of God.

Parsifal looked to the heavens and asked aloud, "Is this the new home of the Grail? Is this where I am to keep your sacred cup, my Lord?"

He took the Grail from his bag, held it tightly, and with no regard for his own safety, walked into the hole. On the other side of the hole, he found himself in a place that seemed free from evil, from selfishness, greed, and ambition. He returned late that night to the home of his love. He told her about Klingsor and explained his quest to secure the Grail. He told her that they could marry, because the Grail is out of his hands and finally secure from Klingsor, his servants, or anyone else who might seek it.

I interrupted The Ancient One's account, asking him, "Do you have the Holy Grail? Did Parsifal give you the Grail?"

He told me that the Grail is in the possession of The Queen of the Land and Shallow Waters. He assured me that she is the purest, noblest being that ever lived in the Sweeter Realm.

"What is The Sweeter Realm?" I asked.

He told me that over the years of his association with Parsifal's descendants, "The Sweeter Realm" is the name they have come to call his home, on the other side of the portal, of the hole in the air created by Parsifal's Grail Blood. In defense of his pride, The Ancient One assured me it was my people who christened the name. I begged him to continue the story.

Relieved of his burden for the first time in many years, Parsifal felt free to pursue his own desires. He married the young woman who rescued him. Her name was Gütel. With a lingering sense of responsibility for the

Grail, Parsifal and his wife built a home in the valley near the place where his Grail Blood opened the portal. Parsifal quickly realized that the portal opened at his approach, always when he crossed the same distance from the portal point. It closed as he left the proximity where his Grail Blood held the portal open. Parsifal spent much time at the portal speaking to the first creature he met in the Sweeter Realm and the only creature from the other side yet to cross — a large, sparkling white swan.

> I interrupted again, this time barely opening my mouth when The Ancient One answered the obvious question on my lips.

> "Yes", he said, "I was the first from my side to meet Parsifal. He entrusted the Grail to me. I brought it to the Queen. There is no safer place."

> "Please", I said reverently and eagerly, "Please continue."

Parsifal opened the portal often and looked forward to his regular meetings with the swan. The swan also enjoyed the meetings, and he waited on his side for Parsifal to let him through. Parsifal and the swan met regularly, for many hours at a time. The swan could vividly sense Parsifal's thoughts. This was an ability new to him. He had no such insight into the beings from his own side. Knowing Parsifal's thoughts as he spoke, the swan quickly learned his language. Parsifal no longer spoke his native tongue. He had given it up for the language of his new family. He eventually invited Gütel to his meetings with the swan. The white bird could not read Gütel's mind. This was a connection he had only with Parsifal, probably established as they united in contact with the Grail, when Parsifal handed it to him.

Parsifal and Gütel grew to adore the swan and trust him for his goodness and wisdom. After years of travel and struggle, turmoil and fear, Parsifal was happy. He had done well by the Lord and was rewarded with a home in the most beautiful valley he had ever seen. He had a friend in the swan. And he had Gütel, who he held as precious as the Lord's sacred cup. They had one child, a son named Lohengrin.

One day, when Lohengrin was not yet two years old, Gütel carried her young son on a long walk around the valley. As they approached the portal point, it opened. Gütel, assuming that her husband had opened the portal, scanned the area but saw nobody. She stepped back and the portal closed. She asked herself why the portal suddenly responded to her approach. But then, she looked down at the young child in her arms.

"Of course," she spoke aloud, "Lohengrin has his father's blood — he has Grail Blood."

She stepped forward and the portal opened again. She set her son down and backed away from him. The portal remained open. Lohengrin clumsily toddled to his mother and the portal closed behind him.

Gütel lifted her son into her arms and ran to the house to get her husband. In a frantic retelling of events, Gütel tried to explain what had happened. Parsifal could not understand what she was saying. So, she put Lohengrin into his arms and pushed Parsifal out the door and toward the portal point. The three of them went up the hill together, but as they approached the portal point, before the spot where Parsifal's approach would open the portal, Gütel stopped them in their tracks. She took Lohengrin from his father and ordered Parsifal to remain where he stood. She inched toward the portal point with Lohengrin in her arms until the child opened the portal. A tremendous burden lifted from Parsifal's shoulders in that moment. He realized that the portal was not just his responsibility, that its destiny could extend beyond his lifetime. His descendants could open the portal and retrieve the Grail when the Lord calls for it, whenever that may be.

As Gütel stood between Parsifal and the open portal, still holding Lohengrin in her arms, the swan appeared through the portal, without his usual radiance. There was earnest concern in his expressions and his beautiful head hung low at the end of his long neck. Parsifal and Gütel had never seen the swan like this. They were curious but frightened about the cause.

The swan said, "There is evil in your land. The Queen is afraid of the portal. She accepts responsibility for the Grail, but fears what evil it might attract. She has asked me to receive your assurance that the portal will be secure on your end from any who might enter the Sweeter Realm in search of the Grail. She has her own queendom to protect and her own subjects to serve."

With renewed faith, Parsifal dropped to one knee and swore that he and his descendants would guard the portal and protect the Queen and the Grail as long as his blood line survives. He and Gütel were both painfully aware of the lifelong burden he had just placed upon their young son. The swan knighted Parsifal into duty to the Queen of the Land and Shallow Waters, for the protection of the portal, the Grail, and the Sweeter Realm. Parsifal rose to his feet and, wearing the most solemnly earnest expression, declared himself a Swan Knight. He committed the blood of his line to the same cause, knowing that his Grail enchanted descendants would have access to the portal between worlds. What choice did he have? Their blood would open the portal. Their blood must guard it. Parsifal swore an oath, speaking for and swearing commitment from every child of his line, until God recalls the Holy Grail from the Sweeter Realm.

The swan spoke to the Queen with great animation of the fervor of Parsifal's resolute commitment. The Queen was pleased and she encouraged her subjects to join the swan in his contact with Parsifal and his family and to aid them in their quest in any way that the Swan Knight needed. She proclaimed that her realm had two borders, one with the mysteries of the Deep Waters and one with the land of Parsifal. She had no contact with the creatures of the Deep, so she warmly welcomed relations with her other border.

The Sweeter Realm had no standard language. Each type of creature communicated in its own way. Inspired by his ability to communicate with Parsifal and his family, the swan went to the Queen and proposed the adoption of a unified language for the entire Sweeter Realm. He convinced the Queen that the language of the Germans, that of Parsifal and his family, should be the language of The Sweeter Realm. He taught her a few phrases and explained the rigid simplicity of the vocabulary and grammar. The Queen was delighted with the warm relations the swan had kindled with Parsifal and Gütel. She held the swan in high esteem and agreed to place him in charge of teaching the language to the realm. The inhabitants took quickly to German, and the standardized expressions did much to unite them under the Queen.

The Ancient One was pleased with his efforts and he nurtured in himself a passion for teaching. Parsifal saw little of the swan while the teacher of the new Sweeter Realm language completed his duties to the Queen. But when the swan returned, he offered himself as tutor to Lohengrin. Parsifal and Gütel were not only glad to see their old friend. They fully embraced his proposal. Lohengrin would study under the swan. Gütel provided the new teacher with all of the literature in her possession. Within weeks, The Ancient One devised lessons for the rest of Lohengrin's childhood. The portal opened for Lohengrin every time he approached the spot where his father's blood hit the earth. Parsifal made fewer visits to the portal, leaving young Lohengrin to open the portal and summon his teacher. Every day, the boy toddled up the slope to the portal point, opened the passage, and welcomed his teacher into the valley.

Parsifal spoke with his son of his many adventures with the Holy Grail. The swan described to Lohengrin, with heroic animation, Parsifal's noble oath to the Queen and his assumption of the identity of the Swan Knight. This sparked a fire inside of Lohengrin. He revered his mother and father and was moved by tales of their heroics. Particularly, Lohengrin enjoyed the stories of his father's travels and adventures as he tried to secure the Grail from Klingsor. The Swan Knight's son received the training of a knight, along with the schooling of a philosopher and theologian. He was as quick with scripture as with the sword, and as romantic as he was thoughtful and faithful. The little valley that Parsifal and Gütel claimed as their own was an ideal setting to raise the next Swan Knight, the next servant of the Lord, steward of the portal, and knight of the Queen of the Land and Shallow Waters.

When he came of age, with his head filled with heroic images of his father, Lohengrin felt the hero's call.

He grew resolute in his desire to travel the roads of the world and stumble upon his own destiny, as his father had. Parsifal reminded him of his hereditary obligation to the portal and the Grail. Lohengrin would not be dissuaded. With the impetuosity of youth, he declared his intention to set out on his own. Parsifal feared not only for his son, but for the portal and the Grail. Lohengrin had Grail Blood, which would open the portal upon approach. The idea of that blood roaming the wild world terrified him. Parsifal began having nightmares about Klingsor and his servants. He had vivid recollections of the flowermaiden and the poisoned blade. He forbade Lohengrin from leaving home. Father and son fought for several days over the matter. Parsifal final gave in, but begged the swan to accompany Lohengrin on his travels and guard him against anyone who might seek the Grail. Parsifal made Lohengrin swear to hide his identity and to speak to nobody about his home, the portal, or the Grail. Lohengrin swore such an affectionate oath to obey his father's wishes, taking the sharp edge off of Parsifal's fears.

Lohengrin loved his teacher. As impetuous and confident as Lohengrin grew, he always listened to the swan with reverently attentive ears — and was grateful for his company. Parsifal constructed a small boat with a harness for the swan to pull and for Lohengrin to ride. On the day of the departure, Parsifal fit Lohengrin in his father's old armor, polished to a blinding gleam by an apprehensive and melancholy mother. Lohengrin's long hair flowed out from the bottom of the helmet, in waves more like his mother's light brown than his father's pure black. They set off in a wagon with little but the boat, the armor, Parsifal's sword, and the dreams in their heads.

Parsifal warned The Ancient One, "You only know three humans. There are many out there, many good and many bad. Lohengrin has only known goodness. Please steer him from harm."

With ardent obedience, the swan swore to abide by Parsifal's request. Parsifal and Gütel, with arms wrapped tightly around each other, watched their son and their friend disappear into the woods on the north side of the valley. They sank deeply into their fears. They arose early the next morning and assumed a sentry post near the point of the portal, alternating in a ceaseless watch until their son would return home and all Grail Blood was safe within their little valley. Lohengrin and the swan were gone for more than two years. In that time, Parsifal and Gütel did not know a moment of peace. The Queen of the Land and Shallow Waters had such confidence in Parsifal's valor, and the wisdom and ability of the swan, she rested well in the assumption that the portal was safe and the border of the Sweeter Realm was secure.

Lohengrin and the swan traveled north. The swan enjoyed long flights in the crisp, cooler air of this side of the portal. In obedience to Parsifal's plea, he flew out ahead of Lohengrin, scouting their path and steering them from potential danger, and looking for any opportunity for Lohengrin to feed his hunger for heroics within tolerably safe circumstances. Lohengrin, having grown up with the story of his father's rescue by the hands of his mother, charged into every encounter with the expectation of discovering his true love in an equally dramatic and romantic manner. He admired his mother and ventured into the world trying as much to be like her as like his noble father. Lohengrin thought that his parents fell deeply in love at the moment of his father's rescue, not in the long and mundane weeks that followed, when their love was truly embroidered one small stitch at a time. So, the traveling Lohengrin tried to recreate his childhood image of his parents' epic romance.

One day, the swan flew out to a small community, on the coast of a cold northern sea. He saw a young woman bound to a post of the docks, accused of murder. The woman's name was Elsa. She screamed into the crowd of surrounding people, insisting her innocence and begging for her honor to be championed. The swan flew back to Lohengrin and reported what he had witnessed. Lohengrin strapped his friend to the harness, clad himself in his father's armor, and mounted the boat. The swan was apprehensive. He thought of Lohengrin's parents. He thought of the Queen and of the jeopardy to the border should Lohengrin's identity come to light. Nevertheless, upon Lohengrin's vehement insistence, the swan pulled him to the dock of the community and to the young woman whose fate was in their hands.

They arrived in time to see the mob descend on Elsa. The shine of the swan and of the armor caught the attention of the crowd. How heroic they must have appeared as Lohengrin leapt from the boat. The clamoring mob settled to a low murmur and a few astonished gasps, as Lohengrin walked through them to stand face to face with Elsa.

She looked him in the eyes with confused wonder and whispered, "You."

Lohengrin asked Elsa if she knew him.

Elsa, more enthralled by Lohengrin than in fear for her life, cleared her throat and declared loudly, "Those are the eyes. You are the man from my dreams."

Lohengrin was already wrapped and bound by a sense of destiny. Elsa's proclamation tightened those binds further. He declared himself her champion and called for her accuser to present himself. A young man of Lohengrin's age, but taller and more rugged, approached and accepted the challenge. Although smaller than his opponent, Lohengrin's erect posture and noble, heroic stance made him look twice as large. When the contest began, Elsa's accuser made a single swing of his sword toward Lohengrin. Before the poor man knew it, he was on his back with the point of Lohengrin's sword staring him in the eye. Lohengrin defeated his opponent with ease. The man yielded. The contest was over. Elsa's honor and life were spared. She threw herself at Lohengrin's feet. Eager to rush headlong into his destiny, Lohengrin felt honor bound to repay the woman's weeping effusions of gratitude with a commitment of fidelity and an offer of marriage. Elsa accepted and the crowd erupted into cheers before the swan could lodge a protest.

Once alone together again, the swan reminded Lohengrin of his promise to his father. Lohengrin's identity and his origins must remain secret. Lohengrin agreed and informed Elsa that she can never ask his name or press him for his history. Elsa accepted the one condition of their marriage, secure in the thought that the truth would someday be hers. But her tongue was restless. It wanted to know the thruths behind the majestic, armor-clad hero who appeared out of the mist on a swan-pulled boat and restored her honor with a wave of his hand. Her tongue itched, and the itch could only be satiated by the question, "Who are you?" The dark depth in Lohengrin's eyes as he demanded his stipulation was not to be tested. Elsa held her tongue.

A faction within the community, loyal to Elsa's accuser, rallied against Lohengrin. They made plans to attack the couple on their wedding night. After the wedding, when the couple had retreated to the wedding chamber, Elsa assured Lohengrin that she could keep the secret of his identity, if only he would tell her. Lohengrin avoided the subject as long as Elsa did not directly ask his name. The secrets behind her champion, behind the handsome young knight who arrived to her rescue just as the lynch mob descended upon her, as if out of a fairytale told to children as they settled into bed, were too seductive to resist.

When they laid in bed together, Elsa whispered in Lohengrin's ear, "What is your name."

Just as Lohengrin sat up in response, Elsa's accuser broke into the room with a group of armed men. Lohengrin grabbed his sword, and with nothing on him but what God had had given him at birth, and his shining sword, he defeated the attackers. All of them were dead or disabled. With the danger subsided, Lohengrin slowly dressed, fully clad himself in his father's armor, lifted Elsa to her feet, and kissed her softly.

"Where are you going?" she asked.

He answered, "My name is Lohengrin. I am the son of Parsifal, keeper of the Holy Grail. I am a Swan Knight and sworn protector of the portal to The Sweeter Realm. I am a loyal subject of the Queen of the Land and Shallow Waters. And now, my love, your curiosity has separated us. I must leave you forever."

Lohengrin summoned his friend and teacher and told him that it was time to go home. They walked together to the dock, followed by Elsa, and a growing crowd of people behind her. Elsa, marching into the cold night in only a light nightgown, matched Lohengrin's pace, not daring to gain on him. Lohengrin strapped his friend to the harness and mounted the boat. With a strong sense of satisfaction, the swan pulled Lohengrin away from Elsa and the crowd. Lohengrin turned around inside of the boat and watched Elsa drop to her knees, wailing in violent sobs, and hitting her forehead and forearms against the ground with destructive force.

At the water's edge, she screamed through her sobs, "I am sorry I asked your name. I will tell nobody. I have forgotten it already. Please do not leave me."

A thick curtain of fog drew quickly closed between them, leaving Lohengrin only to hear the cry of his wife slowly fade as he stared into the blinding grey of the thickening fog. They traveled for hours across the water in this exact manner. Lohengrin did not turn back around. He stood facing the back of the boat, staring into the distance behind them until they came aground.

Lohengrin sought no more adventure. He and his teacher wasted no time getting home. When they arrived in the valley, both were astonished at how much Lohengrin's parents had aged in two years, especially Parsifal. When they left, Parsifal was a strong and proud Swan Knight, with a little greying at the temple, but with the fire of youth in his eyes and a noble posture. Lohengrin started at the first sight of his father, now wrinkled and hunched, with much thinner and entirely white hair. In the course of the two years, Parsifal barley had a week's sleep. He was drawn thin with lack of eating. His skin had tanned and cracked under the sun and weathering of his sentry post. Lohengrin's fantasized reunion was shattered as he approached his home and found his father sitting on a rock near the portal point, just beyond his opening point, bent over his folded arms, staring at his feet. The swan let out an involuntary gasp, not sure that the figure he beheld was his old friend. Lohengrin did not gasp. He recognized his father, with all his alterations, at a single glance.

Lohengrin sped his walk toward his father, then advanced in a quick run. His steps caught Parsifal's attention. Parsifal stood immediately, fully revealing his bent and tattered form. But when he recognized his son, his eyes lit like they did when he held his boy for the first time. His posture straightened — though not to the form of his knightly youth. Parsifal yelled for his wife, who ran from the house expecting to see her son. She had often mixed dream and fantasy with the image of Lohengrin's homecoming. In her weary stupor, she did not know if this was another dream until she reached the embrace of her son. Lohengrin towered over his mother. But in that embrace, she held him.

She pulled his head to her breast, stroked the hair on the back of his head, and repeated in a young and vibrant voice, "My boy, my son."

The swan made a low, gentile bow to Parsifal. Promising to return shortly, he asked Parsifal to open the portal and let him return to his home. Parsifal stepped toward the portal point.

Lohengrin shouted, "No!"

Parsifal stopped sharp. Lohengrin looked adoringly at his father, commanded him to rest, then turned to the swan and declared himself the Swan Knight and guardian of the portal.

He said, "If I am to have adventure, it must find me here. If I am to have love, it must come to this valley. I am a Swan Knight and I will never again leave my post."

With that, Lohengrin, still clad in Parsifal's armor, walked to the portal point, opened the portal, dropped to one knee, and bowed his head reverently to his teacher, gesturing toward the opening. The swan walked up to the portal, but stopped in front of Lohengrin and gave him a kiss on the cheek. He declared Lohengrin the Swan Knight before slipping into the portal and disappearing from sight. Lohengrin stood, took his mother and father by the hands, and walked toward their home, hearing the muting crackling of the closing portal behind him.

Back in their home, Lohengrin made coveted gifts to the eager ears of his parents of each minute detail during his years of adventure. Although they were happy to have him home, and perhaps happier still to have the portal secure from wandering Grail Blood, Parsifal and Gütel's hearts broke as Lohengrin tenderly told the tale of Elsa. Not only did they hurt for the pain endured by their son, but they realized that while Elsa lives, Lohengrin cannot remarry. He cannot have children. If the line of Grail Blood should end, sealing the portal forever, the Holy Grail would remain irrevocably in the Sweeter Realm. They were also afraid that Elsa might try to find Lohengrin, and lead others to the portal. Not wishing to burden Lohengrin further, Parsifal and Gütel spoke alone for many weeks discussing the fate of the Grail. Parsifal strongly believed that the Grail still had some hand in the fate of mankind, that its hiding place in the Sweeter Realm was a temporary home, until the day that the Lord would recall the Grail into the service of the rightious.

Parsifal and Gütel were old. They had to decide quickly whether to bring the Grail back and risk its safety or leave it and risk it being eternally buried behind a portal that no human could open once the Grail Blood is dead. After weeks of no conclusion that would bring them peace of mind, Parsifal decided to consult The Ancient One, who in turn consulted the Queen of the Land and Shallow Waters. The Queen, who had never known an enemy, recommended that the Grail remain with her. She insisted that when God is ready to recall the Grail, God will open the portal, as he did when Parsifal needed it most.

The rapid rise of Klingsor's power and ambition made Parsifal realize how precarious was the Grail's safety in the hands of humans. There would be no fortress that could not be breached, no knight that could guarantee the security of the Grail. They decided that it must stay in the Sweeter Realm, at least for now. The Ancient One offered to make regular flights to Elsa's home to ensure that she has kept Lohengrin's secret and that she makes no attempt to find him. Although the decision to keep the Grail with the Queen settled the debates, Parsifal and Gütel felt the passing of each day as a day nearer the permanent closure of the portal and the removal from God's hands the first holy weapon against evil.

Lohengrin was true to his oath. He remained in the valley, keeping a vigilant eye on the portal and meeting regularly with his friend and teacher. Parsifal and Gütel's fear for the fate of the Grail was brought into balance by their pride in their son, who grew wise and humble, strong and holy. Many years passed peacefully. One day, Lohengrin awoke early and walked to the portal. He stood in terror as he approached the portal point and saw that it was already open. He ran to the portal and in the dim light of the infant day, Lohengrin saw his father, lying motionless on the ground, face down with his arms stretched forward, as if trying to crawl. He knelt beside his father and lifted the old man's withered frame quickly into his embrace. Parsifal was cold and lifeless. Lohengrin held his father's body, silently weeping, caressing his father's head and kissing him ceaselessly, until the sun rose fully. Lohengrin built an altar of rocks and wood near the portal, clad his father in his old armor, adorned the altar with flowers from the valley, and laid his father upon it. Next, Lohengrin went into the home and gently woke his mother. He sat on the bed beside Gütel and told her that her husband was dead. Lohengrin held his mother tightly while they wept together.

He abruptly composed himself, stood up, took his mother by the hand, and said, "It is time to say goodbye to father.

Gütel and Lohengrin dressed in their best clothes and walked together, hand in hand, to the altar that held Parsifal. The portal remained open by the blood of Parsifal's lifeless body. Lohengrin lit a torch and carried it toward the altar. Gütel took him by the arm, and without a word, took the torch from Lohengrin and walked to the altar.

She kissed Parsifal and said to him, loudly enough for Lohengrin to hear, "You are the bravest, truest, and holiest man. You are the greatest husband and father."

Gütel gave her husband one more kiss then she put the torch to the wood of the altar and stepped away. Mother and son backed away from the fire and watched as the fire destroyed Parsifal's body. They heard the muted crack as the portal, which was held open by Parsifal's blood, closed as the Grail Blood inside of him was destroyed by flame. Both mother and son held their breath as they pondered the weight of the moment. The blood that fell to the ground and created the portal would never again open it. Even with an arm of his dear mother wrapped tightly around Lohengrin's waist, the Swan Knight had never felt so lonely. He thought about his father and about fatherhood and legacy. He thought about Elsa. The fears that had gripped his parents fell suddenly and forcefully upon his head. His blood alone could open the portal. He alone could retrieve the Grail. Lohengrin felt a crippling sense of his own mortality and a desperate need to leap into the service of the Grail. Only, he had no idea how.

The next morning, Lohengrin walked out to the crumbled, scorched altar to bury what remained of his father and erect a monument in his honor. As he approached, his eyes were stabbed by the flash of the sun's reflection off of Parsifal's armor. Lohengrin ran to the site and saw, upon the collapsed rocks and crumbled, burnt wood, the perfectly polished armor. There were no char marks on the rocks, no human ashes, no skeleton, no signs of his father at all, except for the shining armor. Lohengrin had never seen the armor so resplendent. Even the leather straps showed no sign of touching fire. In fact, they appeared restored to a condition they had not known since before Lohengrin was born. Lohengrin considered burying the armor under the shrine, which he was to build for his father. But the armor was renewed. It shone bright with vitality. It seemed almost living — and it belonged on the living. Lohengrin set the armor aside and constructed a simple, but elegant rock shrine to his father. He spent the next few days sculpting out of wood an ornament for the shrine. It was a little helmet, with the wings of a swan sloping backward from the ears. He placed the carving atop the shrine, at the spot of the altar where he had sent his father's body to God.

The Ancient One was gone when Parsifal died. He flew north to spy on Elsa and verify the safety of the Grail secret. He had been gone for weeks. Once the shock of Parsifal's death settled, and mother and son fully embarked on their new life alone together, Lohengrin began to long for the comfort and wisdom that his teacher could provide. When the swan finally arrived, Lohengrin was standing at the opened portal, staring into the hole, lost in deep contemplation. After Lohengrin told him of Parsifal's death, and the proper words on the subject were exchanged, The Ancient One told Lohengrin that the story of his marriage to Elsa, his heroics, and his mysterious flight had spread. The story evolved as stories do. As Lohengrin sailed away in the fog, away from the wailing Elsa and gathered people, it appeared to the observing crowd that he flew from the surface of the water and was pulled into the sky by the swan. That was the story being told.

Elsa had been banished from her community for her marriage to the mysterious and seemingly magical stranger. In Lohengrin's absence, she was blamed for the deaths of the attackers in her wedding chamber. The same crowd that cheered Lohengrin when he defeated Elsa's accuser near the docks turned on her and sent her into the wilderness with nothing. Upon hearing this account, Lohengrin ran a few steps toward his house to retrieve his armor and sword and rush to Elsa's rescue. When he left the proximity of the portal, the familiar snap of the closing portal stopped Lohengrin in his tracks. His head dropped. His shoulders slumped forward.

He clinched his fists and looked to the sky saying, "I will not leave you, father. I will not leave my post."

He turned to his old friend, beckoned him into an embrace, thanked him for his efforts, turned, and walked into his home. He told Gütel the story that The Ancient One relayed.

Gütel said, "Go to her."

She pulled the armor out of the chest that held it and began putting it on.

"I will guard the portal, son. Go to your wife", she told Lohengrin.

Lohengrin grabbed the armor from his mother and put it back into the chest.

"Word of the Swan Knight is spreading", he said. "The portal needs me now, more than ever. If danger should befall the portal, because of my actions, then my actions must defend it. My place is here."

Gütel knew that Lohengrin was right, but she still saw in her son the young, romantic Lohengrin, searching the world for love. And she mourned the loss she keenly perceived behind his brave, manly, heroic features. Gütel thought of nothing but the lonely life of Lohengrin. She feared her own death for his sake. She fell into deep depression and illness. Her son stayed by her side and nursed her in vain. Gütel drew her last breath with Lohengrin at her side, caressing her and singing the songs of her childhood. Lohengrin buried his mother beside the shrine to his father. He spent the next weeks isolating himself in his house, never opening the portal, never visiting The Ancient One. His mother's death left him all alone, caged from mankind by the bars of his oath and the preciousness of his blood.

CHAPTER 6

New Friends

THE ANCIENT ONE, still pressed to observe Elsa and the growing legend of the Swan Knight, now spreading wildly across the north, had to leave Lohengrin, but feared his isolation. In a voice Lohengrin had not heard since their early lessons, The Ancient One sternly ordered the Swan Knight to join him at the portal. He flew ahead and waited beside the portal point for Lohengrin to approach.

As the lonely and weary man did, and he opened the portal, The Ancient One told him, "You have friends, Lohengrin. You have allies. You have a family."

He nodded to Lohengrin then disappeared into the portal. Lohengrin stood, staring at the opened portal. Within seconds, the great swan returned — with friends. Following directly behind the swan, with eyes that betrayed their apprehension, were two small creatures, unlike anything Lohengrin had ever seen or imagined. They were long and flat, about the length and width of Lohengrin's thighs, but no thicker than the palm of his hand, with four short, broad legs that barely lifted their flat bodies off the ground. They were covered entirely in white hair, except for their faces, which were as white as their hair. Their heads grew to a point, like that of a fish.

The two holes from which they breathed sat equally between their broad mouths and their deep black eyes. They had tiny ears, shaped like human ears and as white as their faces. They had short, thick necks that lifted their pointed chins away from the ground. The Ancient One introduced them to Lohengrin as Scheriers. Lohengrin gave a courteous bow and expressed a polite greeting, not expecting intelligent conversation from creatures baring no resemblance to humans.

One of the Scheriers responded in a voice neither high nor low, but bearing a distinctly feminine air, telling Lohengrin, "It is an honor to finally meet you, Swan Knight."

Lohengrin's face betrayed his astonishment.

The Ancient One tilted his head and looked at Lohengrin as he had so many times, as he asked, "Are you so very surprised when *I* speak to you?"

"Of course not", answered Lohengrin. "And I am not surprised that my new friend here speaks, only that she speaks so well, and in such accordance with what is proper in my world."

The swan was delighted with Lohengrin's answer, although it was not completely truthful. Lohengrin looked again at the Scheriers and gave them another deep bow. The Scheriers, unable to bow their low, flat bodies, turned their heads to the side with their eyes closed, and touched one of their tiny ears to the ground.

"The Scheriers will stay with you. They will keep you company and tell you stories about their home. I must go now. I will return with Elsa and news of your growing legend."

Lohengrin stared at his teacher in excited surprise, then he asked, "What do you mean? You will return with Elsa."

"This valley needs a woman and you need a wife. You love her and she loves you. Now that she is away from her people, alone in the wilderness, I can bring her here and nobody will know. Nobody will notice. Nobody will follow. Do not forget that your mother did not have Grail Blood. Yet, she served the portal, the Grail, and the Queen — and she was a friend of mine. Now, your Elsa can take her place as you have taken your father's. Parsifal swore the service of his line. Now that is in your hands — yours and your wife's."

With that, The Ancient One flew away. Lohengrin and the Scheriers watched together until the magnificent bird was out of sight. The swan flew far and wide, listening to conversations in the gathering places, where people spun tales and recited the legends of mankind. He enjoyed the more fanciful retellings of Lohengrin's adventures, not just because they were comically entertaining for someone who was there and witnessed the events first-hand. The more fanciful the tale, the less danger the story presented to the portal and the Holy Grail. Elsa had spoken. Stories of Parsifal and the Grail intertwined with the adventures of the mysterious knight Lohengrin. Fortunately, the stories were generally told for entertainment and did little to spark the adventurer into action. Once The Ancient One was comfortable with his assessment of the legend, he turned his eyes to the wandering Elsa.

He found her weak, hungry, and sickened with exposure, seated against a tree in the thick forest southeast of her home. Her exposed shoulder pressed hard against the rough bark and bled down her arm. She was scraping her cheek against the tree, as if nestling into a soft pillow. But the rough bark tore her skin and her blood pooled in large drops at her chin. He spoke to her, trying to bring her comfort with assurances of Lohengrin's constant affection. He tried to revive her spirit with tales of Lohengrin's faithfulness and his loneliness without her. He told Elsa that Lohengrin's parents were dead and that the knight spends his days faithfully tending his post. This did not revive Elsa. It seemed to sink her lower.

Elsa spoke in a broken but still beautiful voice, somewhere between a whisper and a lullaby, "Where is he? Where is my husband?"

The Ancient One dropped the tips of his wings to the cold ground, lowered his head and said, "I came to bring you to him. He waits for you and he loves you."

Elsa lifted her head to the sky, exposing the tattered cheek of the once exquisitely angelic face of the Swan Knight's only lover. The Ancient One let out a shriek, not one of disgust for having witnessed something horrid, but one of pity for witnessing the destruction of beauty. Elsa knew that she would never see her husband again, that the swan's arrival came just days too late. She could not go to Lohengrin. She could not stand. She felt the hands of death curl its last fingers around her. With her eyes to the sky, Elsa yelled. It began as a melodic tone, in the soft voice the swan had known and admired. As the scream continued, it became slowly shrill, higher and rougher and painful to the ear. It accompanied the most wretched writhing of her figure. Her arms seemed to bend unnaturally behind her body. Her neck twisted and her bent knees pushed hard against each other. The writhing suddenly relaxed as the shrill scream broke instantly into one short but forceful sigh, followed by a low, soft moan.

She exhausted all of her air with that last moan and did not draw breath again. Elsa was dead. Her last thought was in learning that a long and happy life, in the warmth of a southern valley, in the embrace of her husband and the friendship of fantastic creatures was one finger's length from her reach, offered to her and taken from her in the same moment. The Ancient One had to tell the Swan Knight. But he could not tell everything. A faithful and vivid description of Elsa's end would have broken Lohengrin and left the portal closed without a key. The swan composed a pleasanter end to Lohengrin's love, one whose image could bring the mourning husband some comfort.

As The Ancient One told me this story, 1300 years after it happened, I could see that he was still sharply affected by Elsa's death and even more so for lying to Lohengrin. The swan felt no pity for me, the nine-year-old, sheltered prince upon whom he threw such heart-breaking stories. But he felt acute compassion for the figures of the stories, figures who still held his heart tightly after so many centuries.

When The Ancient One returned from the north, he found Lohengrin in good spirits, rolling around the ground and wrestling playfully with the Scheriers, laughing youthfully. His somber approach warned Lohengrin of ill news before a word was spoken. The boyish figure that had been rolling around the ground with his friends quickly sat rigid and knightly. The narrow focus of the swan's voyage meant bad news on one of two fronts, either the legend of Lohengrin threatened the portal or Elsa was dead. Lohengrin studied his friend's face and saw more sadness than concern. In the silence of the swan's hanging head, he knew that his wife was dead.

He dropped back to the ground, flat on his back. The Scheriers ran to the portal point as quickly as their little legs could take them. They walked a few circles around the point, then laid flat on their bellies, waiting for Lohengrin to let them home. But Lohengrin did not move for hours, nor did he blink his eyes. He just stared at the sky, expressionless, occasionally wiping a single tear that had crept its way from the corner of his eye to slide quickly to his ear. He stayed exactly like that until the first few stars appeared in the darkening sky. Then he rose, walked to the portal point, where the Scheriers had fallen asleep, startled his friends with the crackling of the opening portal, watched the Scheriers disappear into the Sweeter Realm, then turned sharply on his heels, walked into his house and went to sleep.

Lohengrin slept well into the next day. When he arose, he packed a small bag. The swan, who had kept a vigilant and nurturing eye on his friend as he slept, asked Lohengrin where he was going.

The knight answered, "My father swore the loyalty of his line to the Queen. Parsifal's blood must not die."

He walked briskly and with focus, out the door and up the hill. The Ancient One watched him intently, observing closely for some indication of Lohengrin's state of mind, until the Swan Knight disappeared into the thick forest of the hill. Lohengrin's parting words gave The Ancient One hope that his former pupil might seek a wife and provide him with a new pupil, and a knight to protect the portal when Lohengrin is dead. He thought so hard on the idea that he soon convinced himself thoroughly of its truth. He gathered the books given to him by Gütel and

96

began reviewing the lessons he had given to the young Lohengrin. He paused a moment to consider that it would still be several years until lessons with the child of Lohengrin would begin. He laughed at himself for a moment, then with a renewed sense of purpose, he continued to prepare the lessons as if they were to begin early the next morning.

The Ancient One did not expect Lohengrin to return quickly, but the long absence of a Swan Knight in the valley began to worry the old swan. He did not feel that he could fly in search of his old student and leave the Portal Valley entirely abandoned. A few months later, while The Ancient One was preparing year three of his new pupil's training, the tireless swan looked up the hill from a window in the house. He saw Lohengrin walking alongside a woman. She was not as pretty as Elsa, but there was intelligence in her eyes and a strong air of understanding about her. She was older than Lohengrin. Grey hairs peered shyly through the thick brown hair of her youth. Her eyes wore the wrinkles of time, but not hard time. They spoke of years filled with experience and heavy contemplation. The Ancient One walked out of the house to greet them at their approach. Lohengrin had told the woman about his life, the portal, and the giant talking swan. Hearing about a giant talking swan and witnessing one are very different things. She froze when she saw him. Lohengrin did not slow his walk toward the house and his awaiting friend. When the woman stopped, Lohengrin reached back, blindly took her hand, and pulled her forward at her previous pace.

Lohengrin appeared more resolute than joyful. The swan made a deep bow. The sun caught him to perfect advantage. Even Lohengrin had never seen his friend so majestic. Added to the sun on the splendid white feathers was joy, visible and almost tangible, radiating from the bird. Lohengrin introduced his companion as "a very good woman".

The Ancient One began a second bow but snapped upward, looking at Lohengrin, and said, "But what is her name?"

Lohengrin pulled himself out of a trance of thought and apologized, "I am sorry, this is my wife."

The Swan repeated with some impatience in his voice, "But what is her name?"

The woman stood like stone at Lohengrin's side. Sheepishly, Lohengrin answered, "I am sorry. Old friend, this is Nethe, my wife. Nethe this is…"

Lohengrin's introduction was cut short by his surprise at Nethe's sudden drop to one knee.

She buried her chin in her breasts, then looked up slowly to catch the swan squarely in the eyes as she reverently said, "The Ancient One."

The swan continued the second bow he had stopped so abruptly. This bow was lower and slower than the one he had intended earlier. Nethe remained on her knee, so The Ancient One looked slightly downward to keep her eyes. Nethe began to reach up to him.

She paused and asked the swan in a tone so proper and respectful, "May I?"

The swan nodded his consent and Nethe continued her reach until she was caressing the long, soft neck of the most magnificent creature she had ever dreamed of.

The Ancient One felt a warm sense of right with the introduction. Nethe's mind was capable and her heart was intensely loyal. This the swan could see clearly, as if reading her mind the way he read Parsifal's. Kindness and piety flavored the air around her, more satisfying than delicious to the palate. With the introductions behind, The Ancient One asked to be let home after the many long weeks alone in Lohengrin's house. Nethe waited with piqued curiosity as Lohengrin apologized again to his old friend and walked with him to the portal point. Nethe followed but kept her distance.

Every sense in her body and mind leapt when the crackling sound heralded the opening of the portal. She watched with a degree of wonder that her eyes had not felt sense her early childhood. The swan disappeared inside of the portal. Lohengrin turned his back to the hole in the air. As he walked from it, back to his new bride, the portal snapped to a close leaving nothing but the natural scenery, as it had done countless times before. Lohengrin walked beside his wife and looked at her as she was unable to break her gaze from the portal point. Lohengrin reached behind her head, so as not to break her gaze, and pulled her slightly toward him, just enough to apply a tender kiss to her cheek. He walked away and into the house, leaving Nethe staring at the scene, with her memory and imagination filling in the images she had just witnessed. After a few minutes, she joined her husband in her new home.

Nethe took quickly to her new life. She paid a respectful visit to Gütel's family, who maintained close relations with Lohengrin. They were delighted to meet her. Although they were ignorant of the portal and the obligations of the Swan Knights, they compassionately felt Lohengrin's loneliness and were glad that he had married. It took little time for Nethe to earn their admiration. Nethe warmed admirably to her life as a Swan Knight's wife. She treated the Scheriers to delights from her kitchen and stories from her past. The Ancient One was enthralled by her skills in conversation and her deeply philosophical mind. As much as he loved Lohengrin, his visits to the valley from the Sweeter Realm were motivated by his desire to converse with Nethe.

Lohengrin had grown cold in his manner and Nethe brought warmth to the home. She spent more time with the swan than her husband did. Nethe often begged for Lohengrin to open the portal and summon the swan. He was quick to obey his wife, but took little initiative himself to see his old friend. His austerity was only lightened in the company of the Scheriers, whose light-hearted playfulness always managed to coax Lohengrin into a wrestling match.

Nethe and the swan would speak for hours, in such open and comfortable conversation, on subjects of every imaginable field of thought. One of their more common topics was the state of Lohengrin's mind. The Ancient One told Nethe stories of Lohengrin's youth, painting a picture of a warm and passionate knight who sought love across the north. He told her the story of Elsa, of their adventures in Elsa's rescue from the lynch mob, the marriage, the battle in the wedding chamber, the departure from Elsa, the return home, and Lohengrin's oath to the Queen. Nethe wished dearly to see Lohengrin in this way, to bring the heroic fire of love into their life together. The swan told her of Elsa's death and its effect on her husband. Lohengrin had told Nethe about Elsa, but his hardening exterior forbade the expressions of love, regret, and turmoil that still swirled tumultuously inside of him. Being a woman of deep understanding, Nethe's mind filled in the missing pieces of the story, completing the portrait of Lohengrin's coldness. It was Lohengrin's mind that left the valley in search of a wife, not his heart. Lohengrin's mind chose the best woman he had ever met, but his heart was still broken and could not be given to anyone. Both Nethe and The Ancient One understood this.

Nethe felt pity for her husband's pain, but also a new sense of obligation to melt the ice in him and revive the Swan Knight's heart. It was his earnestness that attracted her to him when they met. A deathly serious sense of honor hung plainly in his manner. Nethe found this quality to be entirely unique among her connections. It attached her mind to him, but her heart longed for a husband's warmth. Nethe and The Ancient One conspired to warm Lohengrin's heart and return to the valley the passionate Swan Knight that swore his allegiance to the Queen. They decided that the innocence of the creatures of the Sweeter Realm might cut through Lohengrin's worldly regrets and despairs enough for the passionate child of Gütel to bubble forth. The Ancient One returned to his home with a new quest, to find the sweetest creatures of the Sweeter Realm and bring them to Lohengrin to melt his coldness.

The Ancient One was gone for more than six weeks. Lohengrin spent his days patrolling the peremeter of the valley. When he returned to the house, he often cried. When he was not crying, he was in intense prayer. Nethe's attempts to welcome her husband into the house, with warm and nurturing words and caresses, went unnoticed and unreturned. Nethe grew lonlier each time she set eyes on her husband, each time she touched him. She sat near him and cried with him when he sat and cried. She intensly prayed when he intensely prayed. Still, no matter how strenuously Nethe reached for a tender connection to her husband, Lohengrin remained focused in his spiritual isolation.

Christmas came and Lohengrin showed no signs of recognizing the day. Nethe left the valley alone and joined in a humble celebration in the home of Gütel's family. They welcomed her as one of their own. They prayed and feasted admirably. But it only made Nethe long more deeply for family, and her only family was the increasingly cold and distant Lohengrin and the long-absent Ancient One. Nethe returned from Gütel's childhood home, early in the evening, with a painful hunger in her soul. The night was cold and clear. Snow covered the ground and her feet were wet and cold from her long walk. But she was not ready to retire the sacred day, to yield to slumber without giving Christ's birthday another chance to redeem her. She gathered all of the oil lamps in her house, carried them to the portal point, placed them in front of the nearest tree and lit them. She tied ribbons of different colors to the branches. The ribbons caught the light of the flames brilliantly, dancing giddily in the breeze, against the sharply contrasted darkness of the branches and the forest behind them. They reminded Nethe of the Angels who sang to the shepherds of Christ's birth. She imagined that the ribbons, which seemed to put off their own light, were angels singing to her of the birth of the Lord. She knelt before the tree and began to sing along with the angelic voices in her imagination.

Lohengrin, attracted first by the singing and then by the light, broke from his nightly patrol and walked under an inescapable trance toward his wife, seeming to float over the rocks and stumps and other obstacles in his path. As he approached her from behind, he joined his deep voice to hers. She glanced over her shoulder at him, smiled, and reached her hand back to him, never breaking the mystic melody that flowed almost involuntarily from her lips. As Lohengrin reached her outstretched hand, and his voice came into balance with hers, he crossed his trigger threshold and the portal opened. Through it stepped The Ancient One, followed by a dozen of the pleasantest looking beings either Nethe or Lohengrin had ever beheld, made even softer by the warm light of the lamps, the divine dancing of the ribbons, and the angelic harmonies still swimming effortlessly from Nethe and Lohengrin's lips.

Nethe stood facing the tree. Lohengrin stood beside his wife, clasping her hand as if he would never let it go. The Ancient One stood beside Lohengrin and rested his head on Lohengrin's waist. Two creatures, as thin as the branches that held the ribbons, covered from head to toe in soft, almost glowing, brownish-orange hair, stood breast-high beside Nethe. The waves of their thick, coarse hair resembled the patterns of tree bark. Their facial features were slight, offering little change from forehead to chest. Their eyes sunk deeply into their heads and their noses were little more than a knuckle of a human hand. Their mouths were mere slits beneath their almost unnoticeable noses. They had no distinguishable necks, just a steady slope from the tops of their heads to the beginning of their long legs. Yet their faces expressed vividly their good nature and their instant sense of gratitude and loyalty to their human hosts. Their most remarkable feature were their small hands with long fingers. The flesh of their hands and fingers looked like wood, hard and splintery. Nethe glanced down to them, welcoming them with a joyous face and her continuing song.

Six ankle-high birds filled in the spaces around the feet of the party. They looked like owls, but with awkwardly large, thick wings, and bushy tails dragging behind them, like a wolf's tail, covered in such fine feathers that they looked hairy. The birds were deep brown, like the darkest bark in the forest. Their tiny beaks hooked like an owl's and their large, bright-blue eyes expressed both warmth and intelligence. Two new Scheriers were with the group, alongside the two they had already met. The four Scheriers laid across the feet of Nethe and Lohengrin. They wrapped themselves tightly around the ankles of the humans, resting their heads atop their own rear legs, facing the lighted tree. The Ancient One was the first of the creatures to join in the song, followed soon by the others. They sounded like a hundred voices. And the light from the lamps seemed to grow with the sound, and light half the valley. The snow on the hillside turned light orange. The crackling of the open portal added a fitting percussion to the song. The ribbons swayed precisely to the rhythm.

Portal, lamps, ribbons, and trees, the Swan Knight and his wife, the old teacher and his host of friends, and the crackling portal all joined in orchestrated solidarity to praise the Christ Child and celebrate the unity of their mutual affection. In the heart of the song, Nethe looked to her singing husband, his face glowing in the light of the lamps, the joined voices of their friends seeming to reflect off his cheeks, and she saw in him, united with the earnest devotion that had attracted her to him, the joy of Christmas and the bloom of loving youth. As he turned to meet her eyes, she squeezed his hand a little tighter and leaned her shoulder against him. In that glance, their hearts joined as their minds had already done. They fell in love in that moment, surrounded by friends, song, and the strong presence of the Lord. At that moment, they embarked on a marriage of respect *and* affection.

The song came to such a natural conclusion, as if it had been meticulously composed in advance. The party took the lamps and the ribbons into the house, moving as one, almost as tightly as they stood and sang. The portal closed behind them as they moved the Grail Blood toward the house. When they entered the house, it was already as warm inside as a midsummer afternoon — at least it felt that way to the happy party. The lamps lit the small house more brightly than it had ever been lit. All contributed in hanging the ribbons about the walls and furnishings.

They ate. They told stories. They laughed and they sang. The stick-like creatures introduced themselves as Zweigwesens. They usually spoke in unison. There was nothing about them that might designate gender. Their voices were high, like that of a human child. They spoke clearly and with courtly formality. The little birds clearly understood everything spoken by the others, but they spoke in high-pitched whistles that could not be understood as language by the humans. Their fluctuating tones imitated spoken language, but no words could be distinguished from them. Their contributions to conversation were translated by The Ancient One, and occasionally by the Zweigwesens. Nethe called them Eulesängers. Nobody corrected her and the little birds seemed to accept the name with pride.

Nethe and Lohengrin held each other tightly most of the evening, rarely relinquishing the grip of new lovers, and often catching each other in fixed and devoted gazes at the other's beaming face. In a sense, they were new lovers. The infant love they felt in the house that night was born on the hill just moments before, in front of the portal and their friends. They had never before heard the blending of their singing voices. She had never before seen the smile that he gave to her in front of the lit tree and dancing ribbons. The night gave the couple all of the thrills of new romance, wrapped tightly in all of the comforts of intimate familiarity.

While the celebrations continued in the house, Nethe looked in one moment to find Lohengrin wearing an expression of regret, as he considered his earlier cold behavior. She responded with a look that understood and forgave, one that welcomed his happiness to join hers, and melted and evaporated his regrets, as if they had never existed. Nethe did not have Grail Blood. But at that moment, Lohengrin considered her as noble as any knight or any king in any land. They all celebrated deep into the night and slept, in one giant embrace, the most peaceful and contented rest that any of them had known.

They awoke to a bright, cold morning that seemed to welcome them to an exciting new life, with new vigor, and new friends. The Ancient One and Nethe caught each other admiring the glow of warmth shining from Lohengrin's face as he walked into the fresh air of the morning and drew a deep breath that called a hearty welcome to his future. They smiled at each other, congratulating the other for such unexpected success in their mutual quest to soften Lohengrin's heart. Nethe and Lohengrin saw their friends to the portal. The Zweigwesens gave a simultaneous, courtly bow, promised to return soon, and stepped into the Sweeter Realm. The Eulesängers ran around Lohengrin, rubbing themselves affectionately against his ankles, and imparting their adieus in their high and spirited whistles. They flew around Nethe's head, brushing their bushy tails against her cheeks, then flew swiftly through the portal. The

Scheriers waddled into the portal humming Nethe's Christmas melody. The Ancient One, having spent so much time away from the valley and wanting to revel in the success of his endeavors, remained with Nethe and Lohengrin for a few more days. The three of them enjoyed sweet companionship and rich conversation. When the swan asked to be let home, he offered to bring more kind creatures to meet them.

Lohengrin stood near his old friend at the open portal, tilted his head slightly to one side, and said softly, "My teacher, I put my welfare under your capable wings."

The Ancient One pressed his head against Lohengrin's belly, turned and winked to Nethe, then strolled casually and contentedly through the portal. Lohengrin and Nethe stood staring at the open portal for a full minute, then walked toward the house and gave each other a tender little kiss just as the portal snapped shut behind them.

CHAPTER 7
The Greatest Knight

LOHENGRIN AND NETHE spent the next two weeks alone together fueling the new fire between them. In the holy and devoted passion of those weeks, they conceived a child. Nethe knew immediately upon waking the next morning. Lohengrin knew at a single glance at her smiling face. His sense of relief and accomplishment was immense. They had forged the next link in the chain of Grail Blood. They had made a family out of a devoted, passionate, and pious love. The Ancient One would have a new pupil and the Queen a new knight. The Grail would have another paladin and the Lord a new servant. The couple worked hard that their preparations might match those of the teacher, and the house was quickly suited up to again hold a family.

A few weeks later, Nethe was walking near the portal point when she heard the familiar crack of the opening portal. Excitedly, she looked around for her husband, but Lohengrin was nowhere to be seen. Suspicious and unsettled, she alternated between staring into the portal and quickly scanning the surrounding area. There was nothing and nobody but her and the open portal. She slowly backed away from the opening until it cracked to a close. She stopped sharp and smiled, realizing what was happening. Unlike Gütel carrying the unborn Lohengrin, Nethe was able to open the portal within a few weeks of conceiving the child. Lohengrin, Nethe, and The Ancient One pondered the meaning of this.

The child's blood was strong with Grail influence. Nobody knew what this would mean for the child or for the portal. Nethe, filled with faith, shared none of Lohengrin's concerns. She felt a righteousness growing inside of her, a holiness swelling her faith from within. She was proud to be the wife of a Swan Knight, but much prouder to carry one inside of her. She felt the power of Parsifal's blood in her belly. She delighted in opening the portal and hearing it shut behind her as she walked away. Lohengrin warned her not to use the ability of her unborn child frivolously. But her power over the portal reminded her that her name would be eternally etched into the history of the Holy Grail. It reminded her of her important role as a servant of God. Each crack of the opening portal at her approach brought her closer to Christ and to the destiny of his precious cup.

Nethe could not help herself. She walked to the portal several times a day. This increased Lohengrin's concerns and doubled his patrols, separating the couple from one another. Although the sensations in Nethe subsided and routines returned to normal, Nethe still enjoyed opening the portal, and Lohengrin, understanding that Nethe's ability would be lost after the birth of the child, asked her to open the portal whenever it needed opening, rather than doing it himself. As the child grew inside of her, Nethe opened the portal from farther and farther away — farther than Lohengrin! All agreed that this would have some profound meaning for the child and for the portal.

As the child's birth came near, Lohengrin became increasingly contemplative. When home, he was as warm and loving as he was on Christmas night. But he spent more time on the hillside, usually staring toward the north, lost in thought. Nethe knew that her husband still thought of Elsa and still carried guilt for the children she would never have. Without a word to her husband, Nethe decided on names for the child — if a boy, Elgast — if a girl, Elsa. Caring for her namesake might relieve Lohengrin of guilt for the wife he did not protect, the wife he let die, cold, in the wilderness, with no home and no family. When the time came, Lohengrin delivered his own daughter and placed her in her mother's arms. When Nethe, worn and weary, loudly declared the baby to be called Elsa, Lohengrin understood the motivation and thanked the Lord for his wife's love and wisdom.

He laid beside Nethe, taking her in his arms and tenderly and lovingly placing alternating kisses on his wife's cheek and his daughter's head. Lohengrin embraced fatherhood with a fervor of devotion even greater than what he had given the portal for all of his years as the Swan Knight. At their age, Nethe and Lohengrin knew it unlikely that they would have another child. Elsa would have to assume her father's burdens, as the only carrier of Grail Blood. Lohengrin began speaking to young Elsa about her duties as a future Swan Knight from the moment she was born.

Lohengrin brought Elsa to the portal in the afternoon of her first full day. For the first time since Parsifal's death, the portal was opened by two. It showed its excitement as it tore open with unusual speed and crispness. In anticipation of his duties to the child, The Ancient One built a new nest near the portal point in the Sweeter Realm. From his side, he knew by the unique behavior of the portal that the child was born. He came through with a gift. It was the first feather he had ever lost, kept as a treasure by a sentimental bird. He had sharpened it into a pen as soon as he heard of Nethe's pregnancy, and held it in his nest to be given to the newest keeper of the portal. It still shone as brightly as the feathers he wore.

The Ancient One handed it to Lohengrin, saying, "It is for her lessons, when they begin."

Lohengrin held it reverently and caressed it softly. He thanked his old friend for the gift and began the next day building a box to hold it until Elsa was old enough to employ a pen. Upon the lid of the box, he carved in relief a stunning likeness of his old teacher, pulling a boat that held the Holy Grail. The swan and boat image floated upon a feather, the exact size and shape of the baby's gift. The box and pen held a place of prominent display in the family's home, waiting for the day that it would be held by young Elsa. After presenting the pen, The Ancient One returned to the Sweeter Realm to announce the birth and gather gifts and visitors.

Before the baby was a week old, The Ancient One returned with Scheriers, Zweigwesens, Eulesängers, and many other creatures, each baring gifts. The Scheriers rolled a large, round piece of ore. They presented it as a mystical boulder that had resided near their home for as long as anyone could remember. It was light enough to be pushed by several Scheriers, yet as strong as anything in the Sweeter Realm. They said that resting on it brought a sense of well-being and security. Three Scheriers demonstrated by mounting the rock, curling into tight balls, and exhaling with slowly widening smiles.

Lohengrin and Nethe accepted the gift with a full understanding of its cultural significance to the Scheriers.

The Zweigwesens gave a toy crafted from wood. It was a Unicorn, about knee-high to Lohengrin. When placed on a downward slope, its wooden-jointed legs galloped forward with amazingly life-like movement. Elsa was startled out of sleep by the sound of the toy as it galloped down the hill from the portal, toward the house. She smiled, then let out a quick baby laugh and fell back asleep. Two Zweigwesens fetched the toy back up to the portal. One mounted the toy and rode it back down the side of the hill. The creatures of the Sweeter Realm laughed at the display, but Nethe and Lohengrin did not laugh. They stared in amazement at the mastery of the mechanics and the artistry. Lohengrin had worked wood himself, including the small ornamental helmet on his father's shrine. He had never seen, or even imagined, such an ingenious and masterful piece of mechanical woodwork. The humans' astonished gazes slowly transformed to shared laughter as the creatures took turns riding the toy down the hill. Zweigwesen children can walk at two days old and run by the end of their first week. They expected to see Elsa ride the toy down the hill. They were disappointed but understanding when Nethe explained the timeline of human infant development.

The Eulesängers gave a handful of tiny eggs. This seemed too intimate a gift and Nethe accepted them with an expression of uncertainty. The Ancient One explained that they were not Eulesänger eggs, but stone replicas with tiny holes in them. He instructed Nethe to blow into the hole at the pointed end of one of the eggs. When she did, a whistle came from the egg. It sounded exactly like the song of the Eulesängers. Over time, Nethe learned to play her Christmas melody with the eggs, reminding her of her tiny friends and that magical and holy night when they came into her life. Playing the eggs became her favorite pastime. Their sound was one of the sure ways to coax young Elsa to sleep. Over time, the eggs became cured by the hardened tears from the flow that so often sprang from Nethe's eyes as she played the precious gifts of the Eulesängers to her young child.

Elsa grew up much less lonely than did Lohengrin. Parsifal and Gütel were affectionate parents to their son, but Elsa had the benefit of many more companions. The creatures of the Sweeter Realm became comfortable in the Bavarian hills surrounding the valley. They came from a peaceful place. They had not known war or crime in thousands of years. They were ignorant to the dangers of Lohengrin's world. Even some of the shyer and more secretive creatures of the Sweeter Realm ventured through the portal to play with the young knight. Elsa grew beautiful, with patience and understanding beyond her years. Her hair was bright yellow as an infant. As she grew older, it darkened to match the light brown of her father's.

When Elsa was four years old, The Ancient One began his lessons with her. She consumed the material at an amazing rate. She walked herself to the portal each day and opened it to welcome her teacher and begin the lessons. Elsa began to control the portal with her thoughts, not just her proximity. Nethe watched her one morning walk right to the portal point. It did not open. She sat down, pulled out the pen that was gifted to her at her birth, looked up to the portal point and opened the portal with a glance. One morning, she opened the portal from the house and yelled from her window until the swan joined her there. Elsa studied all morning and spent most of the afternoon playing with her friends from the Sweeter Realm. She was a happy child, made of an unusual alloy of innocence and understanding.

One day, when she was five, Lohengrin found her sitting on her toy Unicorn, near the portal point. The portal was closed. In its place stood a Unicorn, tall, with wide, powerful shoulders. It was light grey, with a pitch-black mane and beard. Its horn had loose spirals, so that from the base to the tip, a spiral wrapped around the horn no more than two or three times. In the inset of the spirals, peering, out subtly through the brilliant white, was a hint of deep blue. It towered over the small child as it bent its head low to touch the point of its horn to the center of Elsa's chest. Lohengrin drew his sword and yelled to his daughter. The Unicorn lifted its head, but before it did, Elsa grabbed the horn so that she was lifted off of the toy. Once the Unicorn was fully erect, Elsa slid down its neck to rest seated comfortably on the creature's back.

Elsa was perched heroically on the Unicorn. Lohengrin lowered his weapon and stared in amazement. Not only had he never seen a Unicorn, but his young daughter seemed to have a comfortable understanding with the magnificent beast, as if she had known it and trained with it for years. Lohengrin's scream beckoned Nethe by his side. They watched their daughter nod her head. Elsa was still on the Unicorn's back. It could not have seen her nod. But it responded nevertheless, and walked slowly and majestically to the astonished parents. When the Unicorn stood beside Lohengrin and Nethe, Elsa stood up high on its shoulders. It twisted its neck toward her so that she could grab the horn. Once she had ahold of the horn, the Unicorn lifted Elsa off of its shoulders and placed her gently in Lohengrin's arms.

The Swan Knight and the Unicorn stared deeply into each other's eyes. The Unicorn broke the gaze to bend its head downward and touch Lohengrin in the chest with the tip of the horn, just as it had done with Elsa. In the moment that the horn touched Lohengrin, he felt the creature's thoughts. The Unicorn was pleased to meet Elsa's parents and honored to be the first of his kind to greet this new world. Lohengrin felt his own thought travel from him, through the horn, to the Unicorn. Its black, bushy, expressive eyebrows responded to each of Lohengrin's thoughts as he wished the Unicorn welcome to his home and concentrated to think the most peaceful and honorable thoughts. Lohengrin had the feeling that the Unicorn read much more than the simple thoughts that he tried to send across this magical connection.

Satisfied with the greeting, the Unicorn pulled its horn away from Lohengrin, rubbed its large mouth against the top of the giggling head of Elsa, and galloped to the portal point. It stopped at the portal point and turned to look back at Elsa. With a subtle blink of her eyes, Elsa opened the portal and the Unicorn trotted through. When Lohengrin spoke to The Ancient One about the encounter, the swan was amazed. He had not seen a Unicorn in a hundred years. They hid, excluding themselves from contact with any creature. This was a testament to Elsa's power and suggested that she might have a destiny in both worlds. Within the secret corners of Lohengrin's heart, the thought elicited great pride and great fear.

The Ancient One maintained a diligent eye on the Lohengrin legend growing in the north. Many told of the knight named Lohengrin, who had to choose between his love of a mortal woman and his devotion to a divine quest. In other communities, the story evolved into a choice between the love of a mortal woman and that of a mythical goddess. The swan watched with wonder and apprehension as the stories of his former pupil were acted out on makeshift stages. The stories branched into variations both mortal and mythical, all stemming from the loose tongue of Lohengrin's first wife and Lohengrin's own magical appearance and disappearance with the giant swan.

Beside the legends of Lohengrin, grew the legends of Parsifal — the peasant who became a knight, his defeat of the Red Knight, his quest to find the Grail, his vanquishing of an entire army of Saracens. These stories surprised the swan. Parsifal had told him little of his adventures prior to the conflict with Klingsor and nobody lived to explain or authenticate the legends. The Holy Grail played heavily in the tales of Parsifal, which surged inland from the western coasts like wild fire. The legends of Parsifal and those of Lohengrin united to connect Lohengrin to the Grail. There was nothing in the tales that directed adventurers to the portal point, so The Ancient One tempered his rising fears and returned home to report his discoveries to Lohengrin.

The Swan Knight's heart skipped a beat when he heard about the spreading rumors of his father and the Holy Grail. The Ancient One brought him solace when he described the nature of the growing legends. The stories were told at firesides and sung in drunken halls. They blended with local legends and family histories. There was no evidence of an earnest quest to follow the path of Parsifal to locate the Grail. Lohengrin's own legends had swelled into such absurd fantasy that no degree of ambition would act upon them. The swan also reminded his old student that the Grail is out of reach of any who might seek it. The old magician Klingsor was surely dead.

The Grail was in the possession of the Queen of the Land and Shallow Waters. It was hidden deep in the Sweeter Realm. Parsifal secured the Grail from the perils of his world and Lohengrin secured the portal. This speech soothed Lohengrin tremendously. Nethe also reminded her husband that God had opened the portal for Parsifal and that Lohengrin should trust in the pact between his noble father and the Holy Redeemer. Still, Lohengrin kept a more rigid eye on his daughter and limited her access to the portal.

Lohengrin's faith in the security of the Grail grew as he witnessed the powers of his daughter grow. Her connection to the portal and to the inhabitants of the Sweeter Realm was profound and mystical. In the swell of his anxieties, Lohengrin would often lean upon the sphere of metal ore gifted by the Scheriers. It brought him the same sense of well-being that it had provided to the Scheriers for countless generations. The rock became less necessary when The Ancient One returned one day from a long flight and reported that the Grail was rumored to rest in Jerusalem. Nevertheless, Lohengrin doubled his preparations for Elsa's eventual appointment as the Swan Knight. He pressed his friend to push harder with his lessons. Lohengrin was growing old and Elsa would assume his post at a much younger age than he would have wished.

Elsa was fascinated by the stories of her grandfather and of her destiny as a Swan Knight. Lohengrin often scolded her for climbing on Parsifal's shrine and removing the wooden helmet carved in his honor. She played with it, pretending to be Parsifal, fighting wicked flowermaidens, being rescued by a local woman, opening the portal, meeting a giant swan, and securing the Grail, all as it had been told to her by The Ancient One.

Lohengrin had to pry the sculpture from his daughter's hands to return it to the shrine.

Elsa's abilities grew, as did her calm wisdom. One day, when she was about twelve years old, the quiet of the valley was disturbed by the march of a small army. Lohengrin, fearing the worse, donned his armor, drew his sword, and stood alone to face them. The leader rode forward on horseback and asked Lohengrin if he and his soldiers could pass peacefully through the valley. Both relieved and impressed by the cordiality of the request, Lohengrin nodded and allowed the men to pass by their home and over the next hill. As they did, a few of them looked back to see a Unicorn sprint through the portal just before it snapped shut. They returned at dawn the following morning, with around twenty men, armed and hoping to plunder the magic they had witnessed. Nethe barred the house as Lohengrin walked out to meet them. They drew their swords and encircled Lohengrin. He attacked the band and killed half of them before being overwhelmed.

Just as the surviving marauders piled on Lohengrin, the sweet voice of Elsa rang out, holding a single high note. It caught the attention of everything and everyone between the mountains. The marauders abandoned the defeated Lohengrin and ran in unison toward the unarmed twelve-year-old girl, who stood just on the other side of the portal point from the advancing men. When the men were right on Elsa, she opened the portal and watched them disappear inside. She quickly shut the portal to Lohengrin's desperate scream of despair. Elsa held up her hand, which muted her father's cry. Lohengrin stumbled to his daughter, who had walked slowly and confidently to meet him half way.

Elsa shook her head and told the Swan Knight, "It is done. It is over."

Lohengrin's astonished and bewitched gaze into his daughter's calm eyes was broken by the sound of the opening portal. He looked past Elsa to see the lifeless bodies of the marauders piled outside of the open portal.

Elsa drew Lohengrin's attention back to her as she said, "Come, their bodies are our problem."

Lohengrin, Nethe, and Elsa burnt the bodies of all twenty men and buried their remains along with all of their armor, weapons, and possessions. Lohengrin slept poorly that night, his mind being passed back and forth between the tight grip of fear and the nurturing wonder at his daughter's abilities. By morning, he decided to give her a set of armor. His father's armor would never fit Elsa's slight figure. And she was something more than he, more even than Parsifal. She deserved special armor.

There would be no place to purchase armor for a slight-figured young woman. Had there been, he could not afford to buy it. Lohengrin decided to forge the armor himself. He ran many designs through his head, some common and familiar, some unique. The helmet design was easy. He would forge a helmet exactly like the wooden carving on his father's shrine. He consulted his wife and his teacher and decided on a design for the armor. He built a kiln and needed only the metal to begin. He awoke early one morning to buy the supplies to forge the armor. He was startled by commotion outside of his door. He opened the door and saw several Scheriers rolling their sacred ore to Lohengrin's feet. They looked into the house, past Lohengrin, to Elsa, who stood silently behind her father, seemingly directing the Scheriers with the slightest of gestures.

Lohengrin knew what he was meant to do. He spent the next year smelting the stone, extracting the lightweight, pitch-black metal from the rock and forging it into Elsa's armor. The armor was magnificent and polished brilliantly. It was as thin as a shirt and harder than any rock. The helmet was identical in design to the wooden ornament on Parsifal's shrine. Small swans topped the shoulders of the breastplate, intricately carved in fine detail to imitate The Ancient One. Each portion was fitted precisely to Elsa's figure so that when she ran fully clad it hardly made a sound. Lohengrin, Nethe, and The Ancient One presented the armor to Elsa in a ceremony that included her oath to the Grail, the portal, and the Queen and a symbolic transfer of the knighthood from father to daughter.

Every creature that had ever ventured through the portal was there to witness the oath of the new Swan Knight. Lohengrin swore that things would continue mostly as they had been. The ceremony was more to acknowledge that Elsa's ability to defend the portal had surpassed her father's. The swearing of the oath and the presentation of the armor did not signify Lohengrin's retirement from service, or even mark the slightest reduction in his diligence in protecting the portal. It served more as a last will, as an assurance of continuity should anything happen to Lohengrin. There, at the open portal, surrounded by friends and family, Elsa stood stone-still and proudly erect as her father clad her in her new armor. It was a cloudy day, but the sun still appeared to reflect off Elsa's long, flowing hair. Just as Lohengrin finished strapping his daughter in, two more Scheriers came through the portal, followed by a being so unlike anything the humans had ever seen, from either side of the portal. It was tall, barely shorter than Lohengrin.

It looked like a statue of water, as it stood perfectly still in a shallow but reverent bow to Elsa. The objects behind it could be seen foggy and distorted through it. Portions of it hung loosely off of it, like clothing, but appearing more to be a part of the creature than something worn. A long appendage hung behind its head, like hair, but of the same clear, water-like appearance. It bore the figure of a human woman, naked but clothed. As it stood still, nothing of it moved, like the figure of a portrait standing before a living background. When it rose from its bow and turned to face Lohengrin, tiny waves rippled across every part of it. In an almost silent whisper, it expressed a cordial greeting to Lohengrin. It turned back to Elsa, in beautiful movements that looked more like the haphazard currents of the breezes than the conscious stumbling of a human body. As it walked to Elsa, it seemed to be carried by the tiny ripples across its body. Elsa reached out and touched the side of its face, expecting to reach right through it and pull back a wet hand. The creature was solid and quite dry. Its face was softer than a rose pedal.

It reached both of its small, flawless, feminine hands to Elsa's breastplate and began caressing the armor. As it did, the armor polished. It rubbed every inch of Elsa's armor, leaving it upon completion, glowing as if the clouds had opened for a single ray of sunlight to shine directly on the new Swan Knight. The armor seemed to flash white and silver while remaining pitch-black, changing and glowing with Elsa's slightest movements. She removed her helmet and leaned in to the creature. It bent low and received Elsa's grateful kiss. The kiss was the purest, softest experience Elsa would ever know. It intoxicated her and felt like a blissful eternity, until the creature pulled away and returned Elsa abruptly to the moment. It whispered something in its own language.

Although it spoke aloud and was heard by all, Elsa felt like the message was whispered directly into her heart. It warmed her and returned for a brief moment the blissful feeling of the kiss.

There were no formal introductions, no name given to call this creature. It turned and rippled its way back through the portal in a dance that looked commanded by the whims of nature. It was followed by all of the other inhabitants of the Sweeter Realm, including The Ancient One, leaving the family alone to celebrate the occasion in the peace of their quiet home. In a later lesson, Elsa tormented The Ancient One until he abandoned the agenda for the day to speak of the creature with the magical kiss. He called them Brunnens. The Brunnen that came to the ceremony was one of particular esteem among her kind. The Brunnens worked closely with the Queen and commanded a great deal of respect in the Sweeter Realm. As Elsa listened to The Ancient One's description of the Brunnens, she was humbled by the attention the creature paid her. It only served to strengthen her desire to enter the portal and meet the Queen. The Brunnens are without gender. But their features and manner are so feminine, so nurturing and maternal, their touch so soft and their kiss so tender, that Elsa referred to them all as females.

The armor that Lohengrin made fit so comfortably that Elsa wore it often, for several days at a time, even sleeping in it. She said that it cradled her. It clearly maintained the soothing effect that served the Scheriers. It both emboldened and comforted Elsa. She hated removing it. But like with the feather, Lohengrin built a box to hold it, and it was there that it spent most of its time.

Elsa, now nearly sixteen years old, continued her lessons with her teacher, continued to grow wise, and continued to sharpen her control of the portal and her connection to the creatures of the Sweeter Realm. Elsa wanted to meet the Queen to whom she had sworn her service. The swan reminded her that the Queen would never leave the Sweeter Realm and that the Swan Knight is forbidden to leave her post, on her own side of the portal. She dreamed often of the Queen, constructing the images from the descriptions given by the old teacher — the smoothest, fairest face, embedded like a stone among the most radiant and colorful scales. Of all of the magnificent creatures of the Sweeter Realm that Elsa had met, none could compare to the image of the Queen from the swan's description that she kept perpetually atop her active mind.

Elsa asked constantly about the Queen. There was little to tell beyond the physical descriptions and the stories about how she united her kingdom by communicating with all creatures when they could only understand their own kind. She lived in the Shallow Waters, which is presumably where she kept the Grail. With a thought, she could make quarreling parties see and understand the position of the other. She did not bring an end to quarrels in her kingdom. But she brought understanding and a sense of unified purpose. She ended the ancient conflicts. Most importantly, she held the border between the Shallow Waters and the Deep Waters. She was Queen when The Ancient One was born and few remember a time without her.

Elsa's abilities continued to grow as she matured into adulthood. Not only could she open and close the portal at will, and from increasing distances, she could alter the size and shape of it. One day Elsa entertained some visitors from the Sweeter Realm by opening the portal into the silhouetted images of her guests — a small, Scherier-shaped portal closed and reopened as a large Unicorn shaped portal, even a tiny Eulesänger shaped portal, hovering above the ground. Lohengrin and Nethe's astonishment was only broken by the laughter that the spectacle pulled from them. Elsa was a fun, light-hearted young woman with a hearty, authentic, and contagious laugh. She delighted in everything and everyone. She bore none of the worries that haunted Lohengrin. But then, she had few of Lohengrin's experiences and many more unique abilities. The valley has not known a happier person, before or since. Elsa had all of the companions she could wish. She had family. She was adored by all who knew her.

But Lohengrin and Nethe grew older. They had no contact with Nethe's relatives. They grew distant from Gütel's family. Lohengrin, Nethe, and The Ancient One knew that Elsa would need to marry and start a family of her own. The longing for love seemed to enter Elsa's heart just as this determination was being made behind her back. With a little fertilizer from the swan, Elsa grew determined to find love. Lohengrin begged her to venture out and search for a husband while he was still strong enough to protect the portal. So, Elsa packed for a journey and headed southeast toward Oeni Pons, known now as Innsbruck, Austria. At the advice of her teacher, she left her armor behind and strolled into the forest with no weapons. As the parents and teacher watched Elsa disappear into the woods, they continued to hear her sweet singing. They stood and listened long after the song had faded, then went into their home and told stories of Elsa's childhood — laughing, crying, worrying, and praying that their daughter finds a good man, worthy of his post as a Swan Knight's husband.

Elsa stopped in Partanum, known now as Garmisch-Partenkirchen. She was wise and understood her obligations. She did not submit to the siren call of passion. She looked for a man with few familial ties, one who could easily disappear, a good man, a pious man, one with whom she could share mankind's most precious secret. She found this young man in Partanum. His name was Cunrad and he was an architect and stone worker. He was everything that Elsa sought, pure, innocent, just, and holy. He had left his ancestral home to seek work and had no relations in Partanum. Cunrad fell quickly for Elsa's light spirit and wise eyes. But he wanted to settle in Partanum. He assumed that they would make their home there and live on his skills. He was proud and wanted to provide for his new love in the town where he had established his business. Elsa told him that they must live at her home. She told him that there would be little use of his skills in their new life together. He was convinced by the earnestness and wisdom in her expression, and by the love that had already sewn itself tightly to his heart.

They married at the old church in Partanum that Cunrad had renovated, and they returned to Elsa's home. Elsa was only gone from home for four months before returning with her husband. Cunrad's goodness shone brightly from him. It immediately captured the trust and affection of Elsa's parents and teacher. Cunrad had such a strong faith in the power and presence of God that nothing about the portal and the Grail, The Ancient One and the creatures of the Sweeter Realm surprised him. He was honored to assume his role as a Swan Knight's husband, with all of its sacrifices, and the eminence of Elsa's position as a holy knight only strengthened his love and admiration for her. In the noblest words, Cunrad passionately expressed to his new family the strength of his dedication and commitment to Elsa and her duties as

Swan Knight. The trust and comfort of family encircled them all within hours of meeting.

Over the following weeks, several visitors from the Sweeter Realm came to pay their respects to the newlyweds, each bringing unique gifts. Most of the gifts were food, as is the custom for such unions in the Sweeter Realm. The Scheriers brought a flat round fruit. Its casing looked like baked bread, but was not edible. The inside was pure black with white seeds. The meat of the fruit was so soft that it was almost easier to drink it from the casing than to hold it in the hand. The black fruit was bland, but the seeds were sweet and piquant, releasing onto the palate almost more flavor than it can tolerate. The Unicorns brought a thick nectar, the consistency of honey, but salty and bitter. The flavor was too interesting to be unpleasant, and it gave instant clarity of mind when eaten. It revealed no secrets that were not already known, but it cleared away peripheral distractions from the subject at hand. The Unicorns consume it when important decisions need to be made. After the initial sampling, Elsa stored all of the nectar for future use. The Eulesängers brought candy, tiny triangles of candy made from a bitter plant then sweetened, similar to chocolate, but bright orange. The couple sampled many other treats, all given in hearty friendship from their friends in the Sweeter Realm. Most were consumed immediately. Some were stored.

The Ancient One came with a gift too. It was from the Queen of the Land and Shallow Waters. It was a long weed, a rare weed from the waters near her home. The swan told Elsa that only three or four of these weeds exist at a time, making the gift of one something extraordinary. Elsa bit the weed. The Ancient One began to glow with a piercing white light. Elsa looked to Cunrad. He too glowed, but not quite as brilliantly. She turned to Nethe and Lohengrin. Standing together, they shone so brightly that Elsa had to look away. Elsa asked the swan what was happening to her. He explained that the weed reveals love. When consumed, those who love you the most will appear to glow — the deeper and more committed the love, the brighter the glow.

She asked, "So, I am the only one who sees you glowing?"

The swan nodded, proud of the gleaming luster his love for her must be shining in her eyes. For several days, Elsa's loved ones seemed to put off their own light. In Elsa's eyes, Nethe continued to wear a faint halo several weeks later, all from that single nibble from the end of the weed. Elsa stored the weed more securely than the other gifts. Sensing it would save her in a time of desperation, she stored it on the highest shelf in the house.

With the portal in the hands of a powerful Swan Knight, and with a faithful husband at her side, Lohengrin finally felt free to wander from the portal for the first time since he returned with Nethe. In his many years, he saw the growth of the surrounding communities. He feared for the secret of the portal and for the welfare of his family. He left alone for a castle near the town of Foetes, now called Füssen, where a wealthy and powerful family resided, an alliance with whom would strengthen his faith in the Grail's security. The family was called The House of Welf. A beautiful stone castle stood outside of the town near a lake. It was over the ruins of this castle that my father build Hohenschwangau Castle. I remembered my father telling me that Lohengrin had resided in Hohenschwangau. Hearing the swan confirm his words melted some of the ice that encased my father's image in my mind and reminded me of one of his tenderest moments, when he touched my shoulder softly as I stared into the painting of Lohengrin.

Lohengrin fell in love with the area and the people, but longed for home. With each step away from his valley, the blade of longing cut more deeply into his heart. The lake near the castle had many swans, which only made Lohengrin more homesick. But he was warmly welcomed by the Welf family. By now an old man, his eyes still burnt youthfully with the fire of understanding. The sincerity of his words betrayed his righteousness to his new acquaintances. They had never encountered anyone like Lohengrin. His humble piety shone brilliantly from his face. The Welfs were also good people. They readily offered their friendship. As Lohengrin walked the halls of the castle, or viewed it from the hills around it, he thought of his family. He thought about Cunrad and how the young architect would admire the castle. He spoke so openly, vividly, and endearingly about his family that his hosts felt that Nethe, Elsa, and Cunrad lived in the castle with them.

Lohengrin stayed in the castle for almost a year, kindling trust and the bonds of like-hearted kinship. When he returned home, Elsa held a baby in her arms. He was Bechtold, son of Elsa and Cunrad, grandson of Lohengrin and Nethe, and future Swan Knight. The valley was teeming with visitors from the Sweeter Realm who had come back and forth for the weeks since the baby was born. No greeting could have welcomed Lohengrin home more warmly than the echoing cry of his grandson. Nethe ran to meet him as soon as she was alerted to his approach. She kissed him several times then pulled him by the arm to meet the baby. Between the security given by his new alliance and the birth of a healthy, strong baby, Lohengrin was stripped of the worries that had hung around his neck for so many years. He walked with lightness in his step. He wrestled with the Scheriers like he did when he was young. He held his wife like he did on Christmas night so long ago. In his peaceful mind, blended the happiness and confidence of his youth with the wisdom he had gained since. Lohengrin was the very portrait of bliss.

During the pregnancy, Bechtold showed no unusual abilities, as his mother had. But then, this was the first time that the mother of a future Swan Knight was herself a Swan Knight. The portal still opened and closed at Elsa's command and showed no signs of influence from the unborn child. During Lohengrin's absence, the portal opened for Elsa and only Elsa. Even when Nethe carried her infant grandchild to the portal point, it did not open until Elsa willed it so. As an infant, Bechtold did not trigger the portal by proximity. By the time he was walking, and had seen the portal opened and closed many times, he began to display some signs of controlling it, but it was a weak and haphazard control. He was a quiet child, without his grandfather's charisma or his mother's bright eyes. The portal struggled to open when Bechtold walked to it. It seemed almost hesitant to obey him, not like the quick and excited snap opening for the previous Swan Knights. But there was a subtle comfort to Bechtold. The entire valley was his friend — every rock, every tree, every blade of grass. He garnered more affection than obedience from the creatures of the Sweeter Realm. The actions of the portal reflected the nature of Bechtold's relationship with the entire valley. He was a good little boy, but not the seedling of a great adventurer or dynamic leader.

When Bechtold was two years old, his brother Diterich was born. While Diterich was in the womb, the portal showed some unusual behavior, but nothing as ominous as what was seen with the unborn Elsa. Within days of his birth, Diterich opened the portal instantly upon approach. By that time, Bechtold had begun elementary lessons with The Ancient One. One year after Diterich's birth, Elsa and Cunrad had their first daughter, Hildemar. The three children were healthy and happy. The family outgrew the house. Fortunately, Elsa married an architect and stone worker. While still expecting Hildemar, Cunrad began designs for a new home for the Swan Knights. He designed a grand lodge. Its structure demonstrated his experience with churches and his dedication to the Lord. It had an attached chapel, a large kitchen and dining room, eight bedrooms, and a training room for the knights.

Cunrad built a scale model from sticks and rocks. It was a magnificent display of his skills. He said that the building must befit the glory of his wife and her station, yet remain humble enough to evade attention and ward off envy. The little model perfectly reflected Cunrad's vision. It was as cozy as a rabbit's burrow and as glorious as a hallowed cathedral. The exterior was simple and understated, yet it seemed to open into an interior twice as big as its walls should hold. Cunrad built a gazebo in front of the old house, under which he displayed the model for the admiration of his proud family and friends. Cunrad began construction on the new lodge, placing it directly behind the old house, between it and the portal. He did so just in time. Soon after breaking ground on the new lodge, just three months after Hildemar's birth, Elsa was pregnant with their fourth child.

Lohengrin awoke with a start one morning with concerns greater than the capacity of their house. Elsa was to have her fourth child. Only one would assume the title of Swan Knight. What would become of the others? They all had Grail Blood. They all would have access to the portal — and so would their children and their children's children. He could not confine them all to the valley as the generations passed and the Grail Blood multiplied. The idea of portal access spreading throughout the region chilled him to the marrow. To that point, nobody had deeply considered the long-term maintenance of the Portal Valley or the proliferation of the Grail Blood. Lohengrin consulted privately with The Ancient One, who took the matter to the Queen.

The council of three determined that no child born outside of the valley can know about the portal. Any child born in the valley will be taught by The Ancient One and steeped thoroughly in the responsibilities of knowledge. Any child of Parsifal who leaves the valley will swear an oath of secrecy to the Lord God. The oath would preclude them from sharing the family secret with anyone not living in the valley, spouses and children included. This was the only solution to the perils at hand. Lohengrin took a drop of the Unicorns' nectar. The effects of the nectar reinforced the determination of the council. They could not allow a town to grow around the portal. That would draw travelers, tradesmen, and laborers. The population of the valley must remain limited to the Swan Knight's immediate family and any close relations content with the simple life of a subordinate portal custodian. The Portal Valley was a quiet, obscure, secret little corner of the world. Every effort and sacrifice must be made to keep it so.

CHAPTER 8

Great Loss and Glowing Love

BY THE TIME the fourth child was born, a girl they named Birgit, construction on the lodge was well underway. Cunrad's oath of loyalty to the family was put on brilliant display. He worked all day, every day, and well into the night. At the end of the day, he assumed his corner of the old house with a smile and a heart full of love and appreciation for his family, for his position as a Swan Knight's husband, and for the service that Divine Providence graciously permitted him to render his God. The wearier his body at the end of the day, the fuller and more grateful his noble heart. When the lodge was nearly complete, Lohengrin spoke with Elsa and Cunrad about the secret council and its determinations. The Swan Knight and her husband painfully agreed. Cunrad began to consider the future of the valley and the growth of the family. He tilled a large plot of land and prepared it for crops. The next day, he and Elsa left the valley to buy seeds, leaving Lohengrin and Nethe with the children. They did not go far and returned within five days. They entered the valley just after sunset to the smell of burning wood. There, outside of their smoldering, collapsed old house, were the three older children. They were huddled together, weeping loudly. Bechtold and Diterich stood facing the house. Hildemar stood tightly against Bechtold's leg, facing away from the smoldering ruins.

Elsa grabbed Bechtold by the arm and pulled him from the grasp of his little brother and sister. The boy was not yet six years old.

She asked her son, "Where is your baby sister? Where are your grandparents?"

Bechtold pointed to the smoldering pile of rubble, then broke free from his mother and ran into the woods. Cunrad ran after him, leaving Elsa with her grieving little children. Diterich had just turned four years old. He was stouter than the rest and pulled himself together enough to explain that Nethe and Birgit were trapped in the fire. Diterich explained that he had been playing with blocks. His sister and grandmother were in another room. Lohengrin was outside, presumably on his regular patrols. By the time Diterich noticed the flames, every wall of the house was on fire. Lohengrin rushed through the door and ordered the children out of the house. He remained to free his wife and grandchild. Diterich described watching the collapse of the house, with his baby sister and grandparents still inside, while he and Bechtold watched from the outside and Hildemar clung to her brother exactly as Elsa had found them.

Elsa instinctively ran a few steps toward the ruins, determined to save her family. She stopped as she drew close enough to see the extent of the destruction. She realized that her loved ones were dead. She walked slowly to the rubble, followed closely by her surviving children. Elsa called quietly for her mother. The children, standing just behind her, echoed the plea through their sobs, in the most pathetically tragic little voices. Elsa stood with her toes against the burnt, fallen wood and stared into the rubble in silence, while the children called grievously for their grandparents and sister.

As the children continued to call out, and the only response was the crackle of the smoldering rubble, their calls grew louder, more panicked, and more desperate. It rang in Elsa's ears with violent, stabbing pain. The sound also reached Bechtold, who was hiding in the woods from his searching father. Bechtold ran from his hiding place, toward the portal. He opened the portal and yelled into the hole for his teacher. He repeated this call only a few times before the swan appeared. Cunrad ran to his son just as The Ancient One arrived. The screaming boy at the portal, panicked father, the smoldering house, the rancid smell of burnt destruction, the wailing calls of the children for their lost loved ones, the Swan Knight standing frozen at the rubble, all entered the swan's senses together. His thin knees buckled under his despair. He recovered enough to wrap his wings around Bechtold and coil his long neck on the boy's head like a crown. Cunrad ran to his wife and children. Elsa stood as pale and motionless as a marble statue. The children continued their desperate calls until Cunrad wrapped them all in his arms and fell to the ground, gathering them in and squeezing them, as if he wanted to put them inside of his chest.

The weeping was broken by the sound of Elsa throwing logs and sifting through the rubble. She found her parents and child. Their bodies remained in a tight embrace. Nethe's charred lips were still pressed against the head of the baby. The Ancient One and Bechtold joined Cunrad and the children. They all watched as the Swan Knight worked dangerously through the remains of the house. Elsa burnt herself badly as she removed debris from the bodies, but she showed no signs of pain. She just whispered prayers as she cleared debris. Bechtold saw his mother's hands burning.

He cried out, "No mother!"

Cunrad instructed Bechtold to hold his brother and sister. Then he joined his wife in clearing the bodies from the ruins of their home. The Ancient One tried to wrap himself around all of the children. As he coiled his neck around Hildemar, he noticed a pile of objects on the ground beside them. It was the box with the plume and two containers, one with the Unicorns' nectar and the other with the Queen's weed. Bechtold did not wait for the swan to comment.

He spoke up immediately as his teacher noticed the items, saying through his tears, "I saved the gifts. I saved them. At least I saved the gifts."

The Ancient One kissed Bechtold repeatedly and told him what a good and brave knight he is.

Once free of the rubble, the bodies were laid together at the foot of Parsifal's shrine, just outside of Lohengrin's portal trigger point. The clear night sky gave way to a thick sheet of clouds and a late spring fall of snow. Cunrad gathered his family under the gazebo and huddled them closely together — all except his wife, who knelt beside her lost loved ones in a constant mumble of prayers. At dawn, Bechtold opened the portal for the swan, who returned to his home to relay the terrible news. Bechtold opened the portal several times that day and called into it for his teacher. The swan did not return. Elsa and Cunrad buried the bodies beside Parsifal's shrine, wrapping Birgit tightly in Nethe's arms and lying them beside Lohengrin. The mounds of dirt over the bodies was all that broke the whiteness of the freshly fallen snow.

With his hands blistered from digging, Cunrad said a quick prayer at the graves and returned immediately to the construction of the lodge. First, he walked to the gazebo and altered the model. For the sake of brevity, he broke from his design. The need for shelter was desperate and he was determined to finish within a week. In his determination and desperation, Cunrad worked faster alone than he had with the help of Lohengrin. In just a few days, the lodge was livable. There was still much to complete, but the family was indoors at night.

Elsa was not. She remained at the grave, not eating or sleeping. She was weak and weathered. Every day, Bechtold opened the portal and called for The Ancient One. When the teacher finally returned, he saw Elsa and was reminded of the death of Lohengrin's first wife. He begged her to go indoors and rest and eat. She did not appear to notice him. She just knelt and mumbled, as she had for days. The swan told young Bechtold that he feared for his mother's health. Bechtold ran to the gazebo, where the wedding gifts sat beside the model of the lodge. He took the Unicorns' nectar and brought it to his mother.

"Here mother", he said as he reached his small hands forward, holding the nectar.

This silenced Elsa's prayers. She turned to her son, took the nectar from him, kissed his cold, little hand, then dipped her finger into the nectar and put it in her mouth. The tonic seemed to work. Her tense shoulders dropped and relaxed. The rigid, wincing expression on her face melted into one of calmness. She looked down to the mounds of dirt at her knees, then dropped flat on her belly, over the graves, and cried. The nectar did its job. It cleared away all peripheral concerns, leaving poor Elsa a clear and focused picture of what she had lost. She fell into desperate despair, convulsing and striking the graves with her hands and feet. Nobody knew what to do. Elsa remained like that through the day.

As the sun began to set, The Ancient One entertained images in his head of the light-hearted Elsa singing as she disappeared into the woods in search of a husband. This stood in mortifying contrast to the broken woman before him. He thought of the wedding and the pride he felt as she stared at his glowing form after biting the weed. This image was replaced with an idea.

"Go get the weed", he told Bechtold.

After Bechtold fetched the weed, the swan instructed him to give it to his mother.

By now it was quite dark. The moon was low in the sky and gave little light to the valley. Bechtold brought the weed to his mother and said that The Ancient One wants her to have some. The tenderness and almost maternal nurturing in the boy's voice soothed Elsa enough to sit up and look at him, and in motion more instinctive than intentional, she took the weed and nibbled on the edge. She looked at her son as he began to glow in her eyes. The swan had gathered the family around her. They all glowed. Elsa stood abruptly and jumped off of the graves. A bright light shone up from the ground, through the mounded dirt. The weed revealed the love of her lost parents and child. Such a brightness came from the graves that Elsa had to turn away. The children did not understand what their mother was experiencing, but the swan knew and Cunrad knew. Cunrad tilted his head to the side and smiled as he imagined what his wife must be seeing. Her reaction made it clear to him that the light of Nethe and Lohengrin's love, and that of the baby, filled her enchanted eyes.

To Elsa, the glow from the graves lit the snow around her and joined with the glow of her gathered family behind. The entire valley seemed to shine like the face of the sun. It warmed Elsa. It brought color to her drawn, pale face. She knelt down beside the graves, and shut her eyes tightly in defense against the brightness as she kissed the ground. She thanked her parents for their love. She blessed her little child. She turned to her surviving family, ran to them, and kissed them all in a repeating pattern of grateful, affectionate kisses. After a long embrace and many declarations of love and gratitude among them, Cunrad gathered his family into the lodge. The Ancient One joined them and they all ate and drank in honor of their lost loved ones.

The swan slept in the lodge that night. Before going to sleep, he begged Elsa for a small nibble of the Queen's weed. She graciously and humbly handed the weed to her worn and weary old friend. She knew that he needed the weed's gift. Elsa grinned as the swan's eyes squinted from the bright glow he perceived from her. He crawled into Bechtold's bed, curled up tightly against the boy, who rested his troubled and sleepy head on the bird's long neck, like a pillow. Before he closed his eyes, The Ancient One admired the glow of his own white feathers under the light of Bechtold's love for him.

Their friends from the Sweeter Realm came to say their goodbyes to Lohengrin, Nethe, and Birgit, after an appropriate period of time determined by The Ancient One. The Scheriers told stories of wrestling with young Lohengrin. The Ancient One told the story of Nethe's entrance into the family and the long conversations they used to have. The Eulesängers whistled a story that nobody understood. But they listened nevertheless, and smiled and nodded in agreement. The Zweigwesens told the story of the magical Christmas night that brought many of them together for the first time and lit the fire of passion in the Swan Knight's marriage. Elsa loved the stories. As she listened, the giggle of the light-hearted girl she used to be returned to her throat. Elsa wanted badly to play on the Eulesänger eggs the tune that her mother played for her. The eggs had been lost in the fire. So the Eulesängers returned the next week with new eggs. Elsa caressed them for a few moments, then put her mouth to one and played the melody of the angels who danced in the tree for her mother on Christmas night.

Cunrad completed the living spaces of the lodge, and the kitchen and dining room were functional. The training space was open to the air, but it was warm now and training took place outdoors. The only room left to complete was the chapel. Cunrad worked hard on it, with many helping hands, of all shapes and sizes from the Sweeter Realm. When it was finished and furnished, several Zweigwesens dragged a large cross through the portal. They constructed it on their side to keep it a surprise. Cunrad mounted it atop the roof of the chapel, lending a holy authenticity to the facility. The daily prayers in the chapel reminded Elsa of her holy obligations. It strengthened her and united the family to the cause of the Holy Grail. Every morning, before breakfast, the family gathered there to pray together.

Cunrad cultivated the tilled plot of ground with the seeds they had bought. He dedicated a portion of it to flowers, so the graves and the shrine could be adorned for most of the year. The children grew strong and beautiful. In the wake of the fire, the valley blossomed into a fertile, holy, and happy place. Elsa still wept by the graves from time to time. Sometimes she would chew a nibble of the Queen's weed and watch the graves glow. Eventually, they stopped glowing, but for the rest of her life, Elsa could close her eyes and vividly remember the brilliant light off the graves, lighting the snow around her. The memory was enough to provide for her what the weed no longer could.

Her spirits fully rebounded and her true character fully restored, Elsa's abilities continued to grow. She communicated complex notions to the creatures of the Sweeter Realm with only a thought, not in language that could be recited later, but in understanding. She was cunning and beautiful, diplomatic and fierce. Many perils came to the valley. Elsa dealt with them all, sometimes talking, sometimes hiding, and sometimes killing. She coordinated efforts with her friends and with her mastery of the portal in ways that no mortal danger could defeat. The Unicorns became more regular visitors. Elsa often rode them around the surrounding hills. She knighted them into service to the valley and posted them on regular patrols.

The children grew. Bechtold had his mother's heart but few of her abilities. Diterich had her abilities but not her heart. Bechtold was sentimental, affectionate, and social. Diterich isolated himself at every chance. He developed many of his mother's abilities, including subduing the portal's reaction to his approach until he wanted it open. He could not open it at a distance or open it with thought. He could only keep it from opening when he approached. Bechtold was much like his grandfather, holy and dedicated, but more of a servant to the portal than the portal was to him. Hildemar grew beautiful and loyal, more like her oldest brother than her closest brother. She reminded The Ancient One much of the young Elsa, in her spirit, in her joy, and in her love of all that surrounded her.

Bechtold and Diterich grew distant. Diterich was proud of his growing powers and believed that Parsifal's armor and the knighthood should pass to him. Neither boy had the abilities of their mother, but Diterich's were significantly closer. He could feel the Grail Blood inside of him. He felt his blood charge with energy each time he opened the portal. But his shoulders did not sense the weight of the responsibility that came with his sacred blood, the responsibility of the oath sworn by his great-grandfather, binding the blood inside of him to the service of the Queen. Bechtold felt the full weight. He consciously put it on every morning like a shirt.

In Diterich's mind, the knighthood should pass to the more powerful. It was clear who that would be. Bechtold wanted to think nothing of it. His mother was the Swan Knight and he did not want to imagine an end to that. All of the children received equal training from The Ancient One, but Bechtold's lessons included, in addition to the knowledge and the skills, the burdens of knighthood. Bechtold wanted the burden but not the power. Diterich wanted the power but not the burden. He wielded his abilities carelessly and flippantly. The creatures of the Sweeter Realm loved them all, but Bechtold and Hildemar reminded them of lost loved ones, and their favored affection was difficult to hide. This only served to isolate Diterich further. He spent most of his free time practicing the skills of combat with the tools of war. He became very good with them.

As Diterich grew into young adulthood, he became increasingly lonely. He felt a strong connection with the knighthood and longed for a relationship with the grandfather he never really knew. He had more pity than love for his own father. Cunrad did not have Grail Blood. He could not open the portal. He was merely a loyal servant to the cause. Diterich did not understand his parents' relationship. He did not see the strength of his father or understand his importance to the Grail. To him, his father was weak and subservient. He was pathetic. Elsa honored her husband. She revered him. So did Bechtold, Hildemar, and the creatures who came through the portal. Diterich was perplexed. To him, every being in the valley was exceptional, even Bechtold — everyone except Cunrad. Diterich spoke down to his father, displaying the superiority he believed he inherited through his mother. Elsa did not see this weakness in her son. Cunrad had too much love for them both to speak to his wife about it. Diterich's distance from his father grew in proportion with his fascination with his Grail heritage and his obsession with his growing abilities.

Diterich stopped attending the morning prayers with his family and spent the time beside Lohengrin's grave, speaking aloud to his grandfather of his disgust with his father and brother. Elsa could not help but become aware of the rift. She stood behind Diterich one morning and overheard him talking to the grave. In disgust, she interrupted her son, defending her noble husband and devoted eldest child. Diterich turned on his mother. He blamed her and Cunrad for Lohengrin's death, cursing Elsa for leaving her post. Elsa's face grew stern. It frightened Diterich. Without a blink, Elsa opened the portal behind her. Through it ran five Unicorns, summoned by the Swan Knight with the slightest of thoughts. They posed themselves majestically in a semicircle behind Elsa. The center Unicorn lowered its horn. Elsa reached blindly behind her and grabbed the horn with precision, as if she had set it there herself. The Unicorn lifted Elsa, who swung around gracefully to sit on the Unicorn's high shoulders.

She told her son, "You understand nothing!"

Then she rode away into the hills, leaving the remaining four Unicorns standing in front of Diterich. They looked sternly down at the young man, with their shaggy faces and bright eyes. Diterich dropped his head and the Unicorns disappeared into the surrounding woods. As great as Diterich's abilities were óver his humble father, so Elsa's were over him. He had been so absorbed with his own talents that he never stood them beside his mother's in comparison. Elsa's devotion to her husband had reduced her in Diterich's thoughts. Her display with the Unicorns pulled from beneath Diterich's feet the proud platform of superiority upon which he had been standing and growing for years. He was humiliated but not humbled.

Diterich did not have his mother's abilities, and he knew he probably never would. He grew insanely jealous. He wanted to command Unicorns. He wanted to be the Swan Knight. Secretly, he fantasized about a fire taking Elsa, Bechtold, and Hildemar, eliminating all Grail Blood from the earth but his. Hints of this secret fantasy snuck through the cracks of conversations without him knowing, deeply offending all who heard and pieced together the hints. Diterich's admiration for his mother turned to bitter envy and blame, even hatred. The Ancient One tried to counsel him, which only spread his anger onto his teacher. Diterich stopped attending the lessons with his brother and sister. He disappeared into the surrounding hills for days at a time. In the gathering room of the lodge, Elsa and Cunrad confronted him one day, reminding him of his lineage and his responsibilities to the family. In a violent fit of yelling, Diterich told Elsa that she did not understand her responsibilities. He said that he is more like Lohengrin and he should be the Swan Knight — not after Elsa died, but immediately. He accused her of weakening the knighthood and the portal with her affection for her weak husband and not much stronger eldest son. Next, in a low growling tone, with clinched teeth, he told Elsa that he hated her.

Cunrad interrupted, "That's not true."

Elsa walked to the container that held the last piece of the Queen's weed. She ate it. Diterich did not glow. The weed had lost none of its potency. Cunrad shone brighter than ever, but Diterich was just Diterich, cold and resentful as ever. In a broken voice, and with tears welling in her eyes, Elsa told him to go.

"But first", she demanded, "You must drop to your knee and swear to The Lord that you will keep safe and silent the secret of the Grail, the portal, and the Swan Knights."

Finally presented with control of something, Diterich could not help but wield it. He smirked at his mother, turned to his father with a look of pitiful disgust, and then walked out the door. Cunrad took a few steps toward the door and called for Diterich to come back. Elsa silenced her husband with a soft touch on his shoulder. Cunrad broke into tears. Elsa's sympathetic love responded in kind. They held each other there, at the threshold of the lodge and cried for their lost son. The next day, they told The Ancient One. He wanted to fly away and find Diterich, and force the oath of secrecy from him. Elsa forbade it. She had faith in Diterich's goodness and reminded the others that the blood of Christ's cup is in him. They must leave Diterich to Christ's influence.

They never again heard from Diterich. They never heard about him. His was the first Grail Blood to leave the valley and never return. The first of many descendants of Parsifal to wander from the valley and build a life away from the portal. Elsa and Cunrad — and years later, Bechtold and Hildemar — spent much time in contemplation over Diterich, what places he had seen and people he had met, the love he may have found and the children he may have raised. Did he ever find peace? Did he keep the Grail secret? Will his children ever come to the valley? Bechtold was disturbed by the lost Grail Blood, the children and grandchildren of his brother, roaming who-knows-where, spreading throughout the world, perhaps aware of their heritage and their power over the portal, perhaps ignorant to it. He expressed his concerns to his mother and father. They consulted The Ancient One, who consulted the Queen. Elsa proclaimed that the valley must be strengthened, but warned of the perils of bringing in outsiders. Cunrad suggested that he reach out to his family. But his family home was too far away and he had not seen them for decades. The Ancient One reminded them of the Welf family, who resided in the castle to the west, with whom Lohengrin spent so long cultivating friendship. The Welf family was powerful and Lohengrin reported them to be honest, faithful, pious people. Cunrad volunteered to go to Foetes and rekindle the relationship. He took his daughter with him.

There was another relationship Cunrad wished to strengthen. During their travel he shared deeply and personally in conversation with Hildemar. Bechtold's austerity and Diterich's defiance consumed the attention of their parents and teacher. All the while, there sat Hildemar, quiet, obedient, faithful, bumble, and good. Cunrad spoke to his daughter of the fire and the loss of Birgit, his admiration for Lohengrin and Nethe, and the story of his love for Elsa. Hildemar had grown so quickly, and was an adult before Cunrad knew what had happened.

He spoke to her as an adult, like a friend. Hildemar could almost physically feel the bonds between her and her father thicken and strengthen as they walked and spoke, ate and rested, and walked and spoke again until they reached the castle outside of Foetes. Hildemar revealed the quiet yet profound wisdom inside of her reticent heart. Cunrad was proud of his daughter, proud of the wise, beautiful, and holy young woman she had become. In their long conversations while traveling, he learned from his daughter. The lessons of The Ancient One had found fertile ground in Hildemar's young mind. Her calm, happy wisdom was profound and Cunrad was wiser for his conversations with her. He wondered how long she had been like that and how he could have missed seeing it.

At the castle, Cunrad introduced himself to the Welfs as a messenger from Lohengrin's family. When they found out that he was the husband of Lohengrin's daughter and the father of his grandchildren, they embraced him heartily and welcomed him as family. They immediately recognized Lohengrin's eyes in young Hildemar. When they voiced the recognition, Hildemar blushed, inhaled deeply, and thanked them. They asked about Lohengrin and his wife. Cunrad told the story of the fire with great animation, pausing to wipe his tears and regain his voice from the severe emotional strain. His hosts were touched deeply by the earnest account from his broken heart. Cunrad's loyalty and goodness revealed itself lustrously. He seamlessly assumed the kinship that Lohengrin had painstakingly constructed so many years ago. And Hildemar — the traits that had just revealed themselves to her father attacked the sensations of the Welfs instantly.

One evening, at supper, the Welfs asked Hildemar to share what she remembered about her grandfather. She told what she had pieced together from the stories she was told and the bits of imagery that stuck to her young mind. Hildemar was not one to erupt in effusions of sentiment. When her account became too emotional to express, she simply paused until she could continue. As she spoke of her memories of her mother in the days after the fire, she stopped in the middle of a word, held her breath, and wiped a single tear from her cheek. A young Welf prince, of open and sincere character, was sitting beside her. His name was Aldwin. He was tugged hard at the heart by Hildemar's story, by her deep love of her mother, tugged harder by her attempt to withhold the flow of her emotions. Instinctively, he reached to her and took her by the hand. She turned to him, looked him squarely in the eyes, and released her long held breath. She felt encircled and embosomed by his sympathetic gaze and the gentle, reassuring squeeze of his hand. Cunrad recognized the look between them. He had known it himself when he first met Elsa. Just as he had finally connected to his daughter's heart, he must soon give it away. That reality was as certain to him as the food in his mouth.

Everything in the behavior of the Welfs confirmed the praiseful words of Lohengrin. Aldwin was a good man, a gentle man, although perhaps a bit naïve from a comfortable and sheltered childhood. Added to his personal qualities was his prestige and power. One would never know it upon meeting him, but Aldwin was to inherit the estate and title of his good father. Cunrad had not forgotten what spurred the visit. He would never trade his daughter for the benefits of the Welf family connection. But receiving those benefits as an addition to his daughter's happiness was an unexpected blessing and one he believed gifted by God.

They stayed for less than two months in the castle. Before departing, Hildemar received an offer of marriage from Aldwin. Both fathers endorsed the proposal and sealed it with a drink and a strong, brotherly embrace. Perhaps it was the relation to Lohengrin, or a subtle sensation of the sacred blood inside of her. Maybe it was her own behavior. But in the eyes of the Welf family, especially Aldwin's, Hildemar stood so far above every young woman they had ever met, so superior in character, so superior in beauty. To their besotted eyes, a light went out in the castle when she walked through the gates to return to the valley.

Many secrets remained behind the lips of Cunrad and Hildemar during their visit with the Welfs. They discussed them openly on the road home. As ideal as the union would seem to be, there were many logistical concerns to be penetratingly considered and decided upon, among the family and the friends who would be affected by them. At home in the lodge, once the congratulations were shared, those concerns were attended to.

The Ancient One reminded them of the decision of the council, "Either Aldwin must come here and be shown everything, or she must go there and keep the secrets to her death."

Elsa and Cunrad were comfortable with either decision, so they left it to Hildemar's heart. Hildemar hated the thought of leaving her home, her parents, her teacher, and the wonderful creatures who had filled her childhood with joy and magic. But she knew that one more man in the valley would do little to secure their future. Her presence in Foetes and in the castle with the Welf family had much to offer her mother. And after all,

Hildemar was not to become the Swan Knight. That honor belonged to her brother. Aldwin was to inherit his father's title and bear great responsibilities. She decided to go to Aldwin and remain with him there. From that seat of power, she could do more to secure the portal than she could from within the valley.

Nobody doubted Hildemar's commitment to the secret of the portal. She had never been cursed with a loose tongue. Everything would remain safe behind her silent lips. After deciding to live in the castle with Aldwin, despite the confidence in her decision, Hildemar cried every night until she began to pack for her move. Many creatures from the Sweeter Realm came through to bid her farewell. They thought they would never see her again. The Ancient One said what he knew she needed to hear, that she reminded him of her grandfather and grandmother, that her command of the portal was stronger than Parsifal's, that she would forever be a part of the Grail story, and that she would always have a home in his thoughts. His words allowed her to untie the final tethers that held her heart to the valley. They liberated her to focus on the man she loved and the home she would make with him.

Many of the creatures brought fantastic gifts for Hildemar.

In her wisdom she refused them, saying, "Nothing so wonderful, so fantastical can go with me. I carry your secrets with me, and I would do nothing to endanger you, my dear friends."

One Brunnen stepped up to her, rippling and waving like the breeze. It touched her hand with such seductive softness that it almost enticed her to stay.

It said to her, "Then take our love. That is something you can show to everyone and not betray our secret."

With that invisible gift, the coffers of Hildemar's heart were filled with everything she would need for her journey and new life. She left for Foetes with her father, mother, and brother. Several creatures accompanied them to the top of the first hill before turning back. The Unicorns stayed with them longer. The Ancient One stood by the portal point and waited for the creatures to return. From a great distance, Elsa knew exactly when they all stood around the portal point. She opened the portal for them and closed it behind the last one to pass through. As she traveled, Elsa's connection to the creatures began to fade — all but the Unicorns. She had never traveled so far since her powers had peaked. She determined to accompany her family until she felt her connection with the portal and the Unicorns weaken, at which point she would turn around and return to her post. She made it all the way to Foetes. At the gate of the castle, she opened the portal for the Unicorns to perform patrols of the valley and surrounding hills. Without sharing their vision, she knew what they experienced and she shared the experiences of her voyage with them. She did not see through their eyes, but she knew what they experienced. And they knew her, as if their horns were pressed against her chest.

Elsa was able to place her heart where it belonged, on her daughter and the wedding. Her powerful and complex mind maintained awareness of the valley, through the experiences of the Unicorns, opening and closing the portal at each Unicorn's request, while holding in-depth conversations with her new relations in the castle.

I interrupted The Ancient One's chronicle at this point, asking, "Will I have such power? Will I be like Elsa?"

Embarrassed by such a bold presumption, blurted out without thought, I scanned the area to be sure that my father did not stand near. I stared back toward the lodge, at first looking for my father, but then overlaying the images that had been described to me so far upon the backdrop of the lodge and the valley I had come to know well. My imagination took me back more than a thousand years. I envisioned my brother Otto, riding one of the Zweigwesens' toy Unicorns down the hill toward the lodge, Cunrad running along beside him, laughing, while I sat at the portal in intense study with The Ancient One. For a moment, I allowed myself to believe that Otto and I were the youngest sons of Elsa and Cunrad. The Ancient One was such a wonderful storyteller, I felt that I knew them all that well. When The Ancient One reached his long wing to my chin and turned my eyes to face him, I thought I was seeing the swan of the first few generations of the Swan Knighthood, not the much older version that stood before me when I was nine years old. I was reminded of the truth by his eyes — eyes that had seen and suffered so much more than the stories he had covered to that point.

He answered my earlier question about Elsa, "Nobody, in all of the centuries of Swan Knights, matched Elsa's abilities. She was the greatest Swan Knight."

My fantasies of controlling Unicorns and the portal from great distances, sharing in their experiences and saving the Grail were only moderately discouraged by his response. My dreamy, nine-year-old imagination still saw myself as the next Elsa, the next "greatest Swan Knight". So I begged him to continue.

Hildemar and Aldwin's wedding was a lavish, opulent ceremony, under the splendor of rich surroundings and exotic foods. As magical as Hildemar's childhood had been, their lives were simple, their meals plain, and their possessions paltry. She was royalty now, which meant that they all were by marriage. The ceremony set the line of Parsifal down a road from which it would never stray. Afterward, Elsa, Cunrad, and Bechtold began the long walk home. Cunrad and Bechtold talked, laughed, and shared many opinions of their new relations. Elsa was silent. Her heart was heavy. Although thoughts of Hildemar living in the castle with a good, gentle, sincere, and noble man, with whom she was deeply in love, brought a subtle smile to Elsa's mouth, her eyes remained sad. For each thought of Hildemar's happiness, there were three thoughts of the valley without her. Elsa's family and her heart were full when Birgit was born. Now, from four children, she had one.

Although Elsa did not intentionally communicate her sadness to the Unicorns that awaited her return, they perceived it, and they gathered at the top of the hill where they had escorted the wedding party when they left for Foetes. As they sensed Elsa's approach, four of them ran out to meet her. They ran much farther from the portal than they had ever been. Each of them carried a family member back into the valley, and one burdened their belongings back to the lodge. Many creatures waited just inside the portal, in the Sweeter Realm, jumping and twitching, excited to greet them at the lodge. As she topped the last hill into the valley, Elsa opened the portal. The expectant creatures all ran enthusiastically to meet them at the door to the lodge. The greetings and congratulations were short. They all knew that the family needed to be alone together and to rest from their travels. As the last one returned through the portal, it closed. The crackling snap of the portal gave way to a silence the valley had not known since Parsifal wandered into it many years earlier.

In the following weeks, Cunrad completed the training room of the lodge. Elsa and Bechtold could train all year and in any weather. Bechtold's agility and skills with the sword improved remarkably. He learned to ride the Unicorns masterfully. He never developed his mother's ability to commune with them, but they served him loyally and often communicated with a touch of their horns to his chest. He loved them, and they sensed the loyal goodness in him. Bechtold was humble and behaved more as a servant to the Unicorns than a master. He was humbled by their diligent service to him. He was greatful for the friendship of such beautiful and majestic creatures. And his humble gratitude showed.

He learned a powerful and permanent lesson one evening. Five thieves, who had been traveling west along the Graswang Valley, turned northwest at the valley end, crossed the river and encountered the well-lit lodge. Elsa and Cunrad were inside and Bechtold was patrolling the perimeter of the Swan Knight valley. Bechtold saw the men creeping toward the lodge with weapons drawn. So powerful and sudden was his swell of fear that it triggered the portal to open. The sound caught the attention of the thieves — and of Elsa. The men ran toward the portal and

Bechtold met them in between. Elsa stood and watched her son as he easily defeated the thieves. But he did not kill them. He could not bring himself to do it. Two Unicorns and The Ancient One appeared through the portal.

The Unicorns stabbed their sharp horns toward the thieves. Bechtold hollered for them to stop. They obeyed his command, but one of them walked to Bechtold and touched the point of its horn to his chest. In the instant, Bechtold saw the images that the Unicorn wanted him to see. He saw the Unicorns' fears. He saw wild, evil, Godless men laughing as they ran through the Sweeter Realm, slaughtering the creatures there, slaying Unicorns and removing the horns. He saw one evil man holding the Holy Grail above his head, laughing a sinister laugh then drinking the blood of the slain creatures from the Lord's holy cup.

When Bechtold awoke from this vision, he was standing over the defeated thieves with blood running from his raised sword and dripping off his elbow. He looked down and saw the beheaded bodies of the thieves, his teeth still clinched tightly with the rage he felt in defense of his friends and in duty to the Holy Grail. He looked to his mother. She wore a face of pensive understanding. An innocence died in Bechtold that night. From its grave arose a Swan Knight. As he stood there staring at his mother, then turning to the Unicorns, and then The Ancient One, his very identity altered. The depth of understanding and responsibility that lives perpetually inside of a Swan Knight swelled inside of him, from a tiny point in the center of his heart, to fill everything under his skin. He never forgot those men, never purged the memory of their faces from his mind. He knew that the swell of his own fears opened the portal. Had it remained closed, the men could have been driven from the valley alive. In addition to the lessons of that night, Bechtold learned to control his fear. Never again did he accidentally open the portal. Never again would he reveal it to outsiders.

CHAPTER 9

Ending the First Era of Swan Knights

HLDEMAR'S NEW LIFE was too full of changes to mourn the loss of her old life. She was a wife, a noble in a wonderful castle, and within a year of the wedding, an expecting mother. She was always an imaginative girl, but in her freest fantasies, she could never have imagined such happiness. Aldwin and his family were good to her — better than good. They doted upon her. They saw her gentle wisdom and deferred to her young mind on many household decisions. As Aldwin assumed a greater portion of governing the region, Hildemar governed equally, albeit quietly and behind the scenes. As she grew older, Hildemar's eyes shone more like Lohengrin's. Aldwin's father replaced his lost friend with the granddaughter who carried so many of his noble traits. Hildemar was friend to the father, wife to the son, and mother to the next generation of the Welf dynasty. The family, and therefore the region, truly centered on her. In the depth of rare quiet contemplation, she thought of home, of her mother and father, her brother, her wise teacher to whom she owed so much, and of the wonderful friends from the Sweeter Realm. She wondered when her family might visit again. She wanted to send a message, but could never send someone into the secret and sacred valley. So she just waited for word.

Shortly before her first child was born, a young traveler arrived at the gate of the castle with a sealed letter from Bechtold. In it, he bragged to his sister of his improving skills, relayed the incident with the thieves, and told some anecdotes of the funnier goings-on around the valley, an athletic competition organized by the Scheriers, complete with an obstacle course and stone throwing contest, which involved Bechtold, the Scheriers, The Ancient One, a few Eulesängers, several Zweigwesens, and many others. He described with great humor the Eulesängers' attempts to toss heavy stones. In the middle of a race, two Scheriers bumped into each other. They abandoned the race and began wrestling. The spectacle was so hilarious, it brought the entire competition to a pause.

Of course, Bechtold won the competition and was proudly crowned king of the day by The Ancient One. Hildemar laughed and cried out loud as she read the letter, the transition between the two often indistinguishable. Aldwin begged for a recitation of the letter. Of course, she could not reveal the secrets within. Being a good husband, Aldwin wanted to share the stories that brought teared laughter to his wife. Being a good man, he did not press her on the subject. He simply cupped her pretty face with the palms of his hands, wiped the tears from her cheeks with his thumbs, kissed her on the forehead, and left her to read in peace.

Bechtold ended the letter with a demand that Hildemar never respond. Elsa would be furious to find that such delicate details were sent by messenger. Bechtold concluded, writing that he did not need updates on her well-being. His faith in her calm wisdom, which he admired in her since she was a young child, and the goodness of the Welf family, were all the assurance he needed of her happiness. The compliment was warmly received. Hildemar held the finished letter tightly against her breast, took several deep breaths, as if trying to inhale her brother's love directly into her lungs, then dutifully burnt the letter. She kept the ashes of the letter in a small cup among her treasured trinkets.

The next generation of Grail Blood came into the world under the frescoed ceiling of Aldwin and Hildemar's lavish castle bedroom. Ermenrich's first cry echoed through the halls of the castle with a strength that foreshadowed his destiny. Hildemar was true to her oath. She did not speak a word of her family's secret outside of the valley. Ermenrich and the four other children who followed him into the world knew nothing of Pasifal or Lohengrin (outside of the legends that had spread in fanciful form throughout the region), nothing of their grandmother — the greatest knight the world has ever known — nothing of the wise old swan or the portal to the Sweeter Realm. As far as they knew, they were a fortunate family of nobles, whose mother married into privilege from some obscure family in the country.

They always felt that special blood flowed through them, but never thought that it was bequeathed to them from the mythical Parsifal, through their simple mother. Aldwin and his father knew that Lohengrin was a knight, but for reasons they did not understand and would not ask, Hildemar insisted on the simple identity she assumed. They trusted her rare form of humility and perpetuated the history she invented.

As nobles, the children were given an elite education and trained in combat and strategy, as well as religion and philosophy. Hildemar was pleased to watch her children develop in this way, with good hearts, strong bodies, and sharp minds. She felt deeply that her children, or their children, would someday be called in defense of the portal. As she grew older, she knew that her older brother's opportunities to produce an heir to his position drew narrow. Her mother, now a grandmother, must soon put away her armor and pass her responsibilities to her descendants. Without revealing the truths that she kept caged within her teeth, she prepared her children in every way she could for the sacred responsibility any one of them could inherit.

Back in the valley, The Ancient One was regaling Bechtold with another forced retelling of the stories of Parsifal and Lohengrin when he became abruptly and visually pensive. The swan halted suddenly, in the middle of a story. He walked to Parsifal's shrine, touched the structure gently and lovingly with his outstretched wing, and cried. Bechtold, being Bechtold, intimately sympathized with the wave of emotion that rushed upon him from his dear friend and teacher. The wave crashed against his tender heart. In tears of his own, he walked to stand beside his friend. He wrapped his fingers around the bird's neck, just beneath the beak, and gave a long stroke downward, while pulling the swan to nestle tightly against his hip. Cunrad and Elsa saw this from the field of crops where they were working. They dropped their tools and joined their loved ones in front of the shrine of Parsifal, beside the graves of Lohengrin, Nethe, and Birgit.

The Ancient One turned to Elsa and said, "One hundred years, my Love. One hundred years ago today your grandfather was attacked, rescued by your grandmother, healed by the Holy Grail, and dropped his blood to open the portal for the very first time."

Elsa let out an involuntary gasp as she placed her hand to her heart and opened herself to experience the full weight of the swan's words. Bechtold pulled The Ancient One's head to his and kissed the bird atop his upper beak.

The Ancient One continued, "You cannot understand how it is for me... Your lives are so short... like a year of mine. I fall in love with you, so deeply in love, just to watch you age and die. Parsifal and I were friends and equals. Now I watch his granddaughter grow old before my eyes. I watch her son show the first signs of old age. I have sworn to belong to your family through time, but it hurts. As each of you were born, I loved you like my own... loved you... just to lose you. Lohengrin's birth feels like last year to me, and I remember everything, his first steps, his first words, the delight and wonder in his young face the first time he opened the portal on his own, his first swing of the sword, his brave and foolish impetuosity as we embarked on our adventures together... and I remember his death. I can close my eyes and live it like it was last night. I remember every moment I have spent with *you*, my love, and with you, Bechtold. Long after you are gone, I will remember Diterich's smile... and his departure. I will remember Hildemar's last embrace before she went away. When I swore my allegiance to Parsifal, I could not have imagined the burden on my poor heart, the joys... and the burden. I do not know how much more I can take. I cannot lose you, my treasure, my little Elsa, yet I must. Someday, I must."

The swan fell on top of his weakened legs and wept a deep cry, from the depths of his heart. The sound was alarmingly dismal. Nobody had ever heard such a sound from the noble bird. Nobody had ever thought of him that way or considered how his life had changed since being so tightly intertwined with the portal and the family of Parsifal.

Elsa pulled herself from the pit of sorrow into which she had been dropped, and asked, "You loved Parsifal, didn't you?"

The swan answered, "He was my first and only brother. I have never known such a burdened heart, nor such a faithful one."

Elsa raised her voice and declared to the hills around them, "Tonight we celebrate Parsifal... and the bond he forged with our eternal friend, our teacher, our brother. Let us set the example tonight for every hundred-year celebration this valley will have the pleasure to host."

The announcement lifted the spirits of all. The Ancient One's heart went immediately from bearing the weight of his post to perching atop it, with the pride that his faithful service deserved. He looked at Elsa, still posed with her chin lifted from her proclamation. Through the wrinkles of her face, he saw the little girl he remembered so vividly — and he laughed a laugh as new and surprising to the others as his cry had been just a few moments earlier.

The rest of the day, until dusk, was spent preparing for the celebration. Cunrad built a stage for the theatrical reenactment of the great moments of their lives. Elsa strewn decorations from the lodge to the portal. Bechtold coordinated with The Ancient One to receive guests from the Sweeter Realm, who all brought their favorite treats to share. The celebration was a tribute to all who had shared their lives together in the valley. It was jovial, nothing like the scene at the shrine that morning. The shrine and graves were adorned with flowers and lit brilliantly with lamps. The Ancient One mounted the stage wearing a dress and holding the wooden helmet from Parsifal's shrine. He imitated the young Elsa playing with the helmet. A Zweigwesen played the part of Lohengrin, farcically scolding the feathered little Elsa, prying the helmet from under the swan's wing, and returning it to the shrine. The laughter was hearty and rich. Elsa's convulsing giggle shook free a tear that had clung to her bedewed eye. Her loving husband watched her as all signs of old age in her face seemed to melt away. Through it surfaced the very image of the woman he fell in love with.

The night was declared as a tribute to Parsifal and The Ancient One. Tribute to that quarter was certainly paid. Bechtold gave a masterfully dramatic rendition of his great-grandfather, stumbling into the valley for the first time and being attacked by the flowermaiden. He even reenacted the fateful kiss before being stabbed. It was a hilarious moment, as the flowermaiden was played by an Eulesänger, whose hooked beak met quite clumsily with Bechtold's lips. She wrapped her large wings around Bechtold's face and perched her feet on his collar bones. The stab of the knife into Parsifal's side was a thin stick, pushed lightly against the top of Bechtold's shoulder — the lowest point on his body that the Eulesänger could reach with the stick wedged under her wing. Cunrad, with a cloth wrapped around his head like a bonnet, played the part of Gütel. In the highest pitch his deep voice could manage, he yelled at the Eulesänger, frightening her away. He hoisted his son upon his shoulder, yelling "I'll save you, good knight" as he carried Bechtold from the stage.

Most of the theatrics centered on Elsa. A Scherier pretended to be Elsa, commanding the portal to change shapes. In reenactment of the changes in the portal, representatives of each Sweeter Realm breed in attendance bumped the previous one from the stage and assumed the part of the portal, now in the shape of that breed. Bechtold stared at his mother. The comical representative of her amazing abilities brought to the surface his intense admiration for her, which only deepened with every improvised scene from her youth.

The night witnessed many other hilarious theatrical reenactments, many shared remembrances, the breaking of bread in the Lord's name, the sharing of new and exotic foods from the Sweeter Realm, and more tears and laughter than the entire world expelled that night. When the celebration was over, the visitors began to clean the mess they had made. Elsa stopped them, kissed each one of them, and thanked them for their contribution to the most joyous night she had ever known. She insisted that the reigning Swan Knight is responsible for cleaning up and that it was her pleasure to do so. She sent them away and sent her husband and son to bed, despite their vehement protestations.

Elsa remained outdoors until well after dawn, striking the constructs of the celebration. The warm evening had turned into a cold night and before morning, Elsa wore the chill heavily in her chest. Bechtold awoke early and found his mother still hard at work, shivering and weakened. His first insistence refuted, he lifted his mother in his arms and carried her to bed. Cunrad wrapped himself tightly against her and remained with her in bed until her temperature and color recovered. Elsa slept all day and through the next night. She awoke the following morning still weak and sickly. Cunrad and Bechtold had finished what Elsa could not, returning the home and valley to normal. Elsa donned her armor and began patrolling the valley. Cunrad reprimanded her stubbornness harshly and insisted that she remain indoors and accept the nurturing attention of her family. Elsa looked at him and laughed. The laugh turned into a cough that buckled Elsa's knees and nearly dropped her to the floor. Cunrad caught her, kept her on her feet, and began to pull her toward a chair. Elsa had never been sick or weak. She did not take it well.

She broke herself from her husband's grip and insisted, "I am the Swan Knight."

Cunrad replied sternly, "Bechtold is strong and capable. If he needs you, he will tell you. Rest for now!"

With a shaky hand, Elsa sheathed her sword and walked out the front door. The emotions of the celebration served to strengthen Elsa's already strong connection to her family and the commitment to her position as the Swan Knight. She patrolled a much wider swath of the surrounding hills than normal, which took her late into the night. She entered the lodge that night at a near crawl. The armor, which she normally removed as quickly and easily as a pair of shoes, was heavy and burdensome. Cunrad and Bechtold reproached her gently but quite seriously. In an immediate but fragile retort, she reminded them that she is the Swan Knight and the decisions of the valley are hers to make. She had never spoken to either of them that way. They were terribly worried about her and they summoned The Ancient One and expressed their concerns to him.

The next morning, Elsa repeated the routine from the morning before, this time being confronted at the door by The Ancient One, who sided with Cunrad and Bechtold.

Elsa reminded her old teacher, "Do not forget, in my time, I am much older than you. Would you have told Parsifal or Lohengrin to stay in bed?"

"Yes!" the bird insisted, "and they would have listened."

Elsa was driven by something deep inside of her, something stronger than reason, stronger even than friendship and family. She still began each morning with prayers in the chapel. Over the next several days, her morning prayer time grew shorter, and she left them more resolute in her commitment to duty. Each night she returned weaker, more fragile, sometimes barely able to speak. All were at a loss as to what could be done, short of physically restraining her. Weak and fragile as she was, they were still not certain they could defeat her if it came to that. Cunrad was an old man and even Bechtold was beginning to pass his prime. But Elsa's decline was quick and alarming, and something needed to be done.

One night, lying in bed, sleepless and worried, Bechtold got an idea. He arose, snuck his mother's armor to the portal, summoned The Ancient One, and instructed him to take the armor into the Sweeter Realm. The Swan Knights are forbidden to enter the portal. Elsa could not retrieve the armor.

"She will order you to return it." Bechtold warned. "Do not give in."

The swan saw the wisdom in the plan. He took the armor through the portal and hid it in the Sweeter Realm. Elsa was in such a weakened state; she did not perceive the opening of the portal that night. She slept through an event that always aroused her, even at great distances. In the morning, her ritual was broken when she noticed the missing armor. Bechtold interrupted her panicked tirade and firmly ordered her outside. Entranced by his rare sternness, she followed him toward the portal point. Elsa started to open the portal. Bechtold raised his hand at her in a firm command to stop. Elsa let the portal close. When they reached Bechtold's trigger point, the spot where Bechtold opened the portal by his proximity, the swan came through and presided over an abbreviated version of the oath ceremony, inaugurating Bechtold into the position of Swan Knight. Elsa allowed the ritual to continue to completion, uninterrupted.

Afterward, she demanded, "I want my armor back. My father made me that armor."

"I know, my love", The Ancient One replied, "I was there."

Bechtold drew his mother's attention and said, "Your armor is safe where it is…"

The swan interrupted, "And it will remain there. Bechtold, the Swan Knight, has no use for it."

Elsa's shoulders raised and her fists clinched tightly at her side as the rage of betrayal swelled in her. She held this position with her long held breath as she switched her embittered glare back and forth from her son to her teacher. She had not felt such betrayal since Diterich left. But there was such holy righteousness in Bechtold's expression, and the love of a father in the gleaming white figure of the bird. Elsa slowly exhaled. Her escaping breath took with it the tension in her shoulders. With the next inhale, her embittered form was washed away by love and understanding. The little boy that Elsa's eyes had always seen in her son was replaced by the stout figure of a man, a strong man who rivaled Parsifal and Lohengrin in his gallant frame. She wanted to show her pride in her son and her reverence for The Ancient One's wisdom with embraces of each. But she simply nodded her head in deferent submission and returned to the lodge. She went to bed, but before she did, she prayed in the chapel. She prayed for her son, that he might become the greatest Swan Knight and live his older years under the love and care that Elsa now felt warmly wrapped in.

Each morning after her retirement, Elsa awoke stronger and more like herself. Once fully recovered, she made short patrols of the area. Bechtold permitted them, as long as they were short and peaceful. He knew that they did her good. Elsa lived many more years in this way, honored and revered, loved and respected. Although no longer the Swan Knight, she maintained command of the valley and household until she died peacefully in her sleep, held lovingly in the embrace of the truest husband that ever lived. In the last year of her life, Elsa rediscovered joy. She again saw the beauty in everything and everyone. She often thought of Diterich and Hildemar, but even those were thoughts of gratitude for the precious gifts of the Lord.

When Elsa died, the portal opened. It remained open after Bechtold buried her. Bechtold could not close it. He ran toward it and ran away. He placed his toes against it and raced away from it, riding at top speed well over the nearest hill. It would not close. Nobody knew what to do. Bechtold prayed to his mother to close the portal. It remained open. The Ancient One flew wide patrols over the area. Many creatures of the Sweeter Realm were called into service and assigned sentry posts along the perimeter of the valley. The crackling of the open portal called out like a beacon to any wandering traveler or passer-by. The Queen was notified and given constant updates on the security of the portal.

It went on like this for a few weeks, until one morning, when Bechtold, Cunrad, The Ancient One, some Unicorns, and a few other creatures were gathered around the portal. The portal began to grow. Next, it shrunk into the shape of a swan, then grew again, into the shape of a large Unicorn. The Unicorn-shaped portal bowed its head slowly to the ground, then raised its head to the sky, then crackled and snapped to a close. A few seconds later, it opened normally from Bechtold's proximity and behaved normally from then on. Everyone felt the same thing — that Elsa had said goodbye to them all that day. A few days later, Cunrad joined his wife. As Bechtold buried his father beside his mother, he was surprisingly peaceful. The Ancient One stood beside him and told him how sorry he was to see him lose both of his parents in so short a time.

Bechtold smiled at his old friend and said, "First and foremost, my father was a husband — *her* husband. His life was for her, in service to her. I did not expect him to stay with us much longer. They are now as they were always meant to be... together."

The private and simple ceremony was exactly as Cunrad would have wanted. It was a celebration of his marriage and his reuniting with his wife.

The peaceful air of the ceremony was broken the next morning, when Bechtold awoke lonely. He was born into a full valley, with Lohengrin, Nethe, Elsa, and Cunrad, and joined shortly by three other children. Now, he was the only human left in the valley. Being openhearted as he was, he confided his lonely feelings in his friend and teacher. The swan knew that Bechtold would need him, and he rose early and waited one step from the portal point on his side for Bechtold to summon him.

The swan reminded him, "*I* have no family. Your family is all I have ever had in this valley. Now we are the same. We have only each other."

Bechtold's face betrayed his following thoughts. No sooner did he part his lips to speak than the swan answered the question that his mouth had not yet uttered.

"No, your sister has her own life, in her own world. Those worlds must be kept separate as long as they can."

Bechtold dropped his chin in reluctant agreement, but replied, "I have no wife, no children, and I am older now than Lohengrin was when he left the valley to find a wife."

The Ancient One, knowing better than his words, told Bechtold that he still had time, that love could still find him, that he could still produce the next generation of Swan Knight.

Bechtold shook his head. He said, "I will serve the portal and the Grail as long as I am able, as long as the Lord wishes me to. But I will not die in the arms of a loving spouse, as my mother did, and I will not be buried by my children. Hildemar's children must assume the burden when I am gone. You must teach them."

The swan insisted that Hildemar's children were too old to learn now about the portal, too old to train and study. He reminded Bechtold that the lessons begin when the children are very young. Bechtold, perhaps knowing his sister better, assured the teacher that Hildemar had her children ready to assume any responsibility the Lord might choose for them.

The debate continued for the next several years, cresting and waning in frequency and intensity. Eventually, Bechtold proved himself right by growing deathly ill. He was unable to walk up the hill and open the portal, unable to move at all. The Ancient One built a nest for Bechtold, right on the Swan Knight's trigger point. The portal remained open as the Swan Knight remained lying in the nest. This allowed his friends from the Sweeter Realm to come and go and say their goodbyes. The nest was painful to build. The Ancient One knew that he was building Bechtold's deathbed. On his deathbed, Bechtold took his last opportunity to claim victory in their long debate. He joked about dying. He did not mind dying. He knew what he was to the Lord, to the Grail, and to the portal. He played the role written for him, and he played it well. Bechtold was never vain, nor did he ever cling to the pleasures of the world. His home, his destiny, his life was in that valley. He also knew that his little sister was far greater than he, in many ways. As he closed his eyes for the last time, with a joyous smile on his face, he described to The Ancient One what he envisioned. He pictured Hildemar's children, cladding them with his imagination in the shiniest armor. Stout and able were the lot of them. It was this image that Bechtold rode to meet his Lord in heaven.

With nobody to mourn him but the creatures of the Sweeter Realm, Bechtold's burial was a formal but subtle affair. The Unicorns stood statuesque in a semi-circle around the grave. The Eulesängers sang. The Zweigwesens read some of Bechtold's favorite passages of literature. Even The Ancient One, who loved Bechtold dearly, did not cry. He was set at peace by Bechtold's calm and confident departure from this world. Besides that, the swan had weightier concerns on his mind. The portal closed as Bechtold's body was carried from the nest to the grave. The valley sat unguarded by a Swan Knight. The portal could not be opened. The creatures who attended the funeral were trapped on this side. The swan had no choice but to fly to Hildemar himself and hope that she still lived. He left immediately after the funeral, assigning the remaining creatures a post to guard, but ordering them to stay hidden.

He arrived at the castle just before dusk. A flood of joyous emotion filled the bird when he saw Hildemar finishing her evening stroll outside the castle. She was old. Her hair was as white as the swan's feathers. Her face bore all of the lines of age and motherhood. But it was undoubtedly Hildemar. He would have known her at twice the distance. In the middle of the night, when she and Aldwin were asleep, he snuck in through a window of their sleeping chamber, scrawled a quick note begging her to come home, dropped it in one of her shoes, and flew quickly back to the valley. Aldwin, long since head of the household and the region, was early to work, before his wife woke. Hildemar woke alone, as she usually did, and leisurely dressed.

When she found the note, she ran down the hallway. She read while in a full sprint toward her husband. She finished reading as she swung open the door of his study. She kissed him quickly, told him that she loved him, and said in a fast, almost unintelligible voice, that there was a problem with her family, that she was leaving immediately, that she may never see him again, and that she is taking Ermenrich with her. He tried to stop her, but the weight that her wishes carried in the castle only increased with time. Nobody told the castle matriarch what she can or cannot do. Aldwin trusted that Ermenrich would bring her home safely once her business with her family was done.

Hildemar had many fine horses at her disposal. She and Ermenrich took the two fastest and rode to the valley with few chances to rest. They spoke very little as they traveled. Not only did they ride too hard for leisure conversation. Hildemar's mind raced with the possibilities behind The Ancient One's brief and cryptic note. By the time they reached the last row of hills before home, she had eliminated the possibilities, one by one, until concluding that her family was dead and the responsibility of the Swan Knighthood rested on her and her children. She wished that she had taken one of her younger children. Ermenrich was to inherit the governmental title that his father inherited from his father. He had been groomed for the position for decades. How could he rule his region and serve as the Swan Knight? This was a question to be answered later. She pushed it out of her mind and rode fiercely into the valley, nearly losing her able son behind her.

When they arrived in the eerily quiet valley, and passed the dark and empty lodge, as weary as they were from their journey, they rode behind the lodge and dismounted the horses between the lodge and the portal point. Hildemar walked her son toward the point. She knew every rock, every tuft of grass around it, and she knew exactly where her approach would trigger an opening of the portal. She stopped just short of that point and instructed her son to keep walking. Ermenrich could not imagine why they left the castle in such a panicked hurry, or why they stood in this obscure valley near an abandoned lodge, or stranger yet, why his mother instructed him to walk away from the lodge, up the very ordinary hill behind it. She warned him to prepare himself to be startled. Through a nervous laugh, he asked what was going to happen.

"Just walk forward", she commanded.

Ermenrich opened the portal, which did not startle him as much as the giant swan that swooped excitedly from the top of a nearby tree, where he had been watching his old student instruct her son. He landed right in front of Ermenrich. When the swan began to speak, Ermenrich dropped to his knees, weakened by astonishment, and sat back on his heels.

The Ancient One looked right through Ermenrich, to Hildemar, as he spoke through a heavy sigh, "Oh Hildemar, thank God you have come. God bless you, child."

"Child?" she responded. "My friend, I am an old woman now, with children of my own, and a grandchild on the way. My oldest daughter expects her first."

After a long and adoring stare at one another, Hildemar broke the silence with an eruption of laughter, joined soon after by the swan. Ermenrich remained frozen in silent wonder and disbelief. He turned to the swan, then back to his mother, then to the crackling open portal. The sound of the portal was a delight to both Hildemar and the swan, for different reasons. The swan heard through the crackling the continuity of the knighthood. The portal opens differently and sounds differently for each child of Parsifal. Hildemar reveled in the portal's unique reaction to her son.

Ermenrich, still sitting on his heels, pointed into the portal and asked his mother, "Did I do that?"

"Yes", she said.

He turned his head to The Ancient One, still pointing into the circle of crackling nothing, and stuttered, "D... d... did... did I do that?"

The giant swan smiled and nodded his head.

Ermenrich looked into the portal and whispered to himself, "I did that."

He turned back to Hildemar. "Can I close it?" he asked his mother.

"Just step away." She said.

Ermenrich rose to his feet and walked slowly backward. The portal closed. The Ancient One pushed him forward until it opened again, then called out into the surrounding woods. All of the creatures who had been trapped by the closed portal appeared out of the woods and ran through the opening, nodding to Ermenrich as they sailed by him, and passing a few quickly spoken pleasantries as were permitted by their speed. Ermenrich looked around to be certain that no more friendly creatures were rushing from the trees. The swan nodded to him. He slowly stepped backward again and closed the portal.

Ermenrich asked, "What is it? Has it always been there? Is it always in that spot? Why do I control it? What does it have to do with me? Those creatures, who were they?" He looked to his mother inquisitively.

Hildemar said, "There is a history you must know. And I will leave it to the teacher to teach it to you. Sit down, my son, and listen closely. You have so much to learn."

She left her son in the warm and loving wings of her old friend and walked her eager heart to her childhood house, glancing wistfully at the graves as she passed, stopping at the freshly broken ground that was obviously the grave of her brother, and blowing a single, slow kiss to Bechtold. She stepped to the graves marked as her mother's and father's. She knelt down and rubbed the ground, patted it lovingly, stood, and resumed her walk to the lodge. Once in the lodge, Hildemar stopped to weep over every board in the floor, every furnishing, every bittersweet reminder of her family and her childhood. She even paused a moment to picture young Diterich playing with his blocks in the corner of a room. After the day's lessons, Ermenrich and The Ancient One joined Hildemar in the lodge. The swan spoke tenderly of the final moments of Elsa's life and of the mysterious behavior of the portal. He detailed the peaceful passing of her father and of her brother. Every hair on Ermenrich's body stood erect as he listened to the loving words of the swan. He had just learned that he is descended from Parsifal and carries Grail Blood. He just learned about the portal and the Swan Knighthood. None of that meant as much to him as hearing the swan speak to Hildemar about her family.

Ermenrich studied with The Ancient One every day, from dawn until late in the evening. He stoutly and proudly bore the heavy and profound responsibility the old swan laid on his shoulders. He was proud of his father and the long, noble, Welf line that bore him. He loved his mother dearly, and now had a family tradition from her line even more glorious, holy, and mythical. During the lessons, The Ancient One often caught him sighing deeply and looking toward the lodge, where his mother spent most of her time bringing the home back in order for her son and the family he must raise there. Ermenrich sighed tenderly toward his mother, her humble reticence standing nobler, more pious, and so much more admirable in the light of her pedigree.

As a boy, Ermenrich heard the legends of Parsifal and Lohengrin. He ran around his family estate with a cup, pretending to be Parsifal, striking furniture with his wooden sword, warning the chairs not to try to take the Holy Grail from his hands. He stood on his bed and pretended that a giant swan pulled him across the sky. These memories seemed hours old to him, as he looked into the eyes of the very swan after whom the legends arose. He paid his mother a holy reverence that she had never seen from him before. When he looked at his mother, he realized that she was cradled in the arms of Lohengrin himself, that she spent her childhood playing with the fantastic creatures that flew by him as he stood frozen in astonishment on his first day in the valley. It took him days to hold his mother's hand, and share the intimate tenderness of mother and son. He viewed her as a goddess, sprung to life from the pages of his childhood storybooks, who had been hiding her identity in a mortal castle for all of his years. He regained his filial intimacy with his mother precisely as he began to see himself as the next page in those storybooks.

After three weeks of industrious study by the son and domestic preparations by the mother, The Ancient One presided over the oath of another Swan Knight. The swan praised and thanked Hildemar for preparing his student so well — just as Bechtold said she would. When he told Hildemar how Bechtold praised his sister and predicted the noble excellence of her children, how he swore to the worried old bird that Hildemar would have her children well taught and prepared to assume the knighthood, Hildemar ran to Bechtold's grave and watered the infant grass above it with the tears of a grateful and doting little sister.

The Ancient One told Hildemar many stories of the valley during her long absence. He told her about the hundredth anniversary celebration, with many fine details about the theatrics on her father's stage that night. He told her about Elsa's stubborn reluctance to bequeath her duties to her son. Hildemar shook her head and wore a scornful face at this report. But a giggle snuck through her nose, unable to breach her tightly pressed lips. Elsa's behavior during that time was so quintessentially Elsa that it endeared itself to Hildemar, despite her remonstrance.

The old teacher and Hildemar exchanged many stories, many laughs, and some of the most penetratingly bitter remembrances either one of their sweet hearts had ever felt. A few days after Ermenrich swore his oath, Hildmar surprised him with the announcement that she would leave for the castle early the next morning. Ermenrich assumed that he and his mother would live out their days together in Parsifal's valley, in Cunrad's lodge. She reminded him that she has a husband, three other children, and very soon a grandchild waiting for her at her home.

"The lodge is yours now, son." She told him. "So is the valley, the crops, and the duties of the Swan Knight."

Ermenrich spent that night sleepless and alone in the Swan Knight's bed, while The Ancient One and Hildemar snuggled tightly together, as they did when she was a child, and slept soundly in one of the lesser bedrooms. The next morning, as promised, Hildemar set off for the castle, taking both horses with her. Before she did, she said her morning prayers at the graves, conversing casually and intimately with God, her mother and father,

her brother and baby sister, and her grandparents. Ermenrich watched from a distance as the conversation came to a natural conclusion.

Hildemar kissed her son, told him how proud she was of him, said, "Tell the old bird I love him", mounted her horse with a grip on the reins of the other, and rode away.

She returned home to the anxious arms of her family. She gathered them, holding her new granddaughter, who had been born just a few days earlier, and told them that Ermenrich was serving Christ on a mission she could not share with them. The quiet matriarch spoke with such authoritative finality, while caressing the head of the infant, that nobody dared question her. Within three years of Hildemar's return, Aldwin died, having never heard from or of his son again. But he died proudly and confidently, knowing that his son employed his childhood training and education for some holy cause, that he was special in the eyes of the Lord, and that he would embrace him in heaven one day. With Aldwin's death, the estate and title passed to Ermenrich. Nobody pressed the issue while Hildemar lived. The house and lands were hers, as they had been for many decades. The ever-intuitive Hildemar, sensing that her time was near at hand, sent her second daughter, the only one of her children not restricted by marriage or duty, to Ermenrich with a message to come home to see his mother before she dies.

Ermenrich met his sister on the ridge of one of the valley's peripheral hills, having spied her well in advance. He had cleared the valley of all visitors from the Sweeter Realm, sending them into the woods, and he welcomed his sister into the lonely lodge. She wanted to ask him about his life there, but was silenced by the remembrance of her mother's solemn proclamation. Ermenrich allowed his sister to rest for a few hours, then insisted that they begin the journey home. When they arrived, Ermenrich found his mother weaker, visually older, but quite herself.

She told him, "I must hand you a burden that nobody has held. Your father is dead. You must rule his land now… but you are also the Swan Knight. You must fulfill your oath to the Lord, and to the Queen of the Land and Shallow Waters. You must protect your people and the Grail. You must be a servant to both.

Remember…," she said, "No child of Parsifal born outside of the valley can know of the portal and the Grail. You are the only exception there has ever been. Keep my valley safe. Keep it secret."

Ermenrich reached around his mother's neck and held her head like a chalice. He bowed toward her and kissed the thin, wrinkled skin of her forehead.

Still holding her so, he slid his mouth against her ear and whispered, "I know mother. I am the Swan Knight… and I am your son."

He pulled his head away from her, winked at her, and relaxed his grip into a gentle caress on the side of her face. Hildemar smiled at him. But she worried. She knew that either one of his titles would test the strongest spirits, the sharpest minds, and the stoutest bodies. He must fill both, and he would not be allowed to fail at either.

In Hildemar's last hours, she spoke aloud to her parents and brother, as if they stood right in front of her. There was nothing worrisome or uncertain in her dialog. She spoke to them as if in casual conversation around the dinner table. Ermenrich isolated her. He feared that precious secrets would be spoken in her conversations with the departed. Alone with her, he watched her laugh and reminisce with long lost loved ones. He inwardly praised his own foresight when she began to talk about the Scheriers and the Eulesängers, the Zweigwesens and Brunnens. She asked her mother to make funny shapes with the portal. She stared into a wall and laughed, as if the portal became a Unicorn right in front of her, in her favorite room of the castle. She closed her eyes, giggled some more, kissed the air in front of her several times, wrapped herself in her own arms, squeezing a loving embrace, then died in front of her son. As she exhaled her last breath, calmly and peacefully, her face wore the color of youth. Ermenrich told her aloud how beautiful she was. He picked her up and kissed her repeatedly while he carried her to her bed, where she remained in state for the visits of family and friends.

The people loved her. They mourned her and every person under Ermenrich's rule attended her funeral. After the funeral, Ermenrich tended to his duties to his people. Within a few months, he returned to the valley to find the sentries in their place, ready to be let home by the Swan Knight. All was quiet. All was well. All was secure. Ermenrich painstakingly constructed a plan and schedule for his attendance to the portal, while maintaining his duties to his father's lands. He laid the plan forth for The Ancient One's approval. He appointed the swan as custodian of the plan, an honor the swan accepted with a blend of honor and apprehension. Ermenrich reminded him that the valley is not without a Swan Knight while he is in Foetes, and that his power and position outside of the valley contributes to the portal's security.

The Ancient One, remembering Lohengrin's efforts in making the first connection with Ermenrich's grandfather, admitted the truth of the claim and took quickly to his new post, assigning patrols to the various recruits from the Sweeter Realm and strictly regimenting their schedules. He secretly prayed that Elsa's communion with the portal and the creatures would pass to her grandson. It did not. But Ermenrich was true to his word. He appeared in the valley precisely as he had scheduled. He reviewed his well-organized list of needs and duties and was as true and devoted to the portal as any Swan Knight had been, though he spent so much time away and The Ancient One had to adjust to life in the absence of the human companionship he had enjoyed almost constantly since he met Parsifal in the Sweeter Realm.

The Swan Knight was a powerful noble. He took a noble wife in his grand castle. He had several children. The rule his mother had laid before him in her final days, that no child born outside of the valley can know of it, was not realistic. One of his children must inherit the knighthood, or it must go to one of his nieces or nephews, none of whom was born in the valley. He, The Ancient One, and the Queen struck a new law. Since the Swan Knights now had secular titles, and none were born and raised in the valley, the two eldest children of the Swan Knight would be brought to The Ancient One at the age of nine to learn the history and begin their training. It must be two. If one were to be lost, the other would be ready to assume the role. The children would train in the valley and swear their oath when they come of age. The new laws became known as the Laws of Ermenrich.

Ermenrich abided by the decision. He brought his two eldest children to the valley. They trained and learned to be Swan Knights. His daughter assumed the knighthood when Ermenrich became too old to travel back and forth. Before becoming Swan Knight, she married into another noble family of the region. The descendants of Hildemar grew in power and wealth, keeping their family secret and abiding by the Laws of Ermenrich. Their noble connections bred more noble connections. They married good, pious spouses. The husbands and wives that married Parsifal's descendants learned of the portal, along with the First-in-Training (the oldest child of the Swan Knight) and the Second-in-Training (the next oldest). The younger children remained ignorant of all regarding the valley and the Grail.

Power consolidated and the Swan Knights ruled larger and larger areas around the valley, eventually enveloping the Portal Valley itself in the secular territory of the ruling Swan Knight. This added a welcomed convenience. Lohengrin's vision, his purpose for traveling forth and kindling the flame of kinship with the Family of Welf, came to complete fruition. The lodge became just another royal retreat, secluded and private, to which the Swan Knight could travel easily and without arousing suspicion. The Swan Knight could spend months at a time in the valley. The First and Second-in-Training could live there.

CHAPTER 10

The Royal House of Swan Knights

THE GRAIL BLOOD spread throughout the noble families of Bavaria. The influence and prestige of the Welf family, Aldwin's family, crested and waned. The Swan Knights skipped, through marriage and birth, from one noble dynasty to another. Political control of the valley changed hands many times, but it remained remote. It remained obscure and secluded, and it remained under the diligent eye of the reigning Swan Knight, The Ancient One, and the host of creatures dedicated to the protection of the valley. The best Swan Knights were the women who married out of political title. They were able to raise families in the valley. Some Swan Knights never married and left the knighthood without a direct heir. But there was no shortage of Grail Blood in the region and The Ancient One kept a rigidly accurate family tree. He knew exactly who was in the line to become the Swan Knight. Ermenrich was not the last adult to enter the valley later in life and assume the Swan Knighthood.

The valley saw its share of adventures and danger. The Swan Knights spilled much blood in the valley. They fought and they learned. Some held positions of great secular power, demanding their time and attention. Others held few or no secular responsibilities, and were able to live in the old lodge. More legends grew from the ranks of the Swan Knights. Ermenrich's great-granddaughter, Veronika, was a Swan Knight. Her adventures before taking the sacred oath grew into the legend of Tristan and Isolde, only the legend switched the genders. The figure of Tristan grew from Veronika, and Isolde from her lover. I wish I had time to write of every Swan Knight, as their stories were told to me by The Ancient One. Each story is dear to me. But I write as quickly as my hand and pen will let me. I must connect this account to the present, to my life, and time is tyrannical. It pushes me relentlessly forward and my end draws near. I cannot present each generation as they ought to be — as they were taught to me. It pains me to think that the stories I omit may soon be lost forever, gone from the minds and the tongues of the living. But I have no choice. Please forgive the brevity of my account.

The lodge was destroyed and rebuilt, expanded and reduced. Bechtold was the last Swan Knight buried in the valley. The graves, and even the shrine of Parsifal, were overgrown by bush and tree, and were eventually indistinguishable from the landscape around them. The Ancient One still sat and prayed over the bones of his friends and students. But to the Swan Knights, several generations removed from Bechtold, the site of the graves was just another of many sacred pieces of the valley, attached to stories they all learned from The Ancient One when they were nine years old.

Near the end of the first millennium A.D., the Grail Blood married into the Wittelsbach family. In 975, a young Swan Knight named Elika von Walbeck married a Wittlesbach named Berthold. They had one child, a son named Heinrich. When Heinrich Wittelsbach became the Swan Knight, upon the death of Elika, the Swan

Knighthood attached itself to the Wittlesbach dynasty, who would carry the burden to this day. In 1117, in Kelheim Bavaria, Swan Knight and Count of Wittlesbach, Otto IV, had a son. He called his son Otto. The young Otto was a fiery redhead, born with a spirit to match the flaming hair of his head that he wore above his passionate eyes. When young Otto was nine, he began training in the valley with The Ancient One as Second-in-Training under his older brother, Hermann. Unlike most of the recent young Swan Knights before him, Otto lived most of his training years in the valley, raised and taught by the swan and the creatures of the Sweeter Realm, who were besotted by his passion and charismatic energy. Otto trained with Hermann, who like Elsa's son Diterich, left the valley in anger and never returned.

Otto was much younger than Hermann and was only eleven when Hermann went away. He spent most of his days in the valley as the only knight-in-training. He had a strong awareness of his uniqueness and a thirst for adventure and fame that reminded The Ancient One sharply and lucidly of his first student, Lohengrin. Although Otto was a good, obedient student, he was strong-willed and full of ideas. No student of the swan had ever frustrated him like Otto. But as much as Otto frustrated, he also impressed. For example, he never took to the sword, the standard weapon of every Swan Knight until Otto. Otto mastered the sling and rock. He could disarm a sword with a simple stick, picked up off the ground. He truly was an inventive warrior.

Otto's creativity shone in other arenas as well. He had a natural eye for architecture. The Ancient One's lessons on human history fascinated him, particularly the evolution of the arts. He loved theater. At fourteen, he designed and constructed an addition to the lodge. It was a theater, fully enclosed, but designed to imitate the open Ancient Greek amphitheaters. It was a small, intimate theater, with seating for thirty. It had columns surrounding the seating area. The ceiling was black with stars to imitate the night sky, making the columns appear to shoot into the night sky and connect to nothing, even though they supported the roof of the theater. Otto loved the history of his family. He identified strongly with Cunrad and dedicated the theater to him, in memory of one of Otto's favorite stories, one whose retelling he demanded almost daily — the one hundred anniversary celebration. Otto stood on the stage of his making and presented The Ancient One and many of the creatures with an encore to the performances of that night. To the audience, most of whom witnessed the anniversary celebration first-hand, Otto's performance was a tender reminder of days gone by and gave them a powerful and needed sense of continuity. Performing on the stage linked Otto more closely with the image of Cunrad.

Few artifacts from the early years of the portal survived to be admired by Otto. One that did survive was Cunrad's axe, the very tool he used in the construction of the lodge and of the stage for the anniversary celebration. The axe hung mounted on a wall of the lodge with a small inscription beneath it that read, "Cunrad's Axe". To the terror and fury of his teacher, Otto liked to pull the axe from its mount and swing it over his head while spinning in circles and hollering a cry that sounded like something between an agonizing appeal for help and an attempt to recite the real name of The Ancient One. The swan never knew what to make of the spectacle, but the seemingly wild and haphazard flailing of the axe never struck an item Otto did not intend to strike. He had remarkable control of the tool.

"If the sword fails him," thought the bird, "perhaps the axe will serve him well."

As painful as it was for the swan to desecrate and endanger the artifact, he allowed Otto to train with Cunrad's axe. Otto needed little training. He took to the weapon naturally. He could spin it in his hand, toss it and catch it, and throw it to pluck a single leaf from a tree from an amazing distance. The Ancient One gained such confidence in the boy's abilities with the axe that he allowed Otto to knock berries off of his head with it. He thrilled in the experience, while trusting Otto explicitly. Everything about Otto was thrilling, for all who inhabited and visited the valley. The Queen herself was so intrigued by reports of the boy that she entertained the idea of paying him a visit. The visit never happened, but it was spoken of as inevitable until the idea slowly faded and was forgotten. But Otto was unpredictable, exciting, dynamic, and charismatic, and the Queen always enjoyed hearing about him.

Since Hermann left, Otto's younger brother, Conrad was groomed to be the Second-in-Training. When Otto was seventeen years old, Conrad turned nine and was introduced to the valley, the portal, and the teacher. Conrad was a quiet and peaceful boy, starkly contrasted in character with Otto. Otto assisted with Conrad's training, delighted to have a playmate and partner. The two boys did not bond easily. Conrad could not be stirred to violence. He did not want to act in the theater, or train with weapons. He focused his training entirely on the stories of the Grail. He spent his personal time in the chapel, in silent and intense prayer and meditation. It did not take The Ancient One or Otto long to realize that Conrad would never make an effective Swan Knight. Otto grew bored of Conrad, which spread to a boredom of the valley and his training.

At eighteen years old, he was ready to leave. His father, the Count and reigning Swan Knight, was still young and strong. This was the time for Otto to take his skills into the world and sow the seeds of his own legend. Many young knights since Lohengrin had followed his example, but none reminded The Ancient One of young Lohengrin like Otto. Otto almost used the exact same words as he pleaded with the swan to let him sally forth into the world. This time, there was no Parsifal to guard the portal, only Otto's father, Count Otto Wittlesbach, a nobleman Swan Knight who rarely came to the valley, even more rarely since Otto became a man. There would be no swan to pull Otto around in a boat and scout the area in front of him for danger. Otto was on his own — and that is just how he wanted it. His father saw him off, fitted with sturdy armor and a new battle-axe.

For twenty years, Otto roamed the world, drawn to every adventure that teased his path, frustratingly seeking that elusive event that would carry his name through the ages. He joined the army of the Holy Roman Empire. In June of 1155, when Otto was thirty-eight years old, he traveled with the army to Rome for the coronation of Emperor Friedrich Barbarossa. The Emperor traveled with the caravan. Otto was excited. Surely, if ever his moment would come, it would be in the defense of the Emperor himself. The caravan arrived in Rome without incident. Rome was secure. The coronation went off without so much as a rowdy "Hurrah!" The only thing less appealing to Otto than returning to the quiet of the valley and his placid little brother was sitting around Rome in polished armor, carrying a weapon that had never been swung in the fury of battle, never vanquished an evil enemy, and did nothing to sculpt his name into the stone of eternal legend.

The coronation ended and the caravan began the slow march back to German land. During the slow and hot march north, Otto finally resolved to return to the valley, assume his position as the Swan Knight, and hope that adventure and legend would find him there. Lulled by the entrancing rhythm of the marching army, Otto's mind drifted to The Ancient One's lessons of the Swan Knight history. His face winced and grimaced when his memory recalled the quick, boring stories of the obscure knights, those whose time passed peacefully and easily. He smiled as he vividly recalled the old swan's voice rising in volume and animation as he told the stories of battles in the valley, of the portal consuming villains at Elsa's command, and the Unicorns slaughtering the evil band, of Lohengrin's valiant victory in his wedding chamber. Otto's shoulders twitched and shrugged as his mind reenacted the adventurous stories he heard as a child.

Near Verona, in northern Italy, Otto was snapped from his fantasies by the holler of men. By the time he regained the moment and looked around him, his army was in the throngs of battle. They were ambushed in an attempt to kill the Emperor. Weapons swung all around him. Clanging, screaming, and splattering blood filled the air. This scene was so like what Otto imagined as a child, when he swung Cunrad's axe around the lodge, he was taken back to those moments. Before he knew it, his virgin battle-axe was spinning in his hand, tossed and caught, and flinging the blood of its enemies behind it. Otto spun and yelled. He was not afraid. This was the moment he had waited for the last twenty years. He defeated more of the enemy than the rest of his army combined. If the chaotic noise of the battle, if the clanging and screaming could have been replaced with music, Otto would have appeared to be dancing beautifully to it, in movement choreographed by Salome, herself — his long, flame-red hair seeming to lift him into the air as it flowed out from under his helmet and into the air around him. He leapt and he slid and he spun his way through the enemy, dropping them lifeless in his wake.

The passage that was meant to trap the Emperor's army from escaping the evil ambush trapped the attackers. None survived Otto. The only thing more satisfying in Otto's eyes than the signs of valor on his axe and armor was the look of awe, wonder, and gratitude on the Holy Roman Emperor. The Emperor lived, as did most of his army. Every man who returned safely from Rome had Otto to thank — and they thanked him. They praised him. They sang songs of his heroics. If a definitive characteristic of a legend is that it must grow larger and more heroic than the event that spawned it, then the story of Otto's battle at Verona is no legend. Nothing could be added to the story to make it grander than the truth of that day, short of Otto sprouting wings or throwing fire from his eyes. He danced so beautifully through the enemy ranks, so gracefully, so unlike the clumbsy and frantic gestures of battle, that Otto appeared as one of St. Michael's angels floating through the evil horde in sculpted attitudes. If anything, the images in the memories of the witnesses reduced the grandeur of the event with the passing of time.

Forever cognizant of his obligations to the portal, Otto did not ride the wave of his heroics into immediate political advantage. He returned to the valley, eager to spread the news of his victory to those who would be deaf to the rumblings of the outside world. Otto arrived to find his father at the lodge, dining with The Ancient One and

Lohengrin's two Scheriers. The Count was happy to see his son. Conrad never stayed in the valley while his father was there. He had gone to one of his many ports of study and prayer. The Count told Otto that this would be his last visit to the valley. Word of his son's heroics at Verona reached the Count's proud ears. He knew his son would return to the valley. He went to the lodge and waited for Otto's triumphant homecoming. He was ready to pass the knighthood to his son. In fact, he had been ready for many years and only awaited Otto's return.

The story of the heroics at Verona and of the political favor gained for the family by the victory set the Count at ease. Otto joined his teacher, the friendly Scheriers, and his father at the dinner table. He wasted no time. The hero of Verona dove straight into a dramatic and sensational retelling of the battle. He lulled them with a long account of the mundane hours and days that led to the ambush. When his story brought them to the battle, Otto jumped atop the table, giving his captivated audience a true sense of the surprise of the moment. As he relayed the details of the battle, his descriptions and reenactments were so colorfully vivid, the Count and the creatures could feel the heat of the Italian sun on their heads. They could smell the air of the battle, hear the sounds, and feel the southern breeze blow through Otto's red, flowing hair, as if they had lived the moments themselves.

Both the teacher and the father puffed their chests in pride as Otto relayed every bloody detail. Truly Otto was ready to assume the Swan Knighthood, which he did in a ceremony that took place the next day. Otto still wore the signs of battle on his uncleaned axe and armor. At the request of The Ancient One, he reluctantly allowed the Brunnens to polish his regalia. It was brighter than it was the day the Count presented it to him. Otto's regret for the loss of the souvenirs from his battle was washed away by the unearthly shine, as the sun hit the axe and armor. After the ceremony, Otto got a new axe. He hung his battle-axe on the wall of the lodge, just beneath Cunrad's axe, with a sign beneath it that read, "Otto's Axe".

The Count remained in the valley for three months after the oath ceremony. Conrad stayed away the entire time. Within a few more months, the Count died, elevating his son to the title and the responsibility of political rule. His last words were in praise of Otto. After the Count died, Otto reflected on their last time together in the valley. He realized that his father was saying goodbye and did not expect to live long. Otto's heroics and return allowed the Count to die in peace, knowing that his son was an able count. The death handed Otto the title, with all of its secular responsibilities. But Otto was not ready to leave the valley. His spirit needed stability after decades of wandering adventure. It needed the secluded placidness of the valley. He spent little time in Kelheim, the Count's primary residence. He spent little time governing his lands. Even if he had settled in Kelheim and committed himself to the affairs of state, his celebrity would have been a gross impediment. There was no place in the Holy Roman Empire that Otto could roam without being lifted upon shoulders or toasted with exuberance. For decades, he had craved the valor, but never the celebrity that followed.

Almost as soon as Otto's father left the valley, Conrad returned, and the brothers began to reconnect. The Count's death, as deaths so often do, brought the brothers closer together. Despite their differences, Otto was proud of his brother. Conrad was pious, just, and full of goodness. He spent most of his youth in the valley, praying and tending to the domestic affairs of the lodge, the portal, and the visitors who shared it with him. He grew close to the creatures of the Sweeter Realm. His peaceful faith and loyal heart attracted them to him. He did not draw admiration quickly, with fiery passion and physical beauty, as Otto did. Conrad purchased affection slowly, one small payment at a time — payments of kindness, sturdiness, compassion, and a sneaky, quiet sort of wisdom, that burrowed itself in the recipient's ear, only to reveal its profound nature much later. By the time Otto returned from his adventures, Conrad had assumed a subtle but undeniable patriarchy of the valley. The wise old bird found an intellectual equal and a friend in Conrad of Wittelsbach. The brothers spent enough time in the valley together to establish and solidify a mutual, brotherly love and friendship. Otto, having spent his fill of wanderlust and impetuosity, was now as desirous of retirement as Conrad. In the few months immediately following the death of their father, the brothers bonded deeply and authentically.

But the valley felt crowded with both of them, and Otto's personality left little room for a second patriarch. Within nine months of Otto's return, Conrad left the valley to study and learn from the world around him. He did not know that he was walking into a world that deified his brother. Otto's fame seeped into every corner of the region. Stories of his heroics at Verona echoed off the walls of every watering hole. Conrad was not envious of his brother's fame, but he did regret the attention it brought to him. Toasts were offered to the brother of The Red-Head everywhere Conrad traveled. He decided to study in Paris, where corners still remained unlit by Otto's notoriety, corners in which Conrad could sit, study, and pray quietly.

In 1161, frustrated by Otto's reluctance to receive the awards he deserved for his valor at Verona, and wishing to make some payment toward that debt, Emperor Friedrich Barbarossa awarded Conrad the powerful position of Archbishop of Mainz. To Conrad, this was just another toast raised to his brother, but he desired the position and he accepted it. It gave him both the means to seclude himself for study and a platform from which he could serve God on a grand scale. The Ancient One flew regular visits to Conrad in Mainz, and later in Salzburg, when Conrad became archbishop there.

From time to time, Conrad visited the valley. After one visit, lonely for home, he took a Brunnen back with him, hidden among his things. The Brunnen never returned to the portal and the Sweeter Realm. She was Conrad's personal friend and companion. Nobody knows what became of the creature. But Conrad grew a reputation of talking to spirits. He was even seen conjuring a spirit in his study one night, or so it appeared to a curious eye. The public debated the truth of the claims, but Otto and the creatures of the Sweeter Realm knew that it was the Brunnen that was seen in the study with Conrad that night, with candle light passing through her water-like body. She became Conrad's closest friend.

The Archbishop learned the language of the Brunnens, a melodic language that uses specific notes to conjugate verbs and set tense. The Brunnens have two passages in the throat, allowing them to speak in harmony with themselves, and express complicated thoughts quickly. The vocabulary of their language is simple and rigid. The different cases of a sentence are expressed through the musical note in which it was spoken. For example, if a word is the subject of a sentence, it is spoken in G. If the same word is spoken in F, it is the object. They harmonize with the two halves of their throat if a word served as both. If they want to say "I hurt myself." They would speak their one word for self, in both G and F at the same time, one through each of their two throats, followed by their word for hurt. Whether they say that they are, have, or will hurt themselves is expressed in the musical note they use in their word for hurt. They slide their notes flat or sharp for emphasis and to express emotion. This created confusion as the Brunnens first learned German from The Ancient One and challenged Conrad in the learning of their language.

Conrad commissioned his music master at the catherdral in Mainz for intense musical lessons to help him better understand the Brunnens' language. He relished the challenge and learned to understand Brunnen perfectly and even speak it, albeit crudely. When they speak German, the Brunnens use only one side of the throat, but when they speak their own language, they sound to human ears like two people. Rumors spread of Conrad holding demonic rituals in his study. Through the doors and walls, servants heard strange melodic chanting, in what sounded like multiple voices. When the Archbishop left the room, nobody else was seen. Charges of demonic rituals died shortly after hitting the streets. Conrad was a good bishop and a holy man, and beyond reproach in the eyes of most.

As the years passed, Otto's energy and ambitions rebounded. He embraced his role as Count, which included the necessary basking in the fame of his growing legend. The same ambitious heart that drove him around the region in search of adventure, that eventually brought him into the Emperor's caravan, redirected toward the welfare of the people under Otto's influence. He gave freely, and his dynamic charisma encouraged others to do the same. Kellheim and the surrounding area flourished under his leadership. He steered the exuberance of his devotees into more productive arenas, initiating several holidays dedicated to charity and forbearance. With each success, Otto became more energetic, more youthful. But time did pass by, and Otto did age.

Otto's flaming red hair grew white. He had no wife, no children. The Ancient One knew that Conrad would never leave the church to assume his brother's post. If he did, it would only be a temporary solution. Otto needed to marry. In one of the swan's visits with Conrad, he discussed his concerns. Through his position in the Church, Conrad had friends and connections far and wide. He thought of a young lady from the House of Loon, in Belgium. He arranged a visit between his brother and Agnes of Loon. Otto was fifty years old. Agnes was seventeen. Otto's notoriety was still rich and pungent across Europe. Agnes had grown with the stories of Otto's valor. As a young girl, she fantasized about being rescued from hordes of villains by the Red-Headed Knight. She was eager to meet the man behind her childhood fantasies. They met under Conrad's supervision in Salzburg. Otto had lost none of his charisma, none of the intoxicating allure of his figure or manner. Agnes fell for him at first sight.

She was a sweet and innocent girl, ready to devote herself to any life that came with the hero she adored. Otto attached his love for his brother to the girl, assigning her Conrad's traits and adhering her quickly to his affections. Within days of the introduction, Conrad performed the ceremony and married Otto to Agnes in Salzburg. The newlyweds left for the valley immediately after the ceremony. As they traveled, Otto tried to prepare Agnes' young mind for the wonders that awaited it.

Agnes delighted in the stories of the magical wonders and beautiful creatures that Otto described to her while they traveled. Her mind was still pliable enough to bend her known notions of reality around the fantastic things her new husband told her. Otto's descriptions must have been accurate and detailed. The images in Agnes' mind must have struck near the traits of the creatures she would soon meet. When they presented themselves to her, she showed no signs of surprise. She embraced them like old friends.

Agnes would have been content to keep company with the creatures at the portal all day, and hold her legendary husband all night — for the rest of her life. But the life of a Swan Knight's spouse was not that simple. Otto's duel identity and complicated life threw Agnes into the whirlwind of a Swan Knight's life. In 1169, she gave birth to their first child, a boy they named Otto. At nine years old, according to the Laws of Ermenrich, Otto began his training. Young Otto was much like his father. His sister Heilika was just two years younger. When she reached nine years old, her parents brought her into the valley and introduced her to her teacher. The next three children, Agnes, Richardis, and Ludwig, all within three years of Heilika, remained in Kelheim, where all of the children were born. The youngest three were told nothing of the portal and the Grail, nothing of the family legacy.

Within weeks of studying under The Ancient One, Heilika showed great promise as a budding Swan Knight. Her imagination was free and unpredictable, much like her father's. Like her Uncle Conrad, she preferred books to weapons. She steeped herself thoroughly in the stories of the Swan Knights. Where the stories fell short in detail, Heilika's imagination made them full and dramatic. The Ancient One often caught her telling the stories to her favorite creature visitors, elaborating and taking a great deal of creative license. At first he corrected her, believing that she remembered the stories incorrectly. He quickly realized that she knew the stories perfectly, but she relayed them to her audiences as she thought they should be, always including dramatic scenes of romance when there were none and enriching them when there was.

Every story was a love story to Heilika. The swan stopped correcting her and encouraged her creativity. He thought that such an imagination at her age could do her little harm, and he enjoyed hearing her mutations of the very stories he had told her. He was wrong, as he eventually discovered. Heilika's imagination *could* do her harm. She pulled a love story into every lesson. In the middle of sword training, she would drop her sword and run into the arms of an imaginary prince. During riding training, she would dismount her Unicorn and run to the aid of an imaginary knight who had been stabbed by an evil, enchanted flowermaiden. The Unicorns, with their expressive, bushy eyebrows, relayed their perplexed exasperation in a few, reproachful glances toward the girl's teacher.

Young Otto and Heilika trained enthusiastically together and loved each other dearly. Neither felt the full weight of the responsibility for which they were being trained. Heilike was swept by the romantic tales of love and marriage in the family history. She was particularly infatuated with the story of Lohengrin and Nethe, and the Christmas night around the portal. With all of her developing skills and promise, Heilika was dreamy. She stared for hours at the ridges of the hills around her, expecting at any minute for a valorous knight to ride into the valley and fall in love with her. The Ancient One said that she could have been the greatest Swan Knight since

Elsa, if not for the command over her mind that her adolescent fixation on love ruthlessly exercised. She looked for love everywhere and took every opportunity to leave the valley and meet young men. Otto was obsessed with glorious battle. He turned every lesson into an epic opportunity for legendary valor. When the two children trained together, they brought some balance to the lessons. But every lesson ended with a tangent into some imaginary scene. No lesson ever came to its designed conclusion and no wisdom ever came from their failures.

The swan encouraged them to take their fanciful imaginings into their father's theater, hoping that they could learn to confine them to that arena. The whole valley was their stage, and the world beyond when they had a chance to leave the valley. To the children, life was dreamy and always had a happy ending. The Ancient One tried to balance them by emphasizing the credits of the less exciting Swan Knights and their soberer spouses. Cunrad, Hildemar, and Ermenrich — the subtler heroics of these figures could not keep the children's attention over the likes of Parsifal, Lohengrin, and Elsa. Their own father's life did little to attract them to the mundane. Count Otto was often in the valley with his children. The tales he so dramatically told of his own adventures erased every effort The Ancient One made to balance the children.

There was a depth and a seriousness to the Count that the children could not see. Even when he sternly spoke to them of the grave, harsh realities of the world and of their positions as sacred guardians of Christ's cup, the children saw what they wanted to see in their father. Like most of Europe, they only saw in their father the hero of Verona, the rallies and cheers, the toasts and the swooning devotees. The political realities of the world around them soon brought permanent change to the family and to the Swan Knighthood. The life of a lesser count — the life of his children — is a free life, without political concerns beyond their tiny corner of the world. Such would not long be the life of Count Otto and his children. A grander destiny awaited the hero of Verona. Greater responsibilities awaited the Wittlesbach.

CHAPTER 11

Rule of Bavaria

THE WELF DYNASTY held the Duchy of Bavaria and were entirely ignorant of the Grail Blood that hung in abundance from their family tree. When they fell out of favor with Emperor Barbarossa, the Emperor revoked the duchy, using the dispute as the excuse he needed to finally reward Otto as his honor demanded. In 1180, the Emperor granted the duchy of Bavaria to Otto. Otto became Otto I, Duke of Bavaria, a title of governance that forbade his beloved time in the valley. He was no longer a lesser count. He governed one of the largest and most powerful regions in the empire. His opinions and his decisions weighed heavily in the affairs of Europe. He relished the opportunity to secure his sacred valley under the power of his new title and delighted in the dynastic benefits for the Swan Knighthood. But those advantages would have to be secured from a distance, from the seats of Bavaria's political power, not from his humble lodge in his obscure valley, with his children, his teacher, and the fine creatures he loved.

When Heilika was still nine, Duke Otto left his whimsically distracted daughter to the tantalizing influence of the mystical old valley, its magical visitors, and its long history of romance. One year later, in 1181, the Duke's oldest son, young Otto, fell abruptly ill and died, leaving the dreamy Heilika alone in the valley, with one less distraction from her fantasies. In accordance with the Laws of Ermenrich, Duke Otto and Duchess Agnes brought their third child, Agnes, into the valley to begin as Second-in-Training under Heilika, who became the presumptive heir to the knighthood when her brother died. Young Agnes had just turned nine years old.

Agnes worked and studied much more industriously than Heilika. Despite her sister's natural talents, Agnes' skills surpassed those of the First-in-Training, which only served to drive Heilika further into her fantasies. The Ancient One begged the Duchess to come to the valley and rein in her daughter's wandering mind. Duchess Agnes had little effect on Heilika's behavior, but she came and she tried, and the time brought her closer to young Agnes. The Duchess spent most of the next two years in the valley, more bonding with young Agnes, whose maturity placed her as a needed peer for her mother, than reining in the wild fancy of Heilika. She was content to remain living in the valley with her daughters, away from her husband, until Duke Otto I, The Redhead, the savior at Verona, the Swan Knight, died in his bed at Kelheim, leaving his oldest surving son, young Ludwig, as the new duke. At only ten years old, Ludwig became Duke Ludwig I of Bavaria. The Duchess had to return to Kelheim to serve as regent to the young duke. The Swan Knight was dead. The next one must rise to take his place.

At only twelve years old, Heilika was sworn to the duty of the Grail and the Queen of the Land and Shallow Waters as the youngest Swan Knight in the storied line. She was nothing like her predecessors. She never bonded with the creatures of the Sweeter Realm. She had no interest in them. Her early talents had been rusted over by neglect and indifference. Once her mother had left, she traveled farther from the valley, all alone, and stayed away for weeks at a time. In 1184, at thirteen years old, just four years into her training, Heilika married. Fully consumed by her passion, she left the valley and immersed herself entirely in her husband's life, leaving young Agnes as the lone focus of the teacher's attention. Heilika's departure brought Otto and Agnes' fourth child to the valley. Richardis was eleven and she missed her sister Agnes terribly since Agnes had left home three years earlier to become Second behind Heilika. She entered the valley for the first time, and was introduced to the mysteries of the portal, just as her sister Agnes stood at the portal, taking the Swan Knight's oath in replacement of her departed older sister.

Richardis had no idea what she was witnessing. There was a giant, stately swan, presiding over a ceremony that centered on Agnes. Agnes, who assumed the knighthood a few months younger than Heilika did, dropped to a knee and swore allegiance to some queen Richardis had never heard of. The strangest creatures attended and celebrated. This was Richardis' first introduction to the valley. The eleven-year-old girl spent the first day in a thick fog of disbelief, carried along with the flow of the hectic day's goings-on. The next day, The Ancient One wasted no time revealing the history of the family and trying to recover poor Richardis from her strange first day. Duty, more than wonder, attached Richardis to her new life.

The two girls worked hard. The Swan Knight was still so young and more time was spent in study than on patrols. The Ancient One insisted upon that point. Their father was dead and their mother governed Bavaria as regent over the young Duke Ludwig. Ludwig had his hands full of intense study, preparing him to rule when he came of age. He was ignorant of all concerning the Grail. The Ancient One assumed many of the duties of the Swan Knight, keeping the schedule of patrols, tracking which creatures came into the valley and when they returned home. The Unicorns loved the cooler air of this side of the portal, and they had come to inhabit the valley and surrounding hills almost constantly. They took the extra patrols in the absence of a fully-grown Swan Knight.

The valley had never seen anything like it — Agnes and Richardis, both quiet, practical girls, with humble, unassuming tastes, were the only humans in the valley. What they lacked in the natural abilities of Elsa or their father, they filled with a strong bond of sisterly love and devout faithfulness to duty. The girls had no desire to plant the seeds of their own legends. Under those two young girls, the youngest Swan Knight and her little sister, the valley and the Swan Knighthood saw its most austere sobriety since Parsifal. Both girls accepted the responsibilities of their positions, but they did not desire the honors. Richardis only wanted to serve her sister well until she could marry, leave the valley, and bring her brother Ludwig, the young Duke, into the family legacy. Agnes wanted to serve the Grail exactly as she was required to do, and pass the knighthood on so she could slip into the obscurity of the many Swan Knights whose reigns were uneventful.

She prayed in the chapel of the lodge, every night and every morning, "Nothing on my watch, Lord. Please hide our valley from the world."

Duke Ludwig was less than one year younger than Richardis. He had his father's zeal for glory and a charismatic air that drew the eye and caged it for his pleasure. Agnes and Richardis agreed that he would better live up to the legendary heritage of the Swan Knights. They bode their time in judicious agitation for their brother to come of age to serve the duchy and the knighthood as his father did.

The girls' mother was ruling a large and influential duchy as regent. Otto I had left young children when he died, leaving the political security of the family in a precarious state. Many ambitious eyes turned to Bavaria. Like her daughters, the Regent also envisioned Ludwig as the Swan Knight, as well as Duke of Bavaria. To secure the secular title, she arranged a marriage between Richardis and a powerful regional count. They married in 1186, when Richardis was only thirteen. The arrangement and its political benefits required Richardis to abandon the valley and live with her husband's family, which she dutifully undertook. This brought Duke Ludwig, barely thirteen years old, to the valley to train.

It became quickly apparent to all that Ludwig was born to live in the valley. He showed no signs of astonishment when his sister Agnes walked him forward to open the portal for the first time, the time-honored duty of the reigning Swan Knight. Only, the privelige is usually performed from parent to child, not from a child-Swan Knight to her younger brother. Nothing in the appearance or traits of the creatures seemed unusual to Ludwig. By the end of his first day in the valley, he spoke comfortably and casually to the creatures of the Sweeter Realm, with the familiarity of an old friend. He retold the stories he had just been taught, as if he had witnessed them himself. He offered suggestions for the improvement of his lessons and the security of the valley. It was like he had been born in the valley and opened the portal every day since infancy. No doubt, the rigorous schooling his mother put him through in Kelheim served him well in the Portal Valley. In silence and without him knowing, she had trained him to be a Swan Knight.

Agnes was relieved by her brother's natural abilities and inclinations toward a life as a portal custodian. Within a year of Ludwig's arrival in the valley, Agnes began to speak of resigning the Swan Knighthood to her brother. Ludwig had a way with the Unicorns and he commanded the respect and admiration of all of the creatures who came to the valley. Agnes spent many long days and nights alone with her brother, sharing all that her young mind could share to prepare Ludwig for the Swan Knighthood. There was little else that Agnes could teach her brother. His skills progressed well beyond those of the reigning Swan Knight. He also showed an admirable balance between his father's energetic charisma and his sister's devotion to duty. As soon as the snow melted in the spring of 1188, Agnes began to travel, not in search of adventure, like her father, but in search of retirement. By the middle of autumn, at sixteen years old, the youngest Swan Knight ever was married to Count Henry of Plain.

A tremendous weight lifted from Agnes' shoulders as she passed the Swan Knighthood to her successor, still safe, still secret, still secure, as she had prayed for every day. Agnes made regular visits to the valley for the next two years, never telling the secret to her husband or new relations. In 1190, Count Henry died unexpectedly, burdening Agnes, at eighteen years old, with the full responsibilities of the household and the Count's lands. She never came back to the valley. When Agnes left, passing the valley to Ludwig, The Ancient One presided over another oath ceremony, this time altering the oath to underscore the permanence of the position. He was uneasy with the recent years' coming and going of young

Swan Knights. He prayed over the place where the shrine of Parsifal once stood, to his first human friend, that the spirit of Parsifal might seize young Ludwig and maintain its grip as long as the boy lives.

Agnes of Loon remained as Regent of Bavaria during Ludwig's training in the valley. After young Agnes assumed matriarchy of the House of Plain, and Ludwig's positions as Duke of Bavaria and Swan Knight were firmly solidified, the Regent let go of the world and fell into the embrace of her waiting husband, serene in her faith in the future of her family. His mother's death weighed heavily on Ludwig's heart. She had held his hand every day after his father died and he was thrusted into the daunting role of Duke of Bavaria. Ludwig struggled to imagine life without her. For the first three years of his training, he was content with the company of the portal and its Sweeter Realm visitors, not thinking very often of his dear mother. Suddenly, she was gone, and Ludwig found himself in constant thought of his family. His penetrating recollections punctured his deepest memories and released an eruption of sharp and poignant admiration, particularly for his mother, and for young Agnes, and Richardis.

After being compared to his father by every friend and relation since his early childhood, Ludwig began to identify less with his legendary father and more with the subtler greatness of the women in his life. He thought often of his sister Agnes, of the long nights at the dining table of the lodge, spent consuming every morsel of wisdom that the youngest Swan Knight had to offer her brother. The seeds of Agnes' early influence grew and blossomed in Ludwig. He grew more serious, more fearful. He loved the valley and was always disinclined to leave it. But the sobering of his contemplations barricaded his thoughts within his home and the sacred oath that held him there. He saw the growth of the world around him. He feared its encroachment and his inability to pass the Swan Knighthood down as peacefully as he received it. These fears were further agitated by the political circumstances that plagued his reign.

Ludwig's twenties were filled with conflicts between the Holy Roman Empire and several dukes and counts under the Emperor. Within weeks of the death of Count Henry of Plain, and the end of the visits by his beloved sister, Emperor Barbarossa died. His death placed Bavaria in the center of a vicious power dispute. The House of Welf disputed the claim of Barbarossa's son and heir, Heinrich, to the throne of the empire. Heinrich took the throne but did not live long upon it. When he died in 1197, the dispute was renewed. The kingship of Germany was claimed by two families, the House of Hohenstaufen, and the House of Welf. The throne of the Holy Roman Empire sat empty in dispute. The eyes of the entire Empire turned to Bavaria and Ludwig wanted to turn them away. Although the reigning Welfs were ignorant of their connection to Ludwig and the portal, Ludwig was not. He had a painful decision to make. A side had to be taken — either for the bonds of kinship and the line of Grail Blood with which he felt an intimate connection, or for the peace of the region and a return to the normalcy and obscurity of his holy little valley. Painful as it was, the decision was clear. It pained Ludwig to side against the blood of Parsifal, against kinship, but the mandates of his oath to the Queen were clear.

These political circumstances weighed heavily on the Duke and Swan Knight. He was not certain where the conflicts would take him. He hosted few celebrations in the valley, few moments of leisure. He took up the sword that his father had abandoned for the axe and sharpened his skills on the stone of his fear and his faith. Even without the mystical connection of Elsa, Ludwig bonded deeply with the creatures. Never had there been such a sense of solidarity, of single-purpose between a Swan Knight and the creatures of the Sweeter Realm. The Queen's distant eyes maintained a vision of Bavaria from Lohengrin's day, despite the swan's warnings to the contrary. She kept a blissful ignorance, but her subjects adhered themselves firmly to their allegiance to Ludwig, under Ludwig's heightened sense of impending calamity. Political disputes meant battles. Battles meant armies, marching across the center of the conflict — across Bavaria. The fear of armies sweeping through the valley plagued every moment of Ludwig's toubled thoughts. The Swan Knight drilled his companions relentlessly until they could disappear in an instant when Ludwig whistled. Holes and hiding places were never more than two steps away.

The Ancient One observed the dutiful preparations and praised God that Ludwig held the knighthood.

He told Ludwig, "Thank God your sister Heilika is not the Swan Knight. And thank God your sister Agnes left her influence in your heart before she married."

The primary defense of the valley fell on the Unicorns. Ludwig feared for their lives and wanted to fit them with armor of their own, but they refused, which only intensified his nightmares. He feared for the Unicorns almost as much as he feared for the Holy Grail. He woke every night from the same dream. In it, the Unicorns stormed an approaching army, trampling Ludwig in their path. When he pulled himself back to his feet and looked up, the valley was quiet — and all of the

Unicorns were dead on the side of the hill in front of him, their horns cut out of their heads and their shaggy, bloodied faces still wearing their noble pride and valor. Ludwig often awoke from this dream cursing himself and scratching violently at the sides of his face.

Every step Ludwig took, every thought in his head, was bent upon one concern — securing the valley. A strong alliance was the surest way to do so. In 1204, he left the valley and married. It was a political marriage. He married Ludmilla of Bohemia, and he did it to gain an ally out of a former enemy. Ludmilla's uncle, Ottokar I of Bohemia was a powerful duke of a large, wealthy, and influential duchy. The alliance with Ottokar made Bavaria a less tempting target in the regional power struggle. Ludmilla was a widow, with three children from her first marriage. All three children remained in Bohemia. The marriage certainly bolstered Ludwig's power. It was seen as ambitious, as a move of political offense, not as the defensive, cautionary maneuver that it was. Ludwig was watched, his every movement recorded and reported to both sides of the conflict. He could not return to the valley. He could not risk its detection. He kept his wife in the dark, deciding that she could learn of the family secret once the perils at hand had passed. In 1206, Ludwig and Ludmilla gave birth to their only child, a son named after the Swan Knight's heroic father, Otto.

With Bavaria secured to the north by his marriage, Ludwig turned his attention south. The throne of the Holy Roman Empire was won by Otto IV of Welf in 1209. Pope Innocent III supported Otto IV at first, but when Otto tried to extend his power deeper into Italy, the Pope switched alliances and threw his support behind Friedrich, the son of the deceased Emperor Heinrich. All of the powers of Europe were thrown into the conflict, including

King John of England and King Philip II of France. Poor Ludwig. A continental war would bring soldiers from all sides across Bavaria, sadly situated in the center of the turmoil. Ludwig abandoned the valley and committed himself and the Bavarian army to the political maneuverings that would keep foreign soldiers out of his valley. His soldiers did not know it, but they fought for the Unicorns. They fought for the Scheriers. They fought for the portal, the Queen, and the Grail. Before he left the valley, Ludwig opened the portal and summoned a force to guard and protect the portal. Representatives of all known creatures of the Sweeter Realm responded to the call. Ludwig placed The Ancient One as head of the force of creatures.

Ludwig spent little time with his wife and child. The baby Otto and Ludmilla found themselves imprisoned in the palace in Kelheim, imprisoned by Ludwig's fear. Otto hardly knew his father. All he saw was the worried Duke, working tirelessly and traveling constantly. Ludmilla admired Ludwig's tireless efforts and quickly sank herself into the effort in every way she could. She assumed many facets of governance abandoned because of the many draws on Ludwig's attention.

Back in the valley, the creatures were left without a Swan Knight. They watched with terrible anxiety as marching armies crossed the area, often skirting the edge of their own sacred valley. The Graswang Valley was a common passage. It brought armies just south of the Portal Valley. From the hills surrounding the portal point, and from the lodge on occasion, the clatter of marching armies could be heard. The guarding creatures prayed for Ludwig's return, but the Duke's efforts to secure the portal through political and military means consumed every moment of his time. So the creatures of the Sweeter

Realm, who left their homes and abandoned themselves in Parsifal's Valley (as The Ancient One always called it), were left to their own plans, their own abilities, to secure the portal while keeping the secret of their own existence. The sound of marching armies rang perpetually in their ears, even when none were nearby. The Ancient One was so sickened with fear that it began to take its toll on his health. He lost feathers, and those that he kept lost their radiant whiteness for a dirty, jaundiced yellow.

Ludwig was absent for years at a time. In the valley, there were no children to teach, no human companionship, and more importantly, nobody to open the portal for reinforcements and relief. The creatures lived off of the land, a land that offered none of the foods they had at home. One cold spring evening in 1212, a Welf army under the banner of Emperor Otto IV passed near the valley. The lonely, comfortable lodge drew the attention of the knights. The foot soldiers made camp at the far southeastern end of the Grail Valley, on the opposite end from the portal. The knights rode toward the lodge to plunder and enjoy a night of shelter. The creatures scattered into their designated hiding places and watched a couple dozen knights enter the lodge. These were Welf knights — nobles. It was possible that one of them carried the Grail Blood and could pass by the portal and trigger an opening. Centuries of cooperative safeguarding was in jeopardy, and there was no Swan Knight in the valley. The Welf knights sacked the lodge. The sun set and they built a bon fire of the furniture, clothes, and books of the Swan Knights. The creatures watched, ready to attack a stout, well-armed band of fighters they could not defeat in open combat. The Ancient One instructed them to wait and watch through the night, and hope that the army would leave their poor valley in the morning. There was nothing of value to tempt a return, if they only leave without seeing any curiosity — creature or portal.

As difficult as it was to watch the invaders destroy and defile the Swan Knights' possessions, the destruction of each triggering tender and vivid memories associated with them, The Ancient One placated his rage with the image of the dawn, and the peacefully departing army. The image was shattered when one of the knights walked out of the lodge carrying Otto's axe.

The swan heard him tell his companions, "It read, 'Otto's Axe'. This is the Redhead's axe, the famous axe from the battle at Verona, Duke Otto of Wittelsbach's famous axe."

The raiding knights knew that the valley and the lodge belonged to Ludwig, their enemy, the enemy of their sovereign, Emperor Otto IV of Welf. The valley was no longer some obscure setting between here and there. It became a target. The rage from the night's spectacle, and the realization that the axe made the valley and the lodge infamous to the knights, combined to spring The Ancient One into action. As the knight swung the axe in the air and danced around in imitation of Otto's legend, the sickly old swan flew at him and flapped around him, biting at his face and squawking a hideously angry and defiant scream. The other knights laughed at their companion, as he swung Otto's axe at the giant bird. When the spectacle lost its humor, the knights saw in the wise old teacher a meal large enough to share. When the other knights converged upon him, The Ancient One flew away into the woods. These knights could no longer be permitted to leave the valley alive. The secret valley was notorious to them now, and the attack of the giant swan was exactly the curiosity that the creatures had hoped to avoid revealing. There was still the fear that one of the knights might trigger a portal opening with his distant, hidden Grail lineage. These were Welfs, possibly descended from Hildemar.

The Brunnens hatched a plan. They would appear before the knights, seduce them and lure them into the woods with their hypnotic songs, where the other creatures would wait to destroy the danger. The creatures moved in silence to the other side of the lodge, to pull the knights away from the portal as the Brunnens drew them into the woods. The terror of the creatures, as they planned and prepared the dangerous mission, was swallowed by their sense of duty to the portal and their Queen, and their sense of vengeance for the defiling of the holy home of the Swan Knights. All six Brunnens that had remained in the valley when the Swan Knight went away crept their way toward the dwindling bon fire, around which all of the knights were gathered. The men had removed their armor, which they had placed in the lodge for the night. Just as they stepped within the light of the fire, and their almost clear, water-like figures came into sight, revealed only by the rippling of their flesh as they moved, the Brunnens began to sing.

The beguiled knights went silent, one at a time as their attentions were drawn to the mystical creatures. The plan was not working. The knights did not rise and follow the Brunnens into the ambush. They simply sat, frozen in bewilderment. One brave Brunnen, followed by another, then another, rippled her way to one of the knights, still frozen in enchanted captivation, and touched his face with the softest little hand known on either side of the portal. The other Brunnens did the same, reaching to the enemy and caressing their faces. Then, simultaneously, the Brunnens slowly backed away. Impulsively, driven by something much deeper than consciousness, the knights rose to their feet and slowly followed the Brunnens toward the trees, matching the steps of their captors, reaching their hands toward them but not daring to gain on them.

The Brunnens led the knights into the thick of the surrounding woods, into the passionately fierce circle of the Queen's loyal subjects. The Brunnens walked to the knights and allowed themselves to be touched by the still outstretched hands of the men. The Unicorns attacked, followed by the others. There were no war cries, no hollers of vengeance. The creatures silently attacked the knights. The knights did not fight back. They stood there and were pierced by Unicorn horns and torn by Scherier teeth and punctured through the eyes by the long, hard, wood-like fingers of the Zweigwesens. The knights dropped to their knees, still reaching for the Brunnens, then fell dead on the floor of the woods, with no signs of pain or distress on the lifeless faces, still wearing the intoxicated glare that took control of them as they rose to follow the Brunnens into the woods. The knights were dead — all of them. The immediate danger was over, but the rest of the army still camped at the far end of the valley, and they knew that their leaders were staying at the lonely lodge.

The creatures hid the bodies of the knights. Then they waited for the fire to disappear into darkness. When the fire was gone and the valley was dark and silent, The Ancient One, followed by the Scheriers, Brunnens, and Zweigwesens, entered the lodge and removed the knights' armor into the woods. The Unicorns touched their horns to the knights' horses. The horses followed the archaic command of the Unicorns and rode away into the woods and over the far hill. In the morning, the camp of soldiers awoke. By mid-morning, the camp bustled in anticipation. When the knights did not rejoin their army by midday, one of the soldiers came to the lodge.

All of the signs of the evening remained. There were the embers of the bon fire, the destroyed items from the lodge, remnants of food on the ground — but no knights, no sign of them whatsoever, no sign of struggle, no blood, no horses. The soldier called for his leaders. Only his own sterile echo off the walls of the lodge answered him. The soldier must have assumed that the knights abandoned their army and rode on without them. For a few more hours, a nervous bustle hovered over the camp, until it slowly dispersed. The remaining army, devoid of leadership and direction, wandered aimlessly away from the valley, and dispersed in several different directions, presumably toward their homes. The valley was safe, at least from the peril of that army. But where was the Swan Knight, and how many encounters like the last night were coming to the valley?

The next couple of years brought many close encounters with the movement of various bands of soldiers and traveling knights. None came as near as the Welf army whose knights sacked the lodge. Eventually, Friedrich II defeated Otto IV, ending the Welf claim to the throne and dissolving the greatest danger the portal had ever faced. In 1215, Otto of Welf abdicated the throne to Friedrich. Ludwig, who had abandoned his family, abandoned the valley, to fight for the security of the portal in a way that no Swan Knight had ever done, not with the sword or axe, but with the hands of politics, was free to resume the life he had always wanted. Friedrich took the throne of the Holy Roman Empire just a few weeks before the Duke's son, young Otto Wittelsbach, turned nine years old.

Pope Innocent III, powerful and influential in Eurpoean politics, decreed, from that point forward, the German royalty would elect their king, who would sit on the throne of the empire. This forbade the growth of princly power from threatening the power of the Pope. Political manueverings became more important than military might, the secret handshake a better weapon than the sword.

With the piling, oppressive fear of the previous decade finally removed from Ludwig's shoulders, the Swan Knight took his son to the valley for his ritualistic first opening of the portal and the introduction to his teacher. Ludwig took his wife too. Although rarely with her husband during the political conflicts, Ludmilla worked equally hard to secure the interests of Bavaria. They did not marry for love, but their bond was forged through furious endeavor toward a shared interest. For a while, Ludmilla could hardly recall her husband's face when she closed her eyes at night. But even in his absence, she grew to love him. She saw the earnest honor in his actions and sensed the fear he had for the portal, though she did not the truth behind the fear.

Ludmilla's first husband, Count Albert III of Bogen, and their three sons, were politically ambitious. Their fears were of personal loss, their actions driven by personal gain. Ludwig's selflessness and dedication to an effort much bigger than one man's wealth or political title kissed her heart tenderly. With each brief reunion during the years of conflict, Ludmilla greeted her husband with increased affection and admiration — until she realized that she was in love with him. When he came home at last and told her that he did not intend to ever leave her again, she professed such grateful love and devotion that he firmly resolved to bring her into the family fully, by entrusting her with the most precious thing he had to offer — a secret, a sacred secret.

It was Ludwig's first return to the valley in a long time. The creatures who had been guarding the portal, locked from their home by the long absence of the Swan Knight, gave Ludwig a loud and exuberant homecoming, spoiling the traditional surprise introduction for young Otto. Ludwig, Ludmilla, and Otto were spied by a patrolling Zweigwesen. Every creature in the valley met them on the ridge of a hill, at the farthest point that the creatures of the Sweeter Realm were allowed to wander. The new Knight-in-Training and his mother experienced the wonderful creatures for the first time, watching Ludwig run into their welcoming arms. They surrounded the Swan Knight, who dropped to his knees amidst them and laughed as they piled on him.

In the joy of the reunion, the jovial party forgot about the mother and son, who stood exactly where Ludwig had left them when he jumped from his horse and ran to his old friends. The laughter and the antics in the reunion pile drew a chuckle from Ludmilla, one that sneakily liberated itself from her frozen astonishment at the strange creatures and at her husband's affectionate familiarity with them. The nine-year-old Otto could only be detained by bewilderment very briefly before the excitement of the scene in front of him drew him to join atop the pile. The Ancient One waited behind a tree near the portal point to spring the surprise, as he had done so many times before. He preferred to appear through the portal when a new Knight-in-Training opens the portal for the first time, as he did with me. But that was not an option with young Otto. Still, he enjoyed flying down to surprise a new student just as the portal opens. When the swan saw the Swan Knight's family and all of the creatures barreling down the hill, toward the lodge, laughing in unison and walking so tightly against each other that they looked like one giant, strange creature, the joy of the scene eradicated any disappointment at the loss of his planned surprise.

The Ancient One stood at the portal point and waited as the entire party rounded the lodge together. By the time they reached the old teacher, nothing about a giant talking swan would stupefy Ludmilla or Otto. The swan simply bowed to them and gestured toward the portal point. Ludwig bowed in return, then stood behind his son, as so many did before and would after, holding him by the shoulders.

He gave his son a little push forward and said, "Walk slowly."

Then he stood near his wife, took her hand, and told her, "Watch this."

When the portal opened for Otto, he pointed at it and resumed the laughter that he began when he jumped onto the pile on the ridge of the hill. The Ancient One walked directly in front of Otto and began his time-honored speech about learning and responsibility.

Ludwig interrupted, "Not right now, old friend. We have so much to celebrate and so much to talk about."

The teacher agreed. He and the rest of the creatures nodded, bowed, and kissed their Swan Knight as they returned through the portal that was still held open by Otto, all promising to return before sunset, with their families, for the night's festivities.

It was a grand celebration. Friedrich retained his throne as King of the Germans and secured the Holy Roman Empire with his defeat of Otto IV of Welf. The guardians of the valley, during the long absence of the Swan Knight, those brave creatures who vanquished the Welf knights in the forest, could reunite with their families in the Sweeter Realm. Strong political stability across Bavaria, Germany, and the entire Holy Roman Empire settled the tumultuous waves of danger that had crashed relentlessly against the shores of Parsifal's Valley for more than a decade. The celebration was grand, but not loud. There was a calmness in the air, a collective sigh of relief across Bavaria and the Sweeter Realm. As happy as the celebrants were, they were also tired, in desperate need of repose and recovery. At the one hundred anniversary celebration, the valley needed elation — so it was an elated celebration. In 1215, the valley needed rest — so it was a restful celebration.

They all told stories from their years apart. The Ancient One told the story of the defeat of the Welf knights. Ludwig was expressively disturbed by the report. Firstly, he was bitterly mortified to hear of the sweet creatures risking their lives to perform the duties of the absent Swan Knight. The lodge was in perfect order, except for the missing items destroyed by the knights. The swan had insisted that the creatures recover the lodge before the return of the Swan Knight. The axe of Otto I hung where it belonged, on the wall near Cunrad's axe. The dutiful diligence of the creatures humbled Ludwig as he sat around his loyal friends. Secondly, Ludwig had no idea of the seductive power of the Brunnens' song and touch. They never had such an hypnotic and debilitating effect on the Swan Knights.

Ludwig knew that anyone who experienced the alluring effects of the Brunnens, and survived to leave the valley, would form an obsession and never leave the valley alone while the spell of the Brunnens remained in the head. The celebration, which already bore a degree of sobriety not usually associated with the word, ended with a proclamation from the Swan Knight. The Brunnens would be almost as zealously guarded as the portal itself. They must not be experienced by anyone outside of the Swan Knight's family. Ludwig imposed strict regulations on their passage between realms. These special abilities of the Brunnens proved their usefulness against the Welf knights. They were a weapon that could destroy enemies — but could also lead to the destruction of the valley, the portal, and possibly the Sweeter Realm.

The sticky film of the war experience clung tightly to them all, and would not wash off quickly or easily. But that night, the night of the homecoming celebration, the warmth of relief and of deep, authentic affection swaddled the party under the same blanket. They slept well that night. They slept happy. They slept in love with each other. They slept relieved of their recent burdens, but they slept with reinforced commitment to their duties and to each other.

The morning broke brightly in the valley. The trees seemed higher, the grass greener, the crack of the opening portal crisper as Ludwig saw his friends back to their homes. The Ancient One stood at the portal, as the last creature in the valley, kissed his old student, bowed to Ludmilla and young Otto, and swore to return early the next morning to begin lessons with his new pupil. The swan was still visually weak and sickly. Ludwig ordered him to stay in his nest for three days.

The Ancient One was deeply desirous of a return to normalcy. Beginning immediately with Otto would have been good for his spirits. But it would have been bad for his health. He insisted that he should return early the next morning to begin Otto's lessons.

Ludwig spoke lovingly but firmly, "Recover old friend. Rest, you have earned it, and I love you and praise you, I honor you for your performance in my absence."

The swan raised his head high and opened his proud beak to deny himself, as he so often did. When his head dropped, unable to be held high by his weakened neck, he muted his protest before a single word escaped. He gave his friend another kiss and turned to the portal.

Before he entered, Ludwig continued speaking, "I will open the portal in three days. Return to us then. Begin Otto's training. I must go to Aachen then to attend the recrowning of my friend Friedrich as King of the Germans."

"Aachen is so far away", relied the swan. "Will you be gone long?"

"No, old friend. A quick ceremony and I am on the road home. I promise."

The worn old teacher disappeared into the portal. Ludwig turned and walked away toward the lodge, taking Ludmilla by the hand. As the two of them walked down the slope to the lodge, the crackling of the open portal remained. Otto, still in fascinated awe of the large circular nothing, stood there, holding the portal open with his presence.

"Come son", yelled his father.

Ludwig heard the scampering footsteps of his son, followed by the snap of the closing portal. The family, alone in the quiet of the empty, peaceful valley, enjoyed three sanguine days under the tender embrace of each other's affection.

After three days, early on a cool, cloudy, late-July morning, Ludwig stood packed and ready for his long journey to Aachen, far to the northwest. He took his son to the portal. There was no surprise this time, no slow, uncertain, anxious creep forward, looking back to the parent and reigning Swan Knight. Otto knew what awaited him. Halfway between the lodge and the portal point, he broke free of his father's held hand, and ran to the portal without looking back. He opened it, still startled, still pulling a surging inhale into his chest. No sooner did the portal assume its form than the teacher walked through it, brighter and stronger than he was at his last passage through the portal.

Otto's eagerness blinded him to everything but the giant swan in front of him. Ludwig walked up behind Otto and kissed him on the back of his head. Otto did not notice. He just stared at his teacher with eager, hungry eyes. Ludwig smiled at his old friend, winked, and walked away. He kissed his wife in the middle of a long embrace, not the embrace of a political marriage, but one of lovers, afraid to pull away from each other, as if the separation would tear them deeply, and fearing the violent amputation of the other from their being. They pulled away from each other to look at the other's teary face. After lengthy effusions of love and devotion, Ludwig promised to return as soon as he was able, and not one moment later. Dressed in the humble clothing of a farmer, the Duke of Bavaria mounted his horse and rode away from his family and his beloved valley.

Ludwig stopped at the ducal residence in Kelheim. He dressed in his royal regalia, changed horses, and resumed his journey to Aachen, accompanied by five Bavarian knights. The Duke arrived in Kelheim unannounced and left quickly — too quickly for an important message to reach his hands. It was from the Master of Ceremonies in Aachen. In it, Ludwig was instructed to prepare a speech for introducing Friedrich at the crowning. Ludwig's support of Friedrich tipped the scales in the king's favor. Friedrich acknowledged this. In his eyes, Ludwig swiped the crown of the Holy Roman Empire off of the head of Otto IV of Welf and handed it to Friedrich personally. The messenger who carried the note, who arrived in Kelheim two days before Ludwig and waited for the Duke, chased the knightly caravan on foot, to the edge of town, before abandoning his commission. Ludwig, with his heart in the valley, rode with his knights to Aachen, with the intention of silently witnessing the ceremony, then racing back to his family as quickly as his secular responsibilities would allow. The ride was peaceful and pleasant. The calm but heavy air of a land recently done with war hung over every town, every community, every individual they encountered along the way. As they approached Aachen, the air became lighter and easier to draw, energetic and celebratory.

At the crowning, Ludwig and his knights took seats near the back of the congregation. Just moments before the trumpets heralded the entrance of Friedrich, the Master of Ceremonies pulled the Duke from his seat and told him that it was time for his introduction of the King. After a few comical exchanges, Ludwig understood what he was expected to do. The trumpets sounded and Ludwig took the eyes and ears of the congregation. Ludwig's homesick musings had irritated his emotions and pushed them into the seat of control over his mind. He gave a tender, personal, but impassioned and rather uproarious speech about the merits of his friend and king. Ludwig's words stirred the audience into a patriotic frenzy. Friedrich entered, almost lifted into flight by the fevered hysteria of support. Ludwig's service in the conflict that won Friedrich the throne was propelled more by his oath as the Swan Knight than by his loyalty to Friedrich. And he felt as much gratitude toward Friedrich, for securing the lands around the valley, as the King and Emperor felt toward Ludwig. Nevertheless, Ludwig was a war hero to the King.

After the crowning ceremony, Friedrich met privately with Ludwig and told him that he would be committing German soldiers to a new crusade in the Holy Land. Pope Innocent III had declared the Fifth Crusade two years earlier, but Friedrich was in the midst of fighting Otto IV. With that war over and the crowns of the Holy Roman Empire and the Kingdom of Germany united on one head, the Pope's support of Friedrich needed repayment. Pope Innocent III wanted to take command of the crusade out of the hands of European kings, so Friedrich was unable to command imperial forces himself. He wanted Ludwig to command his forces in the crusade. He proudly and confidently bestowed on Ludwig the title of Commander of Imperial Forces. Ludwig's loneliness, his love for his family and friends in the valley, and his sense of obligation as the Swan Knight, all gathered together in his throat, nearly choking him in front of Emperor Friedrich. After a few coughs and a disciplined subduing of his emotions, Ludwig mournfully accepted the honor.

He dined that night with Friedrich and the other nobles. The exuberance of the others, their zeal for war and eagerness to embark, sharpened the blade that stabbed at Ludwig's aching heart. The Duke left early the next morning, alone, leaving his escort of knights in the midst of the frenzied celebrations in Aachen. He stopped in Kelheim to settle the affairs of state and he changed into his humble clothes and returned to his family. The news of the crusade dropped a gloomy pall over the valley. When word of Pope Innocent III's death reached Ludwig, he mourned the death of the Holy Father of the Church, as a devoted Christian should, but he celebrated inwardly and looked ahead to the peaceful years ahead of him. The next pope, Honorius III continued the plans for the crusade. Ludwig spent the next five and a half years dividing his time and attention between the valley, his secular duties as Duke, and the suffocating honor of preparing the Imperial Forces for war. His duties never gave him more than two weeks together in the valley, and kept him away for months between returns. Even under this grueling schedule, Ludmilla and young Otto spent much more time with the Swan Knight than they did during the conflict with Otto IV of Welf. They made the most of their time together in the valley, and they often rode together to Kelheim and Regensburg and the other seats of Bavarian politics, when the Duke's responsibilities ordered him there.

CHAPTER 12
The Lost Grail Blood

IN 1217, the crusaders left for Egypt. Ludwig needed more time to gather and prepare the armies of the empire. After months of fighting and thousands of lost crusaders, the Pope's forces took the city of Damietta. From there, they moved toward Cairo. The Pope's crusade could wait no longer for the Imperial Forces. Ludwig had to join the fight. For the next couple of years, all of Ludwig's time and attention went to gathering and organizing the armies. He never saw his valley and rarely saw his family. In the spring of 1221, Ludwig took the Bavarian army and the joining armies of the empire to unite with the crusade in Egypt. He did not wear the armor of a Bavarian knight. He wore his Swan Knight armor — Parsifal's armor, that had been passed through the Swan Knights since Lohengrin pulled it out of the cinders of his father's funeral pyre. Over it, he wore the war tunic and regalia of the Duke of Bavaria. With the armies in tow, he could not pass by the valley to say goodbye to his family, nor could he send a messenger. Ludwig was in Egypt before Ludmilla and Otto knew he had left Bavaria.

Ludwig's forces joined the crusaders at Cairo. Taking Cairo would open the door to Jerusalem, but the Nile River was flooded. There was no passing it. The crusaders were trapped. They retreated toward Damietta, pursued by an enemy that increased in numbers with every town and settlement they passed. The armies of the Pope were captured and imprisoned, Ludwig and his Bavarian knights among them. Rank was not respected in the Egyptian prison. They were stripped of their armor and tunics, and all rank regalia. Dukes, counts, knights, foot soldiers, squires, and servants were all thrown together, all treated the same. But the prisoners continued to recognize rank. When food rations came, portions began at the top. Servants ate what little was left when royalty had their fill. Knights ate well — that is to say, they ate plenty. Servants often went days at a time without a morsel. Ludwig ate first, with the other nobles, but unlike the others, he rationed his portions to little more than he needed to survive. Knowing that they would need their numbers to escape and return home, he passed the remainder down the ranks. That was the excuse he gave the other nobles for nearly starving himself. In truth, Ludwig felt the pain of others with piercingly vivacious compassion. His sacrifices were not the strategic calculations of a military leader. He did not consider anything beyond the suffering of the moment. His immediate desire to relieve suffering, to inspire, and to bring hope kept his stomach growling while other German nobles slept full of food.

One knight of the Order of Teutonic Knights grew rapidly thin and weak. Ludwig noticed and watched him with concern. He was young, no more than seven or eight years older than Ludwig's own son, Otto. The secret behind his deterioration came clear when Ludwig watched him at feeding. The knight took his entire portion and passed it around the servants, instructing them to eat their fill and pass what remained up the ranks. To the protests of the loyal servants, he insisted that he would eat when the food made it up from the servants to the knights. Of course, the food never made it that far. One knight's portion could hardly feed more than a few servants, let alone pass upward from the ranks of the many servants. Ludwig approached the knight with a few pieces of bread he had spared from his own portion.

"Please", Ludwig said, "take the bread."

The knight responded as he was expected, "No my Duke, you must keep your strength."

Ludwig told the knight that he would sooner feed the rats than eat that bread while such a good and noble knight starved. The knight took the bread and immediately struggled to his weakened feet to give it to the servants.

"No!" Ludwig ordered him. "They are already better off than you. You must eat it."

The knight tried to hand the bread back to Ludwig, but the Duke told him, "When we leave here, I will need you, a selfless knight, for the perils of the journey home. I will give my next three meals to the servants so that you can eat your own rations tonight."

With that assurance, the knight ate the bread and swore his allegiance to the good Duke of Bavaria. Ludwig was true to his word. He passed the entirety of his next three meals among the servants. The servants were grateful, but not surprised. The reputation of the Duke of Bavaria had preceded him into the prison. Word of Ludwig's sacrifices from his own portions had already passed through every rank.

The Christian army remained in prison, living in this way. While the other nobles ate their fill, Ludwig and the selfless knight fed the lower ranks. They were in prison for less than a year when the Pope negotiated their release, but that would have been plenty of time for men to starve to death. Dozens of servants, who would surely have perished of starvation, walked out of the prison with their masters because of the sacrifices of Ludwig and the good knight.

The Egyptians returned most of the armor and weapons upon the release of the prisoners, but not directly to the individuals from whom they were stripped. Everything taken from the crusaders, except for some choice pieces that were looted by Egyptian soldiers, was thrown into a pile for the crusaders to sort through on their way out of town. Many of them grabbed anything that fit them and suited their rank. Others sought painstakingly for swords that had been passed through the generations of their families. The peculiar pieces, and those clearly marked for a particular owner, mostly found their way back into the rightful hands. The Teutonic Knights left Egypt in the armor and tunics of the order. Bavarian knights wore Bavarian tunics and carried Bavarian shields. Many special pieces were missing from the pile. Ludwig did not find Pasifal's armor. Nobody in the Pope's army would have taken it. It was stolen by some Egyptian who had no idea of the significance of his souvenir. Ludwig regretted taking it on the crusade, but took comfort in the assumption that the new owner was ignorant to its origin. Perhaps the armor hung on an Egyptian wall. Maybe it was worn again in battle. In any case, the priceless relic disappeared from the members of this history and was never seen again.

As The Ancient One relayed this part of the story to me for the first time, and told me about the loss of Parsifal's armor, I felt enraged.

"The armor should be in the hands of my grandfather" I thought to myself, "and in time, it would belong to me."

I thought about the images of Lohengrin that had so thoroughly captivated me. I knew those images well. I could picture the armor perfectly. I had often visualized myself in Lohengrin's armor. I was furious at the Egyptian who took it. My thoughts were clearly evident to my teacher, who relieved my fury by relaying his own sense of loss from the missing armor. He reminded me of when he watched Parsifal fit the armor on Lohengrin, when they left the valley for their adventures in the north. I had almost forgotten already that he had much greater reasons to mourn the loss than I had. The swan spoke of some of his memories of the armor, ones not included in the history he had relayed to that point. My greedy self-pity was washed away by the realization that the figure in front of me — my teacher — was a much greater treasure. He was the one constant possession of all of the Swan Knights, much more than any armor or axe, or the lodge, or even the Grail itself. Each word from his beak was as pure gold to me. I pleaded for him to continue the history. Of course, he eagerly complied.

In all of the time they spent together in prison, Ludwig never learned the name of the good knight. He enquired among the ranks and learned that he descended from the Lords of Tannhausen. During the ride back to Germany, Ludwig found the knight.

"Tannhäuser!" he called to him, "Come to me in Kelheim and you will be honored for every life you saved in that prison."

Tannhäuser responded, "All honor and praise should go to you, my Duke. While the other royals grew fat in prison, you have nearly wasted away."

"Any good I did, my holy friend, I did by your example. If ever you find yourself able to benefit from what I may offer, please come to me."

Tannhäuser promised he would. Ludwig and the good knight separated among the returning crowd and did not see each other again on that journey. Ludwig suspected that the knight avoided him to keep himself clear of any praise or promotion that the Duke's notice might provide among the other knights and nobles. If Ludwig really needed to find him, he knew where he must look — tending to the lower ranks, sharing his horse and food, and committing himself to seeing that every member of the caravan returned home alive and as well as could be expected. Ludwig thought often about the Tannhäuser and tried to imagine him in different settings, at home and among his people. What sort of man was he in the mundane moments of a peaceful life? Ludwig hoped he would meet Tannhäuser again, but doubted that the proud knight would presume upon his bond with the Duke for personal gain.

On the shore of the Mediterranean Sea, the caravan left their horses and many of the supplies given to them by their captors. They sailed to Italy and passed through Rome. Many travelers remained there for a while, resting and securing supplies for the rest of their journey home. Some saw Rome as just another point between the Egyptian prison and their families. Ludwig was offered the accommodations in Rome that the Duke of Bavaria and Commander of Imperial Forces would expect. He denied them, and instead ate a simple meal with his own Bavarian knights then pressed onward for home. The crusaders traveled together as long as they could, losing groups as their roads diverged. Ludwig and his knights rode ahead of the others, not lingering in Rome as long. They rode directly to Kelheim, with as few stops as possible. Ludwig would not part with his knights without paying them for their service from the Bavarian treasury. He did not entertain going directly to the valley without tending to this paramount point of justice. Although all were nobles, some of his knight came from smaller estates, ones whose income in the absence of the head of the house was tenuous. Others were the fourth, fifth, or sixth son of a Count Someone or a Duke of Somewhere, with no expectation of significant inheritance. Ludwig rewarded them well.

The Duke spent more than two months in Kelheim, restlessly pushing his exhausted mind and body in the completion of state matters that had long gone unattended. Despite his reluctance to reward himself for his service, it was good to be in the Wittelsbach seat, the primary ducal residence. He was warmly welcomed by the people, who showered him with gifts. And he quickly regained his health and figure. The most precious gifts to Ludwig were the wooden tokens. The people of Bavaria were encouraged to make wooden tokens and hold them during the Duke's captivity while they prayed for his safe return. Upon word of the captives' release, officials of Kelheim began collecting the tokens from across Bavaria. They trickled in over the two months that Ludwig was in

Kelheim. They numbered in the thousands. Many were obviously made by children and squeezed by young Bavarian hands, while young Bavarian lips prayed for the safe return of their beloved Duke. Ludwig made the tokens into a set of wooden armor and a wooden shield and sword. He carried them during ceremonial events. The people cheered raucously whenever they saw their Duke wearing and wielding the tokens that they had made during his captivity.

The Swan Knight was forty-nine years old when he returned to the valley. His son was sixteen and progressing admirably in his training and education. Ludmilla, who had married twice in her life, knew more about running a royal household than either of her husbands. During Ludwig's absence, she prepared Otto for his duties as Duke of Bavaria. The Ancient One — and in their ways, many other creatures of the Sweeter Realm — prepared Otto for his eventual role as the Swan Knight. They also spawned in him a passion for music. Otto hosted musical concerts in the theater that his grandfather built. He sang magnificently, harmonizing and blending his voice with those of the sweet creatures who had tutored him musically. The Eulesängers gave him a set of their musical eggs. He played it well, but never mastered it as Nethe had. His finest instrument was his voice.

The story of the deadly siren call of the Brunnens, leading the invading knights to their deaths, was by this time deeply romanticized by those who told the story. Otto admired the beauty and the power of such a gift. He tried to imitate his Brunnen tutors, mimicking their songs and movements as well as his human body would allow. The Ancient One often told Otto that his father, the Swan Knight, would have been much the same if not called away from the valley by the wars that plagued his time. The swan assured him that music would bring him and his father together when circumstances finally united them. Otto could not wait for his father to return to share in his primary love and finally forge the bond that circumstances had so cruelly denied them.

When Ludwig rode over the last hill and into his valley, it was safe, warm, happy, and abundantly overjoyed to embrace his return. Absence and long hours of contemplation had endeared each to the others. The Ancient One was right. Ludwig cried when Otto first sang for him. They sang duets, though Ludwig's voice, ravaged by the trials he had faced, could not compare with Otto's. Ludmilla was quick to join them and music became the first point of bonding between them all. They gathered every morning in the chapel and sang their prayers in harmony to the Lord. The bond of love between them all was quickly tighter than when Ludwig departed. From that point on, Ludwig consulted Ludmilla and Otto on every decision that he made, for the valley and for Bavaria.

Ludwig traveled often between the valley and Kelheim, but he usually took his wife or son with him. In their first year reunited after the crusade, Otto and Ludmilla accompanied Ludwig to Kelheim, where Otto met a woman five years his senior. Her name was Agnes and she was the daughter of Count Heinrich of the Palatinate on the Rhine. The Bavarian officials in Kelheim invited Agnes specifically to meet the handsome young Otto. They knew that if the two were to marry, Bavaria could lay a political claim on the Palatinate and its electorship. Ludwig was entirely ignorant to the plot.

Agnes was a magnificent beauty, well accomplished with skills and talents. She was particularly musical, taking quickly and naturally to any instrument of music placed before her — and she sang. She sang like the creatures whose lullabies had christened Otto's sweetest dreams since he entered the valley at nine years old. The flames of admiration needed little kindling from the political plotters who arranged the meeting. During their second stroll together, Agnes sang for Otto. When he joined her and exposed a passion and talent for music to equal hers, Agnes too fell in love. They married within two weeks. The wedding was held in Kelheim. The couple sang their vows. Rumor has it, the ceremony was so romantic, touching every heart in attendance, that weddings in Kelheim doubled in the following year.

After the ceremony, Agnes and Otto remained in Kelheim with Ludmilla. Ludwig returned alone to the valley. As the Swan Knight approached the lodge, he saw a figure on the slope, near the portal point. When he drew closer, he saw that the portal was open. Directly in front of it stood a man, in full armor, with his sword drawn and pointed at the portal. Ludwig panicked.

He drew his own sword and screamed at the man, repeating, "Who are you? Who are you?"

As he rode closer, he looked around the portal for evidence of his friends. He saw no blood, no bodies. He brought his attention back to the man and noticed that he wore over his armor the tunic of a Teutonic Knight. Ludwig's furious terror calmed slightly. He dismounted his horse within a few steps of the man and held his sword high. He looked closely at the man's face and recognized him immediately. It was Tannhäuser. Ludwig put away his sword and stared at the knight in bewilderment.

Tannhäuser had opened the portal. He had Grail Blood. The Swan Knights always knew the day would come, when lost Grail Blood would wander into the valley. He thanked God that it was someone he already knew, admired, and trusted. Tannhäuser still stood facing the portal with his sword drawn and pointed at the crackling circle.

"How it must have startled the poor man", Ludwig thought. He called to the good knight.

Tannhäuser turned to Ludwig then back in defensive posture to the portal, "Get behind me my Duke!"

Ludwig grinned at the frightened knight. The Duke obeyed and stood directly behind Tannhäuser, who shook his sword at the portal, as if he expected it to grow teeth and bite at his master, hollering at it, "Come at me! Do your best!"

With this, Ludwig's grin grew to a hearty laugh. He grabbed Tannhäuser by his tunic and slowly pulled him backward. Tannhäuser stepped in accordance with his Duke's command until the portal snapped shut. Tannhäuser continued to stare forward at the portal point, holding his sword forward and shaking it occasionally, until Ludwig reached over the knight's shoulder and pushed on his forearm until the point of his sword touched the ground. When it did, Tannhäuser turned to Ludwig with an inquisitive expression. Ludwig's grin and occasional chuckle told Tannhäuser that all was well.

"Come drink with me", Ludwig told him. "Your life is about to change."

Tannhäuser followed the Swan Knight into the lodge, entranced and dragging the tip of his sword on the ground behind him.

Tannhäuser still wore the same armor and tunic he wore when they left Egypt. It still held Egyptian blood and Egyptian dirt, exactly as it did when Tannhäuser pulled it off of the pile of armor and weapons returned to the crusaders. Ludwig often said that Tannhäuser wore the blood on his armor and tunic as a way of keeping the slain alive. He loved and honored every child of God, even his enemies, and he wept each time he pierced human flesh with his sword. He remembered them all, and wanted to carry a part of them with him as he wandered the world. This is a man nature never intended to be a soldier.

The knight had been wandering ever since he left the company of the returning crusaders, with no direction, praying all day and night to God for a clear path for his young life. He wandered quite accidentally into the valley. Weathered and hungry, he knocked on the door of the lodge and called for help. When nobody answered, though he could see food and every domestic comfort through the windows, he would not enter without permission. Though hungry and exhausted, he would not steal. He walked past the lodge and up the slope, until he reached the portal point and triggered the opening that had him so terrified when Ludwig encountered him.

While Ludwig had long recovered his health and figure, Tannhäuser was as pale and drawn as he was when Ludwig gave him bread in the prison. Ludwig fed his friend, then told him that they were both descendants of a long line of knights dedicated to the protection of the portal. He told him nothing of Parsifal or the Grail. Tannhäuser had opened the portal. He knew it was there. Sending him away in complete ignorance was not possible. Ludwig decided to send Tannhäuser for supplies early the next day, and summon The Ancient One for consultation on the matter. The swan also praised God that the inevitable wanderer was the very same knight that Ludwig had honored and celebrated so enthusiastically in his reports of his crusade and imprisonment. They agreed to keep things as they were. Tannhäuser would be introduced to the creatures of the Sweeter Realm and told of the Swan Knights, whose duty it was to protect the opening into their world. There was no reason to tell him more.

When Tannhäuser returned, Ludwig swore him into an oath of secrecy and dubbed him an honorary steward of the portal. God finally revealed to Tannhäuser the path for which the weary knight had prayed so fervently. Ludwig had a trusted friend in his life. Otto had a seasoned warrior to assume the combat training of the next Swan Knight. As the truth of Tannhäuser's new circumstances settled upon him, as he realized that his days of wandering were over and both home and purpose were right there, in that little happy valley, he began to remove the armor he had donned every morning since Egypt. Ludwig hardly recognized him under the smile that he had never seen on Tannhäuser's face.

Tannhäuser was twenty-four years old. He had seen so much war, starvation, and death. He had seen the heights of human cruelty and he wore heavily around his neck every expression of pain and misery that his weary, sympathetic eyes had witnessed. Ludwig set him up in a room at the lodge. Tannhäuser had no possessions to adorn the room and make it his own, but he began whittling wood in the images of people he did not want to forget, and soon had a melancholy collection of wooden faces meticulously placed about. He had a great capacity for imagining beauty. So, by the time Ludwig introduced him to the creatures from the Sweeter Realm, his heart was prepared.

Of all the facets of his new life, the company of the sweet creatures was his most treasured. For the first time in his life, Tannhäuser was surrounded by minds as open as his, and hearts as innocent and compassionate. He quickly grew to love the creatures — truly love them. He relished the stories they told and the games they played. But he never bonded with the Unicorns. One touched its long horn to Tannhäuser's chest. Its eyes grew sad. It shed a single tear, then bowed to him and ran away into the woods. There was something in that momentary connection that unsettled the Unicorns. They paid him the reverence his goodness deserved, but never carried him on rides around the valley, and maintained a cordial distance when in company with him.

Tannhäuser reveled in the company of the other creatures. He bathed in the sounds of their voices when they sang. The Ancient One tried to pass pieces of pertinent knowledge to Tannhäuser, but he was far too consumed with experiencing the lovely creatures, who stood in such stark contrast to the cruel hearts his life had thrown in his path. There was no room in him for academic matters. Life in the valley brought him pleasures he had never known. He had no interest in hearing about the responsibilities that came with those pleasures.

The Ancient One complained to Ludwig, but the Swan Knight excused his steward, saying, "He has had a hard life. Give him time. He will come around."

The swan warned, "I do not doubt his goodness, but he is too care-free now. His hardships have driven him to seek only beauty and pleasure. The wonders of the

Sweeter Realm come at a cost. He does not understand what is at stake."

Still, Ludwig excused his young friend and refused to burden him with the perils of understanding, saying, "Would it be better to make him understand, to reveal what is at stake? Should we tell him everything? His heart is finally light. I will not burden it now, not with matters he need not know — he ought not know."

The Ancient One could not help but concur. But although his mind was with the Swan Knight, his heart still haunted him with low-whispered prognostications of terrible things to come, things brought about by Tannhäuser. Withouot revealing much, he tried to impress upon the good knight the serious burden that accompanies the wonderful life of a portal custodian. Tannhäuser's ears heard the old teacher, but his heart was far beyond the reach of the worrisome swan.

Otto and Agnes returned to the valley as radiantly in love as ever. Ludmilla accompanied them. Their introduction to Tannhäuser was as warm as it was surprising to Otto. Otto heard his father speak of the kind knight who saved the lives of the servants. He also saw in the knight's eyes a thirst for beauty that was intimately familiar to him. But the warm introduction was not without turbulence. Tannhäuser did not wait for Ludwig to explain the truth behind his presence in the valley.

He patted Otto firmly on the shoulder a couple of times and said, "Watch this."

He ran with almost unhuman speed to the portal point. Intrigued and bewildered, Otto chased him, followed by a curious but hesitant Agnes. When Tannhäuser arrived at the portal point, and the sacred family secret revealed itself in bold, crackling splendor, Otto froze and stared at Tannhäuser with eyes of fury and an expression of extreme fretfulness. Ludwig, who at nearly fifty years old followed well behind the others, leapt rather youthfully between them.

He stood with his back to Tannhäuser, looking at his son, and he said, "Tannhäuser is a lost cousin. He knows about the portal... only about the portal. He will serve the Swan Knight as his steward."

Otto's rigid features relaxed. He understood what his father could not say, that Tannhäuser did not know about the Holy Grail. A few creatures came through the portal. They had been waiting there for Tannhäuser, whose earnest compliments and company they began to cherish. The creatures surrounded Tannhäuser and cuddled him. Even The Ancient One, critical as always, placed an outstretched wing on Tannhäuser's shoulder.

Otto looked passed his father, directly into Tannhäuser's eyes, and said, "Welcome to our wonderful valley, and thank you for being with my father when I could not."

Agnes' world turned upside down that day. She knew that her new husband had a fanciful imagination. During their voyage home from Kelheim, Otto tried to prepare her for the wonders she would experience in the valley. He described The Ancient One and the many fantastic creatures that awaited her in her new home. He told her many tales from the family history, including the legends she had heard as a child. Agnes laughed as she listened, never doubting Otto's honesty, but believing that her creative husband spun wild tales for her entertainment. When Tannhäuser opened the portal and those wild imaginings walked through, Agnes fainted.

She came from a practical, political family. Her music was her only escape from the rigid decorum that came with the strong political ambitions of her family. Otto's stories on the journey home were almost too fanciful for her to visualize. When they stood in front of her and shattered her notions of the world, the shock was severe.

For days, Agnes spoke little, ate little, and slept little. She jumped every time a creature of the Sweeter Realm entered her scope of vision, shuttered every time she heard the giant swan talk. Ludwig knew that music was the glue that bound the young couple to each other. If anything would adhere the creatures to her heart, it would be the same glue. He quickly organized a short concert in the theater. Tannhäuser was made Master of the Ceremony. Ludwig sent The Ancient One through the portal to bring back the featured artists, a choir of Brunnens.

The performance included comical dancing by the Scheriers, which turned into an impromptu wrestling match as soon as one Scherier accidentally bumped another. The Zweigwesens presented an ability nobody knew they had. To the sound of Tannhäuser's singing, they attached themselves to each other, latching and connecting to form complicated feats of architecture and geometric shapes in perfect balance. When they connected, their bodies seemed as one, as a single structure. The course, orange-brown hair of one blended seamlessly into the next. Ludmilla stood right in front of them and swore that she could not tell where one Zweigwesen ended and the next began, which pair of eyes associated with which patch of orange-brown hair. Their formations changed to imitate the great monuments of history, as seen in the Swan Knight's books. They made a wide structure that touched the floor at one minute point, probably the single toe of a Zweigwesen. Nobody knew for sure. When they blended together, the only thing that betrayed them as living creatures, not works of wooden architecture, was the blinking of their eyes and an occasional wide smile.

The Ancient One hushed the company and rather dramatically introduced the Brunnens. Tannhäuser had not yet seen the Brunnens. His eye was ever on the search for beauty, and he had never seen anything as beautiful as their almost clear, rippling, feminine figures sailing like leaves on a stream across the floor and onto the stage. His fascination turned to utter ecstasy when they began to sing. He convulsed in an hysterical fit of passion, until his eyes gripped one particular Brunnen. His fits washed away entirely as he fixated on the one. The Brunnen that stole his attention seemed equally besotted by him. Still singing, still in perfect harmony with the others, the one Brunnen rippled forward to Tannhäuser. She touched him on his handsome face, not like they touched the Welf knights, not in a one-sided, manipulative seduction, but in a tender touch of affection, where passion flows in two directions.

The Brunnen stood nearly touching Tannhäuser's mouth with her singing lips. She sang directly into the knight's soul. Tannhäuser's arms swayed in flawless unison with the song, as if his movements created the music that filled the small theater and flowed through the cracks into the quiet valley. Everyone, even the Brunnens who continued to sing, stared at the two of them, in amazement of the undeniable mystical connection between them. The song stopped. The company remained silent, staring at Tannhäuser and the Brunnen. The Brunnen, no longer singing, continued to breathe into Tannhäuser's mouth, which hung open as his glassy eyes peered into his seducer and his arms hung flatly at his side, no longer possessed by the song. The other Brunnens reached for the one. Her skin began to ripple backward toward the others. She followed the pull of her skin and walked back to the chorus, not smoothly like a leaf on a stream, but harshly and reluctantly, still locked in a mesmeric stare into Tannhäuser's eyes.

Awkwardness stole the air of the theater. Otto broke it by jumping up, pulling his wife onto the stage, and introducing her as the sweetest new voice in the valley. He began to sing one of the songs they had sung together at their wedding. Continuing to sing alone, Otto gestured to his wife to join him. She stood still and silent, weighed down by the film of novel exoticism that had settled over them all from the spectacle between Tannhäuser and the Brunnen. Otto tugged at her hand and looked at her with eyes that enshrined her and gilded her with the most reverent adoration. The look shattered the confused wonder that had encased her mind since she saw Tannhäuser open the portal on her first day in the valley and brought her thoughts back to the bond between her and her husband. She joined her voice to his. By the end of the first verse, the wonders of the valley no longer confounded her. The only thing remarkable to her was the adoration of the husband she loved.

Their performance was not as magical, not as mystically arcane as the song of the Brunnens, but it was the most innocently romantic display the creatures had seen since Lohengrin held Nethe's hand in front of the Christmas tree. The awkward connection between Tannhäuser and the Brunnen was forgotten for the moment. The concert served its intended purpose. Agnes warmed. She smiled and giggled. She spoke to the creatures. She embraced them and received their kisses and their heart-felt welcome to the family and to the valley. The goodness in her, which had shone clearly and affixed itself so quickly to the affections of Otto and his parents, poured from her and bound tightly the kinship and loyalty of the creatures. Tannhäuser remained dazed by his experience with the Brunnen, whose gazes toward him were rarely broken. But he buried it just beneath the surface to celebrate with some degree of authenticity the happiness of the newlyweds.

When the concert ended, the creatures returned through the portal, which Ludwig held open. Tannhäuser stood at a distance and watched them all disappear. When Tannhäuser's Brunnen stepped through, he winced as if in sharp physical pain. When Ludwig stepped away, and the portal snapped shut, Tannhäuser dropped to his knees with an exhale that seemed to evict all air from his chest. He fell as if he had been held on his feet by his connection to the creature, until the snap of the closing portal severed it violently, dropping him to the ground.

Ludwig walked up to his kneeling friend, ran his fingers through the knight's hair, and said, "Come inside, Tannhäuser. Celebrate with us."

The steward obeyed his Duke and joined the family in the lodge. The pure love that showered from Otto and Agnes onto anyone who drew near them seemed to further frustrate the lonely man. Every infatuated glance exchanged between the newlyweds pulled air from Tannhäuser's chest, suffocating him. With a forced and obedient smile, he embraced the Swan Knight's family and excused himself to bed.

In the morning, and well into the day, through the closed door of Tannhäuser's room, the Swan Knight and his family could hear him alternate between pacing across his floor and weeping in his bed. Tannhäuser's devotion to Ludwig was stout. So Ludwig had to be the one to interrupt the steward's lamentations and invite him back into the world. Ever the obedient knight, Tannhäuser was certain to respond to an order given by the Duke. Ludwig opened Tannhäuser's door and respectfully ordered him to begin combat lessons with Otto. Tannhäuser pulled his wits about him, apologized to his master, gathered what he would need for the lesson and joined the family in the main hall. He walked right passed Ludmilla, as if he did not see her.

"Good afternoon, Tannhäuser." She said to him.

Mortified by his failure to acknowledge her, Tannhäuser turned sheepishly to her and said, "Forgive me Duchess. Good afternoon to you."

He turned to walk out of the lodge. She stopped him, shouting, "Not so fast young steward. You have not eaten."

Only then did Tannhäuser notice the food she held in her hand, at the end of her outstretched arm. He bowed to her, a low, reverent bow. She reached with her other hand and lifted him erect by the chin.

"We are not in Kelheim", she said, "Here we are family."

With that, she raised herself high on her toes and puckered her lips to him. He leaned down to her and received her maternal, nurturing kiss on the crown of his head. She winked at him as he took the food from her. She ordered him to eat every morsel before stepping one foot outside of the lodge. He blushed brightly and obeyed the valley matriarch.

For the next several days, Tannhäuser worked hard with Otto, teaching the lessons he had learned in battle. It was clear to Otto that his tutor was distracted. Every evening, after lessons, Tannhäuser opened the portal and sat beside it, staring into it. Occasionally creatures would come and go. They tried to entice Tannhäuser into the games they used to play and the conversations they used to have. They could not wiggle him free from the tyrannical grasp of his infatuation. Ludwig watched him attentively. Tannhäuser leaned forward toward the portal, stood to his feet, then sat back down.

He repeated this several times before Ludwig came to him and said, "We cannot go through. It is forbidden."

Tannhäuser answered, speaking more to himself than to his Duke, "I want to see her... her world. I want to see her world."

Ludwig repeated, slowing his words and pronouncing with exaggerated clarity, "We cannot go through. It is forbidden."

Tannhäuser leaned toward the portal again. Ludwig seized him by the shoulder with one hand, and with the other, he turned Tannhäuser's head to face him.

"These are not *my* rules. I am their faithful subject, as my father was, as you must be if you are to remain in the valley."

Again mortified by his uncharacteristic insubordination, he begged the Swan Knight for forgiveness.

Ludwig shook his head, patted Tannhäuser on the head as if he was a child, and said, "I will help you through this. We will get through it together."

Ludwig pulled him to his feet and beckoned him into the lodge. Being with the creatures made Tannhäuser lonely. Being with the Swan Knight's family made him even lonelier.

No Brunnens had come through the portal since the night of the concert. One day, as Tannhäuser stood at the open portal, they arrived with The Ancient One, but came without Tannhäuser's love. Ludwig and Ludmilla were in Kelheim on state business. Otto patrolled the outer mountains with the Unicorns. Agnes committed deeply to the domestic affairs of the lodge. Tannhäuser stood at the portal, watching the Brunnens appear one at a time. Anticipation shot through him like lightening.

When the last Brunnen walked through, and Tannhäuser did not see his love, he demanded, "Bring her to me... or take me to her."

He took one quick step toward the portal. The swan stepped in front of him and insisted that he step back and close the portal. Tannhäuser fell to the ground and broke into shaking, debilitating sobs. The sympathetic old bird wrapped the broken man in his wings and rested his cheek atop Tannhäuser's head.

"She cannot come to you. Her people forbid it. She has been exiled from the valley by her own kind."

Tannhäuser stopped shaking, pulled himself from The Ancient One's embrace, and looked calmly into his eyes, as if completely free from what had ailed him.

"I am sorry," he told the swan.

"No, no, no, my good man", the swan reassured him.

Tannhäuser pulled himself to his feet and said, "Please forgive me."

He looked at the swan, then at the Brunnens. He took a deep breath and ran through the portal. It immediately snapped shut behind him, leaving The Ancient One and the Brunnens as helpless as they were vexed.

CHAPTER 13

A New Breed

THE ANCIENT ONE stood for a moment, staring at the empty portal point, disconcerted and scared. He looked at the Brunnens, who all wore faces of shame. He cursed furiously in his own language, and flew in search of Otto and the Unicorns. He found them on a distant ridge and reported the events. Otto grabbed the horn of the Unicorn he rode. Through his grasp of the horn, it read his intentions and relayed them instantly to the others. The Unicorn that carried Otto sped toward the portal point, while the others split in different directions. Otto and The Ancient One arrived at the portal point at the same time. The Brunnens still stood exactly as the swan had left them.

Otto dismounted the Unicorn, opened the portal, and sternly commanded the creatures, "Go! Find him and bring him back."

The Brunnens rushed through the portal with The Ancient One closely behind. The Unicorn that carried Otto touched him in the chest with its horn. With a thought, the creature received its order to return to the Sweeter Realm and tell the Queen what had happened.

"He is a good man," Otto thought to the Unicorn. "He is family. Be gentle with him."

The beast pulled its horn away and galloped through the portal. The commotion called Agnes from the lodge.

She ran to her husband and said softly, "He has gone through, hasn't he?"

Otto confirmed her insight with a simple drop of his head.

"Do you want me to stay with you?" she asked.

"Yes, please, my love."

Agnes held his hand and tenderly kissed each knuckle. Otto and Agnes stood by the portal for several hours, their hearts rising more tightly into their throats with the slow lengthening of their united shadows on the valley floor. Otto would not walk away. He would not close the portal until he heard from one of the creatures. She would not leave his side or let go of his hand. Just as the sun closed its eye on the valley, The Ancient One appeared through the portal.

"He is gone — hidden deeply in the Brunnen homeland. Not even the Queen can find him there. He is lost... until he wishes to be found."

Otto took a deep breath, held it, and released it with the following words. "Let us pray this comes to nothing."

A month went by in the Swan Knight's absence. Otto and Agnes tried to resume their lives in the valley. Every afternoon, The Ancient One met them at the portal to give the most recent report. But there was nothing to report, except that Tannhäuser met his lover and the two of them disappeared deep in the thick, untamed wilderness of the

Brunnen homeland. Redundant as the reports were, Otto liked receiving them. They relieved him on two points. Tannhäuser could cause little damage isolated in the depths of a hidden wilderness with his lover. Also, the thought of Tannhäuser and the Brunnen living happily alone together brought a secret smile to Otto's romantic heart. With each report, Otto saw the fine hairs rise on the back of Agnes' neck. He knew that her subtle response was to the same romantic thought. While talking sternly, they both secretly wished Tannhäuser and the Brunnen a happy and peaceful life together, despite their serious apprehensions.

Ludwig and Ludmilla returned late in the evening. As they approached the final ridge before the valley, they were startled by the silhouetted figure of Otto, mounted high on his favorite Unicorn, perched on the very edge of the ridge, framed by the large rising moon directly behind them. Their warm and musical boy cut a fierce figure that momentarily stole Ludmilla's breath. In the absence of Otto's genuine laugh, in the stone-rigid statue before them, an aroma of dire seriousness filled the still air between them, broken only by the huff of the Unicorn's exhale. In a deep and hesitant voice, Otto told them that Tannhäuser had gone through the portal, in words that fought their expulsion from his mouth, clinging desperately to his teeth and the tip of his tongue. They were equally reluctant to enter Ludwig's ears. The Swan Knight asked twice for his son to repeat the news clearly, hoping some missing word would reveal itself and alter the terrible message. With each repetition, Ludwig's skin seemed to squeeze his insides more tightly.

Although nothing could be done, the family rode furiously to the lodge and rushed to gather around the table. Agnes served them all a warm drink made with a root. It was known for its medicinal effect in the settling of nerves. Whether the root, the loving concern with which it was served, or simply the comforts of cherished and familiar surroundings, the racing hearts and lacerated minds in the room calmed.

Ludmilla kissed Agnes and Otto and proclaimed, "We will discuss this matter in the morning. We come home to find you here and well. Our home is in order and the sparkle of love still brightens my son's eyes. Tonight is about us. Tomorrow is about Tannhäuser."

The calm sense of Ludmilla's words removed the thorny vine that had coiled itself around Otto's heart since Tannhäuser's departure.

Over the next several days, the Swan Knight family discussed the matter of Tannhäuser. Nothing could be done to retrieve him. But what would they do if he returned? This question brought forth many suggestions. Killing Tannhäuser was out of the question. He swore an oath of silence and they all believed he would honor it. Otto suggested that he never be allowed to return. He posed a much greater risk to the portal on this side than in the Sweeter Realm. Otto proposed that they turn him over to the custody of the Queen. She may protect her realm from him in any way that she deems appropriate. Ludwig had seen more deeply into Tannhäuser's goodness than the others. He believed that their love and counsel would bring all into right. Many other ideas came forth, some extreme, even absurd, which were quickly discarded. Others deserved further consideration and took their place in the backs of their minds, to be sorted if the day should ever come.

Months went by, and the fears and anger associated with Tannhäuser's violation subsided. Life in the valley felt normal again, except for the subtle voice, in the back of the mind, that whispered secretly to them all that the story of Tannhäuser and his Brunnen lover was not fully written, that each of them still had some part to play before the final page is turned. For more than a year, a thin, almost invisible film of awkwardness hung between the Swan Knight family and the creatures of the Sweeter Realm. None was bold enough to address it, so it lingered and slowly faded until the waters of normalcy rinsed away its final remnants.

Months had passed after Tannhäuser left, before Ludwig realized that he had not received any Brunnen visitors. He asked The Ancient One to invite them on behalf of the Swan Knight and his family. The Ancient One told him that the Brunnens have strict laws of decorum, and a violation by one is shame on all. They did not believe themselves worthy of the Swan Knight's company. They exiled themselves, not just from the valley, but from contact with any other creature. They closed the borders of their homeland, while they served some unknown penance, certain to be as severe as it was secret.

Every week, Ludwig sent The Ancient One with a message, inviting the Brunnens to resume to old good-humor with the Swan Knight and his family. The swan left the messages at the border of Brunnen land. Each week he added another letter to the neglected pile.

He reported to Ludwig, "This is extreme, even for them. There must be more to this than we know."

Ludwig replied, "If there is more, it is not for us to seek and discover. The truth must come through the portal to us, if we are to share in it."

The Ancient One agreed and urged Ludwig to obey his own words and leave Tannhäuser to the will and judgment of God. The matter was settled. Although the beautiful Brunnens and their dulcet voices remained in the thoughts and prayers of all, they were never openly discussed except on the anniversary of the Welf army invasion, when the power and heroics of the Brunnens were lauded openly and cups were raised in tearful reverence to the creatures whose seductive powers had ensnared the affections of all of them, in different ways and to varying degrees. After each such celebration, all thoughts of the Brunnens were tucked neatly in the back of their minds, easily accessible for the next time they were needed. Distractions from Tannhäuser and the Brunnens abounded, political and personal, crowned by the long anticipated announcement that Otto and Agnes expected a child.

Elisabeth of Wittelsbach was born in the spring of 1227. Otto took Agnes to Trausnitz Castle, in Landshut. Ludwig commissioned the construction of the castle in 1204, as a wedding gift for Ludmilla. The political conflicts that plagued the next several years forbade the castle to fulfil its romantic intension. Elisabeth was born in the castle to doting parents. Agnes glowed with love for her child and husband as she held Elisabeth for the first time, finally filling the castle with the love that motivated its commission.

The birth of the Duke's grandchild had all of the political ramifications that such a birth would have. Political fires ignited monthly, and Ludwig worked hard to extinguish them, spending a greater portion of his time in Kelheim. A few years of peace and relative political placidity in the empire had dulled Ludwig's senses to the treacherous political maneuverings of the regional powers around him. The snakes in the system usually slithered right up to Ludwig before he heard them hissing. Agnes kept a keen eye on the political interests of her husband. She saw dangers closing in. She recommended to her father-in-law that he grant Otto a secular knighthood and give him the Palatine on the Rhine. Ludwig saw the wisdom of the scheme. He excersized his claim on the Palatinate, which he granted to Otto and Agnes. Agnes ruled over her childhood home.

This was an undeniably wise move for the dukedom. Agnes' shrewd political upbringing gave her a natural instinct in such matters. Ludwig trusted her explicitly. Otto, Agnes, and the baby Elisabeth moved to Heidelberg, on the Neckar River, east of the Rhine, far from the valley and far from Ludwig and Ludmilla. But as Count Palatine, Otto could help secure Bavaria from the west. Travel to the valley was long and strenuous. Visits were sparse, but so were the visits of the Duke and Duchess. When they came to the valley, they stayed for several weeks. Ludwig and Otto coordinated their trips to keep one of them there as much as possible, overlapping their visits by only a few days before separating them again.

Ludwig and Ludmilla were in the valley when Otto and Agnes' second child was born. Ludmilla wrote a letter to Agnes, which she received the day before the boy was born. In it, she described Ludwig's sadness in missing the birth of the child. On 13 April, 1229, the baby was born in Heidelberg. They named him Ludwig, after his grandfather. Otto sketched a portrait of the baby, slightly altering his features to look more like his grandfather, the Duke and Swan Knight. Under the portrait he wrote, "Ludwig – Your Grandson". The Duke and Duchess had just arrived back in Kelheim, after a melancholy departure from the valley, when the letter reached their hands. Otto's sketch was the ideal tonic to revive their lowly hearts. They took turns reading the letter to each other, passing it back and forth between them and laughing at Otto's sketch until they fell asleep in each other's arms.

In June, when the baby was old enough to bear the rigors of travel, Otto and Agnes left Heidelberg for the valley. As they breached the inner hills, they were greeted by the Unicorns, devoutly holding their sentry posts. The beasts seemed agitated. They huffed and stomped and shook their horns toward Otto. Otto dismounted his horse and went to one of them. The Unicorn lowered its horn gently to Otto, inviting their mystical communication through her horn. Otto took her by the horn with both hands and pulled her to him until he touched the center of his forehead against the point of her horn. Otto could tell that the Unicorn was holding something from him. He strained his mind to read more deeply into her thoughts. He ordered the beast to reveal her secrets.

The only thought passed from the Unicorn to Otto was, "Welcome home. Much has happened." The Unicorn mouthed the words as Otto received the thoughts.

Otto squeezed the horn more tightly and drove his forehead into the point until it breached his skin. The Unicorn pulled herself from Otto's grasp, shook her head, galloped a few steps toward the valley, looked back to Otto and gestured for him to follow. Otto remounted his horse and they all rode to the lodge. All seemed normal. The lodge was clean and in good order. Ludmilla's customary note awaited them just inside the door, detailing the events of their last visit, listing how many of which creatures were left in the valley and which ones were sent home before they left.

Once Agnes tended to her husband's bleeding forehead and she fed the baby, they all went to the portal point together. Agnes walked ahead of Otto, holding young Ludwig out in front of her with outstretched arms, while Elizabeth toddled behind. She giggled and looked back to her husband with each step, anxious for the baby to open the portal. When they stood almost on top of the portal point, they heard a muffled crackling sound, but the portal remained closed. Otto assured her that it was normal, that many Swan Knights could not open the portal during infancy. He took the few quick strides forward to open the portal himself.

They expected to wait for a few minutes before The Ancient One stepped through. Instead, Tannhäuser appeared, dirty and naked. He wore an expression of utter dismay. He ran into the lodge and put on some of his old clothes that were still hanging in his room. Otto told Agnes to wait where she stood. He walked after Tannhäuser. As he passed the point where he would no longer hold open the portal, baby Ludwig held it open and the crackling sound of the open portal changed its pitch to the signature sound it would keep every time young Ludwig would open it, for the rest of his life. Agnes was so delighted to hold the Grail Blood in her hands, blood that came from her own body, that she almost forgot about the strange and unexpected appearance of Tannhäuser. Just as Otto opened the door to the lodge, Tannhäuser burst through, wearing his old Teutonic Knight's tunic. He jumped on Otto's horse and flew from the valley as quickly as the tired horse could carry him. Four Unicorns converged on Tannhäuser as he reached the edge of the valley. Otto yelled for them to let him go. They obeyed. They galloped to the portal, bowed to Agnes, Elisabeth, and baby Ludwig, and returned to their home.

Early the next morning, Otto stepped out of the lodge, half-expecting to see Tannhäuser pining at the open portal as he used to do. He was not in the valley. A small but hungry regret started gnawing on the back of his mind. The Unicorns could have stopped Tannhäuser. They should have stopped him.

"He could be well into Austria by now," Otto thought to himself, "saying who-knows-what to who-knows-whom."

Otto pulled a thought to the forefront of his musings, to counter-balance the doubt. He thought about his father's love for the kind knight, and the knight's love for his father.

He thought, "There is no telling what has happened to him during these years, or what drove him from the Sweeter Realm, alone and in such a rush. But nothing could have tainted his love for the Duke. Nothing could drive him to forsake his oath."

Otto meandered aimlessly as he thought, cutting increasing circles around the lodge until he drifted to the portal point and startled himself with an accidental opening. As a child, he often sat and stared into the portal. The look of nothingness in its center and the electric crackle soothed him and allowed his mind to wander to pleasant places. He renewed his old ritual that morning.

He sat within arm's reach of the opening and stared directly into the middle. Just as his mind began to wander and his heart began to settle from the surprise opening of the portal, he was startled again — by something unexpected. A Brunnen appeared from the portal, followed by another, and several more. Their expressions of apprehension melted into delight as they saw the excitement and welcoming love in Otto's face. Otto had just opened his mouth to tell them how much he missed them, when he was muted by an even bigger surprise. The Ancient One appeared with a girl beside him, a human girl. The girl looked to be four or five years old. Her identity was easy to determine. When she moved, her skin rippled like a Brunnen. As long as she was in motion, even a simple sway, she bore the complexion and features of a normal human girl, except of course for the rippling skin. When she held still, she faded into the almost clear, water-like appearance of a Brunnen. When she held perfectly still, she nearly disappeared entirely.

Otto asked, "This is Tannhäuser's child?"

The Ancient One gestured his large wing to the chorus of Brunnens and replied, "This is their story. You should hear it from them."

The Brunnens told the story, alternating two and three at a time, speaking in harmony with themselves and each other, slipping occasionally into their own language only to backtrack and translate when Otto frustratingly reminded them that he does not understand Brunnen. They said that Tannhäuser wandered the woods of the Sweeter Realm with no direction when he ran through the portal, searching for his Brunnen. He screamed for her, awakening creatures of all kinds. The Brunnens came to him and brought him to his lover. Deep in the quiet of the Brunnen homeland, they encircled the lovers and remonstrated them for bringing shame to them all. They banished the Brunnen to the wilderness, never to return, and directed Tannhäuser back to the portal point to await the opening of the Swan Knight. Tannhäuser and his lover took hands, broke through the circle, and ran away into the wilderness together. The Brunnens immediately closed the borders to their land. They would not allow the lovers to lower them further in the esteem of the Queen and the Swan Knight. Nobody came in or out of the Brunnen homeland. The Brunnens did not hear from the lovers for years. They remained hidden away in the wilderness, until just a few days ago.

Tannhäuser broke through the border and wandered through the Sweeter Realm, wailing in torment, crying, "She is gone. I have lost her."

The girl followed behind her father, crying and calling for him. He did not appear to hear her. The Ancient One found them just as the Brunnen leadership caught up to them. Tannhäuser was broken, a look of extreme agony immovably affixed to his face. He did not respond to anything the others said to him.

He just pulled at his hair and continued to scream, "She is gone. I have lost her."

The Ancient One cradled the frightened girl and asked her what had happened. Her mother had died. When Tannhäuser found her body, he lost his mind. He squeezed her body to his chest until it shattered and fell away between his arms. What remained of her disappeared into the tall grass of the wilderness.

Tannhäuser screamed, "She is gone. I have lost her." He stood and walked, repeating the same words. The girl tried to talk to her father but he did not respond. She cried for him, but he did not hear. The poor child watched as her mother disappeared into the grass. She watched the breakdown and flight of her father. She followed him through the wilderness and across the Brunnen border, into Zweigwesen land, sobbing and calling to him in desperate pleas. To the young girl, this seemed to go on for days, until the swan and the Brunnens caught up with them. When they finally calmed the girl — who until then had never met another creature other than her father and mother — they looked around them and Tannhäuser was gone. In the distance, they still heard his painful wailing. They followed him and drew near enough to see him disappear through the portal, from the Sweeter Realm, into the valley.

By the time they reached the portal point in the Sweeter Realm, the portal had closed. The Ancient One settled the girl to sleep in his nest near the portal point. He wrapped her in his wings while the Brunnens stood around and sang to her. Their voices seemed to soothe her and she slept under the swan's wing with a smile on her face. Several Zweigwesens were summoned by Tannhäuser's screams. They hesitantly encircled the nest at a distance and stood, not knowing what to do or say. They all waited there until Otto opened the portal. The Brunnens stepped through while The Ancient One woke the girl. He brought her through, and there they stood, telling the story to Otto. Otto told them that Tannhäuser put on his old tunic and rode from the valley on Otto's horse.

The company brought the frightened girl to the lodge. Otto woke Agnes and Elisabeth. Elisabeth was two years old. The sight of a young child, of a girl, brought a smile to the face of the orphan. She had never seen another child.

Agnes lifted Tannhäuser's daughter in her arms and immediately noted, "You are as light as an empty egg shell, my sweet."

Otto asked the girl, "What is your name, dear one?" The girl answered in the Brunnen language, giving a long

Brunnen name, spoken in the harmonies of her Brunnen throats.

"I am sorry, sweet one, I cannot say your name. What does your father call you?"

The girl sank into deep, melancholy contemplation at the mention of her father. Her skin began to ripple upward. As it did, she grew lighter in Agnes' arms, until she seemed to weight nothing at all. Her face grew red and tears flowed from her eyes. Agnes wiped the girl's cheeks with the palm of her hand, but they were dry. Everyone could see the tears flowing down the girl's face, but in bewilderment, Agnes slowly recoiled her dry hand. The tears running down the face of the girl were not liquid. Her skin rippled downward to give the appearance of tears. Agnes assumed she was trying to tell her that she was sad.

"My treasure," Agnes told the girl, "We are your father's family. We are your family, and we love you very much. Now, we must give you a nickname, something we all can say."

The Ancient One interrupted, "I have already thought of one. She looks just like Hildemar at that age, the daughter of Elsa and Cunrad. She is half Brunnen, half Hildemar. I would like to call her Brunhilde."

Otto repeated, "Brunhilde… it's perfect."

Agnes squeezed the child tightly between her breasts and said, "You are Brunhilde, our darling Brunhilde."

Agnes set Brunhilde on her feet, among the gathered Brunnens, and told her, "You are welcome in this house whenever you would like to come here."

The Brunnens interrupted and told them that the girl cannot return to Brunnen land. They expressed how much they would like to take her to her mother's homeland, but the law that exiled the mother extends to the child. It is an old law. None of the Brunnens held any ill will toward the child. But the law is specific and not subject to reconsideration.

"We are sorry, she must stay here", the company of Brunnens declared in unison.

The room went silent as the weight of their proclamation settled on the shoulders of the others.

"She cannot leave the valley." The Ancient One insisted. "She is peculiar in both worlds. She would draw attention wherever she went."

Agnes answered, "So she will stay here."

The swan reminded Agnes, "Then one of you must always remain with her in the valley. You cannot continue as you have, abandoning the valley for months at a time."

"No, old friend," Otto said sharply, "we will try to find her father, until then, she is yours to raise."

"But can she open the portal?" the swan asked.

Otto replied, "She is Tannhäuser's daughter, a descendant of Parsifal. She carries Grail Blood."

The swan took a deep breath, seeing the wisdom of the order. He coiled his neck around Brunhilde, then encompassed her completely inside of his wrapping wings.

He poked his head out from the shell of giant white feathers and said, "She will be mine as long as she needs a father... she will be mine."

The Brunnens stood embarrassed by the mandates of their law. They looked as if they wanted to apologize, or offer some advice or assistance. But they knew that they had none to give, none that was needed. They bid their adieus with their traditional touches on the sides of the cheeks with their soft fingers, and slow, tender kisses on the foreheads and lips of their hosts. Agnes and Otto assured them that the Swan Knight Family did not blame them for anything. In fact, they felt their own share of guilt for Tannhäuser's actions.

Agnes, in her maternal wisdom, reminded them that Brunhilde is the result of those actions, declaring to all, "I am proud of whatever part I have played in those events. It brought us Brunhilde, our sweet treasure."

On those words, Brunhilde's skin began to ripple upward again. She gave a slight jump in the air, then becoming lighter than an empty eggshell, floated slowly from that slight push against the floor, to Agnes' accepting arms, on the other side of the room. All watched in astonishment, even the Brunnens, who had no such ability.

Except for the swan, who only whispered, "That is a talent I must develop in her. Agnes is right. She is a gift from God and she will do us good."

Through all of the commotion of the events with Tannhäuser and Brunhilde, it was not until the next morning that Otto and Agnes realized that Elisabeth had witnessed the opening of the portal. She saw The Ancient One and the Brunnens. She saw little Brunhilde float across the main hall of the lodge. Now, Elisabeth was only two years old. She was not likely to remember any of what she saw, or she would excuse it as imagination until she turned nine and learned the truth. Nevertheless, Otto and Agnes used it as an excuse to begin her training early — six and a half years early. Elisabeth was in line to be the Swan Knight, after her grandfather and father were gone. Mostly, they thought that her presence in the valley would be good for Brunhilde. They opened the portal to let The Ancient One into the valley, who walked through almost before the hole finished opening. He was eager to begin bonding with Brunhilde, learning what other special traits she carried, and begin teaching her to control herself and the portal. Otto suggested leaving Elisabeth in his care. The swan accepted with elation, but reminded Otto that such decisions are made by the Swan Knight.

"I assure you," Otto said, "my father would yield to me on this decision. Agnes and I must search for Tannhäuser, with baby Ludwig in our arms. It is much better for Elisabeth to stay here with you."

Convinced to the satisfaction of all, The Ancient One agreed to raise both children in the valley, until circumstances changed.

He told Otto, "You must go directly to Kelheim and tell everything to your father and mother."

"That is exactly what I intend, old friend," Otto assured him, "and do not forget, you will have access to the portal with both children. Control them. Control the portal."

The old bird puffed through the holes in his beak, rolled his eyes, waved his head in a large circle, then stared defiantly at Otto.

"I have watched over this portal for seven hundred years."

Otto raised both hands in a gesture of apologetic deference, bowed shallowly to his old teacher, gave him a wink and a smirk, and walked back to the lodge to prepare for his journey. With the matter settled for the time being, Otto, Agnes, and the baby left the valley for Kelheim.

Otto and Agnes braced themselves for what promised to be a trying period. Political and household duties would have to receive what portion of their time and consideration would be left behind by the search for Tannhäuser. It did not look to be much. They spent their journey to Kelheim painstakingly organizing the next year of their lives. They did not rush to Kelheim, nor did they hurry to the Duke when they arrived. This was not a problem that would solve itself quickly. Otto met with Ludwig quite casually, and only after dining and retiring to the reading room did Otto order his father to have a seat and prepare for news of paramount significance. Ludwig sat regally awaiting the news. Otto delivered it while pacing across the room, glancing up occasionally from his fixed stare at the floor to survey his father's reaction. Each word from Otto pierced Ludwig deeply, which demonstrated itself clearly on his worn and weathered face. Otto's vivid description of the noble knight, and dear friend of the Duke, dirty and naked, crushed by the death of his lover, wandering through the Sweeter Realm in the most passionate anguish, was almost more than Ludwig could bear.

Lucid flashbacks of every moment Ludwig spent in Tannhäuser's company rushed through the Swan Knight's head like a mountain thunderstorm, striking his tenderest nerves with vicious bolts. By the end of the narrative,

Otto stood sweating and shaking in front of Ludwig, shaken by his father's reaction to the news. Ludwig sank slowly from his regal perch to a low hunch in his chair, with his hands clasped tightly between his knees and the weight of his head shoving his neck deeply between his shoulders. In this position, he sat in pensive contemplation for several minutes before breaking the silence with a deep, deliberate inhale, which he held awkwardly long before releasing it with a vocalized moan. Otto relieved Ludwig with a summation of the plans he struck with Agnes for retrieving Tannhäuser to the valley and to his daughter. He informed Ludwig of his decision to leave Elisabeth with The Ancient One and Brunhilde. Ludwig had far weightier concerns than the initiation of Elisabeth's Swan Knight training. He nodded slightly to the news and did not give it another thought. The Laws of Ermenrich must bend to the severity of the situation.

Otto and Agnes had hoped to spend a week in Kelheim with Ludwig and Ludmilla then return to the Rhine to settle affairs there before embarking on the search for Tannhäuser. Ludwig insisted that the search begin immediately. He sent messages to key figures in every town in the region, asking to be informed if a lone Teutonic Knight should pass through. Otto was weary, in need of repose before committing to an indefinite quest of constant travel. Ludwig would not allow it. Agnes and Otto left the next morning with baby Ludwig. Otto was tired and his spirits were low. Agnes lifted him as she always had — with song. Before they left the streets of Kelheim, they were singing together. They traveled happy and fully enveloped in their shared love.

Ludwig did not wait long for one of his messages to be answered. Within six months of hearing the news of

Tannhäuser's return and flight from the valley, he received a letter from Pope Gregory IX. Tannhäuser went to Rome and begged to be reinstated into the Order of Teutonic Knights. He confessed his sins to the Pope, and told him that he had a daughter out of wedlock. He told the Pope that he did not know where the child was or how she fared. Pope Gregory IX gave Tannhäuser a strict penance of self-denial, with which he was dutifully grateful, and ordered him to reunite with his daughter. He denied Tannhäuser's request to be reinstated. Tannhäuser flew from Rome in a rage. He told nobody where he was going. Otto and Agnes' search continued.

During their travels, Otto and Agnes crossed Tannhäuser's path a few times, barely missing him. He traveled from town to town, earning his keep as a poet and minnesinger, a profession far more suitable to his natural sensabilities than soldiering. He apparently shed his Teutonic tunic after Rome. Reports of him had him modestly but respectfully dressed in the fashions of the time and area. Otto and Agnes followed his trail into the diocese of Passau, where they were met with a letter from Ludwig instructing them to return. Duke Friedrich II of Austria had written to Ludwig informing him that the minnesinger called the Tannhäuser worked in Vienna. He did not want to return and he was under the protection of Duke Friedrich II. The letter broke Ludwig's heart, but he was determined to do what he could for young Brunhilde. He returned to the valley and met the child. Otto's reports did not prepare him for how peculiarly inhuman she appeared at times. Ludwig determined that the child must be hidden, for her sake and for the portal. One glimpse of her would surely draw attention to the valley. He told The Ancient One that he would build a secluded palace, high on some peak, unapproachable by those bound by the normal restraints of human limitations.

The Ancient One thought about the peak across from the old Welf castle, where Lohengrin visited, where Hildemar lived, Aldwin's home. The peak across from the castle was exactly what Ludwig imagined. Its slopes were steep, its summit jagged. The old Welf castle was abandoned and falling into ruin. They considered rebuilding the old castle, but it was too accessible, to approachable and inviting. They needed a home for Brunhilde that forbade entrance at a single glance. Ludwig acquired the site across from the castle ruins and commissioned a fortress to secure Brunhilde and all of her peculiarities from the eyes of the world. He asked The Ancient One to continue as he was with her in the valley until the fortress was complete, then live in the new castle with the girl. Ludwig paid for the project from his personal funds. He declared it a private family retreat and forbade trespass under strict penalty.

Ludwig sent Otto to oversee the start of construction, which began at first thaw in the spring of 1231. After the foundation was leveled and Otto was satisfied with the progress, Ludwig called his son to Kelheim for an update. Otto arrived in September, two days after the murder of his father. Ludwig I, Duke of Bavaria and Swan Knight was murdered while crossing a bridge in Kelheim. He was fifty-seven years old. The people of Kelheim, who loved their Duke, lynched the murderer on the spot, before any explanation could be given for the crime. Otto assumed the ducal responsibilities, as Duke Otto II of Bavaria, maintaining the title of Count Palatine of the Rhine. His first duty was to investigate his father's murder. For the first year of his dukedom, Otto obsessed on the subject. As the investigation continued to be fruitless, the obsession occupied a lesser portion of his mind. It did not go away. It was simply buried beneath the relentless flow of responsibilities he faced from the multiple facets of his life. The city of Kelheim, the long-running seat of the Wittelsbach, carried too negative an association. Otto abandoned Kelheim as a ducal residence in favor of Landshut.

Although Otto assumed the full responsibility of the Swan Knight, which he had shared equally with his father for many years, he refused to immediately take the oath. To do so would be to push his father into the line of lost Swan Knights. Otto did not talk about it and The Ancient One would not ask. On the first anniversary of Ludwig's murder, Otto took the Swan Knight's oath. He changed the traditional oath and spoke directly to his father, swearing to continue his responsibilities, pursue his ambitions, and honor all that he honored. It was Otto's ceremony, but the spirit of Ludwig filled the valley and his name found its way onto every tongue in attendance. The celebration went late into the night, with Ludwig, not Otto, as the primary subject of conversation. The oath celebration was the proper memorial service that the funeral could not be because of the shocking nature of Ludwig's death. The night ended with a conspicuous sense of closure for Ludmilla, Otto and Agnes, The Ancient One, and many creatures whose affection for Ludwig was disproportionately higher than the time that fate gave them together. Even Brunhilde, who was no more than seven when Ludwig died, was seized by the atmosphere of the evening. When she saw the sorrow in Otto's eyes, she suffered flashbacks to her mother's death.

During a particularly heavy speech by Ludmilla on the immediate shock of losing her husband, while they gathered around a small fire in front of the lodge, Brunhilde became overwhelmed by the poignant melancholy of the moment. She let out a shrill cry and jumped high into the night sky. The company lost sight of her among the stars above. She floated gently and silently to the ground among them, while they continued to gaze upward, straining their eyes for any distortion in the stars that might give her away. She recovered from her sorrow by the humor of the entire company pointing upward and claiming to see her while she stood still and almost invisible among them.

"I am here", the girl said.

Her form became apparent as she fell to the ground laughing, her soft, clear skin rippling in concert with the laughter. Ludmilla's testimony was taking the celebration to a dark place. Brunhilde's inspiriting laughter brought the night back on course. There was much talk of the sacrifices Ludwig made and the time he spent away from his valley, which prompted promises that they would all help reap the fruit from the seeds he had sown. They made earnest pledges of commitment to one another, all in Ludwig's name.

In the spirit of the night's pledges, Ludmilla moved permanently into the valley. Agnes had spent the previous year gently settling into her role as Duchess, deferring to Ludmilla on all matters in which Ludmilla had an opinion. The celebration gave Ludmilla the closure to dissolve what remained of her household in Kelheim and assume the guardianship of Elisabeth and Brunhilde. Elisabeth was six years old. Brunhilde was no more than nine when Ludmilla moved permanently into the Portal Valley. The girls needed a human, a woman, as an everyday influence on their young lives.

The Ancient One delighted not only in the relief of his guardianship over the children. He relished the company and conversation of a woman he had come to admire greatly through the trials of the previous decades.

She became as cherished a Swan Knight's spouse as had ever graced the valley. Finally, she could enjoy the tranquility that the quiet lodge provided and her indefatigable service earned. She enjoyed tranquility for a brief period. But retirement was not in Ludmilla's nature. The circumstances of her life chiseled her into a different sort of figure.

With Otto and Agnes bearing all the responsibilities of the duchy and the Swan Knighthood, Ludmilla took it upon herself to oversee the construction of Brunhilde's castle. Brunhilde endeared herself quite profoundly to Ludmilla, who took a motivated interest in the girl's future. Ludmilla made regular trips to the site and settled all construction decisions. As the wife of the man who commissioned construction and the mother of the reigning duke, her directives were unquestioned. She altered the initial plan for the castle. She added a tall tower with no entrance except for a single high window, knowing that only Brunhilde and The Ancient One could enter through it. If the castle should be breached, Brunhilde could jump and float to the window and wait there with her teacher until help arrived. The architect and builders reminded Ludmilla several times that the tower had no entrance.

She simply stated, "This is how I want it."

They obeyed.

In November 1235, Agnes and Otto had another son. They named him Heinrich. Heinrich was born in the palace in Landshut, where his sister was born. Their son Ludwig was only six. He had another three years until he would be brought to open the portal for the first time and begin his lessons with the swan as the Second-in-Training behind Elisabeth. Although Elisabeth was in line to be the Swan Knight, she felt like the Second behind Brunhilde.

Both girls knew that Brunhilde would never be the Swan Knight. She was being trained only to be exiled into the new castle upon its completion. Nevertheless, The Ancient One's concern for the danger that Brunhilde posed to the portal, and that the world posed to her, focused his training on her instead of Elisabeth. Elisabeth learned from the lessons given to Brunhilde. The girls bonded tightly.

Under the shadow of such an extraordinary girl, with abilities uniquely hers, Elisabeth never blossomed as she would have had she been trained alone, waiting for her brother to join her as the Second. Elisabeth placed her attention on helping Brunhilde hone her talents. Through this, Elisabeth's childhood and training prepared her more to be the support of greatness than great herself. At only nine years old, she worried about what would come of her when the castle completed and Brunhilde left the valley. One year after Heinrich's birth, Agnes gave birth to Sophie. With three children ahead of her, they all knew that it was unlikely that Sophie would ever become the Swan Knight, or even Second-in-Training. They resolved to raising her in Landshut, and bringing her to the valley as little as possible and to never let her see the swan, the portal, or the wonderful creatures. Elisabeth thought this was unfair.

One morning, she told The Ancient One that when Brunhilde left for the new castle and Ludwig came to begin his training, she would like to continue as she had and serve as the Second behind her younger brother. It was not until she said this that the old teacher reflected on the past years and realized that he had not been training the next Swan Knight as he should. Elisabeth's role had been rather more like Second-in-Training behind Brunhilde than like the oldest child of the Swan Knight.

He sat her down and sincerely apologized for not focusing his training on her, as he was sworn to do. She surprised him with startling wisdom from one so young.

"You have done wonderfully", she said. "There are kings and there are knights, masters and servants. Who is training the servants?"

The swan replied, "I do not know, my love." He did not expect her response.

"You are. The king has no kingdom without his knights. The master cannot run his household without servants. Somebody must train great servants."

The Ancient One dropped his head in shame and an overwhelming sense of failure. Elisabeth lifted his head with her soft little hand, kissed him, thanked him for being so good and so loyal, and told him that he has served God, the Grail, the portal, the family, and her superbly. The sincere gratitude and adoration in her eyes lifted his spirits higher than his wings had ever taken him.

Elisabeth looked him in the eye and simply said, "I love you."

In response, bursting clumsily through a mixture of laughter and crying, the old bird said, "Oh, I love you, my sweet one."

It seemed that Elisabeth had long fancied herself a subordinate. She had no desire to be otherwise. She knew that Brunhilde would never have adjusted to life in the valley without her. Brunhilde's abilities, her confidence, her very character were built on Elisabeth's encouragement, affection, and support. Elisabeth drew more pride from that than she could have from any personal accomplishment. This realization settled upon

The Ancient One during the night, while Elisabeth's words haunted him. Beginning the next day, he focused on training Elisabeth — not to be the Swan Knight, but to do what came naturally to her. He trained her to be a steward, to see what the great ones do not and elevate others to a perch they would not otherwise reach. He thought about the great Swan Knights he had known, and of those whose support made them great. He based his lessons on the examples of Gütel, Nethe, and Cunrad. In this new course of study, Elisabeth soared. Elisabeth, Brunhilde, and The Ancient One grew much closer from that day.

CHAPTER 14

Between the Gentle Courtyard and the Swan Castle

IN APRIL OF 1238, young Ludwig turned nine years old. Although he lived most of his childhood in Landshut with his parents, he had been in and out of the valley to see his grandmother. He knew that the valley was home to wonderful things that did not exist elsewhere. He loved his visits to the valley. Compared to the rigid formality of his father's court and the paved ground of Landshut, the valley was warm and free, soft and gentle. The valley seemed to relieve his father and mother of all of the concerns that weighed upon them at court. For this reason, young Ludwig called the valley his father's "Linderhof", his "gentle courtyard". Linderhof — the name rang so sweetly in his young voice that Otto and Agnes began calling the valley Linderhof. The name stuck. To the Swan Knight Family and the creatures of the Sweeter Realm, it has been called Linderhof ever since.

Parsifal's little valley is just north of the far western edge of a larger valley that the locals know as Graswang Valley. Graswang became a common travel route, brushing near the southeastern edge of Linderhof, with a river and a thin band of dense forest separating the world's most sacred secret from the world. Linderhof, the Swan Knights' little valley, gained a reputation as the Duke's very private retreat, where he and his family went for complete isolation. Locals who knew the area, avoided breaching its borders. Eventually, Ludwig's name for the valley, "Linderhof", caught on, and those associated with the Duke's family came to know the private family retreat by that name. Most assumed that it was named for the linden trees that grow in the area, not from the cute but crude mumblings of a child. The river that runs between the western edge of Graswang Valley and Linderhof became known as the Linder River.

Conveniently, Ludwig asked to celebrate his ninth birthday at Linderhof, unaware of the birthday surprise mandated by the Laws of Ermenrich. Leaving Heinrich and Sophie at the palace in Landshut, Otto, Agnes, and Ludwig traveled to Linderhof. They arrived in the afternoon before Ludwig's ninth birthday. Ludmilla was there, recently returned from overseeing construction on the new castle. She never felt comfortable riding Unicorns, but she knew how much Otto loved them. When alerted to the arrival of Otto, Agnes, and Ludwig, while sitting in the lodge, she asked Brunhilde to open the portal and summon some Unicorns to greet Otto. Brunhilde was not fully human. She was born in the Sweeter Realm. Nobody had ever raised the subject of her passing back and forth between worlds like the other creatures of the Sweeter Realm. She had Grail Blood, but she was also a Brunnen. Brunhilde had not passed through the portal since the day she entered Linderhof for the first time. She shook in fear at the request. She visualized the woods that lead from the Brunnen homeland, through the Zweigwesen lands, to The Ancient One's nest. She recalled each step she took in persuit of her father. She opened her mouth and almost called for Tannhäuser, like she did on that terrible day. But she checked herself, recalled herself to the moment, and dropped to the floor, hugging her knees. Ludmilla had no idea that she would react in such a way. Elisabeth leaned down to Brunhilde and whispered something in her ear. Brunhilde smiled, sprang to her feet, and ran to the portal point.

She opened the portal, stood staring at it for a few seconds, and ran through. Elisabeth followed her from the lodge. Within seconds of the portal closing behind Brunhilde, Elisabeth opened it. She stood at the open portal. Her grandmother joined her and the two of them waited. Ludmilla asked Elisabeth what she had whispered in Brunhilde's ear that cleared away all doubt and fear from her terrified heart. Elisabeth opened her mouth in response, but was interrupted by Brunhilde floating through the portal and landing on a high branch of a nearby tree. Behind her ran three Unicorns. There are always Unicorns near The Ancient One's nest, waiting for the call of the opening portal.

The Unicorns sprinted to the edge of the valley to greet their Swan Knight as he approached. Ludmilla and Elisabeth watched in silence, captivated as they so often were by the majesty of the creatures, until their attention was broken by the rich and jovial laugh of Brunhilde, coming from high in the tree behind them, where she hung by one hand from a branch. Her two Brunnen throats laughed together, like two best friends sharing a funny secret. The sweetness and sheer joy of Brunhilde's laugh reached inside of Ludmilla and Elisabeth and pulled similar laughs from them. Brunhilde floated down to the ground and the three of them ran to the porch of the lodge to await their loved ones.

They were all excited for the reunion, but none as much as Elisabeth. She was raised in the valley and did not have the traditional nine-year-old introduction to the portal. Not only did she anticipate the excitement of Ludwig's first opening. She eagerly awaited her chance to serve and support him as she had Brunhilde. She knew Brunhilde did not have much more time at Linderhof. She knew that The Ancient One would be leaving with her, returning only when Ludwig was in the valley for his lessons. When Brunhilde was gone, and Ludwig was not at Linderhof, the lodge would be home to only her and Ludmilla. Elisabeth intended to savor the chaos of company.

Ludwig's birthday came. He opened the portal according to tradition. Visitors paraded through the portal en queue. Everything enjoyable about the day was made more enjoyable, everything remarkable made more remarkable, by the silent maneuverings of Elisabeth, the consummate servant. The company remained ignorant to that fact, except for The Ancient One, who witnessed his training united in perfection with Elisabeth's natural abilities. They raised glasses to young Ludwig, gawked at the newest abilities of Brunhilde. But The Ancient One admired Elisabeth, every spirit raised higher by her hand and every smile broadened by her efforts. She said what she needed to say, and did what she needed to do, to make the events of the day as ideal as possible for each attendee. The celebration bore Ludwig's name, but it savored strongly of Elisabeth's spirit.

During the evening fire, The Ancient One leaned his long neck to Otto's ear and whispered, "Elisabeth was born to be the right hand of greatness."

After their initial greeting the day before, Otto had given few thoughts to his daughter until that encrypted comment. Either through some mystic transfer of understanding or from the effects of the sweet wine Otto brought from Landshut, his oldest child began to glow in his eyes, with an angelic halo, while he pondered the old bird's comment, as she drifted from creature to person to creature again, saying what they needed to hear, being what they needed her to be. But, in line with her nature, Elisabeth sank quickly from the top of his thoughts, and she resumed the practice of her talents beneath the notice of the jubilant company. At the end of the celebrations, Elisabeth was deeply gratified, though no conversations centered on her, no toasts were given to her, and she remained through the day, at best, second on the thoughts of all except for her venerable teacher. With her gentle, eleven-year-old hand, she guided the events of the day down a path of her choosing, to the benefit of all.

For a few weeks, three children trained in Linderhof, until Otto and Agnes took Ludwig back to Landshut to resume his secular schooling from his secular tutor. Ludwig had an unusual interest in political matters for a boy his age, and he enjoyed his studies. But after the magic of the three weeks with the portal and the fantastic creatures, after playing with Brunhilde and laughing at her light spirit and magnificent talents, parting from his beloved Gentle Courtyard was more difficult than it had been. On the journey back to Landshut, he spoke incessantly about the portal and the Grail, about the history taught to him by The Ancient One, and about the Swan Knights he most admired. He badgered his parents to tell him which of the Swan Knights they thought he most resembled. At least a dozen times during their travels, Otto forced him to renew his vow of secrecy. Ludwig's recitations of the vow were often interrupted by another fevered question, breaking through the monotonous oath like a Unicorn galloping through the portal. For the next several nights, Ludwig slept little. When he did sleep, his dreams spun with images of the portal and visions of heroic scenes, featuring him, clad in armor, vanquishing enemies, riding Unicorns, and drinking from the Holy Grail. As an old man, he used to say that he was born on his ninth birthday, that his spirit entered the world through the portal that day, with the many creatures who greeted him in formal procession.

Ludwig spent three weeks out of every two months at Linderhof. Elisabeth continued to live in the valley with Ludmilla and Brunhilde. In April of 1240, Ludmilla visited the site of the new castle. She was surprised to find that it was nearly finished. She stayed in a finished part of the castle until its completion a month later. She paid the workers and dismissed them, sending one of them all the way to Munich with a list of furnishings to be delivered. She stayed until the furnishings arrived and she saw them situated to her liking. She spent one night alone in the newly furnished castle, walking from room to room, imagining The Ancient One and Brunhilde in each room until she felt satisfied that it would suit them. Before retiring for the night, Ludmilla sat in the courtyard, staring up to the highest tower.

The next morning, Ludmilla left for Linderhof to tell Brunhilde, now fifteen or sixteen years old, that her new home awaited her. She rode through a heavy, cold rain and arrived at the lodge in a deep chill. Elisabeth ordered her grandmother to Landshut, to the Seligenthal Convent, to be treated there until well enough to return. In August of 1240, Ludmilla died in the convent before her eyes could see what her mind imagined, the swan and Brunhilde living in the new castle, across from the old

Welf ruins, in the area she called "Hohenschwangau" in honor of her old friend. When they did assume residence in the castle, they devoted one room to Ludmilla. The room she had slept in during her last night in the castle was left unoccupied. The Ancient One adorned it with mementos of Ludmilla. On the day that Ludmilla died, in the very same hour, Agnes gave birth to her last child. Agnes wanted to name her Ludmilla, but Otto wanted to name her after his cherished wife. They called her Agnes.

The area of Hohenschwangau was home to many swans, though only one was ancient, giant, and could speak. When he made his flights from Linderhof to Hohenschwangau, he flew high to avoid suspicion. Those few who passed by the new castle assumed it was unfinished and unoccupied. Its approach from the base of its mountain was steep and perilous. Brunhilde was safe. Her training resumed. She grew strong and intuitive. She learned to float higher into the air with each jump. With the conjuring of a blissful memory, she made herself virtuously weightless. Her powerful legs thrusted her high into the air, where she rippled her skin upward to float for a moment before descending slowly to the ground.

She learned to fight. The Ancient One introduced her to all tools of combat, but Brunhilde preferred her hands. With a sword or axe, she could not jump so high or hold herself in the air with her rippling skin. Also, in stillness she was almost invisible. Her invisibility did not pass to anything she carried or wore, so she carried little and wore nothing. She committed the largest portion of her training to hand combat. During his only visit to the castle, Duke Otto II gifted to Brunhilde a small knife, strong, but thin and almost weightless. This became Brunhilde's favorite possession. She was never without it.

Brunhilde was not allowed beyond the walls of the castle until 1244, when The Ancient One determined that she was old enough, wise enough, and skilled enough at avoiding detection. He allowed her to wander the area. Each time she went, she wandered farther and stayed out longer. One evening, she found a path. She climbed high into a tree and waited to see if anyone would pass by. She fell asleep in the tree and did not wake until early the next morning. She woke to the sounds of footsteps. Three men walked the path beneath her. They were the first people, other than her father and the Swan Knight Family, that she had ever seen. Brunhilde described them later to The Ancient One as "feeling dark and cold" to her. They were loud and they said cruel things about people they knew. This was Brunhilde's first experience of an ability she would employ to its fullest later in life. She had the ability to see what sort of heart was inside of a person. Whether peaceful or cruel, Brunhilde could read the make-up of the human heart. No rich clothing or fancy words could hold back the clear and honest sensation she got when she saw people. The cruel men she encountered that day surprised her. Their hearts were so different than the noble ones she had met to that point.

The coldness coming from the cruel men made her angry. She growled at them from the top of the tree where she had slept. Startled by her sound, they looked up at her. She kept perfectly still and remained invisible against the bark of the tree. The men scanned the tops of the trees for the beast that growled at them. There was no beast, only Brunhilde, increasingly infuriated by the sensation she got from their cruel hearts. She could not simply let them continue down the path. Consciously, she waited for the relief that would come when they passed out of sight. But her angry heart took control of her actions. As they walked away, she jumped from her tree and landed silently on the path, directly behind the men. She held her knife in her hand, above her head, ready to strike one of them with it.

Her thoughtful side regained control of her actions. Mortified by what she had almost done, she let out a gasp. The men heard her and turned quickly toward her. She leapt into the air. The men must have seen her, because their eyes went upward as she did. But they soon lost her in the blue sky above them. Brunhilde landed on the path, on the other side of the men. She stared at them from behind as they scanned the sky and treetops for the mysterious figure who had startled them. Within inches of them, she could feel the hate and cruelty in their hearts as if it crawled like a swarm of insects over her entire body. Her mind caged the fury inside of her. She leapt to the top of a nearby tree just as the men turned around to resume their course. Brunhilde remained at the top of that tree, grinding her teeth and breathing heavily until the coldness from the passing men left her and her skin stopped crawling from the swarm of evil in the air around them.

Brunhilde returned to the castle and reported the events in full detail to The Ancient One, vividly describing the sensations she experienced.

She asked her teacher, "Surely this talent is a gift from God, a tool crafted by his hand, but to what purpose?"

He answered, "You found this tool in the forest, among men. I feel that it is there you must use it. But first you must know it, gain proficiency in its use before putting it to full employment. God's tools are not to by wielded carelessly or unprepared."

This speech was not necessary. Brunhilde fully sensed her responsibility. She felt the power of her gift, of all of her gifts, from her invisibility to her flight, her debilitating beauty to her new ability to sense the hearts of people. Most of her uniqueness had been with her since infancy. But this new ability came to her, high in a tree, like a present from heaven. This was not something she had purchased, and it did not feel like a part of her being. She woke in that tree with a powerful, divine weapon in her hand, placed there while she slept by God for some purpose He would later reveal. It was not a gift she would have chosen. She did not like the way it made her feel. When she closed her eyes, she still felt the icy cruelty that came from the men's hearts. It deeply disturbed and irritated her. If she could deny the gift or accept it on her terms and to her convenience, she would have. But such is never God's way. So she accepted the gift graciously and obediently, and The Ancient One began immediately devising lessons for its mastery.

"Accept the knowledge it gives you," he said, "but dampen your emotional reaction to it. God gave you this ability, but He also gave you the training of a Swan Knight. With patience and steadiness, the purpose will reveal itself."

Brunhilde made frequent, scheduled outings, followed and observed closely by her teacher. She felt the hearts of men, women, and children, of evil and of goodness. She took diligent note of the sensations that the encounters brought her, and she discussed them with the swan. She learned to dampen her emotional reactions to the icy cold of evil and the crawling insect sensation of cruelty. Seeing less danger in her response to goodness, she allowed those emotions to swell and occasionally burst from her in laughter, tears, and song. The Ancient

One warned that these outbursts could be as harmful as her desire to wield her knife against the evil ones and must be caged behind the same bars. The steady wisdom of the ancient teacher aided Brunhilde immeasurably in the effort. But more useful still were the regular visits from Elisabeth. Elisabeth's talent for knowing what needed to be said and what needed to be done to raise others to their potential only honed with age into a fine and precise art. It was difficult for Elisabeth when Brunhilde left Linderhof, but much more difficult for Brunhilde when Elisabeth left her life forever.

Duke Otto II found himself in volleying alliances between the feuding Pope Innocent IV and Emperor Friedrich II. Friedrich was a Hohenstaufen and kin to Otto. Otto inherited his allegiance to the Pope from his father, but his father was also a loyal friend of Emperor Friedrich. For the security of Linderhof and the Lord's sacred cup, Otto sided with Friedrich. He needed to seal the pact with marriage. The words of The Ancient One materialized in his ear and flew around inside of his skull.

"Elisabeth was born to be the right hand of greatness."

Arranged by the fathers, the eldest daughter of the Wittelsbach and the eldest son of the Hohenstaufen engaged to be married. Friedrich's son was Conrad IV, King of Germany. He was elected King of Germany in 1237 and had ruled admirably, gaining the respect of Otto and Elisabeth. Friedrich sought political advantage. Otto's motivations were different. To Otto, the marriage was a victory in the war to secure the portal until the day that God would recall the Grail into service. Elisabeth was not a dreamy, romantic young woman. Never in her life had she placed herself above the good of others. She accepted the engagement with a proud sense of duty and looked forward to serving God and her father as Queen of Germany. The position gave her indirect political control of her blessed valley and Otto trusted in her ability to steer her good husband righteously. Elisabeth married Conrad and became Queen of Germany in 1246. She left the valley. And Heinrich, at eleven years old, took her place as Second-in-Training behind Ludwig.

The Ancient One could not console Brunhilde in her loss.

He reminded her, "Elisabeth worked tirelessly to enchant a simple birthday celebration with her goodness. How much more of her will it take to rule a kingdom?"

This truth was clear to Brunhilde, who knew her friend well, and only served to further convince her that she would never again see her beloved Elisabeth. Her recovery was inhibited by every dark heart she encountered in her training. She held each one against the holy warmth and brightness of Elisabeth, weaving her loss into a crown of thorns that she had to adorn daily. Over time, this crown of love and loss became an ornament. It ceased to be thorny and painful, and became a talisman that Brunhilde carried into every encounter with every person. Perhaps unfairly, Elisabeth became the measuring stick by which Brunhilde gauged all people. The human race had a lofty standard to live up to in Brunhilde's eyes. The loss of Elisabeth's goodness in her life gave purpose to Brunhilde's ability. It no longer served to simply differentiate the good from the bad. It motivated the hunt for evil and an insatiable drive to extinguish it from the earth.

Heinrich's introduction to the valley and portal passed without the usual festivities. Otto brought him to

Linderhof. Heinrich opened the portal and was greeted by many creatures. Elisabeth did not attend and neither did The Ancient One. He was with Brunhilde, whose emotions combined with her abilities to brew a volatile compound. By the end of 1246, Brunhilde was getting restless and angry. She saw the imbalance in the world around her. Good hearts lost while bad hearts gained. She developed a violent hatred for cruel and immoral people. She was without the company and advice of Elisabeth and the swan was often at Linderhof with Ludwig.

Heinrich's lessons could not be put off. The first few months of training were extensive and The Ancient One shuddered at the thought of leaving Brunhilde alone in the castle in such a state. He could not forbid her to leave the castle. She was a grown woman. In the first weeks of Heinrich's training, the old swan's poor wings took him back and forth, from the valley to the castle. He was in flight more than he was on the ground — and he rarely slept. By late spring, there was little left of him to give to either Heinrich or Brunhilde. Ludwig trained mostly with Unicorns and studied on his own.

One May afternoon, The Ancient One arrived at the castle after his long flight from Linderhof. Brunhilde stood in the tall tower looking through the window at a single man, plainly dressed, leisurely climbing from the foot of the mountain, toward the gate of the castle. The Ancient One joined her at the window. He stared at the approaching man for a moment, then drew a quick, short inhale.

"He has a good heart," Brunhilde told him.

"Of course he does, my dear," the swan replied. "He is your father."

The swan would have recognized Tannhäuser at twice that distance, though he was much altered by time. The Ancient One's words took a moment to settle into Brunhilde's head. When they did, she took a few steps backward, away from the window, as if trying to hide from her father's sight.

"He cannot see you. I can hardly see you and I stand at your side. Come. Let us invite him in."

The swan jumped to stand perched on the ledge of the window. He looked back into the tower and saw Brunhilde sitting against the wall.

"This reunion is long overdue," he told her. "It should not wait another moment."

Brunhilde froze in her position, curled tightly on the floor against the wall, deep in shadow, invisible even to the keen eyes of the giant bird.

"I am here," she whispered, as the swan scanned the room for the slightest distortion in the stone wall behind her.

"Do what you must, my dear, but I am going to greet an old friend," he told her.

He flew from the window and landed on the rim of the outer wall. He stood there and watched Tannhäuser climb the steep mountain face. Tannhäuser paused his ascent to catch his breath. As he did, he glanced up the wall of the castle and saw the tall image of the majestic bird, posed regally and silhouetted against the blue sky by the backlight of the lowering sun behind him.

Tannhäuser's arms fell lifeless at his sides. His face grew blank and expressionless. He stared at The Ancient

One in this way for a moment, until a smile slowly came to the surface of his placid face, like a bubble rising to ripple the surface of a pond. The two of them exchanged smiles, then Tannhäuser reached his arms upward to his old friend and curled his fingers inward in invitation. The Ancient One flew down to him, almost landing on Tannhäuser's feet. Tannhäuser was forty-eight years old, but he look twice that old. He threw his weary arms around his old friend and held him tightly, saying nothing and only breaking the silence with long choppy sighs. The Ancient One was about to tell Tannhäuser that his daughter awaited him in the castle. The swan's first syllable was interrupted by Brunhilde, who sailed over the wall of the castle and floated to land gently behind The Ancient One. She swayed in small circles and slowly waved her arms in order to remain clearly visible to her father. The Ancient One did not know that she stood directly behind him. It was Tannhäuser's reaction that interrupted the swan. He acknowledged Brunhilde's presence by releasing his embrace of the bird and resuming the blank and rigid face he wore when he beheld the majestic swan on the wall. In a half-vocalized whisper, he called his daughter by her Brunnen name.

She responded, "I am called Brunhilde now."

The sound of her voice lifted the edges of his tight, thin lips into the smile of authentic delight. He spoke to her in Brunnen.

"I do not remember those words," she told him. "I have been raised in the valley by the Swan Knight Family."

The Ancient One explained a few details from the day of his return from the Sweeter Realm. Brunhilde cut sharply into the middle of his sentence with a declaration that seemed involuntary, as if the child from years ago possessed her later self and spoke through Brunhilde's full lips.

"I called for you. Why didn't you stop? Why didn't you answer?"

Tannhäuser reacted as a stranger might, one who heard the story but did not witness it. Hardly able to bring his broken voice from his throat to his tongue, he told her that, in all of those years away, he remembered nothing between discovering his lover's body and finding himself riding Otto's horse, on the road to Rome.

The Ancient One suggested that the reunion resume under the more appropriate setting of the castle interior. The castle wall had one gate. It was narrow, barely wider than two men standing shoulder to shoulder. The narrow gate was designed by Ludmilla to slow the infiltration of enemies in the case of a breech. Brunhilde floated over the wall and opened the gate from the inside. Tannhäuser gawked in amazement as he watched his daughter fly through the air. Once she cleared the wall and descended out of sight, Tannhäuser giggled and looked to The Ancient One.

"Oh, there is much more," the sage told him, "Come, come home to us."

They retired into the comforts of the castle. The three of them remained in conversation well into the night. There were stories and apologies, remembrances, explanations, poems and songs. There were tears of joy and tears of anger. The conversation touched the darkest and the lightest of topics. Eventually, Tannhäuser fell asleep on the chair in which he sat the whole evening.

Brunhilde curled herself into the tightest possible ball on his lap, reducing herself to the proportions of a child.

She rubbed her father's thin, grey hair and repeated in the softest, sweetest Brunnen voice, "Father... Father...," until she fell asleep.

In the morning, The Ancient One had to return to Linderhof. The discussions that awaited Brunhilde and Tannhäuser were best had in private, and Ludwig's lessons had been neglected too long. The swan looked forward to lingering in the valley much longer than his concerns for Brunhilde had let him. He was confident that the distraction of the reunion would keep Brunhilde from the obsession that had raged inside of her. Her aversion to the cruelty of the world still burnt in smoldering embers inside of her, but the goodness of her father's heart enveloped her and brought a soothing coolness to the air around her. When he parted with them, The Ancient One noted that, since the reunion with Tannhäuser, Brunhilde reminded him more of her former than her latter self, more of the girl whose laughter lit the hearts of Linderhof. To the comment, she simply smiled, reached for a lock of hair on her father's head, and rubbed it between her thumb and fingers like a charm. The swan set that image into his mind and replayed it to himself with an ever-lifting smile as he flew to Linderhof with a lightness of heart he had not felt in years.

In The Ancient One's absence, Ludwig and Heinrich grew close. Otto and Agnes governed two regions, Bavaria and the Palatinate on the Rhine, allowing little time in the valley. Ludwig and Heinrich, young as they were, were often left alone at Linderhof, under the supervision of the few ancient creatures that answered the call of the opening portal. They grew as close as two brothers could be. Each was the other's only human friend. They studied and trained together. They ate and played together. At the end of the day, they usually slept together on the floor of the main hall of the lodge. Ludwig took it upon himself to guide Heinrich and share with him all that he had. There was no First-in-Training, no Second. They were the children of the Swan Knight, and as far as they considered, both in training to be the next Swan Knights. They lacked the structure and guidance to refute their growing fancies. Relieved of his burden in the castle, The Ancient One committed himself to his vow, to return to the valley the traditions and structure of the Swan Knight training and the Laws of Ermenrich. But the adhesive between the boys had hardened fast. The old teacher's plans had to compromise with the relentless bond of the brothers.

This is how things passed for nearly a decade. Brunhilde and Tannhäuser found peace in each other's company, alone together in the castle. They took long walks around the Alpsee, the lake that abutted the old Welf ruins over which my father eventually built Hohenschwangau Castle, my childhood home. They found human contact only when they sought it. Tannhäuser slowly regained a father's influence. He employed the experiences of his years to teach his daughter. Her talents fascinated him, especially her ability to see into the human heart. She described to him what she felt from the people they encountered together. He transcribed those feelings into exquisite verse and song. He had lived among people for long enough. He was ready to view the world from the lofty, isolated perch of a poet. She had lived away from people and longed to bathe in the tumult of the human experience, to come to grips with the swell of sensation that crashed against her mind in increasing strength each time she saw another human being.

Brunhilde reminded Tannhäuser of the passionate lover he once was. She revived the young knight inside of him. Upon it he wore the experiences of the years that followed. Tannhäuser was whole. He was happy. In his daughter's castle and in the hills of Hohenschwangau he was finally at peace. He was a proud, loving father with an extraordinary daughter. Neither Brunhilde nor Tannhäuser needed or asked for more than God had given them in each other's company. The castle, which Elisabeth had seen as a prison for her friend, was the most blissful building in all of Europe while father and daughter lived there together. Tannhäuser's return was the sweetest gift The Ancient One's heart could have received. His beloved Brunhilde was at peace.

Ludwig and Heinrich trained happily with their teacher, spending more of their time at Linderhof than with their secular tutors. When Ludwig came of age, Otto began preparing him for the dukedom. He pulled him from the valley and from Heinrich. Ludwig always felt lonely when not with his brother. The thought of assuming a position he could not share with his brother made Ludwig even lonelier. He told his father that he would like to share the dukedom with Heinrich, once they have lost their noble father. Otto explained that such an arrangement would be in violation of the law, as would sharing the Swan Knighthood. Outwardly, Ludwig yielded to his father's decisions. Inwardly, he viewed Heinrich as he always had, as an equal, as another part of himself. In Ludwig's mind, sharing the knighthood and the dukedom with his brother would not be a division of the titles, rather the titles would be held by two parts of the same person. That is how both of them saw the other.

Ludwig pressed on as his father commanded until late in 1253, when Otto II Duke of Bavaria died. Agnes was fifty-two when her husband died. She followed the example of her mother-in-law, the admirable Ludmilla, and she retired to Linderhof, as servant and custodian when the boys were there, and as sovereign matriarch when they were not. Ludwig assumed the title, Ludwig II, Duke of Bavaria. He was twenty-four when Otto died. Heinrich was nineteen. The glue that bound the young men remained stronger than that which bound their loyalties to their father's wishes. Although Otto died in November, it was not until February that The Ancient One presided over the Swan Knight oath. Against the strenuous protest of the swan, Ludwig insisted that both he and Heinrich take the oath and serve as Knights together. He presented logistical arguments that even the Laws of Ermenrich could not refute. Two Swan Knights could ensure that the portal remained almost constantly under the eye of a Swan Knight, despite the pull of secular duties. This was a powerful argument on the old teacher. Since the early days of the Swan Knighthood, The Ancient One's strongest desire was to have the Swan Knight in the valley. There was a darkness in his heart whenever Linderhof was without a Swan Knight. When Ludwig assumed the dukedom, he made a similar arrangement. In violation of the law, Ludwig split the Duchy of Bavaria into two sovereign sections, Upper Bavaria, which included Linderhof and Brunhilde's castle, and Lower Bavaria, to the east. Ludwig, being the older brother and rightful duke, assumed the rule of Upper Bavaria. Heinrich became Duke Heinrich I of Lower Bavaria. Ludwig moved the seat of Upper Bavaria to Donauwörth to be closer to his lands on the Rhine.

The split set a precedent that would linger over Bavarian affairs for centuries. But Ludwig could never have relegated his brother to the fate of a younger noble son, and appoint him as some count of somewhere-or-another, or see him join the knighthood of an emperor or pope, as so many royal younger brothers had done before him. The arrangement worked well in the valley. Rarely did a day pass when neither Swan Knight was at Linderhof. They both loved the valley. They both loved the creatures and relished their company. The creatures adored and admired the Swan Knights. The political division of the duchy gave Heinrich control of his own Bavarian army. He concerned himself with protecting the portal and his friends, so he positioned his troops to that end. Ludwig did the same.

One year after his father died, Ludwig married Maria of Brabant. After the wedding, he took his wife to the valley and introduced her to the family legacy. Maria was enraptured by it all — the creatures, the history, the legends. She demanded the full Swan Knight training and education. Ludwig obeyed and asked The Ancient One to teach her like a Swan Knight. She stayed behind, parting with her new husband when he left the valley. When she finally rejoined him, she carried all of the family secrets. The Ancient One warned Ludwig that Maria consumed the knowledge like wine. It intoxicated her and made her giddy. The teacher warned Maria that the knowledge of the Swan Knights comes with immense responsibilities and is to be accepted with sober commitment. He hesitated to let her leave the valley, but could not stop her from joining her husband in Donauwörth. For two years Ludwig had to chase after his wife, whose loose tongue threatened the security of the Grail more than any hunter, or band of Welf knights, more than the evil wizard Klingsor.

After two years of marriage, Ludwig found something among Maria's private possessions that sank his heart. He found letters written by Maria, describing the portal and the creatures. She even mentioned the Holy Grail. Ludwig thanked God that he found them before they were sent, but feared what letters, what secrets had already been sent. He confronted Maria. She insisted that the Grail belonged to all of Christendom and the secrets of the portal were not his to keep. Ludwig warned her that many lives have been lost to maintain the anonymity of the portal and its creatures. She sought the fame that exposing the information would bring her. She imagined the valley filled with thousands of visitors at a time. She pictured the destruction of the old rustic lodge and the construction of a monument that would rival anything in Rome.

Maria demanded the return of the unsent letters. She was determined to see them reach their designated audiences. In the silence of her fantacies, she had constructed a vision where she ruled the world from Linderhof, taxing visitors to the portal and growing rich and powerful. Her stubbornness was the mortar that bound her fantacies and made indestructible the images in her head. She told her ideas to Ludwig. No amount of pleading, demanding, or threatening on Ludwig's part could dismantle the kingdom that Maria had constructed in her mind.

Ludwig told his wife, "I am a Swan Knight, sworn to protect the secrecy of the portal. I cannot let you send these letters or tell a single soul what you have learned."

She responded, "You will have to kill me."

She grabbed the letters from Ludwig and ran from the room. Ludwig had her arrested. He begged her to see reason and accept the responsibility of the family legacy. She refused. She shouted loudly about the portal that exists at Linderhof and about the Sweeter Realm and the Holy Grail to everyone she encountered. Ludwig saw his world crashing around him. He refused to be the Swan Knight who ruined it all, ushered the destruction of the Sweeter Realm, the release of the Grail into the hands of any adventurer able to return with it. He had to silence his wife. He moved his capital to Munich to separate the ears of influence from the ramblings of his wife. Maria remained locked in Donauwörth. As crazed as Maria's words seemed to most, rumors of her claims of a portal and the Grail, of Unicorns and a secret queendom, began to spread.

Ludwig was at his wit's end. He had to silence his wife. He accused Maria of adultery, knowing that the accusation would bring her death. He presented no evidence of her guilt. There was no evidence to present. She had been faithful to him in body. It was her mind and spirit that betrayed him. In Ludwig's mind, that was enough. No horde of lovers into Maria's bed could have betrayed Ludwig more defiantly, more dangerously. In his mind, she was guilty of unfaithfulness. He was not the first Swan Knight to kill for the protection of the portal. But in 1256, he became the only one to kill his own wife. He had Maria beheaded for adultery. They had no children. Ludwig cried every day for three years. He loved Maria, much more than she loved him. The ghost of what he always hoped she would be haunted him nightly.

Elisabeth was twenty-six when Duke Otto II died. But her father's duchy, now in the hands of her younger brothers, was one of several in her kingdom. Under the disguise of an obedient and dutiful domestic, Elisabeth wielded tremendous political control over her husband's kingdom. She had one child, a son named Conradin. The boy was born a year and a half before Duke Otto II died. One year after Elisabeth lost her father, she lost her husband and her crown. The king of Germany died. Elizabeth moved to Munich and reconnected with Ludwig. She made regular visits to Linderhof to visit her mother. She never visited her childhood playmate. Elisabeth would have been happy to see Brunhilde finally with her father and living with the youthful joy that had been robbed of her when she was only four or five. But she delighted in the updates provided by The Ancient One during her brief visits to the valley. Elisabeth never sat still. She still commanded a great deal of respect in the kingdom. Her notoriety and acclaim were deeper and wider than she knew.

She was still a servant at heart and she wanted to serve the Swan Knights in the best way she could. Five years after her husband died, she remarried. She married Count Meinhard II of Tirol. His lands controlled the mountain pass from Italy. Nothing would pass from the south without Elisabeth's knowledge. In 1273, Elizabeth and Meinhard established the Stams Abbey. She dedicated it to prayer for the safety of the Holy Grail, while admitting no knowledge of it beyond the legends. I purchased the ruins of Meinhard's Castle Falkenstein, or as it was known then, Castrum Pfronten, hoping to reconstruct it in honor of Elizabeth, one of my favorite figures in the Swan Knight history. I was very excited to walk the renovated halls that Elisabeth had occupied. It does not look like I will live to see that project completed. It is one of the many joys that must remain just out of my reach.

Neither Conradin nor the six children Elizabeth had with Count Meinhard II ever learned of their inherited abilities. They never heard about the portal or the Swan Knights. They never heard of the Scheriers or the Zweigwesens. They never saw a Unicorn. They carried their legendary blood in silence and ignorance to the grave. Ludwig and Heinrich celebrated Elisabeth's marriage to Meinhard without understanding her motivations. Elisabeth did more to secure the portal than either of her brothers and nobody recognized her or thanked her for it. Although Ludwig and Heinrich were devoted Swan Knights, The Ancient One considered Elisabeth the true Swan Knight of her generation. Both of her marriages were in defense of the portal. The wise old bird saw everything that she did, and in the silence of his prayers, he thanked God for her.

Ludwig mourned Maria for four years before opening his heart for love. In 1260, five years after Maria's betrayal and execution. Ludwig married his second wife, Anna of Glogau. Ludwig and Anna had three children, Maria, Agnes, and Ludwig. Heinrich married young and had ten children. The duel knighthood of Ludwig and Heinrich presented the problems that The Ancient One had feared since they both took the oath. Whose child would be the next Swan Knight? The Ancient One called the brothers together.

He told them, "I am not a Swan Knight, but I have been the teacher of every Swan Knight since Lohengrin. I have been the only permanent custodian of the portal for more than seven hundred years. I have asked for nothing. I have made no demands."

Ludwig interrupted him, "What do you want? If it is ours to give, it is yours."

The Ancient One demanded, "We must reinstate the Laws of Ermenrich. There must be one Swan Knight, who must be the child of the previous. Ludwig, you are the rightful Swan Knight and two of your children will be trained. All others must be kept in the dark."

Ludwig and Heinrich sat in silence. They could not argue with the old sage. They agreed on that day to reinstate and firmly enforce the Laws of Ermenrich. Heinrich denounced his Swan Knighthood and declared himself a steward of the portal, at his brother's disposal. Heinrich's children visited Linderhof, but remained ignorant to the marvels that remained hidden during their visits.

Ludwig never forgave himself for the death of his first wife. He founded a monastery near Munich as penance. Within a year of his marriage to Anna, he had his first daughter, Maria. The valley remained childless, waiting for Maria to turn nine. They brought her to Linderhof, but Ludwig had become cautiously protective of the family secrets. All creatures hid from her when she visited the valley. They waited patiently for her to turn nine. But circumstances arose that hurried their timetable. In 1267, while Ludwig and Anna visited the valley with their children, Maria, Agnes who was five, and their infant Ludwig, The Ancient One flew to the valley from Brunhilde's castle. He walked directly into the lodge and spoke in front of the children. He announced that Tannhäuser was dead. Brunhilde lost her mind. She grieved uncontrollably. She soared around the area, screaming for her father. She had grown more beautiful every year, with more intoxicatingly seductive power than any Brunnen. The Ancient One feared that she would be seen and expose herself and the portal. He begged for the Swan Knight's advice.

Ludwig could not bring himself to order another execution. He ordered that she be banished far from Bavaria, if she could not be calmed and her behavior controlled. The Ancient One had spent much of the last several years with Tannhäuser and Brunhilde in their castle. Many of the happiest days he had ever lived were spent in the castle with them both. He grieved heavily the death of Tannhäuser, and now must send away his beloved Brunhilde. But he knew the wisdom of the dictate. If Brunhilde could not be calmed and consoled, she must leave. The Ancient One and Ludwig went to the castle. Agnes, who adored Brunhlde since the day she came through the portal, begged to go with them. She was sixty-six years old. Although her spirit was still vibrant and her heart as youthfully passionate as anyone in the valley, her body had grown frail, weakened considerably after the death of her darling husband. Ludwig forbade his mother from traveling.

When Ludwig and The Ancient One arrived at the castle, they found Brunhilde sitting in the chair where she slept on her father's lap on the night of Tannhäuser's return. The rest of the room, and most of the castle furnishings, laid strewn about and demolished by Brunhilde's mindlessly violent rampages.

Brunhilde looked up slowly and quietly asked in a voice that was calm and startlingly contrasted to the violent destruction around them, "Why does goodness wither and perish... while evil grows and perpetuates? Evil and cruelty fill the air around me. It seeps into my home from bad people everywhere. I smell it. I breathe it in... God, it is rancid!"

Her beautiful face slowly distorted into a look of painful disgust. She flew into another rage, throwing furniture and destroying everything she could get her hands on. She leapt into the air, floated just beneath the ceiling for a few seconds, then lowered her head and drifted slowly to her knees on the floor. Her rapid breathing slowed to normal. The writhing of her facial features mellowed to stone placidity.

"My father is dead," she said, "Why does goodness die?"

The swan answered, "These things are not for us to know. We can only live well and fight for God and goodness."

Ludwig added, "You cannot endanger the portal, dear one. You must go far away."

"Yes," she replied, "I must go. I cannot stay here where I lived with my father. I cannot save the good or bring my father back — but I can destroy evil."

The three of them stood in silence for several awkward moments, broken finally when Brunhilde announced through her clinched teeth, "I will go north. I will follow the path of Lohengrin. I will be a plague on evil. They cannot hide their hearts from me."

She spoke aloud, but more to herself than to the others. Her face grew angry again and twitched as her imagination took her north. The Ancient One jolted her from her distant musing with a soft touch of his feathers.

With tender, loving eyes, he looked at her and said, "You have divine abilities, my good friend. I always imagined you would use them here, with me, in defense of the portal, not in distant lands to the north."

The rage in her expression softened. She answered, "I am a child of the portal. I exist because of it. I will follow the mandates of my heart. Whatever I do, wherever I do it, I believe it will be in service to the portal… somehow."

There was nothing the swan or Ludwig could say in response.

Ludwig kissed Brunhilde on the cheek and said, "You will always be in my thoughts and prayers. I will leave you to say goodbye."

He left the castle and rode back toward Linderhof alone. The Ancient One held Brunhilde and kissed her repeatedly.

He said, "Do what you must. Come back to me someday, if you can. You will always find home beneath my wings."

Such reassurance lifted Brunhilde and gave her the confidence to pursue her destiny. She kissed the swan and leapt from the window, taking only her little knife with her. She disappeared into the dark sky, leaving The Ancient One with no idea if he would ever see her again.

After Ludwig and The Ancient One left Linderhof to confront Brunhilde and send her away, Agnes grew desperate to see Brunhilde one more time. She took Anna's horse and rode toward Hohenschwangau. Halfway back to Linderhof, Ludwig found the horse with no rider. He knew his mother must have set out alone. He searched the area through the night. As the sun rose, he found his mother on the ground. Agnes had fallen from the horse and hit her head on a stone. Ludwig found her lying in her blood, breathing shallowly. He rushed her back to Linderhof as quickly as his horse could carry them. By the time they reached the lodge, Agnes was dead. They prepared her body and set it beautifully in state near the portal point. The Ancient One returned from Hohenschwangau with a heavy heart. He was in no condition to accept the death of Agnes, a dear and cherished Swan Knight's wife. He did not kiss her cheek or eulogize her goodness. He begged Ludwig to let him home. He gave one quick glance to Agnes's body as he stepped through the portal.

Ludwig opened the portal several times a day until he left Linderhof. The swan did not respond. Just as Ludwig was leaving, he rode his horse to the portal point, opened the portal and called for his friend. Although no sound penetrates the portal, the swan stepped through as if responding to Ludwig's call. He was refreshed and ready to bear the burden of his losses while he kept the valley in the Swan Knight's absence. For the next few nights, he dreamed about Agnes' awkward introduction to the valley and the beautiful songs she used to sing with her husband.

The Ancient One kept his ear to the ground for reports of Brunhilde. Stories came from the north about a woman, a creature they called a Valkyrie, named Brunhilde, who flew out of the sky, into the thick of battle. She sensed the hearts of men on the battlefield. When Brunhilde arrived, might did not determine who lived or died. The Valkyrie sensed the good and evil. She decided who lived and who died. She killed with a flick of her knife, then disappeared high into the sky above the battle. As long as the reports kept coming, as long as drunken men told of the beautiful Valkyrie with the angelic voice, sumptuous figure, and the deadly blade, descending among men wearing only her radiant, bare skin, The Ancient One knew that Brunhilde was well. When the sunlight hit Brunhilde just right, her bare skin reflected into the eye like polished armor. Some reports had the Valkyrie wearing armor. Over time, Brunhilde's actions weaved their way into legend. Nobody knew how long she might live. But the legends of Brunhilde grew with each military conflict in the north.

Generations later, when The Ancient One heard stories of the Valkyrie, he smiled. He believed that Brunhilde might still return to him. He prayed that she would. He thought that her old castle, carrying so many memories of her father, might deter her from returning. He begged Ludwig to build a new castle. Years later, he built another castle on the same peak as Brunhilde's castle, directly behind it. He called the older castle Vorderhohenschwangau and the newer castle Hinterhohenschwangau. He had the newer castle fitted up for Brunhilde's return. She never came back to Hohenschwangau. Both castles sat empty. The Ancient One visited them often and pined over his dear Brunhilde and his old friend Tannhäuser. Alone in the older castle, he spoke aloud to his friends, reliving many of the moments they spent there together. Both castles fell into neglected disrepair and eventual ruin. It was over those ruins, six centuries later, that I built the New Swan Castle, Neuschwanstein.

CHAPTER 15
The Seeds of Dissent

LESS THAN TWO YEARS after Brunhilde left, young Agnes died unexpectedly. She was seven. The following year, at nine years old, Maria entered the valley to begin her training. One year after that, Duke Ludwig's wife Anna died, leaving the Duke with Maria and their only other surviving child, young Ludwig. Her death resurfaced painful memories. With Anna's death, Ludwig suffered the loss of both of his wives. Still haunted by the death of his first wife, he turned to religion to soothe his guilty soul. He raised young Maria as devout as any child in Christendom. She spent more time in the chapel of the lodge than in her lessons with The Ancient One. The Ancient One knew he was not training the next Swan Knight. Maria set her heart on becoming a nun. She was good, strong-willed, yet obedient. She was loyal and pious. The secrets of the portal were safe behind her disciplined lips. She believed that her best service to the Grail would be performed in a convent, in endless prayer. The creatures loved her. But to be with her, they must join her in the chapel. She read to them from the Scriptures and enforced upon them the dire importance of their duties to the Swan Knights and to the Holy Grail. Maria's time in the valley was short, but profoundly impactful. Much of what happened in the following generations can be traced back to Maria's faith and the commitment she instilled in the creatures who called the valley home. But this left only young Ludwig as heir to the knighthood.

One year after Dutchess Anna died, Duke Ludwig II met Matilda of Habsburg. She was the daughter of King Rudolf of Germany. The union held obvious political benefits, but Ludwig did not see them. Her character reminded him of the stories of Nethe, the wife of Lohengrin. She unwittingly pulled Ludwig into trances of admiration by using phrases exactly as The Ancient One had quoted Nethe using. Ludwig looked at her, he listened to her, and felt the simplicity and devotion of the early years of the portal. Matilda's every movement swept the Duke into dreamy, romantic visions of years gone by. She intoxicated him like wine pressed by the feet of Bacchus himself. One year after they met, Ludwig and Matilda married. Ludwig was forty-four years old.

Eleven months after the wedding, Matilda gave birth to Rudolf, and then three girls consecutively. Mechthild was one year younger than Rudolf. Agnes came the following year, and Anna four years after that. Two years after Rudolf's birth, in 1276, on his ninth birthday, young Ludwig, oldest son of the Duke and Swan Knight began his training. Young Ludwig's traditional first opening was ruined by his own potential. Duke Ludwig II walked his son toward the portal point, as so many had, with the intention of following tradition. They were only halfway from the lodge to the portal point when the new Knight-in-Training triggered an opening. Nobody had opened the portal from that distance since Elsa. The Ancient One stepped through the portal and had to scan the area to see father and son hiking up the slope. Rumors of the next Elsa swirled around the woods and halls of the Sweeter Realm. Each creature tried to be to Ludwig what the

Unicorns were to Elsa. Frenzied excitement swirled around the valley from the moment the portal spiritedly opened at young Ludwig's distant approach. Although Maria was in the valley as First-in-Training, Ludwig was not brought to Linderhof to be the Second. Maria only awaited her brother's ninth birthday to pursue her destiny in the convent.

It was one week after Ludwig opened the portal for the first time that Maria joined the convent and said goodbye to the valley, its creatures, and her family. Her most powerful weapon against the evils that would endanger her family and the Grail was the power of her prayers. She committed the rest of her life to praying for the Swan Knights. Ludwig developed very differently. With one older sister dead and the other away in the convent, he was First-in-Training. The excitement surrounding his unique introduction to the portal brought many visitors from the Sweeter Realm, all eager to teach and train a boy whose obvios potential promised an exciting and historic Swan Knighthood. Ludwig received constant attention and intense, pressured training. The young boy handled it all with grace and humility. The Swan Knighthood was to be his, the valley and portal his responsibility. And at nine years old, he understood the full weight of his inherited future.

With each day added to young Ludwig's training, the Duke and The Ancient One grew increasingly confident in the future and security of the portal, at least for another generation. Ludwig grew strong, quick, and clever. By the time he was eleven years old, he was as strong as his father, much more athletically gifted, and almost as smart. He could delay the portal opening until he stood directly under it, or open it from as far as the lodge. He could not will it open as Elsa did, but his trigger point expanded measurably outward every month and he could hold it closed until he wanted it to respond to his proximity. The Ancient One advanced his training rapidly, to keep up with his development. He had a dynamic manner of speech. He was remarkably handsome. The strength of his mind and his body could be easily discerned from the briefest of encounters. While the swan groomed him to be extraordinary among the history of the Swan Knights, the mind of his proud father brewed with political ambition.

Ludwig cut a manly figure at a very young age. His beauty and charisma, his sharp mind and intoxicating energy, could convince the stubbornest to follow him anywhere. If ever the seed of greatness grew in any valley, it grew in Linderhof while Ludwig trained. His father, his teacher, the Queen of the Land and Shallow Waters and her subjects, were all sure of this. By the time Ludwig was fifteen, he had developed his skills astonishingly. He had his grandfather's skills on the Unicorns, which transferred nicely to horseback when he left the valley. The Unicorns adored his company. They had long missed their dear Elsa, and young Ludwig's daily comparisons with the greatest Swan Knight endeared the noble beasts to him. He excelled at all forms of sport and combat. He mastered anything he could throw, swing, jump over, swim across, or ride. Ever since he learned the family history at nine years old, he believed that he would be in a great battle, like Otto I's famous triumph at Verona. He boasted his premonition and the family believed him, especially the Duke. He mastered every weapon and perfected their use while performing stunts on the backs of Unicorns and horses. He put his skills on display wherever he went, in and out of the valley.

The Duke was so proud of Ludwig. With Maria locked in a convent, Ludwig was the only child from his marriage to Anna upon whom the Duke could dote. When Matilda gave birth to a boy in April of 1282, the Duke named him Ludwig, after his oldest son, not after himself. In 1283, Rudolf joined Ludwig as Second-in-Training. For Rudolf, there was no escaping Ludwig's tall shadow. The swan, the creatures, the family were not the only ones lauding Ludwig's greatness. Everywhere he rode, crowds demanded to be entertained by his feats with weapons on horseback. The Duke bragged openly and publicly about the skills of his oldest son. Ludwig's notoriety grew.

Baby Ludwig was raised to be like his namesake in every way. But Rudolf was Second-in-Training. The Duke's youngest was forbidden by law to begin Swan Knight training. He must remain ignorant to the family secrets. As long as Ludwig and Rudolf live, no other children would learn of the portal and the Grail. It was the law. That did not stop the Duke from speaking as if baby Ludwig would someday join his oldest brother as Second, supplanting Rudolf. Even before baby Ludwig was born, poor Rudolf received the paltry scraps of time and attention that his older brother dropped from his abundant table. Rudolf was quiet. Even if all light on him had not been blocked out by the tall shadow of his brother, he would not have caught the eye without effort.

One advantage that neglect offers is time. Quietly, Rudolf grew in strength and ability. He learned to understand the song of the Eulesängers. He whistled back to them in their language. He was the first human to converse with them. The tiny creatures were a trove of wisdom that Rudolf tapped daily. From the description of the Eulesängers, Rudolf drew a map of the Sweeter Realm. It was the first of its kind on either side of the portal. The map has passed through the generations since Rudolf, to me. Some Swan Knights have continued the work of Rudolf, adding and amending based on the descriptions of the creatures of the Sweeter Realm. I have included it here, tucked against the binding of this book. It will never serve me as I had planned. I hope it will be useful to the Swan Knight who discovers this.

Rudolf felt more attached to the Queen's realm than to his father's. He stared at his map and dreamed of riding across the borders of the many lands of the Sweeter Realm. The Eulesänger language is extensive and descriptive. The vocabulary is massive and colorful. To those who understand it, a good description in the Eulesänger language could place a more vivid memory in the mind than firsthand experience. Their descriptions to Rudolf painted a picture infinitely clearer than any other language could hope to paint.

Although they are deeply rooted to their homeland, the Eulesängers are travelers. There is little of the Sweeter Realm they have not seen or been told about by their rich oral tradition. When Rudolf closed his eyes and conjured the images planted by his little friends, he was there, in the Sweeter Realm, flying with the Eulesängers or riding alongside them on a Unicorn. His map was drawn more as firsthand memory of the experiences placed into his imagination by his little friends than as a translation from the experiences of others.

Rudolf had little time to regret the attention not given to him by his parents or The Ancient One. The valley had never seen a more industriously studious Swan Knight trainee. He was not particularly athletic. His skills with weapons could not compare with his brother's. But he understood the portal and its creatures. He could sense the power of the Grail coming through the portal each time he opened it. The Holy Grail — the purpose of the portal, of the Swan Knighthood, spoke to Rudolf like it had spoken to no other since Parsifal. He could hear it, humming to him under the crackle of the portal. But its behavior for Rudolf was not peculiar. Rudolf's special relationship with the portal came only in the silent and invisible feelings he had when he opened it. The crackle sound spoke to him in a language he could almost piece together as conversation. He knew what it said to him, though he could not have translated it. His attempts to describe the sensation to the swan were ignored. But his brother did not ignore him. Ludwig, who had been taught to seek knowledge and improvement, listened to Rudolf and tried to learn from his descriptions of the experience.

Rudolf spent most of his time in front of the open portal, listening to its sounds and trying to interpret the language that he swore it was trying to speak to him. He loved The Ancient One. He loved the Queen's subjects who visited him from the Sweeter Realm. He loved the valley and the lodge. But it was all about the portal. It was the portal that he held dearest to his heart — the portal and the Grail that he keenly sensed through it.

Ludwig, the First-in-Training, grew into a good man, much humbler than his childhood nurturing and all of the praise and attention might indicate. Amid all of the praise for all of his wonderful talents and gifts, he still admired his younger brother. He was proud of Rudolf, admired his unique abilities, and gave him the encouragement that even the wise old swan failed to give. It seems that Ludwig was the only person, other than Rudolf, not dumbfounded by his own fine merits and not caught up in the hysteria of Elsa's second coming. What might have appeared as showing off to an ignorant spectator, as

Ludwig put his abilities on display, was simply practice and preparation to Ludwig, and a desire to perfect his skills, driven primarily by his deep understanding of his responsibilities.

When Ludwig was twenty-three years old, he received an invitation to a combat tournament in Nürnberg. Ludwig viewed the tournament as he viewed every moment of his life — as an opportunity to sharpen his skills and prepare himself for the duties that awaited him. The Ancient One wanted to go with him and watch the certain victory. But the Swan Knight was not in the valley and the swan felt the need to remain in his absence. Ludwig spoke for Rudolf, assuring all that the valley would be safe in his capable hands. None but Ludwig, not even Rudolf, truly believed the compliment. But The Ancient One wanted desperately to see the tournament. Although at first he refused Ludwig's offer for Rudolf to keep the Portal Valley while he traveled to Nürnberg, The Ancient One followed the First-in-Training to the tournament and watched with his proud, keen eyes, from the top of a distant tree.

On the evening before the competition began, the competitors excited the spectators with an exhibition of their skills. Ludwig captivated the audience at the tournament. He rode across the arena, standing on the back of his horse, flinging, twirling, and swinging his axe. He drew his sword and manipulated one weapon with the other. He appeared godly to the crowd, like a figure pulled straight from the legends, appearing in full mythical form right before their eyes.

His attention was drawn from his performance by the sight of a woman in the crowd. It was not her beauty that drew him in. It was the look of adoration in her face as she stared at him. Many eyes had admired him since his early childhood. But her eyes somehow saw deeper, to the goodness behind the athletic spectacle. The Ancient One noticed the woman's infatuation before Ludwig did. She clearly fell in love at first sight. Her penetrating gaze caught and kept Ludwig's eye. Just as he winked at her, he nicked himself in the ear with his swinging axe. He fell from his horse, tossing his axe high into the air. He fell flat on his back and his axe spun downward toward his head. A collective gasp came from the crowd. Ludwig caught the axe by the handle, with the blade almost touching his nose. He sprang to his feet and took a long, low bow for the ecstatic audience. Ludwig's Swan Knight training elevated him far above and beyond all other competitors in the tournament. The skills exhibition made that abundantly clear to all who witnessed it. Combat started the next day. Ludwig was the obvious favorite.

The Duke could not attend, but he had his entire duchy in a frenzy of excitement about the tournament. Ludwig competed for the enjoyment of it and to sharpen his skills in a safe setting. His only ambition in the tournament was to return to the valley better prepared to be the Swan Knight. He enjoyed exhibiting his skills, but not for the glory of it. For Ludwig, it was fun. Standing on the backs of horses, swinging his weapons, allowing his imagination to place his skills in the heat of holy battle was fun. He enjoyed it and he enjoyed bringing pleasure to others.

For many of the other competitors, much more was at stake. Ludwig's impressive display during the exhibition made him some enemies. During the evening before combat, Ludwig found the young woman who caught his attention and nearly cost him his skull. The young couple spoke openly and warmly over drinks and a crackling fire that reminded Ludwig of the portal sound when it has sat open for a long time. Ludwig did not fall instantly in love, as she did, but he could not help but think to himself that her open heart, her sincerity, and her beauty would make a fine addition to the family story he learned when he was nine.

While Ludwig was with the young woman, one of the other competitors sabotaged his equipment. Between the potential wife who had taken his attention and the excitement of the tournament, Ludwig forgot to inspect his equipment, as he was trained to do. In the first round of combat, he could not draw his sword. While he yanked on the handle, his opponent advance on him and ran his sword through Ludwig's neck, precisely and intentionally in the narrow space between Ludwig's beast plate and his helmet. The Ancient One watched in silent horror from his perch atop a distant tree. The most talented and promising young Swan Knight since Elsa dropped to his knees, gasping for air. He fell flat on his face and died.

The competitor was disqualified for violating the rules. He was not arrested for the murder. The officials were terrified of the Duke's revenge. So they reported the death as an accident of tournament combat. Such deaths were not rare. But the precision of the deadly strike and the murderer's calculated approach added to the suspicious malfunction with Ludwig's equipment to leave little doubt in the minds of those in attendance that the son of Duke Ludwig II of Bavaria was murdered. The tournament officials investigated the tampering of Ludwig's equipment. His sword was coated in tree sap to delay his draw. They determined that the murderer's first and only strike was intended to kill. The false story would have been the only news to reach the ears of the Duke if the truth had not flown away on the wings of the family's faithful and eternal servant.

The Ancient One flew back toward Linderhof before Ludwig's body was removed from the arena. In a flight he would usually make quickly and easily, he stopped several times, too sickened, too weak to continue. He delivered the news to Rudolf. Rudolf was sixteen years old. He rode without rest to Landshut to inform his parents. Ludwig was only six when his father married Matilda of Habsburg. Matilda loved the slain Ludwig, and Ludwig loved her. The Duke had already begun crafting a shield in tribute to his son's victory at the tournament in Nürnberg. It was to adorn the main hall of the palace in Landshut. He was working on the trophy when Rudolf arrived with the devastating news. For decades, The Ancient One relived the thrust of that treacherous sword in recurring nightmares. Sometimes he saw it from his vantage point atop the tree. Sometimes he was Ludwig. Sometimes he was the murderer. When he woke from the latter, he usually hid away for hours cleaning himself, trying to wash the dream from his feathers.

After the death of his son, Duke Ludwig II lost interest in life. He rarely left the palace in Landshut. His only joy came in the presence of his youngest child. He thought that if he raised young Ludwig exactly as his half-brother was raised, he could revive his lost son in the body of his namesake. Although Rudolf had accomplished things that no Swan Knight, or even The Ancient One, had accomplished, young Ludwig received all of the attention that Rudolf should have inherited upon the death of his brother. Young Ludwig was eight years old when his brother died at the tournament. His sister Agnes was deep into courtship with Heinrich of Hesse. They married two moths after the murder. Agnes would not join Rudolf as Second. Anna had already committed to the church and joined the convent the same week as her sister's wedding. Anna did not join Rudolf. Less than a year after Ludwig's murder, young Ludwig entered the valley and began his training, not as Second behind Rudolf, but as the only focus of the old teacher, whose desire to replace the lost Ludwig with his namesake was as fiercely consuming as the Duke's. The Ancient One was impatient. He wanted to turn young Ludwig into his brother overnight. His desperation allowed no diversion of his efforts from Ludwig to Rudolf, the First-in-Training. Without thought, he often referred to young Ludwig as "the next Swan Knight".

As Ludwig grew to look more like Rudolf than like the slain Ludwig, the Duke's dream of replacing his lost son dissolved before his eyes. This was compounded by the quick realization that the younger Ludwig bore none of his oldest brother's natural abilies and none of his noble character. The Duke grew sicker every month. In 1294, when Ludwig was a clumsy twelve-year-old, nothing like his oldest brother, and Rudolf had gained skills beyond the understanding of the Duke or the teacher, Duke Ludwig II of Bavaria died of his broken heart. The Ancient One began preparations to administer the oath to young Ludwig, when he reminded himself that Rudolf, not Ludwig, is the new Swan Knight. Only when he rehearsed the ceremony in his head, with Ludwig standing center and Rudolf standing near in support, as he recited the Laws of Ermenrich, did the old swan realize his mistake. It was only at the ceremony, when the largest attendance of Eulesängers ever to gather at the portal came to pay respects to the new Swan Knight, that The Ancient One came to understand and respect Rudolf. The Eulesängers sang to Rudolf and he sang back. The Ancient One knew the fundamentals of the language.

Rudolf spoke far above his head. The teacher felt like a child who had wandered into a symposium of scholars. In his eyes, Rudolf transformed in an instant from the figure of a child to a man as mysterious as he was gifted.

The swan knew enough to translate the gist of the conversation. Rudolf sang of the Sweeter Realm in such clear and vivid language that the old teacher thought that Rudolf had passed through the portal. As the new Swan Knight continued, and sang about distances and heights he could never have seen personally, The Ancient One realized Rudolf's greatness. His guilt reminded him of his failures with Elisabeth while he obsessed over Brunhilde. He shook his head and lowered it nearly to the ground in shame. He looked at Ludwig, who stood jealously in attendance — Ludwig, whose grasp of his own language was elementary at best.

It was not until Ludwig leaned toward the swan and said, "Maybe he will die in a tournament. I will be Swan Knight and things will be set right", that The Ancient One felt the full weight of his failure.

He suddenly saw in the new Swan Knight all of the goodness in his noble blood. He saw the humility of Parsifal, the loyalty of Cunrad, the talent of Elsa, and the intelligence of Elisabeth. His newfound admiration for Rudolf struck his heart forcefully from one side, while his disgust and disappointment in Ludwig struck it from the other. The pain was acute.

By sunrise the next day, Ludwig was relegated to Second-in-Training, in all respects. The decline from his previous heights was severe. Rudolf was the Swan Knight. And when he had children, they would become First and Second. Ludwig would be a minor portal servant at best, and his own children would be forced by law to remain ignorant of the portal. All respect, all reverence and attention due to the title were bestowed on Rudolf by The Ancient One, who boldly declared himself a servant to the new Swan Knight. Ludwig's jealousy swelled to consume his every thought. He had one goal — to remove Rudolf from Linderhof and his title as the Swan Knight and as the Duke of Bavaria.

Rudolf could not linger after the oath ceremony. He had to hurry to Landshut to pay respect to his father and to assume the dukedom in a lavish ceremony utterly unbefitting his humble spirit. In Rudolf's absence, The Ancient One tried to resume Ludwig's training as he had left it. But his disgust in himself and in his pupil was evident. Unsatisfied with life as Second in the valley, Ludwig turned his ambitions to the political arena. He quit his training with the swan and spent his time making the political connections necessary to eventually usurp his brother. Of all of Ludwig's ambitions, it was the respect and obedience of The Ancient One that he most desperately wanted to strip from Rudolf.

Rudolf was not blind to his brother's ambitions. Ludwig did nothing to hide them. In September of the same year, just seven months after becoming Duke and Swan Knight, Rudolf made a political move of his own. He married Mechtild, the daughter of King Adolf of Germany. Rudolf and Mechtild had met once, only briefly, as young teenagers. In that brief meeting, Rudolf whistled an Eulesänger lullaby to her. She responded to the song with such gentle enthusiasm that he considered her immediately as someone he could marry and share his extraordinary life with. For some time afterward, he thought of her and imagined her with him. She did the same. He thought of her again when an advantageous political marriage became a necessity. He sided with her father in the King's conflict with Albert of Austria. As payment, King Adolf gave the hand of Mechtild. By the time they stood at the altar, Rudolf and Mechtild did not view their union as a political agreement. They recalled their lone meeting of their youth. Rudolf admitted to imagining her as his wife when he was a teenager. She surprised him by confessing the same. At the altar, they renewed the romantic sentiments of their youth.

As a tribute to his fallen brother, Rudolf married Mechtild in Nürnberg, including in his vow to his wife a request for his dead brother's blessing. After the wedding, Rudolf wasted no time introducing his bride to the extent of his peculiar existence. After one night in Nürnberg, they were on the road. They dismissed all attendants and rested little until they arrived at the lodge. They received no grand reception. This was not because the creatures did not care to celebrate Rudolf's marriage and Mechtild's introduction to the valley and its wonders. After focusing his attention where it belonged, on Rudolf, The Ancient One came to understand the Swan Knight and what he liked. He collected humble gifts from the various breeds of the Sweeter Realm and arranged them neatly on the chest in the Swan Knight's sleeping chamber in the lodge.

When Rudolf and Mechtild approached the valley, the swan summoned to the lodge the eighteen Unicorns and eighteen Zweigwesens he had brought into the valley for patrols before Rudolf left for Nürnberg, a large number to be in the valley at once. They filed into two lines, forming a corridor of shiny, spiraling horns leading to the door of the lodge. On the shoulders of each Unicorn stood a Zweigwesen. This was not intended to add grandeur to the homecoming. Nor was it to impress Mechtild. It was simply designed to let the Swan Knight know that the valley was well guarded so that he and his wife could relax and enjoy each other's company in the solitude that The Ancient One knew his master would want. The only other creatures in the valley were a chorus of four Eulesängers, stationed in the main hall of the lodge, to sing to and with the newlyweds.

Ludwig was twelve years old when Rudolf and Mechtild married. His mother gave him the freedom of a full-grown man. Ludwig roamed Bavaria as he wished. He came in and out of the valley as he desired. Before Rudolf's wedding, The Ancient One ordered Ludwig from Linderhof, to Landhut or Munich, or even to Heidelberg, the seat of the Palatinate on the Rhine. He told Ludwig to go anywhere, be anywhere but in the valley when his brother returns with his wife. At midday, on Rudolf and Mechtild's second day in the valley together, Ludwig rode into Linderhof. The Eulesängers were in the dining room with the newlyweds, serenading a late breakfast. Ludwig noisily entered the lodge. He yelled for his brother until he found them in the dining room. He took a piece of bread from Mechtild's plate and ate it. Rudolf and Mechtild silently stared at the boy until he finally swallowed the bread. The newlyweds rose from their seats. Rudolf began an introduction of his wife to his brother. Ludwig walked away, out of the lodge and toward the portal point, before Rudolf could mention his wife's name.

Ludwig walked briskly up the hill and opened the portal. He yelled for The Ancient One demanding to see him. At the opening of the portal, the swan came through, expecting to see Rudolf and Mechtild. He was furious when he saw Ludwig instead. Rudolf excused himself from his wife's table and joined his brother at the portal just in time to hear The Ancient One berating Ludwig for his selfishness.

"How dare you scold me, bird." Ludwig belligerently retorted. "When I am Swan Knight, I will banish you from our world forever."

Rudolf did not allow his brother to continue. Nor did he give time for The Ancient One to respond. He was not nearly as offended by the interruption of his breakfast, or by the theft of his wife's bread from under her nose. But he would not stand and listen to the spoiled child speak to The Ancient One in this way. The feathers that had caressed every Swan Knight since the beginning puffed and ruffled in anger. The sight infuriated Rudolf.

He screamed at his brother with a ferocity never before seen in him, "This valley is his, much more than it is yours, or mine. It will be his concern long after you are dead, little boy! Get out! Go to your palaces! Go, let the world spoil you somewhere else."

He calmed slightly, took a few deep breaths, and continued, "When you are wiser, when you are humbler, come back here and I am sure that our noble friend will accept your apology."

"Apologize to this animal? It is he who owes me the apology."

The Ancient One was not offended by this last remark. He realized that there was truth in it. He had done wrong by young Ludwig, not for taking his attention away and putting it toward Rudolf, where it belonged, but for misplacing it in the first place. He knew that he bore his share of responsibility for the display of behavior at the portal that day. He looked Ludwig in the eyes and opened his beak. Ludwig shifted and clinched his body as he prepared his rebuttal for whatever the swan might say.

The Ancient One simply said, "I am sorry for the harm I have caused you."

He maintained eye contact with Ludwig long enough to see the confusion in his eyes, followed by the gradual relaxation of his angrily held posture. The Ancient One tilted his head and looked at Ludwig with a blend of love and pity. He turned to Rudolf, bowed low to him, and walked slowly through the portal.

Once the swan was gone, Rudolf turned to Ludwig and whispered deep and low through his grinding teeth, "Get out."

The unexpected apology and loving look of his teacher combined with the bold and defiant confidence of the Swan Knight to soften Ludwig's anger enough to allow a little understanding into his young and greedy heart. He mounted his horse and rode from the valley with more humility than had ever gathered inside of him in his entire young life. It did not last. His selfish, proud heart soon swelled with indignation at the day's proceedings. He recommitted to his desires and efforts to usurp his brother and assume the titles and possessions he believed were rightfully his.

Three years after the wedding, Mechtild and Rudolf had a son. They named him Ludwig, not after his spoiled uncle, or after his often-neglectful grandfather, but after his great-great-grandfather, Ludwig I, Duke of Bavaria, the crusader who sacrificed his heart's greatest desires to secure the portal. Rudolf was much like Ludwig, the Crusader. He too would have preferred wiling away his hours in Linderhof valley, singing with the Eulesängers and perfecting the details of his map of the Sweeter Realm. Had his tenure presented the same challenges as Ludwig I's, he would have made the same decisions. But

Rudolf's time as the Swan Knight and Duke of Bavaria offered different perils, not from continental conflicts or the crossing of foreign armies on his lands. His perils came from much nearer. His own Hapsburg mother, still hovering over Landshut like a dark cloud that no wind can blow away, set herself against him. As tensions rose between Rudolf and his brother, they rose in direct proportion with his mother. Although he saw no arrant signs of treason — of his mother and brother's political maneuverings to pull him from power and elevate Ludwig in his place — the smell of betrayal was pungent in the air, especially in the political centers of the duchy.

This is why the birth of a strong son was so important. Despite the internal politics that needed Rudolf's attention, he provided his new son what was not provided for him when he was young, the attention of his parents. Perhaps Rudolf would have fared better with the likes of Ludmilla or Agnes as his spouse. Their political shrewdness would have served Rudolf, the dukedom, and the valley well when they were desperate for such skills. Mechtild had the purest of hearts, loving, sincere, pious and true, but naïve. Neither the Swan Knight nor his wife spent the time necessary in the political centers, subduing the waves of dissent spawned and perpetuated by Matilda and her youngest son. Instead, Rudolf focused on teaching his child how to be a wise leader. Mechtild taught him to be selfless and righteous. The Ancient One taught him to be a stout Swan Knight. And young Ludwig's lessons began early. The Ancient One sensed the dangers facing the Swan Knight. He suggested that lessons with Ludwig begin as soon as the child could walk. So, they did. Ludwig opened the portal when he was not yet one year old.

Rudolf needed to find that balance between planning for the success of posterity and tending to the needs of the immediate. He focused too much on his son and allowed the dangers encircling him to grow and close upon him. His thoughts were too far into the future. He believed that the dangers would be his son's not his own. So, he bent every thought around strengthening his son's position. Three years after Ludwig was born, Rudolf and Mechtild had another son. They named him Adolf. Both boys were strong. Rudolf's death would not pass the knighthood or the dukedom to his brother. The laws of Bavaria and the Laws of Ermenrich were on the side of Rudolf's children. This was not acceptable to Rudolf's mother, who still mourned the murder of her stepson, and who blindly placed all of the slain man's merits into his undeserving half-brother and namesake. Matilda often said that she would not be allowed to enter heaven unless she saw Ludwig replace Rudolf as Duke of Bavaria. At this point, she cared little for the Swan Knighthood. She never went to the valley. One might have thought that she had entirely forgotten that facet of the family legacy. Her youngest son, however, did not. He wanted control of the portal. He wanted despotic command over The Ancient One and the creatures who loved his brother.

CHAPTER 16

The Schism

IN 1301, Matilda's years of political maneuverings paid off. She used her Hapsburg influence to appoint Ludwig as regent over Rudolf's territories. The move started a civil war in Bavaria. The war between Rudolf and Ludwig was personal and political. Political land and titles were at stake, but Rudolf knew the real motivations. Ludwig wanted to be the Swan Knight. Rudolf would have yielded the title if he did not fear his little brother's character. The burden of responsibility weighed heavily on him. That is both the reason he would have gladly passed it on and the reason he would not pass it to his brother.

Ludwig's power formed around Landshut. Rudolf and Mechtild focused their power around Heidelberg. In doing so, they yielded large swaths of Bavarian land to Ludwig. With all of the political and military support for Ludwig, securing the Palatinate on the Rhine and digging in there was the only option for the Swan Knight and his family. Although Rudolf was still the Swan Knight, Linderhof was under Ludwig's control. But this was a conflict between armies, to be played out on the battlefields. Rudolf still traveled freely to Linderhof. Rudolf believed the entire affair to be the political desires of his mother, with only the political titles in dispute. The children were not a part of the war. Rudolf was safe to leave his children in Linderhof, under the care and tutelage of The Ancient One, without threat from their uncle — so he believed.

Early in 1311, young Ludwig was alone in the valley with The Ancient One. The younger children were with their mother in Heidelberg, including Adolf, who at ten years old, was a year and a half into his Swan Knight training. Rudolf had two more sons, a three-year-old boy named Rudolf and a one-year-old boy named Rupert. Ludwig was thirteen years old and had been training for twelve of them. One cold February evening, The Ancient asked Ludwig to open the portal and let him home for the night. He had to report the latest in the Wittelsbach turmoil to the Queen. He asked young Ludwig to rise at dawn and open the portal. He would be waiting for him at his nest. Usually several Unicorns would be patrolling the perimeter of the valley. But Ludwig was thirteen and feeling quite confident in his skills. He feared the exposure of the portal more than he feared his uncle's treachery.

When he let The Ancient One through the portal, he ordered the Unicorns home to their families. One insisted on staying behind. Ludwig allowed it but ordered her deep into the woods. When the portal closed, leaving Ludwig alone in the valley, he felt a tremendous sense of satisfaction. The portal was his alone to protect. It opened and closed by his presence alone. Ludwig had a tendency to slip into flights of fancy. His imagination was as strong as his young limbs and would take control of his mind. On that night, when he was alone in the valley, with only a single Unicorn circling the distant perimeter of the valley, he mounted his horse, drew his sword, and rode around the heart of the valley, daring danger to approach. His imagination took him into the midst of the battles of the valley, those romanticized stories taught to him by the swan.

He rode fiercely, swinging his sword above his head, yelling, "I am the Swan Knight! I fight for God. Do your worst."

The Unicorn disobeyed her order. She stood near the edge of the woods and laughed at the foolish adolescent spectacle. When Ludwig finally went into the lodge for the night, the Unicorn patrolled the outer perimeter as ordered. The mock battle must have tired the First-in-Training. Within moments of Ludwig entering the lodge, the lamps were out and the lodge was still.

Late into the night, the Unicorn was on the far side of the valley from the portal point. She heard Ludwig yelling in terror. She rushed to him. When she cleared the forest, she saw two men, with swords drawn, chasing Ludwig out of the lodge. Ludwig ran from the lodge to the portal point. The men caught him just as he opened the portal. One grabbed him by his nightshirt and spun him around to face the intruders, while the other drove his sword through the boy's heart. The Unicorn ran at full sprint. She arrived behind the men as they withdrew the sword from Ludwig's chest and released the grip of his shirt. The men watched in satisfaction as Ludwig fell to the ground, only then realizing that they stood between a large whole in the air and a furious Unicorn. In his surprise, the man holding the weapon that killed the son of Rudolf dropped his sword. The Unicorn immediately impaled the man through the neck with her horn. The other man swung his sword at the Unicorn. She parried the swing with her horn.

The Ancient One flew through the portal and tended to Ludwig. When he saw that the boy was dead, he attacked the remaining murderer, flying at his face and pecking at his eyes. The man landed a blow from his fist on the bird's back, driving him to the ground with a deep and hollow thud. As the man turned his attention back to the Unicorn, two more Unicorns came through the portal. They drove their horns into the man's back, touching them together inside of him. The Unicorn who had been in the valley with Ludwig pierced the man's chest from the front and united her horn to the others. The three beasts lifted the man as high into the air as their extended necks allowed. They held him there as he struggled for breath.

The Ancient One recovered to his feet and asked the dying man, "Who sent you? Was it Ludwig, the Duke's brother?"

When the man opened his mouth, the only thing that came from it was a bubble of blood. He looked down and watched his own blood flow down the furious face of the Unicorn in front of him.

The Ancient One yelled, "Tell me!"

The man opened his mouth again, but nothing came out. His writhing limbs went limp. His head dropped. He was dead. The Unicorns, whose horns connected them to the thoughts of the man, knew that he was hired to kill two young boys, ages thirteen and ten, named Ludwig and Adolf. The man did not know who was behind the assassination. Payment was left for the murderers at their home, along with directions to Linderhof. The Unicorns lowered their heads and the man's body fell to the ground, landing beside the lifeless body of the Swan Knight's oldest son. The Unicorns reported their knowledge to the swan. It had to be Ludwig, Rudolf's brother.

"How dare he?", the bruised and enraged old bird growled through his clenched beak, "How dare he kill his brother's son? How dare he send strange men... killers, into Parsifal's Valley and expose the portal?"

By the time Rudolf returned to Linderhof, The Ancient One had decided not to tell him what the Unicorns discovered. Two men attacked the valley. Ludwig was killed in defense of the Grail. He was a holy hero. That is all that Rudolf's war-weary heart could take. The Ancient One bore the treacherous truth. It clawed and chewed at him inwardly.

Although details of his son's murder were never spoken of openly, Rudolf suspected his brother's involvement. He began to question his own fight to maintain power. His own son had been one of many terrible losses in the conflict. Rudolf lost the heart to continue. After the civil war had raged for twelve years, in 1313, less than two years after the murder of Rudolf's son, the brothers struck a peace treaty, splitting the titles held by their father. Ludwig took the Duchy of Bavaria from Rudolf and allowed him to maintain the Palatinate on the Rhine, of which Ludwig at the time had little interest. He banished Rudolf from Bavaria, from Linderhof, from the portal and the Eulesängers, and from The Ancient One, whose commitment to Rudolf was stronger than ever. Before he did, he demanded that Rudolf come to Linderhof one last time and stay long enough to renounce the Swan Knighthood in a ceremony that passed the oath to Ludwig.

Rudolf obeyed and participated in the ceremony nobly, as if it did not break his heart. Immediately after the ceremony, Ludwig ordered Rudolf from Linderhof. Before he left, The Ancient One privately confessed to Rudolf that he still considered, and would always consider Rudolf the rightful Swan Knight. Rudolf stood near the portal, on the spot where his son took his last breath. At the moment that the oath completed and the Swan Knighthood passed from Rudolf to Ludwig, Ludwig turned on his heels toward the lodge — his lodge — and marched down the slope.

As he triumphantly and ceremoniously processed to the lodge, he shouted over his shoulder to his brother, "You are no longer needed here. Leave Bavaria forever."

The Ancient One fluffed with indignation. During Ludwig's march down the hill, the old sage hatched a plan. He stretched his long neck toward Rudolf.

"Teach your oldest two children the family history, according to the Laws of Ermenrich," the swan whispered, "I will send you help. We will train them far from here if we must, for the day that they regain their rightful place."

The Ancient One did not need Brunhilde's talents to read the coldness and cruelty in Ludwig's heart. He knew that Ludwig was behind his own nephew's murder. He dreaded what dark times must come under his leadership. Rudolf agreed to the swan's plan. He left Linderhof to dissolve what little remained of his household in Landshut and solidify his position in Heidelberg. The Ancient One remained in his home, appeasing the false Swan Knight and protecting the portal from what disasters Ludwig's reign might bring.

Since Ludwig's first child was still in the womb and The Ancient One had no child to teach, he asked for a leave of absence. Ludwig opened the portal, ordered the bird home with taunting scorn in his voice.

He told the old teacher, "I will beckon you when you are needed. Until then, you do not belong in my valley."

With that impertinent dictate, The Ancient One returned to the Sweeter Realm and began making plans to train the children of Rudolf. When word spread throughout the Land and Shallow Waters, thousands of creatures volunteered to help in any way they could. But there was one clan of creatures the old swan absolutely needed, a dangerous breed with a violent past. The plan to train the children of Rudolf could not proceed without them. The other creatures referred to them as the Wühlenvogels. They are birds, with long necks and the snouts of wolves and jaws just as powerful, teeth just as sharp. They stand just shorter than The Ancient One. They have two hard, curled horns on their heads, which they use, with the powerful swing of their long necks, to smash the skulls of their enemies. They have large, clawed feet, which they use to burrow into the homes and hideaways they make underground. They have long powerful tails that can wrap and squeeze, with amazing dexterity and strength, whatever they choose to grab. They live in large underground cities, which they burrow with their collective efforts in a few days' time. They are hunters, predators. They can fly quickly across the sky, run along the forest floor with the speed of a Unicorn, and disappear into the ground in a flash. They wrap their prey with their powerful tails and drag them through their holes in the ground, into their underground cities. Larger or tougher prey, they slam in the head with their horns, rendering them unconscious.

For thousands of years, they were quiet, subtle, killing no more than they needed. Fear of them existed only in the nightmares of the young, perpetuated by exaggerated tales and childhood legends. About two thousand years ago, a community of Scheriers, who both build homes above ground and burrowed them beneath, discovered a Wühlenvogel city. The Wühlenvogels, who cherished their secrecy above all, considered the accident an invasion. They declared war on the Scheriers. The Scheriers did not stand a chance. They were slaughtered by the thousands. Most fled into the homelands of other creatures. No place was safe from the Wühlenvogels.

The Queen tried to intervene. The fury of the Wühlenvogels could not be abated. The Scheriers tried to rally other breeds in their defense. But such was not the way in the Sweeter Realm. One day, when the Scheriers neared extinction, a Wühlenvogel accidentally burrowed into the bed of the Queen's Lake. Water rushed the Wühlenvogel city, killing all within. Tunnels connected every city to another. The weight of the lake pushed water through with little warning until the flood was inescapable. The Wühlenvogels faced devastation like they had never known. The Scheriers tried to help them. Despite their suffering, they felt great compassion for the pain of their enemy. They tried to barricade the torrents in the passages between cities, but too few of them survived the war.

Finally, the Queen intervened. She swam to the breach in the lake floor and plugged it with stones and sealed it with the sands at her command. The waters receded and the remaining cities were saved. The Wühlenvogels swore their allegiance to the Queen and offered her many wonderful gifts.

She refused them all, saying, "All I ask is that you end your war."

They immediately released all Scheriers in captivity and ended all raids. The Scheriers — the only other burrowing breed in the Sweeter Realm — committed all of their labor and resources to rebuilding the Wühlenvogel cities. The Wühlenvogels returned to their ancient ways, reclusive and peaceful. Nobody saw them and few spoke of them.

It was time for the silence of the Wühlenvogels to be broken. The Ancient One asked the Queen to redeem their allegiance by asking them to join him in his plan to train the children of Rudolf. The old swan and a team of Scheriers sought them out and found them. The Wühlenvogels were startled by the first communication with the Scheriers in almost two thousand years. But they honored their oath to the will of the Queen. Thirty Wühlenvogels answered the call and joined The Ancient One at his nest, where they met Unicorns and Zweigwesens, Eulesängers and Brunnens. Many of the breeds that refused to come to the aid of the Scheriers two thousand years earlier united to save the integrity of the Swan Knighthood. The Wühlenvogels did not learn German with the rest of the creatures of the Land and Shallow Waters. They remained hidden, as did the mysterious creatures of the Deep. Many Scheriers spoke the Wühlenvogel language. It was learned in captivity during the war, and taught to the children in school in the many centuries since. The Ancient One studied Wühlenvogel, as he did every other language spoken outside of the Deep. Communication between the thirty Wühlenvogel volunteers and the rest of the company was crude and clumsy, but they communicated and the Wühlenvogels were committed to the cause.

The Ancient One laid forth his plan. Rudolf's family lived in Heidelberg, to the north of the Black Forest. The forest would provide the seclusion needed to establish living quarters for the creatures who remained with Rudolf. The swan asked the Wühlenvogels to construct a villiage under the Black Forest. It would need to hold and hide about one dozen permanent resident volunteers. They were proud to put their unique skills on display, to earn the respect of both realms with their service. The Wühlenvogels observe only two holidays — one in recognition of the day that the Queen rescued them from the flood, the other in mournful observance of the day the Scherier discovered their city and sparked the devastating conflict. The former is a joyous celebration, with food and music. The latter is meant to remind them of their disastrous over-reaction and of the horrors of war. It is observed with fasting and meditation. The Wühlenvogels waited for almost two thousand years for an opportunity to make amends for the misery and death they caused, and unite with the rest of the realm in respect and good-humor. The plight of the Rightful Swan Knight provided the opportunity.

The Ancient One described the needs of the underground villiage — how many of which creatures would need residence there and what sort of security measures were required. Immediately upon The Ancient One's request, the Wühlenvogels huddled. They whispered. They argued. Finally, they agreed. They cleared a large section of the forest floor, just beneath the swan's nest, scratching away the grass and removing all debris. When they prepared a proper canvas for their art, they ran around the area in chaotic concert, jumping over each other, diving and rolling, and sculpting into the dirt their design for the city. When the swirling circus of Wühlenvogels finally settled, and they all stepped off of their drawing, a masterful sketch of their plan, in precise detail, laid on the forest floor, at the feet of the astonished and impressed volunteers. After they all recovered from what they had witnessed, and all compliments and congratulations were expressed, the company of different creatures, from different homelands, with different cultures, discussed the design.

A few changes were made, based on the needs of individual breeds. After those amendments were drawn into the design, The Ancient One halted all discussion.

"This is beautiful, my friends, truly beautiful, but this city could hold more than one hundred. How long will this take to build? This is a grand design, but we do not have generations to complete it. Can you start with something small, something quick?" he asked in the Wühlenvogel language.

The architects looked at each other with smiles and chuckles that they tried to hold in. They looked at each other, at their design on the forest floor, and at the swan, whispering and giggling until they erupted into full, united laughter. Some of the other creatures smiled awkwardly. Most just stared at them. When the roar of Wühlenvogel laughter came to a gradual murmur of giggles, one spoke up.

"We can build this city faster than you could fly over it. Thirty of us could build twice this in a day."

The swan's jaw dropped open, in mirror reflection of most of the Scheriers. None of the others understood the conversation, but through gestures, they pieced together the gist and shared in the swan's disbelief. The spectacle of astonishment prompted another eruption of Wühlenvogels laughter.

One of them grabbed a Scherier with its powerful tail, pulled the startled volunteer to its snout, gave the Scherier a long, slobbery kiss on the lips, and told him, "Just bring us there and take a quick nap. You will have your city before you wake."

"Just bring us there." Those words abrasively entered The Ancient One's head and scratched violently on the inside of the old bird's skull.

"How do I get them there?" he asked himself, silently and discreetly mouthing the words with his bright beak. "Ludwig has control of the portal. I cannot ask him to open it so I can parade a hundred creatures into the Black Forest to train his brother's children."

As the swan sank into deep contemplation on this concern, the Scheriers translated the Wühlenvogels' boast into German for the other creatures. None had any notion that the project would be completed so quickly, that the swan's plan could be so readily put into action. The exuberance of the company snapped The Ancient One from his thoughts. He settled the crowd and explained the dilemma, throwing a heavy pall over the company.

"We will need to know this shared language you speak with the others," one of the Wühlenvogels reminded the swan.

"It is the language of the Swan Knight and his people," the swan replied.

"Then we must know it before we begin. Teach it to us. Let us refine our plans to perfection. These things may happen while you resolve your dilemma."

The entire company watched as the panic left the swan's face, pushed from that stage by a gentle and confident smile. He had not imagined embarking on the plan so quickly until the Wühlenvogels' boast. He recommitted himself to a long and meticulously plotted scheme.

"You are right," he said in Wühlenvogel.

Then he announced loudly to the others, "The children of Rudolf will return to the portal someday, but it might take generations. We must plan to be in the Black Forest for a long time. Our plans must be precise, calculated and rehearsed. The slightest of errors could cost lives... and much more. We must be united in purpose, in details, and in language. Adolf is thirteen. He is already well trained. His brother Rudolf is only seven. Let us plan to be ready in two years, to train young Rudolf when he turns nine, in accordance with the law."

He dismissed the company to their homes, giving each specific responsibilities in preparation for their plan. The Ancient One retired to his nest with his primary concern to ponder — how to get the company through the portal and into the Black Forest with no risk to the Sweeter Realm, the Queen, or the Holy Grail.

The Wühlenvogels went into each creature's homeland and built under the ground exact replicas of their portion of the Black Forest city, so that each breed involved in the plan could adjust to their new home underground before leaving the Sweeter Realm. They each gave their suggestions for alterations. The alterations were made and altered again, until the design for the city was sculpted to perfection. This process was delayed by the Wühlenvogels' slow progress in learning German. They had been isolated from the other breeds for so long. Their minds were tightly bound to their own language. But they studied hard. Their leadership passed a law that the use of the Wühlenvogel language would be kept to a minimum. German became the language of their people and Wühlenvogel was only spoken as it was needed to advance their German. With each addition to their German vocabulary, the Wühlenvogels sewed one stitch to their hearts, binding them to the collective will of the Queen and her subjects. Wühlenvogels stayed as honored guests in the homes of Scheriers. They embraced their inclusion and became as social as any breed in the Sweeter Realm. Having never met a Swan Knight, never seen a human, they became as committed to Rudolf and his family as the Eulesängers who sang with him since his childhood and sang to him the images that Rudolf drew into his map. The Queen witnessed unity in her queendom, like she had never seen before.

As the new Duke of Bavaria, Ludwig settled quickly into the places and positions he had coveted for so long. His first child, a girl named Mathilde, was born in July of the same year. Three years later, when his first son was born, he opened the portal and recalled The Ancient One into service, not to continue with the service he had rendered for eight hundred years, not to begin the Swan Knight training with the eldest child of the reigning knight, but to assume guardianship of Mathilde so the Duke could dote on his son without the burden of a three-year-old daughter. The Ancient One gladly accepted the charge. The child's Grail Blood would allow him to open the portal and embark on his plans in the Black Forest. He gave a stern face to the Duke and advised against the order, knowing that his opinion meant nothing to the false Swan Knight. Ludwig left Mathilde at Linderhof. The Ancient One played with her, fed her, tended carefully to her needs, but raised her as a child, not a Swan Knight's child, all the while, plotting his use of the child's enchanted blood for the inauguration of a coup.

CHAPTER 17

The Exodus

EVERYTHING HAD BEEN IN PLACE for the swan's plans — everything except for his dilemma of how to open the portal and usher the company out of Linderhof and all the way to the Black Forest. For almost four years he waited, banished from the valley with no means of returning. Three weeks into his new duties as the child's guardian, he carried Mathilde to the portal point as she slept, opened the portal with her presence, laid her gently in the grass and slipped through the portal praying that the girl would not wake and walk through the portal herself, or walk away and strand him in the Sweeter Realm, leaving a three-year-old girl roaming the hills of Bavaria alone. His heart pounded as he rushed to Scherier land, far from the portal point. He told the Scheriers to gather the volunteers and meet at his nest in one week, in the middle of the night.

"If the portal opens, come through. I will be waiting for you on the other side. If it does not open, return to your homes but leave one in my nest to await news."

The Scheriers excitedly acknowledged the orders. The Ancient One rushed back to his nest and found the portal open as he left it. He flew through at top speed, fearing it would snap shut before he could squeeze into the valley. He had been gone for several hours. He made it through. On the other side, on the gentle grass of Linderhof, slept Mathilde, just as he had left her. He carried the child back to the lodge, singing her favorite lullaby.

The noble bird felt remorse for his use of the innocent child. But then he thought about Rudolf's slain son. He treated Mathilde well. He even began to love her. She was a sweet girl who missed her home and her family. The Ancient One was apparently the only one who cared about her. He took her in and treated her like his own. He did not think of her as the daughter of her father, but as the great-granddaughter of Otto II. He thought of her as a child of Parsifal. But this small manipulation of the child's trust was easily justified by what was at stake. Mathilde had not seen the portal, had not met the creatures. The swan wanted to keep it that way, at least until she was nine. On the designated night, he kept Mathilde up long past sunset. He let her sip from the stores of wine in the lodge. He held her, rocked her gently, and sang to her. She had never slept so soundly. At midnight, he carried the child to the portal point. As he walked with her, she began to snore. She rumbled like a man five times her size.

He giggled as he thought to himself, "To think, I was worried about waking her. It is the slumber of the forest that is in jeopardy."

He opened the portal with the sleeping Grail Blood. The Unicorns led the way, followed by representatives from the volunteers at the initial gathering at the nest. More than a thousand volunteers remained home. Many more wanted to serve the Rightful Swan Knight than could fit in the Wühlenvogels' design for the city. Each breed held an election. The best and bravest from each homeland in the Land and Shallow Waters joined the cause and walked through the portal that night. The swan hushed them all as they came through, silencing their exuberance.

He stepped through the portal and reminded the thousands of creatures who had come to bid farewell to their loved ones, "There is much for you to do here and in the valley. I will still need sentinels and patrols. Those who travel to Rudolf and serve the Rightful Swan Knight perform a noble duty. But there is nobility in the service of the Queen and nobility in the protection of the portal. Pray for our brave volunteers, but pray also for yourselves. Your task is no easier."

The remaining creatures scattered from The Ancient One's nest, toward their homes, with their heads held high and their hearts prepared for sacrifice.

By the time The Ancient One carried the girl back to the lodge, closing the portal behind her, the valley was filled with magnificent creatures. More than one hundred came through, yet the valley was silent except for the local sounds of the night. The Ancient One set Mathilde in her bed and joined the silent army. The ancient bird gave new meaning to swiftness. He led the company from Linderhof to the Black Forest, arriving in the safety of the woods before sunrise. The Unicorns carried the slower breeds on their backs. The Wühlenvogels gripped them with their tails and flew at amazing speed. Even if they had been seen by human eyes, the company would have flown by so rapidly, in and out of the senses in the briefest moment, that the peculiarity of their forms would have been difficult to grasp by the swiftest eyes. In silence and absolute obscurity, they settled in the heart of the Black Forest.

The Ancient One instructed the Wühlenvogels, "Bring them to the northern edge of the forest. Build your city as quickly as you can. Get them all underground before they are seen. I will return with instructions as soon as I can."

With only a few breaths of recovery from the hurried flight, The Ancient One took back to the sky and returned without rest to Linderhof. When he arrived, he found Mathilde in the lodge, taking advantage of his absence to annihilate the sweets that are usually given stingily. She apologized for taking the sweets.

He laughed and said, "Eat your sweets, my dear, then come take your nap with me."

He waddled into bed and fell soundly asleep. He awoke several hours later with the napping girl curled against him and crumbs of treats scattered over them both. He did it. He got the company to the Black Forest and returned undetected and without incident. He allowed himself to celebrate the unlikely victory for a few hours. After that, his self-congratulations wore off and he worried. He worried for his friends in the Black Forest. He worried about Rudolf and his children. He worried what new surprises might come from Duke Ludwig.

Four days after escorting the volunteers to the Black Forest, The Ancient One was startled from the lodge by the sound of galloping hooves. The Duke and his wife returned to Linderhof to claim their daughter. When Ludwig entered the valley, everything was exactly as he expected it, quiet, peaceful, with Mathilde and the old teacher playing games in the lodge.

"We are taking her for several weeks. We will bring her back when we are done with her," Ludwig told the swan, with no explanation and no specifics. "Stay here, on this side. Watch things until we get back. Tell me if my brother comes."

The Ancient One asked him, with a subtle snideness, too delicate for Ludwig's angry mind to detect, "Should you not summon some Unicorns and Zweigwesens to patrol and guard the valley?"

"No", Ludwig defensively retorted.

The Unicorns did not like and did not trust Ludwig. They hid their disdain poorly. Their icy, sneering glares at Ludwig, through their shaggy faces, from their piercing eyes, dissettled him. In fact, they had frightened him since his childhood.

"No", he repeated, slightly gathering his composure, "*you* must earn your keep. You can guard the valley alone."

The swan simply bowed and flew into the sky above the lodge. The Duke stayed for a few hours, eating and making a mess of the place. They mounted their horses and rode out of the valley.

Before they disappeared over the hill, Ludwig shouted back, "Clean up the lodge, will you?"

The Ancient One did not return to the ground. He circled the valley until Ludwig was out of sight. He turned his thoughts and his wings to the Black Forest. He did not fly with the urgency of the great expedition of volunteers. He arrived at the northern end of the Black Forest shortly after midnight. He flew into the woods, then landed and walked, looking for signs of his friends, for Wühlenvogel holes that would lead into the underground constructs. He called to his friends, walking gingerly and darting his sharp eyes in all directions. Suddenly, he felt himself grabbed and squeezed from beneath. In an instant, he was beneath the ground, in the grasp of a Wühlenvogel's tail, flying over the underground city. He allowed the Wühlenvogel to carry him, swooping high and low and pointing out some of his own proud constructions.

Finally, he reminded the creature, "I can fly. You can let me go now."

The Wühlenvogel hissed a giggle through his sharp teeth and released the swan from the grip of his tail. The Ancient One flew beside him and listened to him brag about the city, in a long tour that skipped over no details. The very last place in the city that the swan saw was his own lodgings. Atop a spire, in the corner of the city, sat a nest, a meticulous replica of his nest near the portal point, built with affection by the Scheriers. They knew the old nest well. They had spent many nights in it, waiting for the Swan Knights to open the portal.

The Wühlenvogel escorted the swan to his new nest and said, "Sleep. There will be much to do in the morning."

In the morning, The Ancient One visited the lodgings of each breed. He was delighted to see the integration of creatures. Although each breed had its own section of the city, designed specifically for their needs and comfort, the swan found Zweigwesens lodging in the Brunnen section, Wühlenvogels bunking with Scheriers, and rather comically, a Unicorn crammed into the main hall of the Eulesänger building. The Queen would have been proud to witness the unity. The city was fully and comfortably inhabited when The Ancient One inspected it. The Wühlenvogels continued working on details and the other creatures added their own contributions. It was a tremendous cavern, lit well with torches. It spanned almost one quarter of the Black Forest. The distance between the forest floor above and the floor of the city was so vast that the swan could fly far above the structures of the city without fear of scraping his back on the forest floor above him. Once he inspected the living quarters, he asked to be shown the entrances, exits, and security measures.

The city had thousands of entrances for the Wühlenvogels. They could squeeze through holes in the ground that were so small they could not be seen by a tall man looking down at them. These creatures, who stood almost as tall as the giant swan, flew at great speeds toward the ground and disappeared into holes so small that they could barely hold a child's finger. The ground around the tiny holes showed no signs of disturbance in their wake. More impressively, they could pull creatures of all sizes through the holes with them, grasped in the clutch of their powerful tails. The Wühlenvogels flew up from the city, through the holes, into the forest, and back through the holes into the city, without retarding their pace in the slightest. The holes were an amenity for use by the Wühlenvogels only. For the other creatures, the Wühlenvogels built entrances and exits, hidden behind foliage and between rocks, for them to stealthily enter and exit the city from the forest floor.

After approving enthusiastically of the entrances and exits, The Ancient One inspected the training facilities. Much of the Swan Knight training was to be conducted above, on the floor of the forest, but the Wühlenvogels built an impressive school and training facility in the city.

As impressive as the Wühlenvogel sketch was, on the ground beneath the swan's nest, the finished city was infinitely more impressive. It was time to put the city and the volunteers to their purpose and invite Rudolf and his family into their new valley. The Ancient One needed to return to Linderhof, in case Ludwig arrived and demanded his service. Ludwig must never know of the underground city. He must never know that the children of Rudolf were trained as Swan Knights. The Ancient One flew to Rudolf's castle in Heidelberg and perched himself on its highest tower. He watched and waited for Rudolf or Adolf. In the years between the peace treaty and the completion of the Wühlenvogel city, Rudolf and his family heard nothing from The Ancient One, nothing of the portal or its creatures. Rudolf waited, as the swan instructed him, for word from his old friend and teacher. Now it was the swan who waited for Rudolf.

For days he waited, until he finally saw Adolf ride from the castle, into the open fields on the other side of the river. The Ancient One met him in the fields.

"I knew you would come," Adolf said excitedly.

"We are ready for you," the swan replied.

"Who? Who is ready?"

The Ancient One remembered that all plans were made after Rudolf and his family left Linderhof. They knew nothing of the wonders that awaited them beneath the Black Forest.

The swan began to answer, but caught himself and simply replied, "There is too much to say. Come. Let me show you."

Adolf followed the swan south, into the northern edge of the Black Forest. Once they were fully under the cover of the forest, the swan instructed his student to dismount his horse and follow him on foot. Adolf obeyed without question. They walked together in silence for a few minutes before the swan stopped sharply, turned back to Adolf, and stomped one foot on the forest floor three times. Within seconds, a dozen Wühlenvogels flew out of the ground and into the forest air so quickly that Adolf could distinguish no physical characteristics of the creatures. They paused in the air for a second, then fell quickly to the forest floor, to stand in a circle surrounding Adolf and the swan.

"We have new friends, my boy," the old teacher said. "These are the Wühlenvogels, and they have committed themselves to your father and to you. They have built you a city, a magnificent city beneath the Black Forest."

Adolf looked down, to the dirt between his feet, trying to imagine a city beneath him. The swan exchanged glances with a few of the Wühlenvogels.

Then one of them asked, "Should we take him in his way or our way?"

The swan responded, "Take him in your way. I will go around to my entrance."

He turned to Adolf and warned him, "Don't be frightened, my boy. This will not hurt."

With that, the swan nodded to the nearest Wühlenvogel, who flew into the air, circled around picking up speed, and snatched Adolf off of his feet. He flew straight up, almost to the tops of the forest trees, turned upon himself and darted toward the forest floor, with Adolf dangling in tow. In a flash, Adolf and the

Wühlenvogel disappeared into one of the tiny holes in the ground. The Ancient One flew around to one of his designated entrances. Once in the city, he could hear Adolf hurrahing in exhilarated celebration, as the Wühlenvogel flew him through the streets of his city.

The Ancient One thought to himself, "Truly this boy was born to be a Swan Knight."

With his pupil, the oldest living child of the Rightful Swan Knight, in the Wühlenvogel city, in the company of the volunteers, The Ancient One could return to Linderhof. During his absence from the valley, Ludwig paid a visit. When the swan returned, he found a note on the door of the lodge.

It simply read, "I know where you have been. You have been in Heidelberg, with my brother. I am the Swan Knight. You serve me now."

In the writing, the old bird could sense all of the spoiled jealousy of Ludwig's youth. He waited in the valley for the cruel and jealous anger of Ludwig to reveal itself. He waited for three weeks. At the end of three weeks, Ludwig's army brushed the edge of the valley on its way to Heidelberg. Ludwig camped his army and rode alone into the valley. His old teacher met him at the door of the lodge.

Looking scornfully down at the swan, Ludwig shouted, "I am going to destroy my brother, then your loyalty will be mine."

Ludwig rode to the portal point, opened the portal, and ordered the old sage back to his home with a simple point of his finger. The Ancient One flew from the lodge, toward the portal, but flew over the portal, high into the air and out of the valley toward Heidelberg. He arrived in

Heidelberg well before Ludwig's army. His warning gave Rudolf time to prepare the city's formidable defenses. Heidelberg Castle is a daunting prospect for any attacking army. Rudolf dug in deeply and defended his city. Adolf remained in the hidden city, to preserve the line just in case his father should fail. By the time Ludwig arrived, a stalemate was the only available outcome. Lives were lost in Ludwig's siege on the Palatinate on the Rhine, but no ground was gained. The siege accomplished only two things. It separated Rudolf and his younger children from Adolf and the Black Forest city, and it weakened both brothers, jeopardizing the Wittlesbach hold on the region.

Ludwig was already in a power struggle with the Habsburgs of Austria. His mother's death in 1304 dissolved the familial connection between the families. The political gorge between the interests of the Hapsburg and those of the Wittelsbach was only briefly bridged by Duke Ludwig II's marriage to a Hapsburg. After her death, that bridge of kinship collapsed. Rudolf would not allow Ludwig to risk his family's control of Linderhof and the portal by weakening them both with a prolonged seige. In a measure of extreme personal sacrifice, he demonstrated his greatness by ending the conflict. For the security of the Grail, he yielded his lands and title of Count Palatine on the Rhine to his brother, with an agreement that he or his children would regain the title once Ludwig's conflict with the Habsburgs ended. Ludwig wanted victory over his brother. The agreement was the only way he would get it. Rudolf yielded Heidelberg and he fled with his family into the Black Forest, where they received a hero's welcome by the loyal volunteers in the Wühlenvogel city. In honor of the image of his lost brother, who he grossly misunderstood, his oldest brother Ludwig, who died at the tournament,

Ludwig took the title Ludwig IV, relegating the title "Ludwig III to the brother who did not live to hold it.

There was no keeping with the Laws of Ermenrich now. All of Rudolf's surviving children lived in the underground city, sharing it with strange and magnificent creatures. Adolf was seventeen. Young Rudolf was eleven. Rupert was eight, and Rudolf's youngest, Mathilde, was five. They all studied in the underground school, all learned the family history, and all trained as Swan Knights.

Much of the training occurred above ground. Despite the meticulously rehearsed drills, the children and the creatures were sometimes seen before they disappeared into the city. The Black Forest quickly developed a reputation for housing fantastic and mythical creatures. These reports attracted more adventurers and storytellers, which in turn caused more sightings. The region soon abounded with fairy tales about the Black Forest and its strange inhabitants. Some of the stories struck near the truth. Some resembled nothing to be found in the Wühlenvogel city or the Sweeter Realm. The Queen heard nothing of the fairy tales. The city was her greatest source of pride and blissful contemplation. She began calling it Einigkeitstadt (Unity City). Bleak as the situation was for the Swan Knight, the Queen had never been happier, never felt more accomplished. Her people were one, and the volunteers, in a strange world for a just and holy cause, were lauded as heroes in the Sweeter Realm.

Rudolf was not happy. He did not mourn the loss of his dukedom. He did not mourn the loss of his electorship in Heidelberg. He feared for the future of Linderhof. He feared for the safety of the Sweeter Realm and the Holy

Grail. Ludwig's greed and ambition weakened both brothers and placed the portal in jeopardy against the many eyes cast upon Bavaria. Rudolf's fear grew desperate. He considered taking his army of creatures from the Black Forest and capturing Linderhof by force. He had no doubt that the creatures could take and hold the valley from Ludwig's forces. But the spectacle would bring the entire world of men upon them. They could never hold out. All would be lost. Rudolf drenched himself in panicked sweat. Finally, The Ancient One remembered a story that Parsifal had told him, the story of a magical sword. The wielder carried the strength of one hundred soldiers. It was called Excalibur. The sword was older than the land itself. It resided somewhere in England.

The Ancient One regretted relaying Parsifal's stories when Rudolf left for England the next morning. He was so focused on the sword and his mission to retrieve it, he forgot to say goodbye to his family, a point mourned by the family, and knowing Rudolf, bitterly regretted by the Rightful Swan Knight. He convinced himself that, as an heir of Parsifal, on a holy quest, the sword would certainly find its way into his desperate hands. Rudolf died in England in 1319, having never found the mythical blade and never bid farewell to his family. He was only forty-four years old. His youngest child, Anna, was born after he left for England. Anna had Rudolf's eyes. She was the beacon that the family hoped would guide their father home. Anna died suddenly and without illness one hour before news of Rudolf's death reached the Black Forest. Mechtild lost her husband and child almost simultaneously. The tragic shock was destructive.

When word of Rudolf's death reached The Ancient One, he mourned deeply. But he knew that Rudolf's family and the legion of creatures living in Einigkeitstadt needed a sense of continuity to lift them from their tragic circumstances. Before Rudolf's memorial, The Ancient One administered the Swan Knight oath to Adolf. So much singing and cheering came from the desperate hearts of the city's inhabitants that it could surely be heard throughout the forest and most likely in the towns nearby. The children of Rudolf alternated in the telling of the family history, to the cheers and tears of the audience of creatures. Two days after the oath ceremony, Adolf, the Rightful Swan Knight, presided over a memorial for his father. They buried Anna in a grave in the center of the hidden city. The grave was inscribed with her name and Rudolf's. The celebration two days earlier gave the company the spiritual strength to endure the memorial and the desperate state of their cause.

Adolf's fiercely heroic figure inspired all. His deep voice echoed strongly off of the forest floor above them. They all had faith in him. He commanded their loyalty and their obedience as if Lohengrin himself had knighted him. Adolf said that they would prevail, that they would regain the portal, and that they would return to their homes as heroes in both worlds. Adolf said it. So, it was true. The line of Swan Knights survived vigorously beneath the Black Forest. It withered in Linderhof, on Ludwig's weak branch of the family. The Ancient One returned to the valley and taught the children of Ludwig — in the rare periods when they came to Linderhof and stayed long enough to be taught.

The teacher tried to delay the Swan Knight training of Ludwig's children. He taught them the history of their family, trying to omit everything that would seem extraordinary in their world, everything that might inspire them to embrace the knighthood. Ludwig cared nothing for the Laws of Ermenrich, nor was he interested in the education of his daughters. He wanted strong sons who could defeat the sons of Rudolf. The Ancient One reminded Ludwig that the greatest Swan Knight was a woman.

He responded, "My daughters are not Elsa."

The swan felt pity for Ludwig's daughters. They showed promise, much more than did his sons. Two months after Rudolf died, Ludwig's son Stefan was born. The Duke's older son, Ludwig, who called himself "Louis" in a forced French accent, was foolish and impetuous. From an early age, Stefan showed intelligence, frighteningly coupled with insatiable greed and a propensity for cruelty, much like his father. Louis was reckless, but much less dangerous than Stefan, whose skills at deception and manipulation revealed themselves shortly beyond infancy.

Duke Ludwig's obsession with defeating his brother only tightened its grip after Rudolf's death. Louis and Stefan spent increasing swaths of time in the valley. The Duke demanded progress beyond the natural abilities of the boys. It was not enough that his children become the next Swan Knights. He needed them to be the best Swan Knights, to legitimize his claim on the Swan Knighthood. He demanded that the teacher foster in the children some extraordinary ability that would serve as a sign to authenticate their claim of the Swan Knighthood. Ludwig had three daughters between Mathilde and Stefan, but all died young. Mathilde was sweet and loved her old teacher. In the few times she was brought to Linderhof, after Stefan came, The Ancient One saw signs of goodness in her that were entirely absent in her brothers. Mathilde would never make a great Swan Knight, but she would have made an excellent portal steward, and a much better Swan Knight than her brothers. She delighted in her visits to Linderhof and she always cried when she was taken away. The Ancient One regretted her departures. He thought about her early childhood, asleep in the grass outside the portal, or cuddled tightly against him with crumbs of her sweets scattered on and around them both.

Mathilde was a positive influence on her brothers. They were calmer, kinder, and more responsible when she was with them. She softened them somehow.

The swan often thought, "If they had her influence every day, they might have turned out alright."

None of the sweet and kind creatures who came through the portal could elicit the same changes in them. Most had been the targets of the boys' cruelty and spent as little time in their company as possible. To the casual viewer — which was Duke Ludwig's involvement at best — the chain of Swan Knights continued seamlessly through him and to his sons. In truth, The Ancient One passed to Ludwig's sons only what he thought would make them better people. His lessons were more philosophical than practical, and the boys had no palate for them.

Back in the Black Forest, the children of Rudolf — Adolf, Rudolf, Rupert, and Mathilde — received much more comprehensive and rigorous training. Adolf was the Swan Knight. But there was no First-in-Training. There was no Second. They had to bend the laws. Duke Ludwig wanted an end to his brother's line. The children were not safe outside of the Black Forest. So they all trained. They rode Unicorns. They flew with Wühlenvolgels (they learned how to straddle the tails of the beasts and steer them by the horns through the tiny holes that took them in and out of Einigkeitstadt). They excelled at mathematics, literature, philosophy, architecture, history, and religion, all taught to them in the underground classroom. When Rudolf yielded the Palatinate to his brother, he had no idea what a precious gift he gave his children. With no political titles or expectations to devour their time, with no need to travel anywhere, their schedule of education and training resembled that of the early Swan Knights, before they were shackled with royal responsibilities.

Only Adolf left the Black Forest. He knew that political connections must be maintained for the day when he or his children would resume the dukedom and control of the valley. He also knew that he must marry, which he did in 1320. He married Irmengard of Öttingen, the daughter of a Bavarian count. The marriage was strategic and the courtship brief. But Irmengard was a good woman. She was sixteen when they married. Adolf was twenty. They took a home in Öttingen until Adolf felt confident enough to take her into the Black Forest and expose his life to her. This took almost a year. They quickly grew close, but the Wühlenvolgel city was a precious and fragile secret. With no portal to escape to the Sweeter Realm, the lives of the city inhabitants were in the hands of the city's secrecy.

Adolf and Irmengard did not know each other well when they married. Her father wanted to sew his family to the Wittelsbach name and agreed to the marriage with little coaxing. Irmengard was attracted to Adolf, but her motivation for marriage was her loyalty to her father. It took months for the couple to truly feel comfortable in each other's confidence. Once they did, love rooted deeply. After Irmengard refused a demand from her father, infuriating him, simply to spend another hour with the husband she had come to adore, Adolf knew she was ready to learn the fantastic truths about his life.

The tales of bizarre creatures in the Black Forest, which had swirled around the region in increasing number, intrigued Irmengard. She had a fanciful imagination and a faith not rigidly caged by facts. While most disregarded the stories about the Black Forest, she believed them to be true, even before Adolf brought her there. The more fantastic the tale, the more inclined her blithe heart was to believe it. She was delighted beyond expression when her eyes authenticated her faith. Adolf and Irmengard arrived at the northeast edge of the forest, shortly before dusk. A particularly tall, dark-brown Unicorn greeted them as soon as the thickness of the forest blinded them to the world behind them. Irmengard tilted her head and slowly lifted a sweet, familial smile to the Unicorn, as if setting eyes on a long-absent lover. The Unicorn lowered his horn to touch it against Irmengard's chest and communicate its welcome. She caught the horn with both hands and stopped its decent. She pulled it to her face and pressed her lips against the side of the horn, near the tip, sinking her upper lip into a deep fold in the spiraling horn.

She closed her eyes and held the kiss. The Unicorn closed his eyes too. Adolf knew that the two had joined in deep and extensive communication. He stood perfectly still, patiently waiting and not wishing to disturb the connection. Irmengard's smile grew wider. Her face lit. Adolf watched the tension in her hands grow as she slowly tightened her two-handed grip on the horn, her lip still sunk into the recess of the spiral. The Unicorn's legs twitched as it ran through the memories of Irmengard's childhood. Adolf stared at his young wife in astonished admiration. No Swan Knight spouse had such an instant and profound connection with a Unicorn. At her first introduction to the fantastic lives of the Swan Knights, she displayed her suitableness for her new post.

Adolf thought, "Perhaps she is a distant cousin, with Grail Blood of her own, bequeathed to her through some lost line of the family."

Irmengard's heart found its home in the Black Forest. Since early childhood, she felt a mystical destiny pulling at her soul, sending her sweet heart a vague but demanding invitation to abandon the world around her and join it in another. Adolf opened the door of her destiny. Irmengard ran through without cajoling.

At the center of the Unicorn portion of Einigkeitstadt, the Wühlenvolgels built a replica of the ancient Unicorn altar that stands at the heart of the Unicorn capital in the Sweeter Realm. The altar is a tall stone obelisk in the shape of the horn of the greatest leader in Unicorn history. At its base is a circle of smaller stones, each with a horn-sized hole. The Unicorns insert their horns into the holes to connect in thought with each other and the spirits of their ancestors. Irmengard skipped quickly though the underground city, delighting at everything but stopping for nothing — until she saw the Unicorn connection ritual at the altar. She stood in tantalized captivation as she watched the last few Unicorns insert their horns into the stones and connect to the collective. Her tall brown Unicorn, who had accompanied her through her tour of the city, looked at her, kissed her head, and pulled away from her to join the connection.

Adolf gabbed at Irmengard's hand as she bolted toward the altar in pursuit of her friend. When his hand returned empty, he took a few slow steps toward her, whispering commands to return, terrified of disrupting the ancient ritual. Irmengard did not hear her husband's plea. Her focused heart would have muted the blast of a thousand trumpets. She ran to the altar and wrapped the stone obelisk with her soft arms, squeezing in a desperate embrace, driving the side of her face violently into the stone. She connected to the Unicorns, albeit weakly. In her later descriptions of the incident, she could not tell which of her visions were her own imagination and which were the memories and thoughts of the Unicorn collective.

With no idea how the Unicorns would react to the intrusion, Adolf watched in mortification from a distance. The Unicorns did not seem to notice her. They remained as still as before, with horns buried into the holes in the stones. The stillness and silence was broken by the shout of a young girl. The shout came from a Unicorn, a small grey and white Unicorn with its head low and its horn still in the stone. The voice was Irmengard's, Irmengard's childhood voice. The cry was a shout from Irmengard to her mother. The Unicorns so vividly lived her childhood that words from her youth erupted from the mouths of the connected Unicorns, beginning with the small white and grey Unicorn, and joined by another and another, until the entire collective shouted, in chaotic concert, scenes from Irmengard's life. The strangeness of the spectacle stole Adolf's strength. He fell to the floor, never breaking his focus on his young wife and the echoing sounds of her childhood voice from the shaggy, bearded faces of the Unicorn collective. Irmengard did not move. She did not speak. She remained as she was, embracing the stone altar — the corners of her lips lifted slowly by the memories that were being uprooted by the curious and probing Unicorns.

The sounds of Irmengard's youth died down and the Unicorns pulled away from the holes. Irmengard relaxed her embrace of the stone and slid down to lay curled against the base of the altar. Adolf sat still on the ground and watched his wife slowly lift her head. With tear-soaked cheeks, she scanned the circle of Unicorns around her, whispering a tender "Thank you" to each. From that point, all remnants of adolescence washed from Irmengard's heart and mind. She was quieter, more thoughtful. Not only did the Unicorns give her the benefit of reliving her childhood through older eyes. They passed much of their own wisdom to her. Her depth of understanding expanded profoundly in the moments she remained connected to the Unicorns, and in the days of silent contemplation that followed.

Irmengard saw no more of the city that day. The Unicorns walked away from the altar, toward Adolf. They each bowed to the Rightful Swan Knight and congratulated him on the goodness and open-heartedness of his new wife. Adolf just sat where he was and nodded to each Unicorn as they passed and presented their salutations. The bizarre emotions of the incident manifested themselves in spontaneous giggles, sporadically bubbling to the surface from deep within him, occasionally shaking free a drop of salty water from his welling eyes. When nobody remained near the altar but Adolf and his wife, the Swan Knight rose unsteadily to his feet, lifted Irmengard cradled in his arms, and carried her to their lodgings, neither of them breaking the focused and impassioned stare into the other's eyes. Adolf stared in amazement of a young woman so suited to his extraordinary life. Irmengard stared in gratitude for the man who took her by the hand and pulled her into the fantastic life she always imagined she would have. Irmengard was swallowed by a squall of gratitude and admiration for her husband, a man who descended from fantasy to bring her from the stale and stagnant world she left behind, into the world of her dreams. Adolf stared *through* Irmengard's eyes, into the purity and goodness of the only human soul to deserve such a connection with the proudest and noblest creatures of the Sweeter Realm. Ludwig's entire army could not have broken the gaze of the lovers, as Adolf carried his wife blindly through the passages, halls, and alleys of the Wühlenvogel city, not with every sword in Bavaria.

When the couple awoke in the morning, Adolf continued with the tour of the city, ending at The Ancient One's nest. The old teacher had been at Linderhof, tending to his obligations to the portal and awaiting the arrival of Ludwig's children. Adolf regretted the absence of the old sage. Irmengard's introduction to him would have been a polished and bejeweled crown atop the start of her new life. The couple sat down at the base of the spire that held the nest. Adolf expressed his regret that she could not meet The Ancient One, the bird that would teach their children and grandchildren. He began describing The Ancient One to her, retelling much of the history that was taught to him, particularly as it related to the nobility of the eternal steward to the Swan Knights.

"What does he look like?" she asked.

Adolf began a physical description of the swan, presenting him in such colorful words of adoration, reaching into the depths of his well of expressions to relay the magnificence and beauty of the great swan. Irmengard smiled at the description. Adolf stared at the ground in front of him, visualizing his friend. When he looked up, he noticed that Irmengard's eyes looked passed him, not to him, as he spoke.

Adolf turned and caught The Ancient One's eyes behind him as the swan said to Irmengard, "After that description, my dear, I hope you are not disappointed. He makes me sound downright folkloric."

Adolf's delight could not be restrained. He laughed and lunged at his friend.

The two of them wrestled on the ground until The Ancient One spoke out, "Are you going to introduce me to this divine creature?"

"She is just that, my friend." Adolf replied with a tilt of his head and another adoring gaze into Irmengard's eyes, "She is divine, a gift to us all by God."

Irmengard met The Ancient One with an open heart and hungry eyes. She was frantic to consume all that she could about her new and magical life. Her eyes tried to pull knowledge and wisdom directly from the old teacher. The swan felt the pull and satiated Irmengard's hunger with small, manageable bites of information. Adolf left his wife in the capable feathers of the swan, while he joined his younger siblings in the combat arena to scrutinizingly inspect their progress. Adolf was much older than the children. He was twenty-one when he took his wife to Einigkeitstadt. Young Rudolf was only fifteen. Rupert was twelve, and Mathilde only nine. The political titles that were rightfully his would have prevented Adolf from fulfilling the most pleasurable aspect of his character — surrogate father to his brothers and sister. He secretly thanked God for his father's defeat against his uncle, and the discharge of the titular obligations that would have been his in Heidelberg.

All of Rudolf's children missed their father terribly. His wife, Mechtild, never recovered from the early loss of her husband. Mechtild never left the Wühlenvolgel city, not even to the surface of the forest. She rarely left the sleeping chamber built for her and Rudolf. She curled up with whatever maintained the smell of her husband and squeezed and smelled and caressed the items until they lost their remnants of Rudolf's scent. In the corner of the chamber was a pile of items discarded when they held more of her smell than his. She did not praise God for her husband's defeat and surrender of the Palatinate. She saw it as the injection of a poison into her poor husband, one that eventually killed him and robbed her of a life they were never able to enjoy together. She blamed her brother-in-law, Ludwig, for everything bad in the world. She often reviewed in her mind the images of her entrance into the valley, after her wedding, when Ludwig stole the bread from her plate and brought such fury to her husband's face by insulting The Ancient One.

Mechtild became a ward of her own children. They cared for her. They nursed her. She was a broken woman. Her children's constant heedfulness was the only glue that kept her together. Mechtild was no mother to her children. Adolf was father, mother, trainer, and brother. The wear on the hearts of the children, as they nursed their mother, was patched and repaired daily by the faith they all had in the strength and leadership of Adolf. They dealt with the loss of their father by transferring his image onto the face of their oldest brother. With keen awareness, Adolf burdened the full weight of his responsibilities to them, to Linderhof, to the political recovery of his father's line, and to the continuity of the Swan Knighthood.

When he knelt in nightly prayer, one thought dominated his words to God, a thought of gratitude, towering high amidst the ocean of concerns that plagued his life. He thanked the Lord for his wife, for bringing him a woman who embraced his life, a woman of such pureness, openness, and goodness of character. Once Irmengard adjusted to the life of a Swan Knight's spouse, once her starvation for its wonders settled into a constant hunger, she became a friend and matriarch to the entire city, to the creatures who left their homes for its protection, to the siblings of the Swan Knight, and to their mother. The Ancient One often noted that she had much of Elisabeth in her, more naïve, more puerile, more youthfully energetic, but with Elisabeth's ability to fill the invisible cracks in everything and everyone around her. The thought that she might carry Grail Blood remained ever in the back of Adolf's mind. Had they lived at Linderhof, and had access to the portal, he would know for certain.

Two years after Irmengard came to the city; her mother-in-law succumbed to the weight of her sadness. In midsummer of 1323, Mechtild fell into a half-sleep. She responded to the stimuli around her, but it was as if she experienced them in a dream. Her speech made little sense and she spoke only in the low whisper that her fading strength allowed. Duke Ludwig's boys were seven and four years old. The Ancient One was often at Linderhof with them, as he was when Mechtild's children realized that their mother would soon be gone. Adolf ordered a Wühlenvogel to speed to Linderhof and fetch The Ancient One.

"Fly high, my friend, far above the sight of men. If you can speak to the swan without my uncle's sons seeing you, please do so."

The Wühlenvogel took Mechtild's withered hand in her powerful claw and kissed her gently. She stepped out of the chamber, shot straight upward, and disappeared through a tiny hole in the forest floor. For the next two days, Mechtild's chamber was filled with the love of her children and of the many creatures who came to say goodbye to the wife of their fallen Swan Knight. Just after noon, two days after the Wühlenvogel left, Mechtild mustered the strength to call for her dead husband in a disturbingly loud and desperate cry. Adolf and the others could not console her. She continued crying for Rudolf, waiting for him to answer her, as if she sought him. The scene was so disturbing, so desperately pathetic, that all in attendance began crying in loud sobs that they tried to hold back for fear of making the situation worse. The stoutest hearts shattered from the relentless hammering of sobs and tears. Just as the pitiful company reached the zenith of their wailing, the Wühlenvogel returned. In procession directly behind her was The Ancient One. The crowd made an immediate passage between the swan and Mechtild.

The faithful friend and servant to the Swan Knights answered Mechtild's desperate calls, "It is I, The Ancient One. I am here for you."

Mechtild's calls for Rudolf stopped. The Ancient One walked to her side.

She whispered to him, "Where is my husband, old friend?"

He responded, "Rudolf is with God. Would you like me to take you to him?"

Mechtild was too weak to lift her lips in a smile, but her eyes smiled as they always had. She nodded in agreement, a slow and subtle lift and drop of her head. The Ancient One crawled into her bed and lifted her into his wings. He held her and caressed her forehead with the soft feathers under his beak. Mechtild curled into a tight ball in the swan's wings. Bliss showed plainly in the woman's weathered face. The sobs of the company turned to the quiet laughter of surprised delight.

Adolf told his mother, "Kiss my father for me."

The thought of kissing her husband must have surged Mechtild's body with energy, enough to raise a full and radiant smile. Just as her smile reached its height, she exhaled her last breath. The Ancient One held her until he knew she was gone.

He laid her down and told Adolf and the children, "Come, children, take care of your mother."

The children surrounded Mechtild, who still wore her departing smile. They kissed her, thanked her, and expressed all forms of the phrase "I love you". The company left the chamber, led by the example of the wise swan, leaving the Swan Knight family to love and mourn in peace. Irmengard began cleaning, fetching, and tending to the needs of the children.

Adolf stopped her, saying, "My love, stop. Be with us and with your mother." Irmengard obeyed. She sat on Mechtild's bed and joined the others in praising and thanking Mechtild for all that she did and all that she was.

CHAPTER 18
Destruction and Reconciliation

IN THE YEAR FOLLOWING Mechtild's death, Adolf grew austere and energetically solemn. The loss of both of his parents accentuated the direness of his situation. The Wühlenvogel city was magnificent and more secure than any castle in Europe. As the Swan Knight, Adolf commanded an army of fierce creatures. But his father's line was stripped of political titles and the valley of Linderhof was in the hands of his enemy. When alone in contemplation, Adolf thought of his parents, how his father died in another country, his mother in a hidden city underground. His father had been the Duke of Bavaria, oldest surviving son of the previous Duke. The sweet hills and soft grass of Linderhof should have been his. Rudolf and Mechtild should have lived much longer, with each other and their children. They should have died old, in the palace at Landshut or peacefully in the family lodge near the portal. These thoughts filled Adolf with anger. He tripled the demands of the children's training, working them relentlessly and often cruelly.

The children were old enough to understand the source of Adolf's harshness. They remembered his younger and softer days. They also had Irmengard. They turned to her for all of the nurturing and care that a mother would give. Irmengard and Rupert developed a particular bond. Although every soul in the city revered her as the matriarch, Rupert saw her as surrogate mother, sister, and friend. They shared many sensibilities and academic interests. Rupert's filial relationship with his oldest brother also lended to his reverence for his sister-in-law. He tended to her and served her in any way she needed. Irmengard spent the year after Mechtild's death organizing gatherings and celebrations. She instituted holidays in honor of each breed in the city, including the Swan Knight family. Rupert was her right hand.

On each holiday, the celebrated breed shared stories, food, and culture from their homeland. Adolf rarely attended. He was driven — a zealot to a cause that could determine the fate of humanity. He carried the burden squarely on his own shoulders, though many would have born it with him, if he would have let them. His mother's death also gave Adolf a strong sense of dynastic responsibility. Rudolf's struggles with his brother survived his death and passed to his children. Adolf knew that his uncle had many children and the fight for the Swan Knighthood and the duchy would span generations. Adolf and Irmengard must produce children. Adolf's admiration for his wife's merits bolstered his confidence in the strength of his line. Still, circumstances were strongly against them. Ludwig gathered political and military strength with each passing month. Regaining the valley by force seemed unlikely. Regaining the dukedom and political sovereignty over Linderhof seemed impossible.

A year and a half after Mechtild died, Irmengard was pregnant with their first child. Ludwig's ambitions hung like a shadow over the Black Forest. Rumors of magical creatures in the forest reached Ludwig's jealous and suspicious ears. Although he could not have imagined a settlement to the scope of the Wühlenvogel city, the vastness in scale and diversity of inhabitants, Ludwig suspected that his brother's children lived and trained there with creatures from the Sweeter Realm. He sent spies into the forest. Fortunately for the city, the creatures had eight hundred years of experience patrolling the hills around Linderhof, keeping it and the portal from the eyes of the world. The defensive procedures in the Black Forest were meticulously planned and rehearsed. But the increased pressure from his uncle convinced Adolf to send Irmengard away to have the baby.

Irmengard did not want to leave the Black Forest. She spent her childhood feeling out of place, a stranger in her own home. She looked to the horizon, knowing that a magical world waited to embrace her. Now that she found that world, she was loathed to leave it. Adolf's aversion to parting with her was only slightly defeated by his desperation to keep her and the baby safe. Irmengard assumed a maternal relationship with Adolf's siblings. After the death of their mother, she gave them the nurturing that Adolf could not. They were excited about the baby and wept at the news that the child would be born so far from them. Adolf sent Irmengard far to the northeast, to a town called Amberg. He had built alliances in the region. Irmengard would be well taken care of. The day she departed was as somber as a funeral. A heavy, dark pall of permanence hung over the adieus. She traveled safely to Amberg and delivered a healthy son. She named him after his uncle, Rupert. When the baby was three months old, and strong enough to travel, Irmengard brought him home to the Black Forest. The reunion celebrated both Irmengard's return and the birth of the child, whose dynastic significance was poignantly on the hearts of all.

Rupert was like any infant, but upon his introduction to the inhabitants of the city, he was revered as a king. He slept in Irmengard's arms as a parade of creatures filed through the chamber in a slow but steady procession, offering trinkets and tributes. The familial warmth of the creatures and the doting adoration of Irmengard softened Adolf. He spent more time in the city. He laughed more. He loved more. Although he still oversaw the combat training of his brothers, the proceedings were more light-hearted, more like the training of their ancestors in the valley. Adolf became less fatherly to Rudolf and Rupert, less rigid and authoritarian. He returned to being their brother. He did not feel the need to raise his father's children like his own. He had his own new child. He was father to young Rupert, and he allowed his brothers to be uncles, doting and influential.

Within two years of Rupert's birth, Adolf and Irmengard had three more children, the twins, Adolf and Friedrich, and later, a daughter they named Elisabeth. In fact, it was The Ancient One who insisted upon the name, after his dear Elizabeth, childhood playmate of Brunhilde, the consummate servant and admirable Swan Knight in her own right. The creatures of the city planned a celebration in honor of Elisabeth's birth. They decided to hold the celebration above ground, in the heart of the forest, on the southern edge of the Wühlenvogel city. Adolf's brothers, Rudolf and Rupert, twenty-one and eighteen years old, wished that the child may live above ground someday, perhaps even return to Linderhof.

Rudolf declared, "Her birth should be celebrated under sunlight, the same sun that shines on our ancestral valley, not by the light of Wühlenvogel torches."

Rudolf, whose admiration and imitation of his brother Adolf radiated from him like the moonlight off of a Unicorn's horn, had grown into a strong man — strong in every way a young man can be strong — of body, of mind, and of spirit. He oversaw the celebration planning. He escorted the company above ground and decorated the small portion of the forest that they committed to the celebration.

During the party, Adolf drew the attention of the company. He stood upon a high stone, holding Elisabeth to his chest. He spoke beautifully and emotionally about his gratitude for the creatures who celebrate his family, while remaining absent from their own. He spoke optimistically about their eventual return to the Sweeter Realm and Elisabeth's years at the lodge. He thanked them and thanked them all again. He raised Elisabeth high above his head and declared that she thanks them. As he spoke, still holding the baby above his head, an arrow shot between the baby's feet and into Adolf's mouth. Adolf handed Elisabeth to her mother and fell from the rock, to the forest floor.

Several creatures encircled Adolf, Irmengard, and the children. Many others joined Rudolf and Rupert in pursuit of the enemy. Nobody knew where the arrow came from. They spread out and covered a great portion of the forest, but dared not leave the shelter of the woods. They returned to the others, who had hurried underground. A Brunnen, who had grown particularly attached to Irmengard, removed the arrow from Adolf's face with her soft and gentle hands. Adolf lived, but his life was in grave jeopardy. The Zweigwesens were the superior botanists in the city. They immediately scavenged the forest for ingredients for a tonic. One Zweigwesen plugged the wound with a roll of leaves, pasted together with a sticky, sap-like substance he secreted from his fingertips. His expression as he inserted the bandage did not instill Irmengard with confidence.

"If we were at the portal," he said to her, "I could fetch plants from the Sweeter Realm that would help. But there is nothing in this forest I can use to save him."

They dared not try to take Adolf to Linderhof. The valley was controlled by Ludwig. It was most certainly Ludwig's archer who delivered the arrow. The archer would have seen the celebration and reported it to Ludwig. Not only was Adolf not safe on the road to Linderhof. He was not safe in the Black Forest. Rudolf and Rupert took their brother north to Neustadt am Main. Within a few days of treatment there, Adolf died of his wound. Rudolf and Rupert could not linger to mourn their brother. They had to return to the forest to prepare defenses against an attack by their uncle.

There was no time to anoint a new Swan Knight. The Ancient One was not in the Black Forest. The absence of his wise counsel was intensely felt. Irmengard tended to the fears and sadness of the entire city, burying her own immense loss to serve her family and friends as only she could. Rudolf and Rupert were fierce fighters and brave men. They had trained as well and as thoroughly as any Swan Knight ever had. And they felt a swelling, consuming anger for the murder of their honored brother. They pulsed with energetic fury, a pulse that could be seen on every inch of their bodies, in every movement, every twitch, every clinch-jawed, teeth-grinding word growled through their tightened lips. They swelled with righteous duty to the Lord, to the Grail and their brother, to the beautiful creatures who prepared for battle with them, to their sister-in-law and their niece and nephews.

They knew the forest and they knew their city. They knew their creature army and its capabilities. They devised a defense of the city, considering only the immediate danger, giving no thought to the long-term dangers of their exposure to Ludwig. They did not wait long. One week after Rudolf and Rupert returned from Neustadt, Ludwig's army arrived at the threshold of the forest. The Ancient One saw the movements of the army from Linderhof. Fearing the worse, he sped to the Black Forest. When he arrived in Einigkeitstadt, the buoyancy of his heart was put to the test. As weighted as it was by the news of Adolf's death, he lifted it high, so that all would be bolstered by his leadership. As fiersome as Rudolf and Rupert were, as confident as the city was in their abilities, it was The Ancient One who united them in task. The eternal keeper of the portal, the teacher to all, the venerable old sage, The Ancient One, with his bright glowing feathers and his wise and soothing voice, rallied the city to common and confident purpose.

The first wave of soldiers invaded the forest with no idea of the enemy they faced. They were slaughtered. Rudolf and Rupert led the defenses, destroying more of the enemy ranks than the Unicorns and Wühlenvogels combined. But the attackers came, wave after wave. Thousands of them poured into the forest. The creatures were stealthy, appearing and disappearing before the enemy eyes. Ludwig's soldiers were confused and disordered. But as the waves of attack continued, they saw their comrades dragged through the floor of the forest, into the earth below, by the swarm of Wühlenvogels. The enemy began digging into the forest floor. They discovered the hidden city and began directing their attacks there. The plans to defend the forest did not account for a breach of the hidden city. Many creatures died beneath the ground, having lost their greatest strategic advantage.

Irmengard huddled in her chamber with young Rupert, Elisabeth, and the twins. Rupert was two years old. The twins were one. Irmengard ordered them to hide while she fled through the city with Elisabeth, pursued by the raging army. Mathilde stayed with the children as long as her heart would let her. The cries of battle mixed with her thorough preparations to send her to the forest floor to join the battle there. She joined her brothers and killed many invaders, leaving the children alone in the city. When Irmengard escaped her persuers, she circled back to collect her sons. She found Rupert screaming over the slaughtered bodies of the twins, Adolf and Friedrich. The Ancient One responded to young Rupert's scream. He hoisted the dead children, one in each wing, and ran through one of his exits into the forest.

The soldiers from both sides froze at the sight of the giant, blood-drenched swan, running to the edge of the forest with the young bodies. There, at the edge of the forest, mounted high on a horse, was Ludwig.

The Ancient One, Ludwig's childhood teacher, laid the boys' bodies on the ground in front of him and called out to Ludwig, "Is this what you wanted? These children, the sons of your murdered nephew, the grandsons of your own brother, these children of Parsifal, Lohengrin, Elsa, and your own dear father, slaughtered by your hand. Is this what you wanted?"

The battle froze as it stood, as if captured on canvas by a painter. All eyes turned to Ludwig. His head dropped low and he began to weep. He could not raise his eyes to the red-stained swan and the bodies of his slain kin. He turned his horse around and rode quickly east, away from the forest. Once he was out of sight, his soldiers continued their attack. All of the creatures in the city fled to the surface, led by Irmengard, who carried Elisabeth and Rupert. The enemy forces were too many. Rudolf, Rupert, and Mathilde stood against Irmengard and the children. The creatures surrounded the humans. The enemy encircled them all. The Ancient One carried the boys' bodies back into the heart of the forest, where he found his people surrounded. His buoyant heart sank to the depths of his gut. He stared in horror as the enemy circle closed in, poised to extinguish the line of Rudolf from the world.

All movement in the forest paused at the sound of a high-pitched noise. It was a scream, but more like song than speech. It was two voices in harmony. No, it was one voice, one Brunnen voice through two throats. It was Brunhilde. She was more than one hundred years old, but she looked exactly as she did when she left The Ancient One and traveled north. She floated from high above the forest to land gently in front of the swan. The enemy turned their attention to the beautiful flying woman. When her skin caught the sunlight, it shined back at their eyes like polished armor. When it did not, the beauty of her bare skin and flawless figure instantly intoxicated them.

Brunhilde took one glance at the slaughtered children. Her soft, pale skin turned red and rugged. She turned to the enemy ranks and flew at them with her small blade drawn. The enemy stood paralyzed by her fierce beauty. They did not lift a sword or shield in defense. Brunhilde flew through them so quickly that only the keen, darting eyes of The Ancient One could keep up with her. Before the company of creatures could lift a limb in assistance, the invading army laid dead where they had stood. Ludwig, who rode desperately east in shame, was the only invader of the Black Forest to survive the day. But he did not escape unscathed. His heart was pierced by the words of his old teacher, and the sight of the slaughtered innocence.

The Ancient One carried the dead boys through the enemy corpses, to their mother. Irmengard lost so much in such a short time. They all did. Before their torn hearts could turn to concerns of recovery, they mourned. The surviving citizens of Einigkeitstadt collapsed in each other's embraces. They wept as one. Brunhilde sought out some Brunnens. She kissed them and caressed them. Then she walked slowly to the blood-stained swan and kissed him.

He begged her, "Please come back to us. We need you now more than ever."

She kissed him again, wiped the tears from her own cheeks and used them to wash the blood from the old bird's beak. She kissed him again, looked up to the sky, and jumped through the trees and out of the vision of the sharp eyes of The Ancient One. He stared up to the points of the forest trees, where she had disappeared, praying, willing her to return. She did not. She was gone and the old swan turned his attention where it belonged, to Rudolf, Rupert, and Mathilde, to Irmengard and the children.

"That was Brunhilde," he told Rudolf, "the child of Tannhäuser, my beloved Brunhilde."

So much has happened to me since The Ancient One first told me the story of the Battle of Einigkeitstadt, in the first few weeks of my training. I understand now why he wept as he spoke. Now, as I soon face my enemy, I wish that Brunhilde would sense the fear and loyalty in my heart. More than five hundred fifty years after her appearance in the Black Forest that day, I do not know if she still lives. But my need for her is desperate. The enemy I must soon face would have quite the surprise if I appeared to him with Brunhilde at my side. I have no way of seeking her and no time to wait for her. Perhaps she will arrive to my rescue, floating from above just in time, as she did for the inhabitants of Einigkeitstadt all those centuries ago.

Brunhilde saved the line of Rudolf, the Rightful Swan Knight. She saved them all. She was the only child of a human and a creature from the Sweeter Realm. Nobody knew how long she might live or how her powers would grow. Once the tragedy of loss subsided, The Ancient One drew much satisfaction from his memory of Brunhilde flying through the forest that day, her young and vibrant face, her sweet voice, her swiftness and power. She was everything he prayed she would be since the day she left him and went north.

The next day, starting very slowly and mournfully, but picking up speed in vigor in each other's company, the survivors of the attack began rebuilding their city. None of the attacking soldiers survived to report the strange things they saw in the forest.

And The Ancient One assured them, "Ludwig will not attack again. I saw his face as he turned and rode away. His was the face of a man impaled by remorse. That wound will not heal quickly."

So they continued. They rebuilt with shaky confidence that their efforts were not in vain. The old swan was correct. Ludwig abandoned all efforts to confront his brother's children. He focused his ambitions elsewhere. His piercing, biting, morbid regret drove him to nobler service than his heart had ever felt. Driven by a desire to secure the portal and to see his forlorn kin in the forest safe, he turned his might toward the advancement of his family. Within a year of the attack, he became emperor of the Holy Roman Empire.

After the bustle of the coronation had settled, Rudolf, Rupert, and Mathilde visited their uncle. Just as The Ancient One had said, Ludwig was haunted by remorse. He delighted in the opportunity to reconcile with his niece and nephews. He promised them safety and granted them the Palatinate on the Rhine in accordance with the treaty he had made with his brother. The young men finally held the lands and title that were taken from their father. Ludwig kept the dukedom for his own heirs, but he reestablished the bonds of kinship, weak and torn as they were. Rudolf and Rupert moved to the castle in Heidelberg. They took Irmengard and the children with them. Young Rupert and Elisabeth made regular trips to the Black Forest to be trained by the creatures who had rebuilt the Wühlenvogel city. In 1330, Mathilde married Count John III of Sponheim and moved away from Heidelberg and the Black Forest.

The reconciliation also healed the wounds between Ludwig and The Ancient One. The old sage returned to Linderhof to fulfill his duties to the children and grandchildren of Ludwig. He still visited the Black Forest, under the knowing and permitting good-will of Emperor Ludwig, where he served more as a headmaster than a teacher to the education of the Rightful Swan Knights. He still performed the oath ritual to Rudolf, later to Rupert, then to Adolf's son Rupert. During his stays at Linderhof, he often flew to Brunhilde's castle near Füssen. He perched himself in the tower and stared to the north, hoping to see her lovely figure floating through the sky toward him. He watched as the empty castle fell into disrepair, and eventually into ruins.

Once Ludwig reached his ultimate political ambition and became emperor, the greed that had enflamed his heart needed a new fuel. The sight of the Swan with Adolf's dead children lingered in his mind constantly, sometimes in the back of his head, like an itch that the fingers tend to without consulting the conscious mind, but usually at the forefront of his haunted ponderings. Once his ambitions were satisfied, that image became the primary navigator of his behavior. Unable to give to his brother Rudolf, or dote on his nephew Adolf and the twins, he showered the Heidelberg Wittelsbach with whatever comforts and political advantage his prestigious title afforded him. He offered safe passage for the surviving creatures, from the Black Forest to Linderhof, where they could return to their families and resume their lives. Rudolf and Rupert returned to Einigkeitstadt and presented the Emperor's offer to them. None of them decided to return. The city needed much repair and they had sworn to remain until Linderhof was back in the hands of the Rightful Swan Knights.

Rudolf and Rupert shared both titles, Count Palatine of the Rhine and Swan Knight. The brothers decided not to take the Swan Knight oath until the city was rebuilt. But there was one oath that Rudolf was prepared to take. Shortly after his return from reconciling with his uncle, he married Anna, the daughter of the Duke of Carinthia. The city needed a wedding. It needed a celebration of life after so much death. More than one hundred creatures made the exodus from Linderhof to the Black Forest. Less than forty survived Ludwig's assault. Each slain creature and each slain human received an individual, special, and uniquely personal memorial. It took months to memorialize the fallen. Between that and the tremendous rebuilding effort, the inhabitants of the city were worn physically and spiritually. Rudolf and Anna married in Heidelberg, but to them, that was the formal wedding. The real celebration took place in Einigkeitstadt. Irmengard arranged everything. It was a small company of celebrants, but a grand celebration.

Emperor Ludwig asked The Ancient One to search the Sweeter Realm for wedding gifts from each breed. The gifts poured in — for the newlyweds and for the surviving creatures. Gifts and letters, tokens of love, and awards from the Queen came through the portal. The Emperor stood at the portal and received them all. He and his sons brought them to Einigkeitstadt. Ludwig dared not enter the forest. The memories and the shame penetrated too deeply. He respected his nephews' authority over the Black Forest and the Wühlenvogel city. Irmengard, Rudolf and Anna, and Rupert met them at the threshold of the forest, accompanied by three Unicorns. They met at the exact point where Ludwig sat on his horse and viewed the bodies of the twins.

The proud Unicorns were honored to serve as beasts of burden for the prized cargo. Ludwig did not need to apologize or express his well-wishes. The soft sorrow and contrition in his voice spoke everything that the Rightful Swan Knights needed to hear. Ludwig was struck instantly by Irmengard's intimacy with the Unicorns. His sons were not. Ludwig's sons, who had been raised by the ambitious, greedy Ludwig, not the contrite father they rode with to the forest that day, did not understand the Emperor's behavior. *They* controlled the portal. *They* studied under The Ancient One. *They* were to be the next Swan Knights at Linderhof. When they met with the Black Forest company, they were polite, but their lingering contempt for the line of their Uncle Rudolf was thinly veiled and easily perceived by everyone gathered at the threshold of the forest — especially the mortified Emperor. Rudolf and Rupert knew that their current comforts and safety would not likely outlive their uncle. Emperor Ludwig knew the same.

When he returned home, Emperor Ludwig sent money, supplies, and knights to serve the Counts Palatine. The Emperor made certain that Heidelberg and the Black Forest would be secure from attack for generations to come. They needed to be. The Black Forest would be their home and training place until the line of Ludwig came to an end and the line of Rudolf continued on to assume the Dukedom of Bavaria and control of Linderhof. Neither Ludwig nor his children knew that Rudolf and Rupert trained under The Ancient One and were revered by all creatures from the Sweeter Realm, on both sides of the portal, as the Rightful Swan Knights. That was a secret best kept within the woods of the forest.

CHAPTER 19

Recovery and the Schism Sealed

AFTER THE CELEBRATION of Rudolf and Anna, and the completion of repairs, the city stood as magnificent as ever, with gilded memorials to the fallen, spread throughout the city, serving as an omnipresent reminder of their oaths and their sacrifices. Rudolf and Rupert took the Swan Knight oath in front of the main monument, in the center of the city. The Ancient One stood in stark contrast against the restrengthened and zealous crowd. He was worn and deeply melancholy. After the battle, he spent increasing swaths of time at the abandoned and dilapidated castle, always looking to the north. His desperate eyes often saw the figure of his beloved Brunhilde, souring over the hills toward him. But his reason overcame his imagination and Brunhilde's phantom image disappeared, leaving him a little colder each time. Each return to the Black Forest made him think more of her, and of the twins whose shattered bodies he held in his wings as their Grail Blood stained his feathers. For most, the gain and the sense of hope that sprang in the wake of the battle overcame the lingering lacerations in their hearts. For The Ancient One they did not. He performed the oath ritual with a hovering sense of doom not shared by the others.

Irmengard, though widowed, maintained the honors and influence of a Swan Knight's spouse. Her intimacy with the Unicorns strengthened under their shared losses and tribulations. Irmengard mourned for each Unicorn slain in the battle. Afterall, she had connected deeply with the collective Unicorn consciousness. They rode through her memories and relived her childhood with her. She did not quite bond with the other breeds as she did with the Unicorns. But they all were hers and she was theirs.

Irmengard and Anna became quickly as sisters. After the oath ceremony, they convinced the Swan Knights to hold a different celebration, one with a more serious tone, one that could reach into the darkness and retrieve The Ancient One's heart. The Knights declared "Swan Day". The holiday was more recognition and remembrance than celebration. It was designed to remind the old teacher of everything he had done and everything he has been to the Swan Knights, the portal, the Holy Grail, the Queen, and the Sweeter Realm. Rupert wrote a letter to the Queen, a secret and sealed letter delivered by the swan. The gloomy old teacher returned with a secret and sealed response.

The holiday began early in the morning. The Rightful Swan Knights gathered the entire city before the central memorial. They christened the holiday with a retelling of the family history, accentuating the wonderful deeds and teachings of The Ancient One, from the time of Parsifal to the present. Rudolf and Rupert shared personal moments when, by a word or deed, the swan shaped them into good and holy men. Irmengard bedewed every cheek with her stories of the swan's goodness, with what he meant to her beloved and departed husband. Each breed sent forth a speaker to express what the swan meant to their kind.

The city reflected its name that day. There was "einigkeit", true unity in the city, bound by their mutual adoration for The Ancient One. At the end of the day, Rupert opened the letter from the Queen. It declared the swan's holiday throughout the Land and Shallow Waters. Just as the Black Forest company gathered at the center of the underground city, similar celebrations took place in the gathering places of the Sweeter Realm, all in honor of The Ancient One. The old bird's feathers fluffed. His posture perked. He held the children of Adolf, young Rupert and Elisabeth, in his wings and lifted his head high, knowing that those children were the product of his centuries of service. Rudolf reminded him and the company that he and his brother and sister would not likely exist if not for the swan's dedication to his ancestors.

"In fact", Rudolf announced, "the line of Parsifal would have probably died centuries ago if not for the noble and heroic service of our dear friend and teacher. With all that has happened, the portal is not breached. The Sweeter Realm is safe. The Grail is protected — because of this wise and beautiful bird."

The Ancient One posed regally with the children, as he did when he held young Lohengrin all those many generations earlier, while a few Wühlenvogels scratched their images into the floor of the city center. When he scanned his proud, teary eyes across the gathered, he realized that they all lived because of his Brunhilde.

He thought of her with pride and gratitude, not with the sense of loss that wrapped him so relentlessly when he sat in the tower of her castle and stared to the north. He looked into the eyes of the children. He savored the sparkle of life that shone from them, knowing that they shine because of his Brunhilde. He knew that wherever she was, she was doing good, saving the righteous and destroying evil. She served him, the Swan Knights, the Grail, and the Lord in her own way, on her own terms, and in her own time. Irmengard watched from a distance as the swan held her children, revived of passion and health. She smiled. She succeeded. The Ancient One came back to them, body and spirit.

Spending less time memorializing Brunhilde in lost isolation in a crumbling castle, the reenergized swan flew back and forth, from the Black Forest to Linderhof, teaching and training with vigorous commitment, the children of Adolf and the children and grandchildren of Emperor Ludwig. Ludwig's children grew less interested in the valley and the portal. The treasures of their secular titles glimmered much more seductively than did the portal and the old rustic lodge. They did not wrestle with Scheriers or ride Unicorns. They did not sing with Eulesängers or delight in the architectural structures of the connected Zweigwesens. The amenities of their palaces kept them from the simplicity of Linderhof, leaving The Ancient One with more time in the Black Forest.

Rudolf and Anna had a child, a girl they named after her mother. Baby Anna spent her time in Heidelberg, away from the wonders of the Swan Knighthood, as circumstances now allowed adherence to the Laws of Ermenrich. Adolf's children, young Rupert and Elisabeth, lived mostly in the Wühlenvogel city, as First and Second-in-Training.

The creatures of the city began reproducing, building families and preparing for centuries in the Black Forest. Rupert, son of Duke Rudolf, married Beatrix of Jülich-Berg, but the couple was unable to produce children.

Rudolf's wife, Anna, died in Heidelberg, in an accident inside the castle. Their daughter grew up in the castle and knew only the secular world around her. She married Charles IV, Holy Roman Emperor and successor to her great-uncle Ludwig. They had only one child, a boy named Wenceslaus. He died at one-year-old. Rudolf never remarried. Adolf's children, Rupert II and Elisabeth, were the only continuation of the line of Duke Rudolf. Elisabeth married and left the forest. She visited often and kept the secret of the underground city and her Swan Knight training until her death. She remained in constant contact with her brother and always prepared to assume the knighthood if needed. Rupert II succeeded his uncles as Count Palatine of the Rhine and Rightful Swan Knight.

Rupert II ruled the Palatinate and the underground city well. The creatures continued to reproduce. Over the next few generations, their numbers grew beyond that which took the original flight from the portal. The line of Emperor Ludwig continued to train at Linderhof and maintain the Swan Knighthood there. But they also held the Bavarian dukedom, the treasures of which were much more alluring to them. Years would pass at a time without a visit to Linderhof, from the dukes or their children. The portal remained closed during those times, sealing the sentries from their families in the Sweeter Realm. Bitterness grew with their isolation. The relationship between the creatures guarding Linderhof and the line of Ludwig dissolved and nearly wasted away. When Emperor Ludwig died, his sons, Louis and Stefan divided the duchy, Louis taking Upper Bavaria, including Linderhof, and Stefan taking Lower Bavaria. When Louis' heir, Meinhard, died without children, Stefan reunited the duchy under his own rule. Stefan's character did not improve since the cruel days of his youth, nor did his respect for the swan or the Laws of Ermenrich. Bavaria and all within its borders were his to rule as he wished. He would not be bound by tradition or existing laws or any code of honor.

The line of Stefan followed in his footsteps, greedily seeking more power. Brothers feuded with brothers. Sons imprisoned their fathers. The duchy was divided and united and divided again. Meanwhile, the Wittelsbach contingency in Heidelberg held the Palatinate on the Rhine, united in love and loyalty. They maintained the patronage of the Queen of the Land and Shallow Waters, as well as the creatures whose growing ranks filled the city under the Black Forest. Unfortunately, Emperor Ludwig learned his lesson too late to affect the character of his descendants. Fortunately for the true Swan Knights, the lines of Louis and Stefan fought each other over Bavaria and had no interest in the Palatinate on the Rhine. There was nothing in the Black Forest to tempt Louis and Stefan's greed and ambition. When they died, so did all outside knowledge of the Wühlenvogel city. The line of Rudolf was free from fear of another invasion from Bavaria. They studied. They trained. They bid their time until the Lord saw fit to bring them back to Linderhof and reunite the portal with the descendants of Rudolf.

The descendants of Rudolf fared differently than their cousins in Bavaria. Adolf's son, Rupert II married Beatrix of Sicily. He and Beatrix had seven children. Only the First and Second-in-Training entered the hidden city and trained with The Ancient One. Their first born, Anna, trained most vigorously. She learned the languages of the creatures in the city. She rode the Unicorns and flew the Wühlenvogels. She mastered the sword and the bow. She climbed trees with the swiftest animals in the forest. She even learned to jump through the tiny Wühlenvogel holes.

She almost died when she first succeeded. There was nobody beneath the forest floor to catch her. She dove through a Wühlenvogel hole and fell from the floor of the forest toward the city floor, screaming for help, until a Wühlenvogel caught her with his tail, mere inches from the roof of a Scherier house. The Zweigwesens built ramps and ladders just beneath the forest floor, so Anna could use the holes safely. Rupert and the others carefully and energetically groomed Anna to be the next Swan Knight.

As an adolescent, Anna rarely left the forest. When she came of age, she became more intrigued with the world around her. She fell in love with Duke William of Berg. She intended to take him to the Black Forest to live with her there as a Swan Knight's spouse once her dear father died. William was the first Duke of Berg. The duties of his post were important to him. So was building a dynastic base for the perpetuation of his dukedom. He would not come to the Black Forest. He would not even come to Heidelberg. Anna had to choose between the only life she knew and the only man she loved. She chose love. So, a powerful and promising First-in-Training took her skills away from the arena that built them. Like Hildemar, she painstakingly raised her children with the skills and merits to be Swan Knights, in case fate threw them into that life, as it did Ermenrich.

Her younger brother, Friedrich, was only one year younger and studied as Second under Anna. He was greatly influenced by Anna's goodness, wisdom, and natural talents. He admired her and imitated her every step. Friedrich adored his grandmother. When he was not following his sister, he was with Irmengard, bonding with the Unicorns and learning Irmengard's skills at soothing the souls of others. When Anna married, her second brother, Johann left Heidelberg Castle and learned the history from The Ancient One. Johann thrilled in joining his brother and seeing the creatures whose images were depicted in art scattered throughout his childhood home.

A replica of Parsifal's lost armor stood guarding the entrance to the dining hall of the castle. Johann had imagined all sorts of adventures with the knight who wore it. Hearing of the original owner, the founding patriarch of the Swan Knighthood, and all of his adventures, enflamed Johann's spirit and drew him headlong into his training. The boys sharpened their skills and their minds. They would have made superior Swan Knights and Counts Palatine. Sadly, neither outlived their father. At forty-six and forty-nine years old, they both joined their cousins in Bavaria, putting their skills to use in a war between the feuding grandsons of Emperor Ludwig. The Rightful Swan Knights kept a close eye on the turmoil in Bavaria. When they believed that a side must be taken and supported in the battle for Bavaria, for the sake of the portal, they joined and fought. They died in battle. Their younger brother Rupert III assumed their place in training.

In 1385, the Count of Zweibrücken, with no heirs and heavy debt, pledged the Palatinate of Zweibrücken to Rupert II and his descendants in exchange for relief from his debts. Nobody involved in the agreement knew how profoundly influential that decision would be in the future of the region and the Swan Knighthood. With the agreement, Rupert and Beatrix's son, Rupert III, became heir of the Palatinates of the Rhine and Zweibrücken and the only Swan Knight-in-Training. When his father died in 1398, Rupert III inherited the Palatinates and the Rightful Swan Knighthood. He began his training late, but he was devoted to his family — and he was charismatic.

He won the respect of the nobles and was elected King of Germany just two years after becoming Count Palatine of the Rhine and Zweibrücken.

When Rupert became king in 1400, he had little time to give to his duties as the Rightful Swan Knight. The Ancient One spoke with great emotion about the Swan Knight's responsibilities to the creatures of the hidden city. He needed only recall to his students the disasters of Emperor Ludwig's line. As duke, Ludwig had neglected the valley and the portal. His descendants continued the tradition. The valley sat abandoned. The traditions of the Swan Knighthood at Linderhof dissolved. When political duties dominate the holy duties of the Swan Knighthood, terrible things happen. Rupert III learned the lessons well. He had strong apprehensions that, by either neglect or conflicts of interests, he could not serve as the King of Germany and maintain his Swan Knight oath.

When he became king, he passed the knighthood to his children, adding to the Laws of Ermenrich that, "The Swan Knight shall hold no responsibility over his oath to the Lord, the Grail, and the Queen of the Land and Shallow Waters."

His eldest son was dead. His eldest daughter married and lived in France. The Swan Knighthood went to his son Friedrich, and one year later to his son Ludwig, when Friedrich died. The Ancient One and the creatures from the Sweeter Realm fervently approved of the new law. It pleased the Queen so much that she struck it into the laws of her own realm. The Ancient One presented the idea to Johann II, the Duke of Bavaria and Swan Knight at Linderhof at the time. As a child, Johann trained with The Ancient One, but he, like all of Emperor Ludwig's line before him, preferred the amenities of his political titles and felt that the simplicity of life at the old lodge was beneath him, as were the incessant ramblings of the old swan.

Johann scoffed at the Queen's new law. He knew nothing of the Black Forest city or of a simultaneously running Swan Knighthood in the line of his Heidelberg cousins. Johann's refusal to adhere to the law, and the enthusiastic embrace of it by the sons of King Rupert, strengthened the commitment of the Queen and her subjects to someday see the line of Rudolf restored to the valley and the only Swan Knighthood. King Rupert believed in concentrating the efforts of leadership, not splitting between multiple obligations. German law allowed him to pass all of his holdings to his oldest surviving son, Ludwig. But instead, he bequeathed the Palatinate of Zweibrücken to his youngest son and eighth child, Stefan. Stefan received no Swan Knight training. He was entirely ignorant of the portal and the Grail, the Sweeter Realm and the Swan Knighthood. When King Rupert died, Stefan moved his family to Zweibrücken, the seat of the Count of Zweibrücken. There, the line of Duke Rudolf I of Bavaria flourished politically, waiting for the day that they would reunite their destiny with the Swan Knighthood.

After King Rupert's death, things continued much in the same way for several generations. The Heidelberg line of Rudolf I held sacred the Laws of Ermenrich, living and ruling in Heidelberg, and taking their oldest two children into Einigkeitstadt to train as First and Second-in-Training. The line of Emperor Ludwig treated the Swan Knighthood as little more than another trinket on their jackets. When Duke Georg, great-great-great grandson of Emperor Ludwig, died in 1503, leaving no male heir, he tried to pass the dukedom and Swan Knighthood to his daughter Elisabeth. But an agreement between the heads of the divided duchy forbade a female heir. The dispute grew to war. Many towns were destroyed — many townsfolk killed. Meanwhile, the Electors of the Palatinate on the Rhine grew in strength and respect. At the end of the war, possession of Linderhof remained with Albert IV, who had been duke and Swan Knight since 1467. The war took its toll on Albert. When it ended in 1508, he was weary of war and of politics. He retired to the quiet of Linderhof.

His two daughters should have been First and Second-in-Training. But his son Wilhelm was the only child training at Linderhof. The war had occupied Albert so completely that Wilhelm grew up in the valley, neglected by his father, but singled out by The Ancient One as the possible redemption of Emperor Ludwig's line. Wilhelm was the first in the line of Emperor Ludwig to live in the valley full-time and receive his entire education from the swan. The Ancient One's influence over Wilhelm was profound and obvious. His training focused more on philosophy than warfare. Another conflict with the Black Forest Swan Knights loomed heavily over the swan's thoughts. Although Wilhelm's goodness and obedience to the swan's teaching were promising, he did not want to put his friends in the Black Forest at any disadvantage. Wilhelm cared little for the skills of combat. He wanted to be a good leader and live up to The Ancient One's expectations of a Swan Knight. The swan spoke to him tenderly and affectionately of his cousins in Heidelberg and Zweibrücken. Wilhelm was raised to revere and admire them.

With The Ancient One's guidance, Wilhelm also sought wisdom from his cousin, The Count Palatine of the Rhine and Rightful Swan Knight, Ludwig V. Ludwig was fifteen years older than Wilhelm. He was influential in Wilhelm's training, often working with The Ancient One in creating lessons. Ludwig V was the great-great-grandson of King Rupert, and the King's wisdom passed intact down his line. Wilhelm's respect for Ludwig saved thousands of lives. In 1524, peasants rose up across Germany in defiance of the nobles. More than one hundred thousand peasants and farmers were killed. Count Ludwig V found himself and his castle in Heidelberg, like many of his fellow nobles, surrounded by thousands of peasants. Rather than sending his soldiers out to destroy the protestors, and capturing and burning the leaders, Ludwig V listened to the advice of his childhood teacher. He invited the leaders of the revolt to dine with him. At dinner, he struck a deal to end the revolt peacefully. Wilhelm witnessed his revered cousin's actions and the peaceful results. He ceased all military conflicts with the protestors in his own lands and he sought peaceful compromise. Germany will never know how the goodness and wisdom of The Ancient One saved German lives during those infamous uprisings. They will never know how the old swan's teaching and influence over the Wittelsbach shaped their society.

After the peaceful end of the revolts, The Ancient One and the Queen were proud of both Swan Knights. The Queen wrote letters to them both, praising them and comparing their leadership to the noblest Swan Knights in the early line of Parsifal. Wilhelm replied to the Queen's letter, launching a mutual correspondence that continued through Wilhelm's life. No Swan Knight, in either Linderhof or the Black Forest, had developed such an intimate relationship with the Queen. The Queen had never felt so connected to the happenings on the other side of the portal. The Ancient One was honored to be the carrier of the correspondence. They wrote to each other weekly, sometimes daily.

The relationship between the Swan Knight at Linderhof and the Rightful Swan Knight at Heidelberg strengthened in the wake of the revolts. They consulted each other often and felt a tight connection. The Ancient One was the glue between them. Wilhelm married Marie Jakobäa, the daughter of Ludwig's sister, Elisabeth. With their union, the schism was sealed. Any product of the union would be descendant from both the line of Rudolf I and that of his brother, Emperor Ludwig. The lines of the brothers, Rudolf and Ludwig, reunited, just waiting for a child of the union. Early in 1528, the child came. Wilhelm named the boy Albert. Wilhelm only left Linderhof when he had to. Albert was raised with his parents, in the valley under the nurturing eye of The Ancient One and under the doting affection of his father.

When Count Ludwig of the Palatinate on the Rhine died without an heir, his brother Friedrich II assumed the Palatinate and the Swan Knighthood in the Black Forest. The transition was easy. Friedrich had studied in the Black Forest as Second behind Ludwig. He was prepared to do what the Second is supposed to do — assume the knighthood with the loss of the First. Friedrich already had the respect of all who knew him. The people of his Palatinate called him "Friedrich the Wise", a nickname that spread into the forest and throughout the hidden city. As Second behind Wilhelm, Friedrich was involved in the decision with the revolts and the correspondence with Wilhelm.

Wilhelm's admiration and devotion to Ludwig V passed to Friedrich. He sought wisdom from any source willing to give it, Friedrich, The Ancient One, and the

Queen atop the list. He was a diligent corresponadant, writing to Ludwig V, and later to Friedrich when Ludwig died, as often as he wrote to the Queen. Although it was Albert's blood that sealed the Wittelsbach schism, it was Wilhelm's desire for peace and Wilhelm's strong and loyal notions of kinship that had healed the old wounds. His son Albert inherited his sensibilities. In 1550, when Albert was only twenty-two years old, Wilhelm died, promoting Albert to the dukedom as Albert V, Duke of Bavaria. The valley had always been his home. His ascension to Duke of Bavaria would not change that. He lived in the valley. He lived for the valley.

The Queen severely mourned the death of her dear correspondent. Neither the correspondence nor the humble wisdom survived in Wilhelm's son. He shared in Wilhelm's love of the creatures and the Queen, in his love of peace and liezure bliss. But in his youth, Albert's love was a childish infatuation, without any sense of the responsibility of love. The creatures were his toys, the portal just a door to an imaginary world. Unlike most of the descendants of Emperor Ludwig, Albert was excited to be the Swan Knight, but it was a frivolous excitement. The weight of his responsibility to the Lord and to the Queen never settled on his shoulders until it was too late.

The Ancient One did what he could to keep Albert in the valley. He did not trust his ability to keep the secret. Albert had married in 1546, when he was only eighteen years old. He married Anna of Austria. It was a political marriage designed to mend the rift between Bavaria and Austria. Although Albert eventually grew to admire his wife, she was Austrian and the Wittlesbach secret did not belong to Austria. For the four years of his marriage while his father still lived, Wilhelm forbade Albert to bring his wife to Linderhof. When Wilhelm died, and Albert assumed the dukedom and the Swan Knighthood, The Ancient One continued the order. Anna spent most of her time at the Royal Residence in Munich, while Albert remained mostly at Linderhof. Anna was a brilliant scholar of Antiquity. Albert commissioned the purchase of many beautiful pieces of Greek and Roman art. He created a museum of Antiquity in the Royal Residence. He declared Anna to be curator and placed funds at her disposal for the care and acquisition of the museum pieces. Anna was busy and happy, leaving her little time or concern for Albert's obligations in the valley. They spent enough time in Munich together to grow a shared affection — and enough time to have children. By 1550, they had given birth to three children. Albert adhered to the laws. The First and Second-in-Training did not enter the valley until the age of nine.

Albert's heart was good, as good as any, but his mind was weak and childish. He had absorbed his father's sensibilities without any of the experiences that had formed them. He knew nothing of the Wühlenvogel city in the Black Forest, nothing of the creatures who lived there. He disregarded stories of strange Black Forest inhabitants as simple folklore. Like his father, Albert sought knowledge and wisdom from many places. But his sequestered childhood, his lack of exposure to other humans, left him a poor judge of character. He sought and took to heart the advice and ideas of people who did not deserve his admiration.

Albert was friends with a Swiss scientist, naturalist, and university professor twelve years his senior. His name was Conrad Gessner. The naïve young duke admired Gessner and was easily influenced by him. Albert traveled often to Bern, Switzerland to attend Gessner's classes. He returned from those visits more like Gessner than like his father or like his revered cousin Friedrich in Heidelberg. Gessner was understandably flattered by the attention of the Duke. He excersized his influence and often entertained Albert for weeks at a time, stitching more tightly the threads of the obsession. Gessner was working on a book of animal and plant life. He was intrigued by the stories of fascinating creatures in the Black Forest. He sent a letter to Albert, telling him that he was going to the Black Forest to research the legends. Albert told him to ignore that nonsense. In the back of his head, he felt the wisdom of his father and The Ancient One trying to overcome his infatuation with the professor. But the young Duke was recently returned from a visit to Bern and the spell had not yet worn off and given way to reason.

"Come to my secret lodge," he wrote to Gessner, "and I will impress you with some animal life like you have never imagined."

Albert enticed his friend by hinting at the existence of Unicorns. That was enough. Gessner came to Linderhof with his sketchbook in hand. Had The Ancient One been at the valley when Gessner arrived, the rest of this story would have likely been very different.

The swan was in the Black Forest, advising the Rightful Swan Knight, the childless Friedrich, on the succession of the Palatinate and the Rightful Swan Knighthood. The swan would have had Gessner sent away before he set foot in the valley. But the old sage was absent and Gessner rode freely and unchecked to the lodge. Albert, wanting to surprise his friend, sent all Sweeter Realm creatures back through the portal. He did not want the surprise ruined by any patrolling Unicorns.

He also knew deep inside that his behavior was wrong. He knew that patrolling creatures would stop his friend.

Childishly, Albert kept Gessner in suspense. The scientist begged to see the creatures promised to him by the Duke. Albert giggled and hinted, but made Gessner wait until morning. In the morning, the fate of Conrad Gessner, of Albert, of the Queen and Sweeter Realm, the fate of The Ancient One, my fate, and the fate of the Holy Grail took a dramatic turn. In his later remorse, Albert described that morning to The Ancient One in debilitating shame. It is Albert's own description that has passed through the swan to me. The teacher told the tale in dramatic and vivid detail. He wanted the lesson to linger on his students like a pungent and rancid odor. I will try to do the same.

CHAPTER 20

The Breach

BY THE TIME GESSNER AWOKE, Albert was dressed and standing impatiently at the door of the lodge, his eagerness to impress his friend bursting through in the form of jigging extremities and adolescent snickers. Gessner expected something peculiar, but could not imagine the world his young friend would soon open for him. Gessner dressed and accompanied Albert out of the lodge and toward the portal point, carrying his sketchbook with him. As they made their way up the hill from the lodge, a subtle but distinct warning gnawed at Albert's heart. The words of his good father, the teachings of The Ancient One, his own good sense, all shouted silently at him. Albert caught Gessner staring perplexedly at his solemn expression, as he fought to expel the dreaded sense of warning.

He shook it off by forcing a broad smile and picking up his pace, saying to Gessner, "Come, hurry."

The two men ran toward the portal point. Albert's anticipation of Gessner's astonishment evicted the last of his inhibitions. He stopped short of opening the portal and commanded Gessner to walk past him. Just as Gessner stood upon the portal point — that sacred spot where Parsifal shed his blood — in imitation of a ritual passed exclusively down the line of Swan Knights for more than a thousand years, Albert stepped forward and opened the portal. The creatures he had sent away waited just on the other side, resting in and around the swan's nest until called again to Linderhof. When the portal opened, they enthusiastically ran through. The crack of the portal terrified Gessner. He came to see exotic, never before seen animals, not some frightening, crackling, menacing hole in the air. He fell to the ground and scooted slowly away from the portal. Once he was a full body's length away from the portal, he settled his fears and recalled his scientific curiosity. Before he could ask a single question, two Scheriers — Lohengrin's two Scheriers — jumped through the portal and onto Gessner's lap.

Albert began to shake violently and involuntarily. He had dreamy, romantic visions of that moment, but once it happened and he watched Gessner's opportunistic eyes glow at the sight of the Scheriers, the full weight of his transgression fell on him. He felt the harsh chastising of every Swan Knight since Parsifal scolding him from beyond time. Images of the invasion of the Welf knights ran through his head. The seriousness of his oath and the long line of lives committed to the secret of the portal took control of his thoughts, instantly sobering him from the intoxication of his childish dreams. Albert aged many years in that moment, both mentally and physically. His eyes ran red with the thought of all of the blood spilled to keep the secret that he had just given away. No poison could have seized Albert's gut more violently than the sudden onset of remorse. In the entire annals of human treachery, no betrayal has ever been more painfully regretted.

The Scheriers played on Gessner for several seconds before they realized that their host was a stranger. One grabbed the other and pulled him from Gessner's lap. They stood between Gessner and Albert, exchanging inquisitive glances between the men. By the expression of mortification that had by that point overtaken Albert's entire body, the Scheriers thought that Gessner's presence was not intended, perhaps an invasion of an enemy. They scanned the surrounding area and saw nobody else. They began to ask a question, but were interrupted at the first syllable by the addition of more creatures from the Sweeter Realm, a Brunnen wearing a large flowered vine around the waist, and two Unicorns.

All traces of apprehension in Gessner were expelled by scientific wonder. He glanced quickly at the Unicorns, who had leapt to Albert's side, in defense of the portal custodian. Then his eyes went straight to the Brunnen, who stood still and silent, locked in a solemn stare with the scientist. Gessner crawled to the Brunnen, stood before her, and ran his hand from the top of her head to a flower on the vine around her waist. The soft and brilliantly colored flower pedals laid against the skin of the Brunnen. Gessner's exploratory caress transitioned seamlessly from the skin of the Brunnen to the pedals of the flower. He continued to stroke the flower pedals, not certain if they were part of the Brunnen's body, until the Brunnen broke her confused stare and ran behind the Unicorns.

The wonders he beheld utterly captivated Gessner.

In a bewildered stupor, he turned to Albert, pointed at the open portal, and asked, "Are there more? What else in in there?"

Hoping to quell his curiosity with a definitive answer, Albert answered, "There is an entire realm with its own unique creatures."

Gessner took a sharp step toward the portal.

Albert yelled at him, "No! Nobody goes through. It is forbidden."

Gessner smiled at Albert and ran through the portal. Albert darted in pursuit of his friend, but a Unicorn bit the back of his shirt and halted his movement. Albert tugged the Unicorn forward one step, but the beast would not let go. Albert knew he could not enter the portal. He realized that by opening the portal for Gessner, he set in motion a chain of events that would not likely end well. His legs went limp. He began to cry. The Unicorn held him on his limp legs for a moment, then lowered him to a seat on the ground. The Scheriers and the Brunnen ran as quickly as they could into the quiet safety of the lodge. One of the Unicorns ran into the woods behind the portal. The other ran through the portal, presumably to retrieve Gessner.

Albert sat on the ground, in front of the open portal, forcing through his continuing sobs the repeated words, "What have I done? God help me. What have I done?"

Albert sat in front of the portal in that manner for hours. His thoughts roamed uncontrolled from crippling shame to self-pity — until the chain was broken by a new thought. As quickly as the thought entered his head, the words flew from his mouth.

He yelled into the portal, "Please do not kill him."

He repeated the desperate appeal, in increasing volume, several times, until his voice left him. After a few repetitions in a raspy, broken whisper, Albert buried his face in the palms of his hands. He clinched his fists, driving his fingernails deeply into his forehead and cheeks, drawing blood. He watched a drop of his blood roll down the side of his hand and fall from his wrist to the ground. The significance of a drop of his Grail Blood hitting the ground so near the portal point was not lost to him. He thought of Parsifal and the flowermaiden who attacked him. What did the spirit of the devout and pious Parsifal think of his weak and childish descendant? This was the thought that tried to suffocate Albert as he stared at the drop of blood on the ground. The giddy young Duke who stood at the door of the lodge just hours earlier seemed like a stranger to Albert, a foolish stranger. In his mind, he scorned that childish figure, as if looking back at himself through several decades, not a few hours. His self-scorn would have killed him had he realized the destructive and deadly course of events he had set into motion that morning.

Albert sat in front of the open portal the entire day, with no food, no drink, and scourging and flogging himself with slaps to his face and scratches to his entire body. He continued in this way late into the night, when he fell asleep, finally silencing the relentless sighs, sniffles, and sobs that had serenaded the open portal all day. He slept sitting erect in front of the portal. His dreams were truly wretched. Every possible horror that could result from his actions that morning played out in his terrible dreams. He later described the dreams in that very way, refusing to detail any of the horrid visions that haunted his brief moments of sleep that night. He awoke with a jump, sweating and shaking profusely. He stood slowly, stared into the portal, and in an almost silent whisper, begged Gessner to come back. He waited a few more seconds then walked slowly down the hill to the lodge.

The Scheriers and Brunnen who had been hiding in the lodge since morning welcomed Albert in and tended to his self-inflicted wounds. Without a word, of either reprimand or encouragement, they changed him into his sleeping gown and laid him in bed. They held him through the night. When Albert awoke, he shook himself free of the creatures who held him. In his sleeping gown, he ran up the hill and opened the portal. He did not flagellate himself as he did the day before. He only alternated between sitting and standing directly in front of the portal, waiting for Gessner or news of him.

This continued for more than two months. Albert hardly ate. He hardly slept. He began to doubt that he would ever see Gessner again. The thought saddened him and encouraged him. He did not want Gessner to die. But far more desperately, he wanted the incident to pass without harm to the Grail or the Sweeter Realm — or the Swan Knighthood and the harmonious goodwill that his father finally fostered after the long generations of neglect by the children of Emperor Ludwig.

When Gessner ran through the portal, he scanned the area in fascination of the surprising flora. As his eyes went up, he caught a glimpse of The Ancient One's nest. He climbed into the nest, hoping to find some strange bird-creature or eggs waiting to hatch. He sat in the nest and watched the Unicorn chase him through the portal. The Unicorn did not look up, or think about the swan's nest above him. He looked quickly around him, trying to pick up any indication of Gessner, sight, sound, or scent, then chose a direction and ran away from the portal in search of the intruder. Once Gessner's pursuer was gone, the scientist began sketching in his book every peculiar leaf and flower he could see from the nest. He climbed down and walked through the woods, tentatively at first, but picking up speed and determination as the images around him failed to meet his thirst for discovery. Gessner roamed from homeland to homeland in the Sweeter

Realm, documenting with sketch and description the many creatures he saw. He saw Unicorns and Zweigwesens, Wühlenvogels and Eulesängers, and many creatures even the Swan Knights had never encountered, spying them from a distance, stealthily and unnoticed, and copying their images into his book.

One day, while studying plant life near the edge of the Queen's Lake, he saw a figure rise from the water, look around, and disappear back into the water. He stepped into the water. It was warm and welcoming. The water itself seemed to say "You are happy and loved. Let me caress you." He placed his sketchbook on the shore and dove into the lake, peering through the clear water. He saw creatures from the Shallow Waters, small, turtle shaped creatures, but without shells, no longer than his forearm. They had four finned legs, like a sea turtle. They had a long tail with a complex fin structure on the end. A row of tiny spikes ran from the base of the neck to the end of the tail. They had a frog-like snout with flat teeth. Directly above the eyes, they wore a triangular flap of flesh that looked like a bishop's mitre. The most prominent feature was a broad pair of wings, attached from the base of the front flippers to the base of the rear flippers. They flapped these wings like birds, only very slowly, as they flew through the water. Gessner called them Vogelkrötes. He later sketched them into his book. Forgive the crudeness of my quick reproduction.

Vogelkröte

When they noticed Gessner. They stared at him with their large eyes. Gessner stared back until he felt the water around him get suddenly colder. A strange darkness accompanied the cold, riding upward from the deep center of the lake with strange, pulsing bursts of current. The little creatures appeared frightened by the changes in the water. They disappeared in a flash toward the center of the lake, swimming as high as they could without breaching the surface.

Gessner swam to the surface. He took several quick breaths as he felt the cold, dark water surround him. The previously clear water grew murky. He could not see his own feet through the thickening darkness. In equal proportion, the temperature followed the darkness. Gessner's legs began to ache from the cold. The water no longer seemed to speak words of nurturing kindness. There was a mindless cruelty to the darkening and thickening currents. Gessner swam a couple of strokes toward the shore when he felt something grab his ankle. He looked into the water but could no longer see anything beneath the surface. The grip on him was strong, causing sharp pain to his ankle. He felt a distinct sense of anger and chaos in the grasp. Anticipating his abduction, he took one long breath. The very moment his lips closed to seal the breath, Gessner was pulled beneath the surface.

He felt himself being dragged quickly downward and toward the center of the lake. The water got quickly colder as the claw pulled him. He could not tell if the temperature truly grew colder as he descended or if the increasing sense of hatred, jealousy, and anger made him feel colder. He had remained as still as possible as the biting grip of the claw that held him yanked him downward. In a moment of desperate self-preservation, Gessner wiggled sharply and found himself free of the grip. He swam upward begging the surface to appear from behind the dark water. It did. The water quickly cleared and the surface was clear above him. The water was so clear above him that he felt that he might grab the clouds above with every desperate reach of his hands toward air.

Gessner made it to the surface. He was far from the shore and did not recognize the nearest shoreline. He swam toward it at the greatest speed his weary limbs could manage. He made it safely to the shore, crawling on hands and knees until the water rose no higher than the middle of his forearms. He rested there, on hands and knees, gasping to catch his breath. Suddenly, his feet grew cold again, from the pulsing current that chased him. Gessner sprang to his feet and jumped out of the water to the dry land at the edge of the lake. He stared into the darkening water, too curious to run into the safety of the woods. His curiosity was satisfied by a single claw immerging from the water, followed by a long muscular arm, attached to the King of the Deep Waters. His name is Löwschock. He and his subjects had been isolated from the Land and Shallow Waters for thousands of years, until Gessner piqued their curiosity by introducing the scent of a human into the waters. When Löwschock breached the border, into the Shallow Waters, he must have sensed the power of the Holy Grail.

According to the legends of the Sweeter Realm, the Waters were once a united kingdom and Löwschock's ancestors were kings. After centuries of war with the creatures of the Land, peace and respect gradually replaced hatred and war. The creatures of both the Land and the Waters decided to unite. The Queen of the Land, a Unicorn named Achima, supported the unification effort. She was the first to extend a peaceful hoof to the creatures of the Waters. Achima was revered by wet and dry creatures alike. Her peaceful nature grew to consume the Land and the Shallow Waters. The King of the Waters did not want peace. The centuries of war rooted deep hatred in him. He rallied the vicious creatures of the deepest corners of the Waters, those whose isolation allowed them to perpetuate ignorant fear and bigotry, long after the creatures of the Land and Shallow Waters embraced unity and peace. The King controlled his hateful legions by isolating them further.

He rallied the anger and jealousy of his subjects, until their contempt darkened and chilled the water around them, creating a border between the Deep Waters and the Shallow Waters, as distinct as the border between sky and land. The dark and cold of the Deep kept friendly and curious swimmers high above the border, while the King despotically ruled the Deep. The Shallow Waters united with the Land, in accordance with the wishes of the Queen and the creatures who lived there. The creatures of the Deep Waters were not the only ones to reject unification. The Wühlenvogels took their entire civilization underground and isolated themselves from the Land and Shallow Waters. So did the Scheriers. In less than a generation, the Scheriers resurfaced and joined their people to the peaceful subjects of the Queen. As fervently as they had rejected unity, they came to embrace it. The Scheriers became the most social, peaceful, and kind-hearted neighbors in the Sweeter Realm. The Wühlenvogels slowly immerged from hiding, as the underground roots and grubs ceased to sustain them. They interacted as little as possible with the Queen's subjects, not inciting conflict, but not brokering friendship. They continued in that way until the war with the Scheriers.

When Queen Achima died, the creatures of the Land and Shallow Waters elected a swimmer from the Shallow Waters, named Kandake, the very Queen adored by The Ancient One, the very Queen who corresponded with Wilhelm. The first desire of the new Queen was to unite the entire Sweeter Realm. She swam to the floor of the Shallow Waters and extended her arm into the cold dark below. A violent, screeching scream shot up into the Shallow Waters with a plume of cold, dark water. Terrified by the immeasurable, violent hatred, the Queen swam back to her throne, which rested near the far eastern bank, just beneath the surface. She feared for the safety of her subjects and for the fragile peace between the Land and the Shallow Waters that came at the cost of many centuries and many lives. She issued a decree.

"The Deep Waters are to remain undisturbed. The hatred and anger that dwells there is to remain there. Peace and love are not welcome there, just as hatred and anger are not welcome here."

That is how it remained for countless generations. The border between Land and Shallow Waters and the Deep Waters sat undisturbed, placid except for an occasional encroachment of a Deep creature into the Shallow and from time to time, even upon the Land. Word began to spread across the Shallow Waters about a new King of the Deep, a furious and fierce monster named Löwschock. After Parsifal entered the Sweeter

Realm and the Holy Grail found a home with the Queen, waves of Deep water began pressing upward licking at the feet of the Shallow Waters. It was said that Löwschock felt the power of the Grail, which served to strengthen his jealousy. But he could not identify the source of the power and he never came into the Shallow Waters to find it. The King's only presence in the Queen's realm was the spreading rumors of his viciousness until the Waters were disturbed by the scent of a human — until Gessner. Löwschock did not know of Tannhäuser. He had gone directly from the portal, through Zweigwesen land, to the depths of the Brunnen homeland, far from the Queen's Lake. He went unnoticed by Löwschock and most creatures of the Sweeter Realm. Parsifal stepped into the Shallow Waters, and he brought the Grail with him. That was Löwschock's first scent of a human and his first sensation of the power of the Grail. When Löwschock caught the scent of Gessner, he moved immediately on what he thought must be his best chance to get the Grail for himself.

There stood Gessner, on the banks of the lake, as Löwschock crawled out of the water toward him. The King of the Deep has the face of a lion with the ears of a goat. He has two long, sharp horns atop his head, which slope harshly backward. He has a thick neck and muscular shoulders and arms. At the ends of his arms are sharp claws, like a lobster's. His torso is pale, fleshy, and slimy. So are his arms, up to the crusty shell of his claws. His lower half is a long, scaled tail, like a fish, from the middle of which protrudes two bony stumps for legs, with webbed feet attached to the ends. From nose to tail, he was the full size of Gessner, half over again.

Löwschock

Gessner was frozen in fear. Löwschock stalled his advance. He snapped his claws and a tremendous figure rose from the water behind him. It was almost twice the size of the King. A large, knobby, scaled head broke the surface. Each scale on its head was larger than a human hand. Its mouth was wide, with its lips wrapping around to nearly meet at the back of its enormous head. From the small, sharp teeth of its open mouth hung loose pieces of meat, the flesh of some poor victim. The meat appeared half-rotten, like it had clung to the monster's teeth for weeks. The knobby-headed monster continued to rise out of the water, displaying a bulky, rounded body with no arms or fins. Rising out of the water behind it was its long, wrapping, knotted tail, which began fat at the base of its bulky torso, and narrowed as it wound and wrapped, until it came to a fine point at the tip of a crusty appendage that looked like an arrowhead.

Löwschock pointed to Gessner and the creature snapped its long tail around Gessner's waist before the scientist could react. Gessner had just enough time to grab a deep breath before the monster dropped its large head and bulky torso back into the water, dragging its long tail and Gessner behind it. Gessner watched the clear, bright water of the Queen's realm slowly leave his sight. But in the last remaining glimmer of brightness, he saw the sparkle of a creature that seemed to put off its own light. It swam right past Gessner and slammed against the bulky body of the creature that held him. The creature loosened its tail and Gessner slipped out of its grasp. A pair of scaly arms, with protrusions that looked hard and spiny but felt as soft as feathers, wrapped around Gessner and pulled him out of the murky Deep, through the light, warm Shallow Waters, to the surface of the lake and to the shore.

The soft creature released Gessner onto his knees. She stood towering over the kneeling, frightened scientist, almost twice as tall as a full-grown man. Her soft, scaled arms protruded from beneath a folded, scaly torso that looked more like worn armor than part of her body. She had no hands or fingers, only the spiny-looking, soft digits that covered her arms. Her face looked human, but distinctly boyish. She wore a long skirt of shiny green scales. From beneath it fanned out a wide tail that she stood upon, covered in the same soft, spiny looking digits that covered her arms.

"Conrad Gessner," she said in a deep but angelically soft voice, "I am the Queen of the Land and Shallow Waters. You should not be here. You have broken a threshold that should not be broken. You have disturbed a border that should not be disturbed. You cannot linger here, nor can you return to your world and jeopardize the secret of the portal."

Gessner replied, "Please send me home. I will tell nobody of this place, of you or the things I have seen here."

In a stern but compassionately sorrowful voice, the Queen answered him, "I am the Queen. I must protect my realm and the hidden secrets of yours. I cannot afford to believe you. There is only one place for you, Conrad Gessner."

Gessner asked the Queen, "How do you know me?"

Before she could answer, Löwschock and the knobby-headed serpent appeared behind her.

Gessner yelled, "Behind you!"

The Queen turned, dove into the water, and flew up through the surface, into the face of the larger creature. She spun in the air and struck the beast in the jaw with her fanned tail. The monster howled in pain and sank into the water. The Queen positioned herself directly behind Löwschock. The King lunged at Gessner, but found his stubby feet bound by the sand. Löwschock angrily hollered at the Queen in a strange, hissing language. The sand that wrapped Löwschock's webbed feet rose to consume his entire scaled tail. Löwschock wiggled and writhed, but could not free himself from the squeezing blanket of wet sand rising up from the edge of the water. The sand rose to wrap the King up to his muscular neck. Löwschock growled at the Queen who sailed mysteriously and majestically upon her fanned tail to position herself between Löwschock and Gessner. Löwschock looked down at the sand that wrapped him, then up inquisitively to the Queen.

The Queen told him, "I am the Queen of the Land and Shallow Waters. Where the Land and Water meet in peace, I am in command. The Land and the Water kiss lovingly where you stand, and they obey me."

The Queen grabbed Gessner and took him beneath the surface, into the Shallow Waters. Gessner felt no need to draw breath while the Queen held him. A strange cliff rose up from the bed of the Shallows, its walls ornately sculpted with images of swimming creatures. The Queen swam directly at it, and through a hole in the cliffside, near the floor of the lake. Inside was an air-filled room. The Queen released Gessner inside of the room and told him that he must remain imprisoned there for the rest of his life.

Meanwhile, Albert sat beside the portal, as he had all day, every day, for two months. The Ancient One returned to the valley and found his master in appalling condition. Albert had aged significantly, both in physical form and in depth of expression. He had always worn a shallow and childishly jovial expression. When the swan returned and saw him, he looked like a man twice his age, who had witnessed all of the miseries of a long and trying life. The Ancient One landed beside him, looked into the portal, then back to Albert, then into the portal again.

When he returned his glance to Albert, he said, "Come, my boy. Warm yourself and eat something. Then tell me what has happened here."

Albert obeyed. The presence of the old sage comforted him. The swan's voice soothed his fears and made him believe that all would eventually be well. Albert cleaned himself, changed clothes, ate, then told the story to his old teacher. The censure that did not escape the swan's beak, showed itself in the bird's fiery eyes. He was furious. But he knew that harsh scolding would serve no purpose. Albert wore the signs of a well-learned lesson in the obvious aging of his young face. Nothing The

Ancient One could say would outweigh the burden that Albert's own shame placed upon him.

"Let me through the portal," the swan said, "and I will investigate the state of things. I will consult with the Queen and return to you shortly."

Having placed the burden into the wings of one so trusted, Albert carried himself to the portal with much greater ease than he had all month. He opened the portal and the swan flew through. Albert walked slowly backward from the portal, until it closed in front of him. He continued to stare at the portal point, thinking of his old teacher. The newly aged and worn face of Duke Albert lifted its first smile and shed a single tear as he thought of The Ancient One. An appreciation for the swan, the likes of which he had never felt before, swelled inside of his chest. Every tender touch of his wing, every test of his patience, every word of wisdom from his beak flooded Albert's memory. For the first time, he understood his father's serious disposition. He understood the stern seriousness of his teacher. With that smile and that single tear, Albert completed the transition between the child who opened the portal for his friend and the Swan Knight who finally slipped into his father's honorable shoes.

Albert opened the portal every couple of hours for the rest of that day, inviting the swan's return. Just after sunset, he opened it one more time before going to bed. A Brunnen walked through. She hung her lovely head and wore a grave expression. Albert's first thought was that something had happened to The Ancient One.

The Brunnen said, "The swan has spoken with the Queen. He will come to you tomorrow at dawn. Open the portal for him then."

Only after knowing that the swan was safe, did Albert consider the welfare of Gessner.

He asked the Brunnen, "How is my friend Conrad?"

The Brunnen lifted her angry head to the Duke and scolded him in the Brunnen language, both sides of her throat firing a furious and staccato symphony in Albert's direction.

When she finished her angry song, Albert said to her softly and contritely, "I am so sorry. I am not the ignorant child who endangered your world two months ago. I am so sorry."

The Brunnen stared him squarely in the eyes, softened her angry features, then sang a soft song to him in the Brunnen language. Although he did not understand it, the song lifted every care from Albert's chest, cradled them and rocked them to sleep, then placed them gently back where they belonged, inside of Albert's chest. The Brunnen kissed the Duke and walked back through the portal. That night, Albert got his first good sleep in more than a month. It was his first sleep as a man and a Swan Knight.

The next morning at dawn, Albert opened the portal, not worn and haggard, in his sleeping gown, but eagerly refreshed and dressed in his finest uniform. He looked like a man who took his life, and the lives of others, seriously. Precisely as the portal opened, the swan stepped through. Albert turned and started walking toward the lodge, assuming that The Ancient One, in his usual calm manner, would prefer repose and refreshment before conversation. The Ancient One did not wait to give his news.

He spoke immediately, "Gessner is alive, but he has summoned a dormant evil. The Queen rescued him from unknown torture and certain death. She has imprisoned Gessner in the Shallow Waters."

Albert's face demonstrated relief, having clearly prepared himself for much worse news.

He asked, "For how long?"

The swan tilted his head, confused and disappointed by Albert's question.

He answered, "He will never leave his cell. On this side, he could jeopardize everything we have fought for these last ten centuries. On that side, he could incite a war we do not know that the Queen would win."

Albert's knees buckled and he dropped to a seat on the ground.

"I did this", he said.

The swan replied, "Gessner was in control of his own actions."

Albert sat still and silent for a few seconds, then shook his head and spoke, "No... no, he followed the dictates of his scientific mind. He adhered to his code. It was I who broke from mine."

The Ancient One felt keen compassion for the anguish displayed in Albert's face, but he delighted in the wisdom that allowed it.

Albert and the swan retreated to the familiar comforts of the lodge. They drank liberally and they conversed openly. The timeless old swan almost forgot that he spoke with a descendant of Emperor Ludwig. The rich sorrow in

Albert's voice and the humble wisdom in his words reminded the swan of Duke Ludwig I, the crusader who befriended Tannhäuser. When it was time to sleep, Albert curled under the swan's wings and slept soundly in his embrace. The Ancient One woke in the middle of the night with empty wings. He heard crying from the main hall — crying and the wild scratching of a pen. He joined Albert in the hall. Albert was writing a letter to the Queen, begging her forgiveness and offering any service within his means for the release of his friend. The Ancient One expressed his doubt in the letter's effectiveness, but agreed to deliver it. Albert searched the lodge for wax and his seal. He found the wax beside his father's seal. He sealed the letter with the seal of his father, the same seal Wilhelm used in his long correspondence with the Queen.

In the morning, Albert and the swan walked in silence to the portal. Albert opened the portal. The two exchanged one long silent glance. The Ancient One rolled his long neck from Albert to the portal.

He looked into the portal, away from Albert, as he spoke, "Give me one week. Her decision will not come sooner."

He rolled his head back to Albert to receive his acknowledging nod, then he walked through the portal. The Queen was in her palace on the shore of the Queen's Lake. The swan found her there and delivered Albert's letter. She took the letter from her old friend, already knowing its contents. She held it in front of her and caressed the seal of her dear Wilhelm. She hesitatingly broke the seal and read the letter. She read slowly and carefully each word, trying to pull from the language and penmanship any sign of Albert's authenticity.

She lowered the letter to her lap and asked the swan, "What do you think?"

The swan dropped his head and answered, "He is sincere, and I believe he is whole-heartedly with us now. I see in him the determination of Ludwig the Crusader, but the weakness of Tannhäuser."

The Queen gave a long pause in contemplation and ordered her faithful subject, "Go to the Black Forest. Tell Count Friedrich, the Rightful Swan Knight, what has happened. Consult with him and report back to me what Friedrich the Wise has to say."

The swan thought, "That is an excellent idea! Friedrich will know what to do."

The next day, Albert opened the portal for the change of the Unicorn guards. He was surprised when The Ancient One was the first to step through.

"I must consult a wise and trusted friend."

With a solemn but compassionate expression, the swan flew away to the west. Albert was confused. What friend could he consult? Who would know of the portal and the secrets within? The swirling questions and doubts began to hurt Albert's troubled head. He dropped the chain of thoughts, yielding to the wisdom of the swan.

The Ancient One met with Friedrich. The Rightful Swan Knight was more astonished by the transformation in Albert's character than by the folly of his transgression. The two of them discussed the situation and Albert's change of character. They discussed the dangers of freeing Gessner, of banishing him to the Sweeter Realm and of permitting him to return. Albert's father was the first of Emperor Ludwig's line to foster a strong familial connection with the Counts Palatine of the Rhine. Friedrich thought of his good cousin, Wilhelm.

Friedrich gave his suggestion, "Albert's father was a good man, a true and just Swan Knight. I know he raised his son well and I must assume that much of Wilhelm survives in his son. Let us put the responsibility on Albert. Albert must keep his friend silent. Albert has control of the portal. All responsibility must be his. Gessner's presence has summoned the creatures of the Deep. We cannot ask the Queen to endanger her own queendom by keeping Gessner in the Sweeter Realm."

The Ancient One agreed and returned to Linderhof. Without a word exchanged between them, Albert let the swan through the portal.

When The Ancient One entered the Queen's cave palace, the Queen held Albert's letter in her hand. The swan reported Friedrich's opinion to her. She placed the letter atop a pile of letters from Wilhelm, kept as treasures for her to peruse in her lonelier moments. She looked at Albert's letter and missed Wilhelm even more.

She turned to The Ancient One, and with exhausted resolution in her voice, she said, "Take him."

The Ancient One swam out on the lake, over the cliff prison, poked his head into the water and called for the Queen's Jailor. Gessner had plenty of time to observe the jailor. He was slightly shorter than Gessner, with a bulbous, scaled torso, a human shaped face with a large nose and scales on his cheeks. Around his eyes, the tip of his nose, and his lower jaw seemed to be fleshy, close to human skin, but slick and shiny. He had short, stubby arms with no elbows, large hands and long fingers. Atop his head was a tall scaled cone, from the back of which draped a long, cape-like appendage, similar in texture to the unscaled parts of his face, flowing down past his shoulders like fabric. A similar cape of flesh flowed over his back from his shoulders to just below his knees. His legs were muscular, clearly made to run on land, but his feet resembled the webbed feet of a swan, only meatier. The same draping flesh hung from his lower jaw, down to his upper chest. He constantly stroked it the way a man would stroke a long beard. This gave him a very human quality that comforted Gessner in his presence.

The jailor obeyed the order of the Queen and relinquished Gessner to the swan's custody. Gessner and the swan walked along the shore of the lake. The sketchbook was still where Gessner had left it.

Excitedly, he yelled, "My book!"

He darted for it and grabbed it in his hands. It took a full century for The Ancient One to forgive himself for allowing Gessner to take the book back with him. But his priority was to get Gessner out of the Sweeter Realm, and the man would not go without the book. While they walked from the edge of the lake to the portal point, Gessner began speaking, not words of regret or apologetic appeals for forgiveness. He spoke of his admiration for the plants and creatures of the Sweeter Realm.

The Ancient One hushed him, saying sharply, "Do not speak. You have done enough harm already. Do not conjure any more evil. Do not even breathe any more than you must."

The swan's patience was not to be tested, and Gessner was happy to be alive and free. He obeyed The Ancient One's stern command. Gessner and the swan waited in the nest above the portal point. One full day went by before Albert opened the portal — one long, awkward, silent day. When Albert opened the portal, Gessner and The Ancient One entered the valley to find him in his uniform, holding the reigns of his horse.

Before acknowledging Gessner, he embraced his teacher and thanked him for his diligent loyalty and friendship.

He gave a cordial embrace to Gessner and coldly ordered, "I am going to Munich on state business. Do not leave the lodge. Do not step foot through the doorway until I return. We have much to discuss."

This was not the silly boy who snickered as he waited eagerly for Gessner to dress and follow him up the hill. Gessner was shocked at the transformation. This was the Duke speaking to him, in full stately regalia and with the firm voice of a man of conviction and authority. Gessner responded as he would to a duke, not to a friend.

Albert looked to The Ancient One and said, "Please watch him."

The swan replied with satisfaction, "I will watch him like a Wühlenvogel. Go, my Duke, take care of your business. Leave the scientist and the valley to me."

The Ancient One called out in the Unicorn language. The valley guards on duty responded, surrounding Albert, Gessner, and the swan.

The Ancient One told them, "This man does not leave the valley."

The Unicorns nodded, huffed, and returned to their patrols. Gessner's mind was not on exotic plants and creatures. Albert's surprising presence pushed those thoughts from him. He turned to the lodge and marched down the hill and indoors, with slow, steady, and deliberate paces, feeling the chastising glares of the others beat against his back.

When Albert returned from Munich, he released the swan from watch duty and suggested a week of rest. There was no rest for the bird. Since Friedrich had no children, Friedrich's nephew, Otto Heinrich, the son of his younger brother Ruprecht, was set to inherit the Palatinate and the Swan Knighthood in the Black Forest. He was untrained, untaught by The Ancient One. Friedrich had no heirs. Neither did his older brother. Ruprecht was the Bishop of Freising. He did not train for the Swan Knighthood. He had two sons and refused to bring them to the hidden city. His older son Otto Heinrich was nearly fifty years old. He had to be prepared for the responsibility that awaited him upon Friedrich's death. The swan flew to the Black Forest and left Albert to speak with Gessner.

The two friends sat at the dining table in the lodge. Albert took responsibility for what had happened. He stressed upon Gessner the importance of keeping the secret. He explained the great risk taken by the Queen and by all who advised her. Gessner seemed to understand. He promised not to reveal the portal or the Sweeter Realm to anyone. He relayed to Albert, in vivid detail, every moment of his experience in the Sweeter Realm. He described the creatures. He showed Albert his sketches. Albert was very interested in the creatures he had not seen. He was particularly interested in the water creatures, especially Löwschock and the large, knobby-headed creature that grabbed Gessner with its tail. Gessner's lingering terror showed as he spoke of Löwschock. But he shook and his skin went pale as he described the bulky creature with the rotting meat hanging from its mouth. In Albert's eyes, Gessner had learned his lesson. Albert was satisfied with Gessner's oath of secrecy and dismissed his friend from the valley to return to his home and his life. The description of the knobby-headed serpent monster disturbed Albert's sleep for weeks after hearing it.

One night, shaken awake by memories of Gessner's description, Albert rose from bed and sketched the creature. Gessner sketched almost every creature he encountered in the Sweeter Realm. He did not sketch the bulky serpent that grabbed him with its tail and pulled him toward the Deep Waters. He could not. The horrible memories shook his hands violently every time he held a pen and thought of the monster. The picture that Albert drew of the monster appeared in a book by Edward Topsell, published in London in 1658, more than one hundred years after Albert drew it. We do not know how Topsell got Albert's sketch. Here is my own quick, crude reproduction.

In the Black Forest, Friedrich met the swan. He had spoken to his nephew. His brother Ruprecht was long dead. Ruprecht's son, Otto Heinrich, the Bishop of Freising, had little contact with Friedrich. After his brief conversation with Otto Heinrich, Friedrich determined that he would not be a good leader to the creatures of the hidden city. Otto Heinrich was to inherit the Palatinate. Nothing could prevent that. But Friedrich thought long about his discussion with the swan over the improvements in Albert. Albert was, after all, a direct descendant of Duke Rudolf I, on his mother's side, and therefore a Rightful Swan Knight. His pedigree and his transformation came at the perfect time. Friedrich and The Ancient One traveled together to consult with Albert and tell him about the hidden city and the Swan Knight tradition in the Black Forest.

When they arrived in the valley, it was the first return of the Rightful Swan Knights to Linderhof since Rudolf I yielded the valley to his brother. They all met in the lodge. They spoke on many topics, but the incident with

Gessner and Albert's transformation dominated. The Ancient One told Albert the history of the Black Forest Swan Knights. Albert reached across the table and took Friedrich's hand, holding it and squeezing it as The Ancient One told the history. Albert was visually disturbed by the story of the invasion of Emperor Ludwig's army. Friedrich explained Albert's own connection to the line of Rudolf, through his maternal grandmother. During the story, Friedrich glanced toward the door every few minutes. The Ancient One finally released his long held laugh.

He looked endearingly at the old man and said, "The portal... you want to see the portal."

Friedrich admitted, "I want to open it with my Grail Blood. I have always wanted to open it."

Albert stood sharply and apologized for his thoughtlessness. "Please," he said, "let me show you the way."

Albert took a few steps to the door, but Friedrich stepped quickly in front of him. Friedrich had received vivid descriptions of the valley through the stories in the family history. He had imagined it since his training began.

Friedrich said politely, "I know where it is. I could find it blind."

Albert and the swan walked behind Friedrich, who savored each step toward the portal point in the historic march up the slope. From behind him, Albert and the swan could hear Friedrich's breaths quicken and shorten as he drew nearer the portal point. He walked directly at it, as if he had walked there every day since childhood. In his mind, he had. Friedrich stopped short of triggering an opening. He closed his eyes and reached his arms forward. To the astonishment of Albert and the delight of The Ancient One, the portal opened without Friedrich taking another step toward it.

The swan laughed and said, "In another era, here in the valley, you would have been the greatest Swan Knight in centuries."

Friedrich turned to his friend and his cousin, revealing the torrent of joyful tears that ran down his cheeks and drenched his collars.

"We will leave you in peace," Albert told him.

"No, my boy… my friend, please be with me."

Albert and the swan stood beside Friedrich and they stared together into the open portal. Albert began to tear, easily imagining the power of the moment for Friedrich. The fair Brunnen with the vine around her waist walked through the portal to check on Albert, assuming that it was Albert who opened the portal. When she saw Friedrich, she thought that Albert had learned nothing from the incident with Gessner and had brought another friend to the portal. She thought that until she realized that The Ancient One stood beside Albert.

"Lovely One," the swan told the Brunnen, "This is Count Friedrich, the Swan Knight of Einigkeitstadt."

The presence of the Black Forest Swan Knight in the valley, at the portal, surprised the Brunnen. Without moving her body in the slightest, her eyes leapt back and forth between the two knights and The Ancient One.

Albert had seen enough long awkward stares for three lifetimes. He broke the moment by quickly interjecting, "Things are different now, loyal friend. They are better. The old wounds have healed."

The realization hit the Brunnen profoundly. Her soft, water-like flesh turned silky smooth. Her body nearly disappeared entirely. Her face remained plainly visible from the movement of her ever-growing smile. She knew that her friends and family in the Black Forest would soon be returning home. Albert's face lit with comfort and warmth as he watched the Brunnen's reaction to his words. He had done enough harm. He knew that his actions with Gessner would go down in the history of the Swan Knights. He knew of one way to redeem his name in that storied history — to be the Swan Knight who seals the schism, who ends the isolation in the Black Forest and reunites the knighthood in Linderhof and brings the Black Forest volunteers home to their families. He stepped up to Friedrich and firmly placed his humble and loving hand on the Count's shoulder. The Ancient One drew in to their right and extended his left wing around both men. The Brunnen walked up to Albert, who stood between the swan and the Count, grabbed his ears with her soft hands and began rubbing the sides of his head with her thumbs. The line encircled her and the four of them enjoyed a hearty and affectionate embrace.

After a few weeks in the valley, Friedrich had to return to his duties in Heidelberg. The swan accompanied him. They stopped in the Black Forest city. They gathered the inhabitants into the city square. The Ancient One told them all about Wilhelm's marriage to Maria, the daughter of Friedrich's sister, about their child, Duke Albert, and about Albert's invitation to them all. Albert extended an invitation to the creatures of the Wühlenvogel city. It read,

My Friends,

I have heard of your great sacrifices to keep the Swan Knight tradition alive in the Black Forest during a tumultuous time in our history. I have heard of your losses and I despair with you. I have heard of your triumphs and I celebrate with you. The Ancient One and your own great leader, Friedrich II, have humbled me by uniting the Swan Knighthood in me, your grateful servant. I open the valley of Linderhof to you, and I open the portal for you to return to your families. I wait eagerly to meet you all. Such noble, such good and loyal friends, my home is yours. Please come to me so we can close the wounds of long ago.

Faithfully Yours,
Albert V,
Duke of Bavaria
Swan Knight
Great-Grandson of Philipp, Count Palatine of the Rhine
Descendant of Duke Rudolf, the Rightful Swan Knight

The Ancient One finished reading the letter and folded it under his wing. The city fell silent. Nobody knew what to say or could immediately decide what to do. The leaders of each breed met that evening and discussed the future of the company. There was little to debate. Friedrich, their Swan Knight, had no children and condoned the union of the Swan Knighthood under Albert. The Ancient One spoke ecstatically about Albert's goodness and sincerity. He reminded them several times that Albert is of the line of Rudolf. As a child of Rudolf through his mother, and a child of Ludwig through his father, the lines come together in Albert. The Ancient One declared to the creatures that they completed their vows. They stayed until the line of Rudolf returned to Linderhof. All were satisfied. The next day, the inhabitants of the city said goodbye to their home. For most, it was the only home they knew. More than half of the residents were born in Einigkeitstadt. The bodies of their fallen were buried in the city. The monuments to them stood in the city.

That night, the Wühlenvogel city hosted its last celebration. It was a legendary party. The swan left early to return to the Sweeter Realm and inform the Queen of the city's decision. The Queen was elated. She spread the news throughout the Land and Shallow Waters. Every breed contributed to the homecoming preparations. They had not seen their loved ones in six human generations. Many waited to meet brothers, sisters, and cousins who had never seen their own homelands. The excitement, the love and unity pushed back any encroachment of hatred and evil from the Deep. After Löwschock escaped the sand, he retreated to his kingdom. The love of the homecoming pressed against the border to the Deep Waters. The border was still, placid, and peaceful. Löwschock's dark, cold water had no strength to fight the brightness that pushed down against it.

The caravan was set to depart the safety of the Black Forest at midnight on 10 September, 1550. They spent the preceding hours sealing all entrances to the city. Any eventual discovery of the city could lead to more dangerous discoveries. They left all belongings sealed inside of Einigkeitstadt. Friedrich and the Unicorns canvased the entire forest floor above the city. All was sealed tightly. From the forest floor, there was nothing to see but a forest, nothing to draw attention downward. The only remnants of the city inhabitants to remain above the city were footprints — admittedly peculiar to any hunter who would know the prints of the native animals. But the prints would not last, so the company fled the forest with Friedrich's complete confidence. Friedrich wanted desperately to meet them all at the portal, to witness the reunion with Linderhof and the introduction to their new Swan Knight. But the creatures outflew the wind and Friedrich's final responsibility as the Rightful Swan Knight was to see them safely from his lands.

After the caravan left, Friedrich walked the Black Forest. The forest floor saw little of the moonlight that night, but Friedrich could have flown a Wühlenvogel through the forest, at top speed, with his eyes closed. His heart was heavy as he thought about the city beneath his feet, imagining it bustling with his beloved creatures, knowing its streets, halls, and homes sat eerily dark and empty. He knew every creature who flew from his forest that night. He was raised with them since he was nine years old. He knew them and he loved them. And he knew he would never see them again. His tears were held back by more invigorating thoughts. He imagined the reunions in the Sweeter Realm. Although he wished a different fate had found him younger, a fate that placed him in Linderhof, as the Swan Knight, he believed in Albert. The portal and the Sweeter Realm enjoyed the security of a strong Swan Knight with firm moral convictions. Friedrich's heavy heart smiled with his sense of hope.

The caravan arrived safely at Linderhof. Albert met them just before dawn. He stood at the open portal with eagerly expecting friends and family from the Sweeter Realm. They did not linger at the portal. They expressed their salutations and gratitude to Albert. Many commented that he looked like some relative or another, all from his grandmother's side of the family. Albert bowed cordially to each creature. The tearfully joyous reunions and introductions lifted Albert's heart higher than he had ever felt it ascend. He felt a powerful sense of responsibility to protect the lives and love his humble eyes beheld that morning. Each Unicorn touching horns with another, each Wühlenvogel licking a long tongue against the snout of another, each Scherier wrestling and rolling with a long lost loved one, the slow, ritualistic caresses of fellow Brunnens, the seamless connection of Zweigwesens with Zweigwesens, swelled Albert's chest with pride and responsibility.

The Ancient One presented Albert with the Laws of Ermenrich, written onto parchment by King Rupert, which Albert held like a precious treasure. King Rupert's amendment struck him most dearly. The Swan Knight shall not divide his attention. That morning, Albert completely forgot his dukedom. He was the Swan Knight, the protector and custodian of the beautiful creatures in front of his dewy eyes. Albert had prepared a speech, a pledge of faithfulness that would certainly have rallied the hearts around him. But this was their moment, a moment of family reunion. This moment was not about the Swan Knight. In the overwhelming emotion of the reunions, he forgot all about his speech. He simply stood at the portal holding it open for each group as they wound down their elated greetings and returned to their homes. When the last set walked through, Albert stood alone — so he thought. Behind him, as proud as ever, stood The Ancient One.

Albert backed away from the portal, refusing to peel his eyes from it, until it snapped shut. He turned away from the portal point and saw the swan standing tall and regal.

"Oh!" Albert said with a start. "I am sorry. You must want to go home."

Albert stepped toward the portal point, but The Ancient One stopped him, saying, "No, my good man, I will go home tomorrow. Today, I will stay with you."

Albert's head swayed involuntarily, to the swirling sensation of gratitude inside of him. He did not want to be alone. He wanted to be the Swan Knight that day. He wanted to be with the creatures whose lives and loyalty he hoped to deserve. He fell on the old bird, wrapping his arms around him and forcing him to the ground like a Scherier greeting. They both laughed and rolled in each other's grasp, until the rollling slowed to a halt in the form of a tight and loving embrace, which they held for several minutes before releasing it just enough to walk together to the lodge, arm-in-wing.

In the lodge, they talked. They drank, ate, and slept. When they awoke the next morning, Albert saw his friend to the portal and out of the valley. He returned to the lodge with his heart beating rapidly in his chest. As the portal closed behind The Ancient One, leaving Albert alone in the valley, the young Swan Knight thought of Conrad Gessner and the danger that the scientist still posed to the swan and other creatures who had bound themselves so tightly to Albert's affectionate sense of responsibility. The spectacle of the reunions the night before affected Albert deeply. His chest still filled with loyalty for the creatures and the pungent sense of love that filled the valley before they all disappeared through the portal. Albert began to regret begging for Gessner's freedom. He wished that the scientist was still locked safely away in the Queen's jail. His affection for the creatures dwarfed any remaining loyalty he felt for his former idol. Albert scratched out a quick letter to Gessner and left Linderhof to attend to the matters of state, recalling only a few Unicorns to guard the valley.

CHAPTER 21
Albert's Battle

A MONTH WENT BY with no reply from Gessner, so Albert wrote another letter, and another, and another. Early in 1551, he finally received a reply. It read,

> Dear Duke,
>
> I apologize for not responding until now. I have been very busy completing my book. You will love it. I will send you a copy as soon as I have one to send. Please do not worry. I wrote nothing of your portal, only enough to tease the palate of some curious friends of mine. I will be traveling soon, so I am unlikely to see you for a long while. Please take care of yourself.
>
> Your Friend and Obedient Servant,
> Conrad Gessner

The letter did not give the peace of mind it was intended to give. "Only enough to tease the palate" What did that mean? As high as Albert's spirits raised in the embrace of The Ancient One, it fell in equal proportion at the ominously cryptic words from Gessner. Albert's mind swung widely, from assuring himself that Gessner would not betray him, to soberly reminding himself of his friend's nature — from rallying his faith in himself and the creatures sworn to serve him to visualizing the entire German scientific community descending upon Linderhof.

Albert rode back to the valley as quickly as he could, half-expecting to find an army of scientists, all with books and pens in hand, gathered around the portal point. The valley was empty and quiet. Only the few Unicorns were there, stealthily patrolling the surrounding woods. The Unicorns seemed surprised by Albert's familial embrace, until he grabbed one by her horn and held the tip to his chest. The Unicorn saw the love in Albert's heart, but she also saw the fear. She saw the images that haunted him — Gessner and the horde of scientists descending on the valley. She asked Albert if his fears had merit. Albert showed the Unicorns the letter from Gessner, which he kept in his breast pocket. The Unicorns told him that they must share his fears with the swan and the Queen. Albert dreaded agitating the Queen's patience again. But the Unicorns were right. Any and all preparations for the onslaught, should it come, must be made immediately. Albert allowed one Unicorn through the portal, to consult with the swan and Queen. As the one went away, three more came. They had been waiting near the portal, eager to take their first patrol under the one, united Swan Knighthood. With a touch of horns in passing, the new patrol became aware of the dangers.

One told Albert, "We keep sharp eyes, my knight. Leave the perimeter to us." The assurance came just in time for Albert's faltering confidence. It gave him the will to leave Linderhof and seek out Gessner, to discover the degree of peril his new publication posed.

Albert returned to Munich to a delivery from Gessner. It was his book, *Historia Animalium*. As Albert flipped through the pages, his heart settled somewhere between what he had feared and what he had hoped. True to Gessner's word, the book made no mention of the portal or of Linderhof. It did, however, detail some of the creatures from the Sweeter Realm. He included the sketches of the first water creature he encountered and of Löwschock, as I crudely reproduced earlier, along with their descriptions. He also included the Unicorn, the Wühlenvogel, the Queen, and the Queen's jailor. Gessner's sketches were exquisite. Time forbids an accurate reproduction in this book.

Das Einhorn

Der Wühlenvogel

Die Königin

Der Gefängniswärter

Each time Albert turned a page and saw a Sweeter Realm creature, his heart jumped. With each jump of his heart, he grew increasingly angry at Gessner. After perusing the book, Albert read the enclosed letter. In it, Gessner boasted to the Swan Knight about the popularity of his descriptions and sketches in the academic world. He congratulated himself for not revealing the secrets of the valley and the portal. These statements only made Albert angrier. All of the fear and all of the contrition Gessner displayed in the lodge must have fled him the moment he left the valley. That is to say, there was no sign of contrition in either the book or the letter. Albert put down the letter and returned to the book. He stared at the sketch of the Queen. He was simultaneously besotted and enraged by the likeness. Ever since he was a child, and his father read the letters from the Queen, he wanted to see her. But he was furious that the only human to ever lay eyes on her was Conrad Gessner, not one of the worthy Swan Knights from the long history taught to him by The Ancient One.

As a nine-year-old crown prince, I had often imagined the burdens of a king. It was not until The Ancient One described Albert's grief, alone in his study with Gessner's book in his hand, that I imagined the burdens of a Swan Knight. As The Ancient One told me the story of Albert V's Swan Knighthood, I foresaw the misery that followed Gessner's part in the family history. It was written plainly in my teacher's eyes. He paused several times, and took deep breaths, as he told me about Gessner and the book. The retelling was still painful for him, even after three centuries.

The book sent naturalists and hunters far and wide in search of Gessner's creatures. The popular tales of the Black Forest concentrated the eyes of the scientific community there. Count Friedrich and his merchants grew rich from the hordes that descended upon the region. Friedrich did not mind. The Black Forest was empty of Sweeter Realm creatures, and as long as they were focused on the Black Forest, they were nowhere near Linderhof. Although he abdicated his Swan Knighthood to Albert, he still took very seriously his oath to the Queen and his responsibility to the portal. He met personally with many adventurers and scientists, gamesmen and trophy seekers. He used his influence to guide them away from Linderhof. Many who came to the Black Forest in search of Gessner's creatures imagined to have seen them, exactly as they appeared in the book, adding fuel to the rumors. Most left disappointed. Some simply expanded the search outward from there. One day, in 1554, an expedition found their way to the hills surrounding Linderhof.

The scouts and huntsmen were experts. They were practically in the valley before being spotted by a Zweigwesen who had posted himself on the western edge. When he noticed them, he disconnected from the tree that he held to and ran into the valley. The scouts were so near by the time the Zweigwesen saw them, that they spotted his retreat. The scouts whistled and hollered to the rest of their party. When the Zweigwesen reported the intruders to Albert and the others, he had no idea of the mass of hunters in the party. Albert rode out to meet them. When he came across the crowd, many of them armed with hand cannons, he identified himself as the Duke of Bavaria and ordered them to leave his private retreat. By then, the intruders were whipped into a frenzy of curiosity and discovery by the sight of the mysterious Zweigwesen.

They ignored the Duke's orders and nearly knocked him off of his horse as they rushed by him in one large and forceful wave. The Duke had no time to be offended by the impertinence. His only thoughts were of defending the portal and deserving the confidence placed in him by The Ancient One and Count Friedrich. He rode after the horde with furious zeal.

It did not take long for the handful of creatures in the valley to hear the thunderous approach of the invaders. The Ancient One waited at the portal point for Albert to return and let him through for reinforcements. But the hunters poured into the valley ahead of Albert. Rather than riding out to meet the intruders, Albert could have opened the portal and sent all of the creatures through. But he could not risk the portal being seen. The creatures could have fled into the wooded hills, but a party that size would have seen them and hunted them down. When Albert's demands were ignored and they rode into the valley, the only option was to fight. There were four Unicorns and three Zweigwesens on the outskirts of the valley when the hunting party arrived. They retreated to the lodge and huddled near the entrance. There were six Scheriers playing behind the lodge. They joined the Unicorns and Zweigwesens. The Ancient One remained at the portal point.

More than thirty men flooded the valley, most on horseback, all armed with either blade or hand cannon. Once the men came to the lodge and stood against the defending creatures, the violence was already set in motion. They could not leave the valley alive. But four Unicorns, three Zweigwesens, and six Scheriers were no match for the armed invaders. Albert rode around the edge of the valley and came to the portal point from the opposite direction, behind the lodge. He opened the portal. The swan flew in.

The most painfully anxious moments of Albert's life was the time he spent holding the portal open, waiting for reinforcements to come through, with no idea what was happening on the other side of the lodge, no idea who might ride around toward him, or how his brave friends fared against the hunters. He heard voices coming from the front of the lodge, but he did not hear the sounds of battle. He stood there and prayed that help would come before his friends were slaughtered. The nearest homeland to the portal is the Zweigwesens'. An army of Unicorns and Wühlenvogels would have dispatched the intruders with relative ease. But there was no time to rally them. The Ancient One flew directly to the Zweigwesen homeland. He returned with sixty-seven volunteers.

The Ancient One came through first. He led the Zweigwesens to stage between the portal and the lodge. As the last few came through the portal, the echoing terror of a hand cannon explosion filled the valley, followed by the cries of battle and several more explosions. Albert ran around the lodge to help his friends.

One old Zweigwesen, who carried obvious weight with her people, shouted to Albert, "Bring them behind the lodge."

"No", he yelled in response as he ran, "I must lead them away from the portal."

She repeated, "Bring them behind the lodge."

She began giving orders in Zweigwesen. Her people climbed atop one another, connecting seamlessly, as Zweigwesens do. They climbed and connected, reaching high off of the valley floor, until they formed into the shape of a tall tree. They looked like a large, old, dead tree, but with one hundred thirty-four eyes, blinking and shifting. The old Zweigwesen's voice could still be heard from the center of the tree. She hollered a command and all eyes on the tree shut — all but one pair.

When Albert reached the front of the lodge, he was met with a terrible sight. Three of the four Unicorns were down, flat on their sides in front of the lodge, wounded and bleeding. The three Zweigwesens who had been on perimeter guard ran to the back of the lodge when they heard their leader's commands. They laid on the ground, near the giant tree formation. They looked just like large roots, extending from the tree and poking through the earth.

The Scheriers had attacked together. They were all on one of the hunters. The hunter still sat on his horse. The Scheriers scratched and bit at his face.

He yelled to the others, "Shoot them!"

One of the other hunters fired his hand cannon at the Scheriers. The shot tore through one Scherier, ripping him in half. It also tore the arm off of another. But it hit the hunter in the face and killed him on the spot. He fell from the horse, along with the surviving Scheriers.

The sight sent Albert into a berserker rage. Forgetting the order of the old Zweigwesen, he ran into the lodge and pulled from its mount on the wall the axe of Otto I, the Readhead. He leapt from the threshold of the lodge onto the back of the one remaining Unicorn. Many of the hunters were frantically reloading their guns. Albert rode for them first. He and the Unicorn killed six men, while other hunters shot at them and missed. Recalling the command of the Zweigwesen, Albert rode around the lodge. The hunting party followed with new motives. At first they sought prizes. Now they fought for their lives and for revenge. They chased Albert behind the lodge, where the Swan Knight sat high on his Unicorn, beside the Zweigwesen tree. Some of the men held their loaded cannons, pointing at Albert. Others reloaded, while some held their drawn swords. The Ancient One watched from the peak of the lodge.

The men slowly encircled Albert and the Unicorn. The surviving Scheriers made their way quietly from the site of the fighting to the back of the lodge. A loud cracking sound, from high in the Zweigwesen formation, drew the attention of the attackers. One Zweigwesen detached himself from the others and fell from the formation. He looked like a branch, breaking and falling from the tree. He fell onto a hunter and knocked him off of his horse. The other hunters laughed at their comrade, believing him to be a victim of natural coincidence. Their laughter was silenced when every pair of Zweigwesen eyes opened simultaneously. The entire tree was blinking and looking at them. With a single cry from high in the tree, the Zweigwesens broke their tree formation. They fell on the intruders. They knocked all of the enemy riders from their horses and grabbed at their weapons and poked at their eyes with their sharp, wood-like fingers. Albert and the Unicorn could not even get to the enemy. The Zweigwesens covered the men until the invaders were either dead or crawling on their hands and knees, with empty eye sockets. Albert dismounted the Unicorn, and the two of them, Albert and the Unicorn, finished what the Zweigwesens did not, ending the pain of the blinded and bleeding men.

After killing the last of them, Albert ran to the front of the lodge to tend to the wounded creatures. When he rounded the corner, he saw that two of the men stayed behind. They stood over one of the fallen Unicorns. The poor beast was disabled, but still alive. One of the men held the Unicorn's head, while the other sawed at the horn, just above the base. He severed the horn just in time to hear Albert's cry. Albert ran to the man and buried Otto's axe into his skull. The man still held the horn in his hand. Albert pulled at the axe but could not dislodge it from the man's head. As the man fell to the ground, still gripping the axe with his skull, Albert seized the Unicorn horn from his hand and ran it through the heart of the other man. The battle was over. The blood of the innocent and the guilty blended on the ground in front of the lodge.

The hornless Unicorn survived. She cried, not for her pain or the loss of her horn, but for the other two fallen Unicorns. They were dead. The Unicorn that had held Albert joined his kind in front of the lodge. He touched his horn against the horns of the two dead Unicorns. Albert watched, but did not speak.

The Unicorn turned to Albert and said, "Their memories are held in their horns. Please tell their stories."

He touched the tip of his horn against Albert's chest. Albert cried loudly and uncontrollably as he received the memories of the fallen Unicorns. He was the first since Irmengard to share such an intimate connection with the noble beasts. Every moment of the long centuries of their lives rushed through Albert's heart and into his mind. Only then did he understand the scope of the loss. When the transfer completed, the look of lost wonder left Albert's face, ripped away violently by fury and anguish.

Not until the transfer did Albert understand the value of the horn and what it means to a Unicorn. He knelt beside the hornless Unicorn. Several Zweigwesens already surrounded her, tending her wounds with leaves from a pouch, chewed into a paste and spread on the cannon wound. Albert held the horn to her. It was long, almost chest high to Albert.

The Unicorn opened her sad eyes to the Swan Knight and said, "I cannot take it back. I can neither wear it nor carry it. Touch it to his horn."

Albert touched the horn to the horn of the standing Unicorn. The horn's memory stores transferred safely and fully. By the time the transfer completed, the Zweigwesen medicine worked its miracle. The wounded Unicorn stood, albeit weakly.

She told Albert, "You saved me with that horn, slaying with it a man who would have killed me. Keep it as a reminder of your heroism."

The Zweigwesens tended to their own wounded and the wounds of the Scheriers. Albert and The Ancient One destroyed the corpses of the invaders.

The hornless Unicorn told Albert, "Please let us home. We will come back with others, to deal with our dead."

Albert asked her when.

"Hold my horn to your heart and you will know."

Albert held the horn to his heart. He felt the thoughts and feelings of the Unicorn who received the memories from the horn. They were cloudy, vague images. Albert's face expressed his struggle to pull them into focus.

The hornless Unicorn interrupted his struggle, "It will get clearer in time."

For a moment, Albert saw himself and the hornless Unicorn through the eyes of the one who received the horn's memories.

Albert never wanted to part with the horn, but could not carry a Unicorn horn with him everywhere. So he constructed a handle and mounted it to the base of the horn, like a sword, then fashioned a rounded sheath to hold it. He retired his old sword and carried the horn in its place. To others, it was just a beautiful, twisted, brilliantly white sword. But in his lonely moments, especially when he was away from the valley, Albert held it to his chest and connected with the Unicorn he rode into battle that day, the one who had received the horn's memories.

Within a few days, and thanks to a heavy rain, the valley appeared normal. Except for the broken sod, a traveler through the valley would not guess that anything extraordinary occurred recently. No further danger came to Linderhof as a result of Gessner's book. The friends and families of the invaders knew that they had gone to the Black Forest. So, Count Friedrich reported that they embarked for Africa when the Black Forest failed to yield anything interesting. There was no reason to doubt the word of the old Count. There was nothing to turn eyes toward the valley. Albert and the creatures held memorials for the fallen. Albert sketched the image of the Zweigwesen tree formation and declared it to be the symbol of the valley.

CHAPTER 22
The History Made Personal

ALBERT AND ANNA had five children survive to adulthood. Wilhelm and Ferdinand trained as First and Second, when they came of age. Wilhelm, who was named after Albert's father at the request of the Queen, eventually inherited the dukedom and the Swan Knighthood. Ferdinand pursued a military career. He rarely returned to the valley as an adult. The next in line, Maria Anna, married at twenty years old. She never entered the valley and she knew nothing of the portal. Her younger sister, Maximiliana Maria, who they called "Milli", never married. When Ferdinand left for his career, Albert brought Milli to the valley. She was already eighteen years old, but she embraced the role of Second-in-Training behind Wilhelm. She spent almost all of her time at Linderhof. She oversaw the renovation of the old lodge. She planted a tree behind the lodge, where the Zweigwesen formation staged their ambush of the invaders. She also erected two horn-shaped monuments on the spots where the Unicorns died.

Albert began introducing Wilhelm to the concerns of state, in preparation for his eventual rule. Wilhelm took keenly to his political duties and found much outside of Linderhof to fascinate him. He married in 1568. He remodeled the castle in Landshut. Although he loved The Ancient One and the other Sweeter Realm creatures, and he took his duties to the Queen seriously, the world outside of the valley held his heart. He yielded the title of First-in-Training to Milli and swore to her that the security of the valley was his first concern when he becomes Duke of Bavaria. It was an appropriate move, approved by the Queen and The Ancient One. The old swan always said that although Grail Blood was all over Europe, the line of Swan Knights protruded out like a vein in the hand, made remarkable by distinct character traits. These traits are what have always constituted the Swan Knights and contrasted them to those who simply bear the blood of Parsifal. Milli held those traits. She was supposed to be the Swan Knight. This was as certain to The Ancient One as the webbing of his own feet.

Inside of the valley, Milli reigned. She developed a particular affection for the Zweigwesens. They brought her plants from the Sweeter Realm and taught her how to make medicines. Milli tried to grow the plants in the valley, but they could not survive. So, she kept several in pots filled with Sweeter Realm soil. The Zweigwesens who lived through the attack on the Black Forrest city prepared several pots of medicinal plants. They knew that they could have saved Adolf's life when he took an arrow to the mouth, if the right medicines were at hand. They worked with Milli to ensure that no more Swan Knights would die when they could have been saved by Zweigwesen medicine.

Milli worked with the Zweigwesen leaders to produce a manuscript of Sweeter Realm plants and Zweigwesen recipes. They appointed their top botanist to stay with Milli and pass the ancient Zweigwesen science to her. The manuscript was written in Zweigwesen, which

Milli learned to read. It had illustrations and descriptions, with specific details, from the collection and storage of the plants to the preparing of the ingredients to the application and dosage of the medicines. Milli kept the manuscript in the lodge. It has since disappeared from the possession of the Swan Knights. A manuscript matching its description was purchased in the early 1600s by Holy Roman Emperor, and King of Bohemia, Rudolf II. There was much speculation as to its authorship and nobody could decipher the strange language in which it was written. When the rumors of its strange drawings and unknown language reached the valley, we knew it had to be the Zweigwesen manuscript. Some say it was authored by a Franciscan friar named Roger Bacon, in the 1200s. Other rumors say that it was authored by a Dominican friar and notable doctor named Albert Magnus. I personally know the Zweigwesens who worked on it with Milli. They tell the story, with great detail and animated nostalgia, of working with Milli to create the manuscript. We do not know where the manuscript is now. It is hiding in some chest or on some shelf in the world, a complete mystery to its owner. But there have been many times in my life, and in those of the Swan Knights before me, when we wished it still rested on a shelf in Linderhof.

Albert grew such confidence in his daughter's abilities and in her affinity for the valley, that he abdicated the Swan Knighthood to Milli. He spent more time in Munich with his wife, meeting her in her world, studying the art of Antiquity. Milli never married. She lived her life for her Swan Knight oath. The valley flourished under the nurturing care and protection of her Swan Knighthood. It was never calmer, never safer. Until Milli, the Unicorns had been the primary guardians of the valley, for their agility, their sharp horns, and their ability to communicate with each other. Over time, Milli replaced most of the Unicorn sentries with Zweigwesens. Although Unicorns can be stealthy, they cannot disappear entirely against a tree like the Zweigwesens can. Also, the Unicorn homeland is much farther from the portal than the Zweigwesen homeland. Under Milli, reinforcements and replacements were always near at hand. The ferocious heroics of the Zweigwesens during Albert's Battle (as it became known) raised them in the esteem of all as fitting guardians of the portal. When anyone entered the valley, each tree passed could be a Zweigwesen formation, waiting to fall upon intruders.

Milli had no children. When Wilhelm's children came of age, they began training with The Ancient One. His oldest child, Christine, died at eight years old, five months before she would have begun training. His son Maximilian and daughter Maria Anna became First and Second. Milli died in 1614, twelve years before Wilhelm. Wilhelm should have returned and assumed the knighthood he had yielded to his sister. He had spent his entire childhood as First-in-Training. But he was sixty-six years old when his sister died, so Wilhelm's son Maximilian, named after Milli, took the Swan Knight oath. He was forty-four. The duchy and the Swan Knighthood passed through the next four generations from Maximilian, down to Maximilian III. There are many quaint stories in those generations but none that came to define the Swan Knighthood. None that you must know to continue the necessary knowledge and traditions of the Swan Knights. And my time is short. I have set events into motion that will soon sweep me away. I must press on.

Maximilian III died in 1777, at fifty years old, away from the valley, and without an heir. The Ancient One was trapped in the Sweeter Realm, just as the five

Unicorns, six Zweigwesens, and one Brunnen were trapped in the valley. They remained so for almost a year. Maximilian's brothers died young and without children. His sisters had married and raised their children far from the valley. Only Maximilian's older sister Maria studied with The Ancient One and knew the family legacy. Eleven months after her brother's death, she opened the portal for The Ancient One and informed him of the death of the Swan Knight. The swan begged Maria to send one of her children to him, to assume the Swan Knighthood and provide continuity. Without giving a reason, she refused. The swan sensed grave earnestness in her refusal and did not ask again. Maria left The Ancient One in the valley with the same creatures who were trapped there when Maximilian died. She left Linderhof and never returned. The portal was closed. Nobody in the Sweeter Realm knew why the portal did not open, why their loved ones remained in the valley without relief. The creatures in the valley were in a panic. They did not know if they would ever have another Swan Knight, if they would ever go home to their families.

In the absence of direct heirs, the succession of the Swan Knighthood followed that of Bavaria. In the case of the line of Emperor Ludwig ending, succession went to the Count Palatine of the Rhine, the descendants of Rudolf, and of Philipp, Friedrich the Wise's father. Should that line fail to provide an heir, behind it awaited the Count of Zweibrücken, the descendants of Stefan, son of King Rupert. The Count Palatine of the Rhine was Charles Theodore. He gained Bavaria with the death of Maximilian III. The Ancient One did not know much of him. Reports were not favorable. The Ancient One waited at the lodge for Charles to visit the family retreat. Charles never came to Linderhof. The valley remained without a Swan Knight, sealed away from the Sweeter Realm.

Charles was the Duke of Bavaria for twenty-two years, and for that time, there was no Swan Knight. The Ancient One and the remaining creatures guarded the valley and waited. They all praised God that Maria had come to the valley and allowed The Ancient One through before abandoning them. Without his leadership, they would have been lost. He kept their spirits alive by promising and reminding that God would not allow the Grail to remain forever sealed behind the portal. He would send them a Swan Knight, one whose character deserved the title and responsibility.

The swan's presence in the valley added another benefit. None of the other creatures trapped in the valley could leave, could travel among people. The Ancient One could — as he often had — fly among the gathering places of humans to gather information and assess situations. He kept an ear on the Wittelsbach. He heard the rumors of villagers, farmers, and soldiers. Through this intelligence, he maintained a Swan Knight family tree. He knew who they were, where they lived, and which would make good Swan Knights. The old teacher was ready to adopt anyone with Grail Blood who happened to wander through the valley. None came.

Charles had no legitimate children, nobody to inherit Bavaria or the knighthood. So, Bavaria passed to the next in line, the Count of Zweibrücken, Maximilian IV, a descendant of Rudolf, the Rightful Swan Knight, a descendant of Stefan and the line that carried Grail Blood in noble ignorance in Zweibrücken — and my great-grandfather.

This is how I became connected to this fantastic story. Every morning of those first weeks of my training, when I walked from the lodge and up the hill to continue my lessons, I yearned for The Ancient One to connect the history to me. I wanted to see how young Prince Ludwig connected to the line of Parsifal. When the teacher mentioned Maximilian, my great-grandfather, a name I knew well, I could finally envision the line from the thrust of the flowermaiden's blade to me and to my brother, Otto.

In April of 1799, shortly after inheriting Bavaria, Maximilian IV, who loved nature and long, solitary rides, toured his new lands. He was nearly forty-three years old. But the rapid changes in his life stripped him of the calluses of sedentary decades. He rode out with the eyes of a young man, with skin that felt the air like it had never experienced an alpine breeze. With much on his mind, he rode southwest from Munich alone one morning, toward Würmsee, a large lake he wanted to see. He rode to the far end of the lake. He intended to spend one night on the shore of the lake before returning to Munich. In the morning, a pull at his heart bade him to keep riding southwest. He continued in the direction that took him from Munich to the lake, riding desperately and tirelessly, but he did not know why.

His desperation settled immediately as he entered the valley and saw the lonely lodge. Two Unicorns spotted him and followed him into the heart of the valley. When Maximilian stopped riding, he inhaled the sweet air of the valley and savored it in his thirsty lungs. The air seemed rich. It seemed right. Maximilian felt at home. As he slowly exhaled that savored breath, he heard the steps of the Unicorns behind him. His mind was too soothed and nurtured by the valley air and the sense of destiny it brought him to be startled by the sound. He turned slowly and saw the two Unicorns standing against his horse on either side.

Maximilian was not frightened, nor was he entirely at ease. He did not doubt his eyes. Something about the look of the valley and the smell of the air, the deep inward pull that led him there, or the inexplicable feelings that his senses elicited in him, prepared him for anything magical. He knew that the Unicorns meant him no harm. They leaned slowly toward him and touched him with their horns, one on the shoulder and one on the crown of his head. The Unicorns saw his goodness. They saw his heritage, all the way back to Rudolf.

They pulled their horns from him and one of them turned toward the woods behind and yelled, "He is here!"

The other turned toward the lodge and yelled, "Come out. The Swan Knight is here."

In the connection of the horns, Maximilian understood enough to see that he held a position of significance with the marvelous creatures who greeted him in the valley. He looked eagerly around him to see whom the Unicorns were calling. The Ancient One flew out of the front door of the lodge. The other Unicorns galloped down to join them from the opposite hill. The Zweigwesens converged from all directions, and the Brunnen appeared from wherever she had been. She mounted Maximilian's horse and sat behind him without him knowing.

The Ancient One invited Maximilian to the lodge, saying, "You have many questions and I have much to teach you."

As he rode toward the lodge, shifting his eyes from one beautiful, fascinating creature to the next, the Brunnen reached from behind him and gently touched his ears. Her fingers were the softest things that Maximilian had ever felt against his skin. He thought that the sweet air of the valley caressed him, until the Brunnen introduced herself in her sweet and dulcet voice.

With such an introduction to the valley, Maximilian did not think that anything the giant swan could say would astonish him. He spent nine days in the lodge learning the history of the Swan Knighthood in vivid detail, but rushed, without rest. At the end of the lesson, the swan asked Maximilian to continue the line, to train with him, and to take the Swan Knight oath. His son Ludwig, my grandfather, was twelve years old, a good age to begin as First-in-Training. His daughter Augusta was ten. My great-grandfather was an intelligent, articulate man. But after learning the history and fully understanding what was at stake, he had no words to express the honor he gratefully accepted for himself and his descendants. The creatures took him to the portal point. The crackling of the opening portal never sounded sweeter to the old teacher. The valley held a Swan Knight again, a good, wise, and humble man, and a child of Rudolf.

Maximilian had left Munich without expecting to be gone so long. Aware of the panic his disappearance would cause, he told The Ancient One that he had to leave, but promised to return in six weeks. In exactly six weeks he returned with his wife, Karoline, and his two oldest children, Ludwig and Augusta. They rode right to the door of the lodge, where they were met by the smiling swan.

Maximilian told him, "I have brought you some students. This is Ludwig and Augusta, the First and Second-in-Training."

This is how my grandfather, the same mysterious and magical old man who inspired so many of my childhood imaginings, joined the story of the portal. His father walked him to the portal that day, in the same way that his son walked me.

My Grandfather's life changed so quickly. He was born into the obscurity of a minor Wittelsbach. He was nine years old when his father inherited the Palatinate Zweibrücken from his uncle, and twelve when his father inherited Bavaria and the Palatinate of the Rhine. This alone would have thrown his life into a page from a fantastical book. But no sooner had he settled into his new Bavarian palace, than he opened the portal and talked to Unicorns, was caressed by Brunnens, and wrestled with Scheriers. In 1806, when he was twenty, when the Holy Roman Empire dissolved and Bavaria became a kingdom, he became a crown prince. Bavaria gained independent sovereignty and my great-grandfather became King Maximilian I of Bavaria.

The world was a magical place to my grandfather — the whole world, not just the valley. I understand why. From nine to twenty, fate gave him more fairy tale surprises than the world usually sees in a hundred generations. He felt truly chosen by God. For good and for bad, he influenced my character greatly. Wherever my grandfather went, whether at Linderhof or in Munich, he was a Swan Knight, right out of the legendary past. He filled my childhood eyes with images of Parsifal and Lohengrin. He not only opened my eyes to the world of mystic legends, he blinded me to everything else. He, like I, took the knighthood everywhere, even into the halls of secular politics.

Ludwig's romantic notions were nurtured and bolstered by his father. When Duke Maximilian IV became King Maximilian I of Bavaria, he made immediate improvements in the arts. He founded a fine arts academy in Munich and built a state theatre. Everywhere my grandfather went, there was beauty and art, music and magic, and everything imagined by the mind could become as real as stone. When Maximilian I King of Bavaria died, and my grandfather inherited the throne, as Ludwig I, King of Bavaria, he was never affected by the sobriety of state affairs. He fell in love easily — truly in love. He saw beauty everywhere. And he built.

He constructed monuments to beauty and legend, lacing every creation, every design with hints of his secret title and mystical family history. He inherited the art collection of Anna, the wife of Albert V. He traveled, collecting what beauties could be purchased and sketching those that could not. He not only surrounded himself with beauty, he surrounded his friends and family. And he wanted to surround his subjects. He began a tradition of construction that survived strongly in my father and in me. He designed much of the more beautiful parts of Munich. I grew up in a world that was a product of my grandfather's mind.

My father was the third generation of Bavarian Kings. By the time he was crown prince, the state of his life was not extraordinary to him. It was not romantic. He did not have the childhood revelations sprung on him like my grandfather had. He was introduced to Unicorns as early in life as he was introduced to people. Having seen both lives, that of the Swan Knight and that of the King of Bavaria, from such an early age, neither was more mystical than the other. He was a practical man, more attached to his own kingdom than that of the Queen of the Land and Shallow Waters. He was sensitively aware of the political world around him. This made him a good king, but less of a First-in-Training.

There was much in the political world to occupy him. The world grew smaller. Treaties and alliances spun a complicated web across Europe. My father knew every fiber of that web. In his own way, he was a devoted Swan Knight, though he never held the title. Like Ludwig the Crusader, he thought that the best advantage for the portal was a Bavarian political advantage, and he worked hard to obtain it. He was military-minded. He knew where every soldier in his army stood at any given moment. He knew the armies of other countries almost as intimately. My brother Otto took after him. While I stared at the pictures of Lohengrin, he arranged his toy soldiers on the floor of some hallway, in some palace, to best defend his sleeping chamber. My induction as First-in-Training at nine years old, my introduction to The Ancient One and the family history, did nothing to pull me more into Otto's world, into my father's. It pushed me deeper into the mind of my grandfather. Every childhood possession of mine, every gift, whether practical or frivolous, became the tool of a Swan Knight in my young mind. By the time I learned the entire history, I had passed the point of no return. I was the First-in-Training, like the magnificent figures in the history I had just learned. There was no world outside of that valley and beyond the intimate interest of the portal and the Grail, The Ancient One and the Swan Knighthood.

CHAPTER 23

A Crown Prince Again

THE HISTORY WAS NOT TAUGHT to me in a single lesson. I interrupted too frequently with questions and fevered pleas for elaboration. I begged for many portions to be repeated. The history I have just scribbled was given to me over several weeks, in vibrant detail and with the sentimental tones of one intimately connected with the events. In fact, The Ancient One often digressed into tangents, each more colorful and exciting than the one before. I would not be the one to recall him to the lesson at hand. I rode his diversions like a stowaway on the ship of a famous explorer. The version I have just written is greatly abbreviated. He did not bypass a single generation. He told many anecdotes I have forgotten, and many I have decided to leave out of this account. He spoke with animated emotion, endearingly of most, furiously of some. Hours of storytelling would pass with little progress toward the goal of connecting the history of the Grail Blood to me.

By the time my teacher had connected the line of Parsifal to my great-grandfather, our relationship had warmed into respectful kinship, or perhaps that was only in the mind of a boy who slowly began to see his place in this fantastic story. I was the most recent shard in a magnificent mosaic, and this gradual realization coincided with my paralleled developing affection for the one who revealed it to me, to the one constancy through the entire story — The Ancient One.

My grandfather was not the most taciturn and secretive man. During my earliest years, he hinted at much that The Ancient One told me in those first few weeks of my training. In my mind, the stories connected to my grandfather's hints like one Zweigwesen to another, further endearing the old man to me. We had already shared a bond since my birth, sharing not just the same birthday, but the same birth hour, and the same name.

Episodes of the history were retold to me, in varying detail, throughout my entire childhood training, each with an intended moral lesson. The history holds examples of every sort of folly and every sort of heroics. Whatever point the teacher wanted to make, there was an example from the line of Swan Knights to prove his point. My teacher knew how intimately I related to the history. He used the story I just scribbled down to hammer his lessons home, to pull my thoughts and behavior where he wanted them pulled. My very character sat in a boat like Lohengrin's, and the swan pulled me as he saw fit. He knew how easily he could manipulate me with the stories and characters of the history I love so much. I hope I did them justice in this retelling.

By the time I learned the whole history, I had come to believe that I would remain indefinitely at Linderhof, under The Ancient One's constant tutelage and companionship, like the Swan Knights of old. I walked each morning to the portal and opened it with my own presence, trying harder each day to affect it with my mind. Although it never happened, the attempts never lost their excitement. Since then, the portal has developed many unpleasant associations. Some of my saddest, my wretchedest experiences occurred in its presence. But for the first several years, the sound of the opening and the sight of the circle of nothing charged me like a lightning rod in an electric storm. I awoke early and often opened the portal only to wait long hours for my teacher to appear. I gave no thought to my future as King of Bavaria. I thought only of my future as a Swan Knight. I determined to build a royal palace near the portal and rule from there, so I could remain in the valley always. In my mind, it would soon be my turn to venture forth in a swan pulled boat, rescuing maidens and sparking legend that would travel the centuries. But Lohengrin was not a Wittelsbach. He did not have to prepare to rule a kingdom.

Back at Hohenschwangau, Major General Theodor Basselet de la Rosée waited for his king-in-training. With his regimented, earthly, secular agenda, de la Rosée had no idea that he awaited the reception of a mind connected to his world by only the thinnest of threads. The Ancient One was not to be my full-time teacher. My lessons with him, although intensely concentrated, were sparse. Each time I left the portal for the lodge, I felt like I had left some vital organ behind. When I had to leave Linderhof and return to life under de la Rosée, I felt like the greater part of me was amputated and left sitting on the rock near the portal point. My father was very proud to steer me to the portal and watch me open it for the first time. True to his nature, he left it to my mother to inform me that I would be returning to Hohenschwangau and soon afterwards to Nymphenburg, with no notion of when I would return. I was nine years old, but I cried the whole night before we left the valley. I planned to get up early and say good-bye to the portal, and possibly The Ancient

One, before I left. But prior to the sunrise, I was carted away with no chance to escape up the hill.

When I returned to Hohenschwangau, my schedule allowed for a bearable transition from my life at Linderhof. The castle surroundings, the ruins of Brunhilde's castle — which I could see from my walks — and the walls of my home, reminded me of the swan and his lessons. I had often stared at the old ruins, before turning nine, before becoming the First-in-Training. But afterward, I knew the castle's origin. I could see Ludmilla directing construction. I easily imagined Tannhäuser climbing the steep approach, toward the gate, being met by The Ancient One, Brunhilde floating down to greet her father. If I strained my eyes, I thought I saw Brunhilde curled on her father's lap, on a chair in the main hall. Ruins that held a magical appeal before my lessons began were all the more enrapturing after. The area around Hohenschwangau was not Linderhof. It was not the portal. But it held many reminders of the history. It was a bearable substitute for my time at the lodge.

Although I was away from the valley, my heart and mind were allowed to linger there — but not for long. When I turned ten, I realized the strength and dimensions of the cage that held a future king. De la Rosée's job was to sculpt a king. The Ancient One's job was to strengthen a Swan Knight. De la Rosée implemented his new academic schedule. I was up at 05.30 and in study at 06.30. I studied Arithmetic, German, and Latin before noon, and History, French, and Piano after. I did not complete my daily studies until 19.00. I had short breaks for meals, riding, and visits with my mother. De la Rosée knew nothing of The Ancient One and the Swan Knights. He saw me only as a crown prince. I cannot blame him. He acted under the noblest intentions and the most loyal devotion to his country and king. He knew I was dissatisfied with his academic regimen, but he could not know how I suffocated. I felt longing so violently oppressive that I often thought I might die of it. De la Rosée had no idea that whatever academic discipline he laid before my eyes, my mind connected the lesson to the Swan Knighthood. I benefitted from his lessons, but not as he intended. I must have seemed so distant and dreamy to him.

It was common for months to pass between visits to Linderhof. Although my mind readily acquiesced when my mother reminded me that my obligations to my kingdom out-weighed all other facets of my life, my heart denounced her for the cruelty of my circumstances. In my young mind, a couple of months may as well have been a year. I was even more isolated than before. Otto was left out of most of my schooling and my rare free time was spent in sequestered musings and my imagination's attempts to assume my heroic place as a Swan Knight. I did not want to study Latin or piano. I wanted to learn to read Zweigwesen, like Milli, or to speak Brunnen, like Archbishop Conrad. Every step I took outside of Linderhof, every book I held, every word spoken to me, tried to pull me from the magical world of the Swan Knighthood and chain me to my secular existence. Unfairly, I judged harshly everybody without Grail Blood, everybody ignorant of my true identity as First-in-Training, from the servants to the nobles.

When I returned to Munich, I demanded that the servants at Nymphenburg and the Royal Residence refer to me as "First-in-Training". They snidely obeyed, scoffing at the impropriety. But I was not concerned about their opinions. I knew what they did not. They wanted to adorn me with the titles appropriate for a crown prince. I cared nothing for the kingship I would inherit. I would be the Swan Knight, like Lohengrin and Elsa, Otto I, with his red hair and axe, like Rudolf, who ruled the Wühlenvogel city, like Albert V, and like my own dear grandfather, whose stories sparked the wonder in my imagination. Even when I was three years old, I saw the obvious weight lifted from my grandfather when he gave up the throne. His favorite Swan Knight was Elsa. He worked his whole life to develop her abilities. They never came, but he still related more to her than to anyone else from our history. In a parallel I am not sure anyone else saw, my father bore many traits of Elsa's son, Bechtold.

My grandfather commented to me once, shortly after I began my training with The Ancient One, "I wonder if Elsa would have made a good Queen of Bavaria. I wonder how a crown would have weakened her or made her a worse Swan Knight."

Years later, he still bragged about the wisdom of my answer.

My answer was this, "How could anyone command Unicorns and soldiers?"

My grandfather continued my thought, "… or ministers of state. Maybe that is why there has never been another with Elsa's abilities. Perhaps the political security sought by Lohengrin when he visited the Welf castle, the advantages gained when Hildemar married Aldwin, have caused us more harm than good."

I reminded him that Ludwig the Crusader abandoned the valley to the creatures of the Sweeter Realm when he focused his efforts on politics of his title. But he was a great and revered Swan Knight from our history. He yielded as much but remained with his theory that political power has weakened the Swan Knighthood. He quoted King Rupert and his amendment to the Laws of Ermenrich.

With all of the excuses and rumors surrounding my father's abdication, I believe he did it to be more like Elsa, to focus his thoughts on the portal and the Swan Knighthood. He never stopped trying to control the portal with his thoughts and commune with Unicorns from great distances. He clearly thought that Elsa would not have made a good Queen of Bavaria, that the skills and talents of a great Swan Knight are not necessarily congruent with those of a great monarch. I gave that much thought throughout my life. I used it as an excuse to avoid my political obligations, to the disappointment, and perhaps the death, of many. In any case, my grandfather served as the perfect excuse for me to reject my obligations.

At that age, I spent much of my summers at Nymphenburg. My relentless schedule of study continued. It was compounded by my inability to escape into the reclusive woods of Hohenschwangau. The old country castle had reminders of my Grail lineage on every wall, which were scarce to be found in Munich. My only escape at Nymphenburg was into the expansive gardens. I walked them regularly and found in them enough isolation to free my imagination. At the Royal Residence in Munich, I had no escape. I longed for Linderhof, which offered me greater wonders with each visit.

I grew close to my Aunt Alexandra. When my grandfather was still the Swan Knight, and my father was First-in-Training, all of her other siblings pursued their lives outside of the valley, marrying for political advantage and moving away. Some of them never learned from The Ancient One, never learned the history.

Eventually, Aunt Alexandra became Second-in-Training, a role she kept when my father became king because my grandfather remained the Swan Knight after abdicating the throne of Bavaria. Aunt Alexandra even served as Second behind me, after I turned nine. She only yielded the title when my brother turned nine and began his training. Until then, if my grandfather, father, and I would have suddenly died together, she would have taken the oath to the Queen. She was unmarried and spent most of her life at the lodge. She kept herself surrounded by Sweeter Realm creatures, never truly connecting to the outside world, even when she left Linderhof. Occasionally she would visit me in Munich and bring brightness to those dark days. She pulled me into her room and spoke of the portal and the creatures. She passed messages for me, to and from The Ancient One, who kept a diligent, however distant, eye on my every move.

My brother Otto did not have my fanciful imagination before being introduced to the portal. He did not slip easily into the role of Second, though Aunt Alexandra yielded it gladly. In our earliest years, when we visited Linderhof, we both saw Unicorns and other creatures. Although they struck me as intensely beautiful, they did not strike me as peculiar. They fit right into the world of Germanic lore I had constructed in my mind. The creatures did not fit so easily into Otto's life. His was the life of a Bavarian prince. He spoke of military strategy with our father since he was very young. Since the creatures were not strange to me, I did not speak of them. Once I knew of the family secret, I held them and their secrets tightly to my chest. Otto did not. He often returned to Hohenschwangau and to Munich with tales of strange creatures. He did not tell these tales defiantly and ambitiously, like Maria, the beheaded first wife of Duke

480

Ludwig II, or with the excited fascination of a child making up stories. He told them in fear and confusion, authenticating the stories, or at least his experience of them, in the minds of those who heard them.

They caught the attention of the servants, of de la Rosée, and eventually of the court doctors. They accused him of having hallucinations. This caused a great deal of panic around the royal residences and beyond. When Otto turned nine and met The Ancient One, and learned the stories, he warmed only slightly to the existence of the creatures of the Sweeter Realm. The story of the Wühlenvogel war with the Scheriers disturbed him. The tale of Gessner's encounter with Löwschock and the knobby-headed serpent terrified him. He often shouted out in the night, while dreaming of the creatures of the Deep. In the middle of the day, he would drift into terrible imaginings, and run to the nearest adult, begging to be protected from the giant serpent. Rumors of his insanity began early in his childhood and continued through his life. I pitied him. I mourned his reluctance to join me in my fantastic world. Even after he became Second, he avoided the valley when he could. The portal frightened him. Each time he opened it, he expected Löwschock to reach through and pull him into the Deep Waters. Although Otto was Second-in-Training by title, my Aunt Alexandra remained the Second in all practical senses.

Alexandra was as afraid of the world outside of the valley as Otto was afraid of the valley. Having spent so much time around the portal, she, like I, struggled to adjust to life outside of Linderhof. Like Otto, she spoke too freely of her experiences in and around the old lodge. One day, I heard servants talking about my aunt. They said that she had long complained of having swallowed a piano. They laughed at her and attached my aunt's complaint to the family's growing reputation of insanity. I knew that there was something to the story, something beyond the understanding of the servants who laughed at her when they thought nobody could hear them. The next time I was with my aunt, I asked her about it.

She told me about small, insect-like creatures from the Sweeter Realm called Klavierchens. The creatures have no spoken vocabulary. They communicate with musical notes, not like the Brunnens, who mix notes with word. The Klavierchens speak only in notes. Their notes sound like the strike of a piano key. They are small creatures, the largest of them only reaching the size of an adult human's thumbnail. One day, my aunt opened the portal just as a swarm of Klavierchens flew across the portal point in the Sweeter Realm. They flew unintentionally through the portal and into my aunt's face. She gasped in surprise of the accident, taking one of the poor creatures into her gaping mouth. The hard and sudden inhale of her gasp pulled the Klavierchen down her throat. She felt it squirming around inside of her. Her tender and compassionate sensibilities were tortured even more as she heard it hollering for its comrades, from deep inside of her. The creature's yells sounded like a frantic piano concerto. The incident scarred my aunt. Long after the Klavierchen was surely dead and digested, she still heard it, like the desperate banging of piano keys. When the sensation struck her, she complained quite vocally of it, whether in the safety of the lodge or surrounded by the many ears of one of the other family residences.

"I swallowed the poor Klavierchen", she would say in a morbid sudden panic. "I swallowed the poor little piano."

As I grew and trained, I slipped further from the world that de la Rosée tried to build for me and closer to the world of The Ancient One. I felt alone outside of Linderhof. I felt that I could never have a friend, never have a wife. The world laughed at and scorned my aunt. They accused my brother of insanity. How could I ever connect with anyone from my father's kingdom or beyond, I, who shoved everything not of the valley or Sweeter Realm into the farthest corner of my mind? The answer came when I was twelve years old. My former governess, Sibylle, saw a performance of Richard Wagner's opera *Lohengrin*. She knew how I loved the murals on the walls at Hohenschwangau. She bought me a gift that changed my life. It was a book of Wagner's opera librettos. I read the stories of Lohengrin and Tannhäuser. Of course, the operas were based on the legends, which varied from the truths on which they were based, the truths that were taught to me by The Ancient One when I was nine. Still, the book gave me a mental passage to the valley when I was kept from it.

I begged my parents to take me to see one of Wagner's operas. They felt that the experience would only push me further toward my obsession with the Swan Knighthood and from my education and preparations to be king. They were probably right. Nevertheless, at fifteen years old, after three years of enacting Wagner's operas in my head, in almost every solitary moment, I secured tickets to see *Lohengrin*. As I sat in my royal box in the theater at the Royal Residence in Munich, I watched the murals of my childhood come to life. I saw the tales, more or less, of The Ancient One with my own eyes. I watched The Ancient One pull Lohengrin across the water to Elsa. From that point on, I had no interest in living when I lived. I wanted so badly to be a Swan Knight of old, before rank and title changed everything.

A year after seeing the swan pull Lohengrin across the stage, I saw Wagner's opera *Tannhäuser*. The music from the overture brought me into the distant past before a single performer stepped on stage. I felt my pulse in my ears and eyes, then across my scalp. Every hair on my body stood erect to receive the sensations of the evening. I attended with a court secretary, who held me still as I swooned and convulsed in ecstasy. The story of Tannhäuser and the Brunnen, of their flight through the portal, the Brunnen's death, and the appearance of Brunhilde was my favorite part of the family history. I would have frustrated The Ancient One with my demands for retellings, had he not loved Brunhilde so much. He enjoyed talking about her. He enjoyed every part of the history related to her. The legends never connected Tannhäuser's story to Brunhilde. Why would they? The Tannhäuser legend survived through the poetry he left behind and the stories he told after emerging from the Brunnen wilderness. In Wager's opera, Tannhäuser's Brunnen lover was the goddess of love, Venus. I suppose it is not very far from the truth. The human world had no other equivalent to the seductive beauty of a Brunnen. Inaccuracies aside, I fell in love that night. A gripping obsession was born. I wanted to have Wagner for my own, to bring to physical life other stories from my family history. From my box in the theater, I could live in the past and purge myself of the monotonous rambling and regimented schooling of de la Rosée. In a couple of years, I was given the chance.

CHAPTER 24

To the Throne

MY FATHER WAS A GOOD KING. In being so, he secured the valley and the portal, and was therefore a good Swan Knight, though, as I wrote before, he never held the title. He preferred his academic symposiums in Munich to wrestling with Scheriers at Linderhof. He played the political games better than he rode Unicorns. But he did much to assist the Queen. Perhaps he did too much. In March of 1864, my father grew ill. Some rest at the lodge and some Zweigwesen medicine would probably have set him right. But he had many political concerns on his mind and he worked endlessly to settle them. By the time we realized how ill he had become, it was too late to move him from Munich to Linderhof. My father was dying and I was on the threshold of kingship. I was eighteen. I was not ready.

I would have gladly taken the Swan Knighthood, if my grandfather could have given it to me while my father lived and remained king. I knew I was not prepared to assume the concerns that slowly took my father's life. I saw the responsibilities of my father's throne as the desease that killed him, a disease I must inherit. On 10 March, as I paced the hallway of Nymphenberg palace, while my mother and brother sat at my father's side, my father summoned me to his bedside. He dismissed my mother and Otto. I sat alone beside my dying father. I think he was as afraid of my ascension to the throne as I was. But he did not chastise my immaturity or give me any parting words of advice.

He simply told me, "My son, when your time comes, may you die as peacefully as your father."

From where I sit now, it does not look like his dying wish will come true.

I watched my father take his last breath. The shock of the loss and the tenderness of his final wish overwhelmed the realization that I was king. I walked out of my father's room to the whispers of the court and servants. My head hung low and was only lifted by the surprising words of a page boy.

He simply bowed to me and said, "Your Majesty."

Only then did I fully realize that I was the king.

Two days later, a council in the Royal Residence named me Ludwig II, King of Bavaria. On 14 March, we buried my father. Otto and I walked behind the procession, down the streets of Munich. I had spent so much of my time in the hidden places of my youth, most of the people of Munich saw me for the first time that day, their eighteen-year-old king, with his "insane" brother, burying their former king.

It was my place to tell The Ancient One about the passing of the king. When my grandfather abdicated the throne, he maintained the Swan Knighthood, serving it constantly, in his own ways. He lived to see the death of his son. My father never served as the Swan Knight. In fact, when I turned nine and became First-in-Training with Aunt Alexandra as Second, my father yielded any custodial title in the valley, leaving the concerns of the portal and Sweeter Realm to those of us who wanted them. The Ancient One continued to call him "Portal Steward", but the title meant nothing to my father.

Somehow my grandfather knew that I needed the Swan Knighthood, that being king would ruin me without the true purpose of my life. He surprised me by renouncing the Swan Knighthood when I met him in the valley to tell the swan about my father's death. My grandfather proudly attended the oath I took in front of The Ancient One. The swan was saddened for my loss and that of my grandfather, who he loved dearly. But he never grew particularly close to my father. Had my grandfather died before my father, and the swan was forced to give my father the oath, his heart would have torn. My grandfather died four years after the death of his son, four years after passing the knighthood to me. This made the passing of the Swan Knighthood as peaceful as it could be.

I look back at my first years as king and I regret ascending to the throne so young. My studies were going well and I was just beginning to understand the affairs of state, when I was pulled from my lessons and placed on the throne. Had my father lived to a more natural age, my life would have been very different. The course of European events would likely have been very different. As it happened, I feared the duties that awaited me in Munich. I often rode into the country to avoid my ministers. I wished for the simplicity of Lohengrin's Swan Knighthood. One day, I left on horseback from the castle at Hohenschwangau. I wanted to be in the valley, where I could pretend that my duties to the Queen of the Land and Shallow Waters were all that concerned me. A few of my men rode with me, but I had been darting around the woods of the valley on the backs of unicorns since I was nine. They were no match for me. I lost them within the first half hour of riding and I turned toward Linderhof. I needed the advice of my teacher.

When I arrived, The Ancient One requested to go home for a few days first. He seemed concerned but would not speak openly with me. I let him through and exchanged the valley guards. When I finally settled into the lodge, I found three Scheriers, sleeping on a shelf in the main hall, stacked upon each other. They were delighted to see me. They dove from the shelf and hit me on the chest at once, knocking me to the floor. Scheriers love to wrestle, so I wrestled with them. I offered to open the portal and let them home, but they were too delighted with my arrival in the valley and were not ready to say goodbye. Since Cunrad built the old lodge, Scheriers have occupied the building more than humans have. I hatched an idea to expand the lodge and include quarters for the Scheriers and comfortable accommodations for the other common visitors from the Sweeter Realm. Scheriers are the brightest company anyone could ask for. Three days with them went quickly. I sent the Scheriers home as I let The Ancient One back into the valley. He seemed relieved from the worries that sent him home in such a hurry, but a lingering uneasiness sat subtly in his eyes.

The swan looked at my initial drawings for the expansion of the lodge. His eyes brightened immediately. He had lived through so many absent Swan Knights, those generations between Emperor Ludwig and Duke Wilhelm, the Queen's correspondent, and the years under Duke Charles. My commitment to the valley was clear. My plans for additions to the lodge made it clearer. We discussed the particulars for an hour. It was my first real conversation with him since I took the Swan Knight oath. It felt good to interact with him in that way. There was a deferent obedience in his voice that was not there before my father died. It reminded me that I was the Swan Knight. My enthusiastic plans for the lodge assured the old teacher that my heart was where it belonged — in the valley and with the Queen. The conversation over the lodge was the perfect introduction to the topic I really wished to discuss. I wanted to leave a legacy. My grandfather changed the face of Munich with his grand architecture. My father elevated the arts. I wanted to leave a mark greater than the expansion of the old lodge.

I was so eager as I detailed the plans that I raised my voice in excited animation. The Ancient One laughed at me. I was insulted and ordered him to stop. He laughed harder. Insult turned to anger and grew as he continued to laugh — until he explained himself.

He said, "When you raise your voice like that, in excitement, you remind me of Lohengrin at your age."

No combination of words, in any language, could have raised my spirits like that. Not since I learned the history at nine years old did I feel such pride. I thought about Lohengrin, and the many other great people in the Swan Knight history. I wanted to inspire my subjects the way Wagner's operas inspired me, with the tales of my family's history. I knew what my legacy would be, and I pitched the idea to The Ancient One. I wanted to bring Wagner to Munich and commission him to tell other great stories from my family history. The operas *Lohengrin* and *Tannhäuser* were already enrapturing audiences.

"Imagine what Wagner could do with the other stories — Elsa, Ludwig the Crusader, Otto I, Rudolf and

Emperor Ludwig, Adolf and the invasion of the Wühlenvogel city."

He loved my ancestors and took great pride in his association to them. He loved talking about them. The idea of commissioning Wagner to set their stories to opera put an undeniable sparkle in his old eyes. But it was snuffed out quickly by his sober concerns.

"Be careful," he warned, "not to let this man become your Conrad Gessner. I recognize the infatuation in your eyes. I saw it in Albert's when he spoke of Gessner."

I am sure his assessment was accurate, but it insulted me at the time. I stared at him with an impertinent anger that he did not deserve.

He broke the awkwardness, asking, "Do you really want to incite the curiosity of the world?"

I answered, "We do not live in the 1550s. This is an age of science. The people will see the stories as opera and no more, tales for the stage, to be enjoyed and forgotten."

"Do not forget, young king," he followed, "Gessner was a scientist."

"Yes," I refuted, "a scientist of his day, when science intended to prove what was not believed. Now it only exists to disprove what is believed. Albert V lived in an age of wonder and curiosity. In this age of skepticism, truth is quite safe hiding in art, where it can affect people without their permission. They no longer seek truth. They love to be entertained and hate to be taught. These operas can plant seeds of goodness — improve the people without their knowledge."

The Ancient One was not yet convinced.

So, I asked him, "Why do we protect the Grail? Is it not for the eventual salvation of mankind? Really, one of the greatest enjoyments of the mind is to be carried away by the wonderful works of this composer — and then, elevated and strengthened, one can face the realities of life again. Is it enough to secure the Grail until God calls it into service again, or are we also to secure the hearts of humans, to keep them on the side of good until our services to the Grail are no longer needed?"

The Ancient One was impressed with the case I presented. After warnings and compromises, promises and deferments, we agreed that the stories could be staged, but under different names and different settings, blended into other legends. I could have my legacy of inspiration without unleashing another Gessner event. We decided to begin with the legend of Tristan and Isolde, the legend grown from Veronika, the great-granddaughter of Ermenrich, and enhance it with other stories from the Swan Knight history, and set it far from the valley. Once The Ancient One saw that no harm could come from it, he embraced the endeavor and offered many suggestion from his endless well of Swan Knight stories, even adding tales I never heard in my many lessons. We spoke as equals. We spoke as friends, uniting my excitement for Wagner's music with his love for the Grail Blood. I never felt more love and admiration for my old teacher than I did that evening, after a day of such jubilant conversation. I slept that night with visions of the stage, of dramatic Wagner music set to Swan Knight stories. I thought about the ovations and the gratitude of the Bavarian people for giving them such a beautiful gift.

When I awoke, the concerned expression that The Ancient One wore when I rode into the valley had returned. I ordered him to tell me what worried him. He told me that the Queen had felt waves from the Deep, strong, dark waves of jealousy and anger, pushing upward, into the Shallow Waters for the first time in centuries. I asked him what it meant. He did not know. He instructed me to send one of the sentry Zweigwesens through the portal with a letter. By the time I rounded the lodge, the Zweigwesen already waited at the portal point. I handed him the letter and opened the portal. I watched the creature walk through the portal and I turned toward the lodge. I took one step away from the open portal and felt something large and heavy hit me between the shoulders. I turned sharply as found a Wühlenvogel, recovering from what must have been a painful collision with my back. He had turned his neck to avoid hitting me with his deadly horns. In doing so, his neck took the brunt of the collision.

I tended to him for a moment before thinking to myself, "Wühlenvogels do not come through the portal. This is the first since the great exodus to the Black Forest."

A foreboding sense of dread consumed me.

"Where is the swan?" he asked me.

"He is in the lodge. You may go to him."

He frightened me saying, "This news is for you too, Swan Knight."

"Then come with me." I said as I started toward the lodge.

492

He stopped me sharply, "I would rather remain near the portal."

I whistled loudly to The Ancient One. Within seconds, he joined us from the lodge. The Wühlenvogel told us that the Queen of the Land and Shallow Waters was dead, killed by Löwschock.

"Where is the Grail?" I asked sharply and impatiently.

"The Queen feared for its safety. She hid it far from the Waters. She left the safety of her home to come to you, Swan Knight, and tell you in person where it lies. She had barely left the Shallow Waters when the King of the Deep attacked her. The entire Sweeter Realm heard her cry. Many of us, and many other breeds, came to her call. When we got to her, Löwschock hung over her, screaming and hissing at her in his language. We surrounded the Queen and frightened Löwschock back into the Waters. The Queen ordered the Wühlenvogels to take her to the swan's nest. She must see the Swan Knight. We took her to the nest. One of us left for the Zweigwesen homeland, to beg for their medicines. When they came, it was too late. The Queen died in the nest."

The Wühlenvogel looked directly and solemnly at The Ancient One and told him, "You are the king now. With her last breath, she told me that you are to be King of the Land and Shallow Waters until an election can be held."

The Ancient One's feathers fluffed and shivered. He swayed and nearly fell from the shock.

"Where is she now?" He asked.

"She lies peacefully in your nest."

493

"Bring her through. Bring her to me." The swan demanded.

The Wühlenvogel went through the portal and returned with several of his kind, carrying the corpse of the Queen. The Wühlenvogels howled like wolves, but a piercing sorrow lined their voices. The Wühlenvogel oath of loyalty to the Queen, all those centuries ago, ran through the blood of each of them, young and old. Their pain was immense and their horrible howls expressed it exquisitely.

The Queen was more beautiful than I had imagined her. The shimmering scales of her dress picked up the sun and changed color with every slight movement of her body. They almost sang, using colors as their voices. Such vibrant life in the scales contrasted morbidly with the pale and deathly grey shade of her face, still wearing the expression of pain and fear. My heart had never been stabbed with such sadness. I joined my voice to the Wühlenvogels' and howled in sorrowful unison with them. The Ancient One simply stood, weak and wobbly, until he brought himself to approach the body and lay a tender kiss on her lips. He whispered something into her ear. It was not German, nor did it sound like his language. Perhaps it was the Queen's native words. In any case, he spoke them with more love, more wretched love, than I have ever seen in any creature from either side of the portal.

"We must bury her on this side." The swan proclaimed.

None of us dared question him. He insisted that we bury her at the portal point, where Parsifal's blood hit the valley. I stepped back and allowed the portal to close. Within half of a minute, the Wühlenvogels had dug the grave. They laid her gently and silently. I could not approach without opening the portal. The Ancient One made it clear to me that it would remain closed until she was buried. I wanted to stand beside them all and watch the Queen disappear from the eyes of the living, under the valley soil. I stood back as ordered and saw nothing but the backs of the mourning creatures. I closed my eyes. I am haunted to this day by the sound of the dirt hitting the Queen's beautiful scales as the Wühlenvogels filled the grave — my only sensual experience of the burial.

Once the grave was filled, The Ancient One beckoned me beside him. As I approached the grave, the portal opened at the center of the broken dirt.

After a moment of silence, disturbed only by the dull crackle of the portal, The Ancient One said in a reverent whisper, "She is now the threshold between realms. May all who pass through the portal be worthy to walk across Kandake, the Queen of the Land and Shallow Waters."

At that, the Wühlenvogels bowed low to the swan, draping their long necks along the ground and saying in unison, "Long may the King protect the Land and Waters."

The Ancient One stared at the portal, where it touched the center of the Queen's grave. He did not notice the salute of the Wühlenvogels until they finished speaking and lifted their chins as far off of the ground as they could, while still pressing the length of their necks against the ground.

"No... no... I..." He stuttered until he composed himself.

He took a few deep breaths and responded politely, "Thank you, my friends."

His eyes shot from the Wühlenvogels to the portal, as he spoke sharply and to himself, "I must find the Grail."

He flew into the portal without another word or glance to any of us. Many times I watched the old swan fly through the portal. It often left me sad and lonely. Never had it hollowed me like his departure did on that day.

As I stared into the portal after him, trying in vain to pierce the nothing with my eyes and cling to his image as long as I could, a Wühlenvogel asked me, "Is there anything you need of us, child of Rudolf?"

I did not notice them all staring at me, waiting for an answer. I snapped myself back to attention and shook my head and gestured into the portal. In a blink, they were all gone from the valley. I turned away from the portal and walked quickly toward the lodge. I knew that the sound of the closing portal would hurt me. I wanted to get that pain done with quickly. I felt so alone that I had forgotten that the sentries and patrols were still in the valley. They met me in front of the lodge.

A Unicorn said to me, "We apologize for leaving our posts. But we wanted to express our sorrow to you, and reassure you of our loyalty."

I ordered them to stay with me. After some protests, they obeyed. We sat in silence together until stomachs growled for food. Over food, they told me stories of the Queen. As I listened to each story, the scope of our loss became clearer to me. But I still could not fully understand. She had been their queen for thousands of human lifetimes. There was nothing on this side of the portal to compare. The stories were personal and tenderly spoken, and they covered a greater portion of time than I could truly comprehend.

The Ancient One remained in the Sweeter Realm for several days before I stopped waiting for him. I had to get back to Munich, and I was eager to extend my hand to Wagner. I opened the portal every day before I left, but the swan did not come through. I understood. He had to mourn the loss of an ancient friend and assume her duties. He needed to discover where she hid the Holy Grail. I felt terribly for him. But I also felt terribly for me. I needed him. I had not yet found my own feet beneath me, as king or as Swan Knight. So, I left the valley in the charge of the Unicorns and I returned to Munich to face the questions and criticism for disappearing and leaving my groomsmen behind.

CHAPTER 25
The Surrogate Mentor

WHEN I LEFT FOR LINDERHOF, I had no mind for the affairs of state. I did not return with more. The Queen was dead, and The Ancient One was King. Would I ever see him again? No Swan Knight had ever seen the Queen. Would the same apply now to our timeless teacher? I had gone months at a time without seeing him, several times throughout my childhood. I survived. Now, it had been days, and my longing for him strangled me. Would I only be able to communicate with him through letters, like Duke Wilhelm? I considered abdicating my throne and becoming the new teacher of the Swan Knights. What was I thinking? At best, I could teach two generations before dying and leaving them without a teacher. Besides, his mind was so vast, nobody could teach the history like he has. Nobody has seen it all.

Such thoughts bounced incessantly around my skull, endearing the old bird to me more and increasing my pain in his absence. My mind sought to replace him, to ease my suffering. I wrote to Wagner. I was already enraptured by him, but I poured my love for the swan into him. Wagner was fifty years old. I was only eighteen. He was such a great man. It was easy to transfer my affections for The Ancient One onto the composer. I did not write to

Wagner as a stranger. I wrote to him as if he had taught and trained me since I was nine.

I expressed my admiration for his operas, but included a framed photograph of me and a small ruby.

I wrote, "As this stone burns, so do I burn to have you near me."

I did not truly burn for Wagner. I burnt for my sweet, old sage. But at the time I did not know the difference. I poured my love and devotion onto a stranger.

Nobody knew where Wagner lived. He was in hiding from his creditors. I gave the letter to one of my secretaries and demanded that Wagner be found and given the letter immediately. Nobody in my government knew what I had gone through in my last visit to the valley. I see now how absurd I must have looked and sounded. They found Wagner in Stuttgart. He responded quickly to my letter and was before me in Nymphenberg Palace within two weeks. When I met him, my emotions were shredded. I shook and stammered and poured myself on him. He must have been shocked by my fretful attentions, but I satiated two desperate thirsts of his, his vanity and his finances. Wagner had expensive tastes. This is why, despite his success as a composer, he was broke. I set him up in an apartment on the Würmsee. My own Berg Castle sits on the northeastern shore. Wagner settled in and began writing *Tristan and Isolde.*

With my surrogate mentor nicely settled in, and beginning work on my legacy, my thoughts turned to my actual mentor. I rode alone through Graswang Valley, to Linderhof. From the edge of the woods, as soon as I set eyes upon the lodge, I rode as quickly as I could to the portal point. I jumped from my horse, opening the portal in midair before landing on my feet directly in front of it. Honestly, I did not expect The Ancient One to step immediately through, as he so often has. I did not expect to see him at all, so I was not crushed when he failed to appear. A Unicorn followed me from the outskirts of the valley, and met me at the portal. Because of the panicked pace of my ride into the valley, followed by my desperate leap from the horse and eager eyes staring into the portal, the Unicorn suspected the worse. He touched his horn to my chest and quickly released a huffing sigh of relief.

With his horn still touching my chest, he thought to me, "I will go through and bring back news of him."

The Unicorn walked leisurely through the portal. A few hours later, I opened the portal and the Unicorn returned, followed by The Ancient One. We settled into the lodge with food and drink. I opened my mouth to tell him that I had missed him, that I needed his guidance, his approval, and his affection more than ever.

He stopped me, saying, "Everything is different now. My pact with Parsifal and Gütel, to teach Lohengrin and all of the Swan Knight children, was made under the Queen. But she is dead and I have inherited a realm in peril. When I last left you, the cold and dark of the Deep had spread to fill the Shallow Waters. Its chill has begun to fill the air between the trees of the Land. The breeds of the Land and Shallow Waters united behind me and elected me their King. I could not refuse them. I was humbled beyond expression, as their love for me, their faith in me, pushed the dark and cold back into the Deep. But darkness did not retreat willingly. I can feel it pushing back. Good creatures disappear every day, not just from the Shallow Waters, or even the shore and the Nomadic Belt surrounding the lake, but from deep into the Land.

Löwschock has rallied his evil. They are active. They are moving. They have been seen as far as the Brunnen homeland. I still do not know where the Grail is hidden. As for now, neither does the King of the Deep. He wants it. That is why he killed the Queen."

In a swell of fear for my friend, I interrupted, "Is he after you? Does he know you are King?"

"He must know. But the creatures of the Land and Shallow Waters have not been this united since the plans were laid for the Wühlenvogel city in the Black Forest. Make no mistake. A war is coming. We do not know what secrets are kept in the darkness of the Deep, what evil waits to emerge, or how many enemies we face. But we are united and optimistic."

"I am still the Swan Knight. My oath to the Queen transfers to you."

"There is little you can do without jeopardizing the portal. You are right. You are the Swan Knight. And the Swan Knight's job is to protect the safety and secrecy of the portal. Fulfill that and you fulfill your oath to the Queen — and to me."

The Ancient One could not linger. The responsibilities of his kingship dwarfed the concerns of mine. When I opened the portal and allowed him to return to his kingdom, my spirits hit a new low. I compensated by throwing my entire heart behind Wagner. I lavished him with whatever extravagant comforts he desired, whatever would facilitate the completion of *Tristan and Isolde*. I morphed every moment of worry for The Ancient One and my friends in the Sweeter Realm into eagerness for the opera. In my mind, the completion of the opera would spell peace and safety for my dear swan.

My fear for his safety was so severe that I tried not to think about him. I gave all of my agitated love to Wagner. But Wagner demanded peace, to concentrate on his work. I communicated with him primarily through letters.

I wrote to him as he neared completion, "My Heart's rapture gives me no peace. Nearer and nearer draws the happy day — Tristan will rise."

My obsession with Wagner and his opera could not be understood. It was simply the mask of greater, secret concerns. My ministers talked. They feared that Wagner had become my Lola Montez, the dancer who stole my grandfather from the throne. But the motives of my grandfather, like mine, went much deeper and holier than the officials or the public could comprehend. So, my troubles wore a Wagnerian mask. In June of 1865, *Tristan and Isolde* premiered, and that mask was beautiful. The performance pushed my emotions over the edge. I cried. I writhed in my seat. The stories I had learned from my noble teacher came to life in front of me, just as they had with *Lohengrin* and *Tannhäuser*. Every bit of fear and love for my Sweeter Realm friends, my memories of the Queen's death and burial, the crushing weight of my inability to help them, all poured through my reaction to the performance.

The opera was a triumph, everything I hoped it would be. But its themes and familiar stories agitated my fears. My emotions overwhelmed me during the ride home from the theater. I halted the royal train and strolled out into the woods alone. Every moment of the opera, and every thought in my head afterward, drew my attention to the Swan Knighthood and the perils of my friends. Oh, why must I be the Swan Knight now, in such difficult times? The pain was acute, but so was the rapture. I felt one with the stories of my family past. The mundane concerns of Bavarian politics seemed like the other side of the world. At least my fear for The Ancient One, and a possible war with the Deep, accomplished what my imagination never quite could. It stripped me of all of my secular thoughts, plunging me fully into my life as the Swan Knight. My passions sprang through my pores. My flesh tingled and I felt vivaciously alive. As a young child, I thirsted for just a drop of my mystical connection to the figures in the Hohenschwangau murals. Now, I paddled desperately in an ocean of it.

Tristan and Isolde thrilled the Munich audience. For a time afterward, they celebrated Wagner's presence in the city as much as I did. I began to believe that my plans were falling into place. The Bavarian performance stirred pride in the Bavarian people. They were inspired. But it did not last. My mind was too full for stately events. I threw no balls, hosted no great dinners. I closed the few doors that are usually open for the people to connect with their king. They wanted me and I was gone from their view. Blame fell on Wagner. The people knew how I doted on him. But Wagner was not to blame. I was a Swan Knight first. In fact, I was only a Swan Knight, not a king in any of the ways the people needed me to be.

I wanted to defend and excuse Wagner, and pass the blame to its rightful recipient. But my Swan Knight oath forbade me to offer them any alternative reason for my absence and distraction. I have long enjoyed imagining that I would have made a good king, without the Swan Knighthood, with only those kingly concerns shared by most European monarchs. I never entertain the thought long. Nothing is more precious to me, nor ever has been, than the Swan Knighthood and my blood connection to Parsifal and the Grail. I only wish my knighthood was not so wrought with misfortune. The Queen is dead, the same Queen to whom Parsifal swore the first Swan Knight oath. Every Swan Knight since has served her. Now she is gone. Many tragedies and dangers have come that I have yet to write down in this account, and I am the Swan Knight — now, of all times.

The people of Munich thought that Wagner took advantage of their king. Perhaps there is some truth to that. He required increasingly expensive and elaborate living conditions to continue his work toward our mutual goals. It was a great expense, but little compared to the cost of my grandfather's improvements to the city. My investment in Wagner was less visible than the grand constructions of my grandfather's designs. My investment remained locked away in a room, thinking and scribbling. Although the results were grand, the process was hidden, so the people grew impatient with the expenditure and disdainful of Wagner. Unable to visualize the greatness to come and unable to understand the investment in Wagner, the tensions finally boiled over. Within a year and a half of my first meeting with Wagner, my prime minister threatened to resign if the composer did not leave Bavaria. I could no longer force my vision on them. Wagner had to go. It pained me to send him away, but in the time since the Queen's death and the loss of The Ancient One's ready companionship, I had grown stronger. Opera would not be my contribution. Architecture and construction were in my blood. It was clear, ever since I awed my family with my childhood blocks, that strains of Cunrad lived in me. I turned my attention there.

Although painful, exiling Wagner from Bavaria was not as difficult as I thought it would be. One year earlier, I would have thought it impossible. He went to Switzerland. He and I both imagined that he could return to Munich after a short period, but the public disdain for him was deep. He remained away for many years. The timing of his departure proved fortuitous. He was a tremendous distraction for me and matters would soon demand my attention.

CHAPTER 26
War, Weakening, and Weddings

IN WAGNER'S ABSENCE, I had less to draw me to Munich. I spent most of my time at Linderhof and Hohenschwangau. I had no teacher, nobody to continue my training. The Ancient One was never at his nest near the portal. He had a throne to attend. In fact, he was rarely ever there. I hear he traveled from homeland to homeland in the Land and Shallow Waters, monitoring conditions and preparing for war with the Deep. I took my training into my own hands, recalling into the valley any creature with something to teach me. I knew that I would play a part in the war, regardless of what the new King said. So, I rode Unicorns and flew Wühlenvogels. I never had a stomach for combat, not even combat training. But I prepared myself for warfare by tightening my bond with the creatures and honing, with them, their own abilities. My full heart and mind were behind The Ancient One and his subjects. My Swan Knight oath was to him and I intended to serve him as my predecessors served the Queen.

Just as I prepared for war as the Swan Knight, war came to my Bavarian throne. For centuries, Austria had been the seat of German power. But Prussia to the north grew in strength, and as German unification became a more popular sentiment, the tug-of-war for German control between the north and the south grew in tension. I could not divert my energy between two wars. I left my Bavarian ministers to handle German politics. Löwschock's violence grew from small encroachments and isolated attacks into all-out war. He believed that the Grail and its powers belonged to the ruler of the Land and Shallow Waters. When he killed the Queen, he expected to rule the entire Sweeter Realm, and assume possession of the Holy Grail. When The Ancient One became King, Löwschock believed that the Grail passed to him with the title. He knew that The Ancient One traveled across the homelands of the Sweeter Realm. He began invading the territories one by one to find the King. His attacks were brutal. With the death of the Queen, the Shallow Waters fell to Löwschock. The border between the Shallow and the Deep erased. Darkness and cold lapped against the shores. There was little The Ancient One could do for the poor creatures of the Shallow. Very few could retreat to the Land. Those who survived became unfortunate subjects of Löwschock.

Löwschock and his minions started their attack on the Land with the Wühlenvogels. He breached the hole that the Queen had closed so long ago, flooding the Wühlenvogels' underground cities. The dark creatures of the Deep swam through the cities destroying the structures and killing those who did not flee in time. Most of the Wühlenvogels escaped to the Brunnen wilderness, where they constructed new cities under the ground, designed as staging points for attack should the Brunnen homeland need defending. Those who did not escape were killed or captured. The captured creatures were brought back as food for the monsters of the Deep, sacrificed and eaten in cruel ceremonies. By the time Löwschock reached the Scherier homeland, it was completely empty. Most of the Scheriers sought refuge with the Unicorns or Zweigwesens. The leaders went to the Unicorns to plan and strategize. The Scheriers had one great fear, above all others. The bulky, knobby-headed creature, the one that grabbed Gessner with its tail, loved the taste of Scheriers above all else. Its allegiance to Löwschock was based on the promise of Scherier meat. The monster liked to savor the taste. It kept a Scherier in its mouth at all times, often still alive, pierced by the cruel teeth.

When these reports reached me through the portal, I could not divert my fury or my resources to petty power disputes between Austria and Prussia. I had no idea where The Ancient One was. Löwschock hunted him, assuming that he had the Grail. My fear for The Ancient One's life surpassed any fear I had lived or imagined in all of my years of fantastic imaginings.

Finally, The Ancient One came to me.

I yelled at him, "Where have you been? Why have you not come to me?"

"Our enemy follows me everywhere," he said. "I would sooner lead him to my own beating heart before leading him to the portal. But I hear he is at the outskirts of the Unicorn homeland. I pray they hold him there. If the Unicorns fall, there will be nothing to protect the Eulesänger homeland behind them."

"My God," I said, struck with the imagery of war. "Let me send my army."

"Then what? Should we keep them all here, or kill them to keep the secret?"

"The creatures fought in our defense, in the Black Forest. Am I to abandon them now?" I asked.

"Emperor Ludwig's attack was not against his nephews. It was against the creatures, out of jealousy for their loyalty to Rudolf. It was not a political invasion. It was an attack against me for planning the exodus."

"Then what can I do?"

"For now, nothing. I know that the Swan Knight will play a role in this affair, before it is complete. Go to Munich. Tend to your own kingdom. I pray the answers will come to both of us."

When he saw the tension rise in my manner, his sharp and rigid posture softened. His fluffed feathers settled. He looked at me like he did when I was a boy. He kissed me and disappeared back through the portal. I felt such a powerful urge to follow him through and give up my world forever. But I obeyed him and rode back to Munich.

When I got there, the ministers were in an uproar. The people scorned me for disappearing and abandoning my political duties. The tensions between Austria and Prussia came to war, and Bavaria had to take a side. It was too much for me. The images of the Sweeter Realm war, described by The Ancient One, still hung in my eyes — Wühlenvogels sacrificed and eaten, Scheriers hanging from the teeth of Gessner's vile serpent . Now my ministers asked me to mobilize my army and send them into a battle that was not their own. I thought about my willingness to send them to the defense of the Unicorns. Was this any different? A side needed to be taken and I did not know or care where Bavaria stood. My ministers advised an alliance with Austria. I deferred to their opinions. With the announcement of war, the people of Bavaria cheered. I felt more support in their thirst for bloody glory than I felt during my father's burial procession.

With those wheels set in motion, and the machine of war moving forward without me, I turned my attention to the war with Löwschock. There were only two people I could turn to for advice, my grandfather and my brother. I began with the only person I had ever known with as great an affection for the Sweeter Realm creatures as I have. I sought the advice of my grandfather. As I described the situation to him, he seemed focused and concerned. But when his chance to reply came, his thoughts were scattered. He spoke of English poetry and of Roman architecture. I waited for his thoughts to unite in the form of some profound and useful advice. They remained scattered and utterly useless to me. I turned to my brother. I should never have described the cries of the Scheriers, stuck between the teeth of the bulky beast. The horror of my description shocked Otto. He curled into a tight ball and separated his mind from his body. He hummed over my words and did not appear to understand another word I said. I left him with my love and pity.

I thought about my Aunt Alexandra. She had not spent much time in the valley since my father died. I asked for her advice on ways we could aid The Ancient One's war effort. She had no advice to give, but offered herself to me. I brought her to the lodge. She turned it into a hospital, staffed with Zweigwesens, to accept the wounded through the portal. The hospital stayed empty. Nobody would risk leading Löwschock to the portal point. Nevertheless, having the hospital ready, and keeping it prepared, gave me slight peace of mind and it gave my aunt something to do to relieve her of her lifelong guilt for swallowing the Klavierchen.

The German War, as we called it, lasted for only seven weeks. Prussia prevailed. The sentiment of Pan-Germanism grew, especially from the north. Germany would soon unite, and the base of power would be in Prussia. That is what the German War determined. The Prussians were thirsty for power, and they had a grand war machine. Although I was relieved by the end of the German War, I knew that Bavarian involvement in European war was just beginning. The sovereignty of every German kingdom weakened as Prussia strengthened. Prussia's victory over Austria and Bavaria fueled its military ambitions. As part of the treaty, I had to promise Bavarian support for future Prussian military campaigns. I worried for my kingdom. I worried for Bavarian identity. I worried for the security of my little valley.

Löwschock wearied of war with the Land. His minions did not move easily on the ground and his absence from the Waters loosened his grip there. The Shallow Waters began to warm and light began to penetrate through the surface again. The Unicorns held their ground. Löwschock suffered losses. He abandoned the campaign for The Ancient One and the Grail, and returned to the Waters to reclaim control of the wet creatures. After the fighting stopped, the King of the Land and Shallow Waters taught me my newest lesson — how to be a king.

I met with him in the valley. As I sat hidden away from my subjects, tucked away in my quiet valley, as I so often was, he told me what he had been doing. He traveled each decimated homeland. He presided over memorials to the fallen, he brought Zweigwesen medicines to the sick and wounded. He traveled with a chorus of Brunnens and Eulesängers, who lifted the wounded hearts of the Sweeter Realm with their songs. The Ancient One was kingly. My own behavior stood in embarrassing contrast to his. My army had just suffered military defeat. My soldiers died and were wounded. My people needed the care of The Ancient One. No — they needed the care and compassion of their king. They needed me. I am not certain if I came to that conclusion on my own or if The Ancient One walked me there without my knowing, as he often did. In any case, he listened as the idea came to my mind and out of my mouth.

"I must do as you have." I declared, as I stood sharply, knocking my chair to the floor of the main hall of the lodge with the backs of my knees.

As I detailed my excited plans for mirroring his actions with my own tour of my own kingdom, the weary old swan listened with an increasingly brightened expression.

When I finished, and I returned my chair to its legs and had a seat, he told me, "Finally — you have become what I knew you would be. You are your great-grandfather, your grandfather, and your father, all in one."

His approval surged me with pride and energy. I left in the morning for Munich and planned a tour of my kingdom. The people would have their king, up close and personal.

I could never see myself as The Ancient One's equal. But during the tour, I saw myself as his peer, or perhaps his shadow, mimicking every flap of his illustrious wings.

I adorned the graves of my fallen soldiers with wreaths from my own gardens. I brought medicines and my own royal doctor to tend to the sick and wounded. I brought money to relieve the financial burden of the families affected by the war. The reception of the people, the gratitude, the love, and the loyalty to their king shines, but it did not shine on me. It shined through me and onto a much wiser king. Again, he bettered me in ways I could not have foreseen and could not have avoided if I tried. I had spent so much effort trying to avoid my kingship to tend to my knighthood. Ironically, I never felt more like a Swan Knight than when I tended to my kingly duties on the tour of my kingdom. I never felt more like the product of my venerable teacher. I never felt more like a child of Lohengrin and Nethe, Elsa and Cunrad, Hildemar and Aldwin, than when I finally presented the Bavarian people with the king that they deserved and so desperately desired.

The tour healed many wounds, mine and those of my subjects. My tour of Bavaria reflected The Ancient One's tour of the Land in one terrible, foreboding way. When the dust settled, both his kingdom and mine were weaker. In both kingdoms, peace did not look to last. We both felt that every gasp of recovery breath could be the last before the chaotic turmoil of war repossessed the kingdoms. I realized, as difficult as it was to admit, that my mother was right. My priorities to Bavaria were paramount, not just in my obligations to my kingdom, but in my duties as the Swan Knight. As I sat in reflection of the success of my Bavarian tour, I recalled one of the early lessons of my old teacher, "To simply pass the Swan Knighthood safely and honorably to the next generation is the noblest quest of the Swan Knight."

"To the next generation" — My tour of Bavaria gave the people the image of a bachelor king, and sparked discussions of a royal wedding and an heir. My ears received the rumors from afar and from the direct questions from my closest relations and associates. I see now that I set an impossible standard for prospective queens. I held every woman against the standards of the Swan Knights and Swan Knight spouses. I looked for some creature like in that English novel, pieced together from Gütel's bravery and Cunrad's loyalty, Ludmilla's warmth, Agnes' maternal nurturing, Elizabeth's service, and the mystic sensibilities of Irmengard. There was no such woman in the world. Had there been, I would not have deserved her.

To inquiries on the subject of marriage, I recited my rehearsed reply, "I have no time to get married. Let Otto produce us an heir."

It was meant to incite a smile and to keep the pall of mystery over me. I wish to always remain an enigma to everybody. That pall is the perfect hiding place for the secrets that must remain secrets. The eccentricities of my family, the rumors of insanity, have been the perfect excuse for behavior associated with our arcane legacy, as if by design. But in truth, it is a happy accident. Our family reputation has been the ideal mask for strange things that would have otherwise drawn attention.

Regardless of the inauthenticity of my excuses, I have not had time to marry. I envy the romantic tales of the Swan Knights of old — ribbons dancing in Christmas trees, sung wedding vows, even Tannhäuser's strange and instant passion for his Brunnen lover. But I faced conflicting interests, Bavaria's need for a royal heir and its need for a constant and present king. Oh, that I could have been king at a different time, and spared myself these painful sacrifices. But both of my titles were in peril, both kingdoms weakened by war and certain to face more. The pleasures of life were never meant to be mine. A mariner in a furious storm has no time to savor the pleasures of being at sea. He thinks only of keeping his ship afloat and saving the lives of his crew.

The Ancient One provided me with an example of true nobility, true kingship. He would have preferred to spend his time in the valley, teaching young Swan Knights and reminiscing over loved ones from days gone by. Instead, he became King under circumstances that grieved him tremendously. He pulled himself away from the life he desired and committed his energy to his duties. I too wanted to be in the valley, but from his example, I learned to be a better king. The Swan Knighthood faced its greatest challenges in many generations. It needed my attention. But so did Bavaria. The two facets of my character shared more common ground than I realized at the time. But they certainly shared one common need. Both needed an heir. Both needed a spouse. With the knighthood and the kingship uniting with that singular demand, I had to open my mind to the possibility. I had only met one woman whose mind and heart met with mine on the same field of play. She is my cousin, Sisi. I enjoyed her company for many reasons. Not only did she understand me, as if she had been raised in the valley and knew about my life there, but she was unavailable, which removed the discomfort of possibility.

Sisi married and, of course, I saw much less of her. She threw a court ball that I reluctantly attended. I despise such events, but opportunities to visit Sisi were few. At the ball, Sisi's younger sister, Sophie, caught my eye. Sophie's character is less demonstrative than Sisi's, so I had hardly noticed her until the ball. She seemed to blossom that night, as if her sister's shadow lifted from her and the warm light of the sun finally invited her pedals to expose themselves. Sophie has many of Sisi's quirks, but subtler and half-hidden behind an almost blinding beauty. I did not enter the ball with the intention of seeking a wife. But the obligation, placed on me by both my sacred and secular titles, hung heavily on my shoulders and constantly on my mind.

Sophie appeared to me unlike she ever had before, womanly, maternal, and just unusual enough to embrace the strangeness of my life. We danced together all night. I prodded her through each dance for hints of her character, not the obvious, not the things I had seen or the reports I had heard, but those thoughts and feelings that had never seen the light of day. Had I judged with a heart not battered by war and worry, perhaps I would have seen clearly and saved us both a heartache and embarrassment. As it was, my every thought wore the chains of obligation. I molded her answers to my probing questions into the shape of a Swan Knight's wife and a queen of Bavaria. We were soon engaged to marry.

The engagement brought more dreaded events, crowded and talkative, and everything I hate most in my existence. Perhaps it was unfair of me, but I blamed Sophie for being the chain that held me to that anchor, forbidding the free sailing of my imagination and the attendance to my duties as the Swan Knight. I bounced from one engagement celebration to another, from one loud social event to the next. I felt such a dire need to flee them all and ride at top speed to my beloved valley and rustic lodge. I felt a frenzied need to attend to the portal and receive updates from The Ancient One. Instead, I found myself dressed like a doll in military uniform, utterly detached from the one aspect of my identity that I had most tightly embraced since I was nine years old. But breaking a royal engagement is not easy. I tried to endear my heart to the situation. I started calling Sophie "Elsa", deceiving myself into believing that I saw in her the traits of the greatest Swan Knight. The wedding was planned as one would expect, opulent and grand beyond comparison. It would have been magnificent and terrible.

Sophie and I communicated mostly through letters. Quick answers to questions posed during a dance at a ball can be interpreted however the asker wishes. But letters are not written by the mood of the night, or the music being played, or by the expectations of the recipient. They are written by the mind and heart of the writer. I quickly realized that Sophie was not the Swan Knight spouse I had convinced myself that she was. Her letters betrayed a plainness and a simplicity that pained me deeply upon gradual realization. I spent long days suffering through my dilemma. I took a few late night rides from Berg Castle to visit Sophie at her home. I sought some slight ray of light that would reconcile me to the marriage. I asked her to sing me arias from Wagner's operas. She sang beautifully. Her renditions were rigidly accurate, excellent reproductions of the greatness of another. But there was nothing of her own heart in her performances. I looked for signs of Nethe and Irmengard. What I saw was a recitation of the traits I sought, not the traits themselves. I wanted her to be the woman I could trust with the holy secrets of the Grail and portal. It became clear to me that she was not. I was auditioning her for the most important available position in the world — a Swan Knight's spouse. I took the audition seriously, too seriously for her. I came across as morbidly austere to her. She appeared silly and childish to me. I wanted a woman warrior to share my burdens. She wanted a fiery passion. We both felt trapped.

The wedding was planned for 25 August — my twenty-second birthday. I began to see the marriage as a terminal illness for both my kingdom and The Ancient One's. I bought myself some time by postponing the wedding until 12 October, stating the coinciding with my parent's anniversary as the motive. As that date approached, I postponed again — this time to 29 November. Sophie's father finally offered me a way out. He demanded that I set a date and abide by it or break off the engagement.

I took this as the sign I sought, convincing myself, "A marriage is for life. What is the postponement of a month or two? Surely they do not want this wedding any more than I do."

Her father's letter is all I needed to write to Sophie and break the engagement. I felt the chains fall from me. I felt liberated to act upon the oaths I had taken.

"Never again!" I swore to myself, "Never again will I allow anything or anyone to stand between me and my duties."

There was too much turmoil, too much promise of dangers-to-come for me to divide my loyalty. I felt some shame, some regret for the disappointment I caused many people with the broken engagement. But I quickly replaced those images with the images of slaughtered Wühlenvogels, images of the lifeless Queen, images from Gessner's book, of the vile beasts that threaten the Grail, the Swan Knighthood, my friends from the Sweeter Realm, and my dear old swan. Those images were far more powerful than those of the royal faces that wore a mildly disappointed grimace because Sophie would have to marry some other noble. I quickly put the whole wedding business far behind me.

CHAPTER 27

The Grandest Construction and the Greatest Loss

WITHIN A FEW MONTHS of breaking the engagement to Sophie, in February of 1868, my grandfather died. Although he had passed the Swan Knighthood to me, I had still looked on him as a Swan Knight, and one that would still play some important part in the story of the portal. In the absence of the busy King of the Land and Shallow Waters, my grandfather's death left me truly alone. I went to the portal and waited. I sent many messengers through to bring him to me. After two weeks, he finally visited me. I tried to hide my desperation to see him, to hide my loneliness and sense of inadequacy.

"I am sorry that I am not here for you, as I would be if the Queen… if circumstances were different."

"But you are not the teacher to the Swan Knights anymore." I replied. "You are the King of the Land and Shallow Waters."

"No, old friend. All of the Waters are ruled by Löwschock. I am the King of the Land, and I may not hold that title for long."

This news frightened me beyond expression. I begged him to tell me why he spoke so grimly. He told me that Löwschock seeks both the Grail and the sole rule of the Sweeter Realm. Both desires drive him to find and kill the King — my dear friend.

"He is tireless," the swan told me, "and will not rest while I live."

After a long, silent pause, he continued, "If he succeeds in killing me, you will be King of the Land of the Sweeter Realm. You must save them. You must find and secure the Grail."

"No! You should remain hidden. You must live."

"What good am I as a hidden king? No, I have work to do, work that endangers me but must be done by me. Worse still, he knows about the Swan Knights. He knows about you. He must never discover the location of the portal. If he does, he will wait there for you. You would never again be able to open the portal. I cannot come to you, not while the danger continues. Seal the portal. Send all Sweeter Realm creatures home and seal the portal behind us."

"When do I open it again? How will I know when it is safe?"

"I cannot answer that. You are the Swan Knight. The portal is your concern. The Sweeter Realm is mine. God help and bless you, my dear young friend."

He gave me a quick kiss, then hollered in the Unicorn language. The Unicorn sentries arrived at the portal in an instant, followed shortly by the Zweigwesens. They all disappeared and I quickly closed the portal. There was such a morbid finality in the crackling sound of the closing. Such immense loneliness followed. I cried near the portal point, just outside of my trigger radius, wanting so longingly to open it but fearing to do so. I could not linger in the valley. I could not even say goodbye to the lodge. I raced to Hohenschwangau to speak with my brother and ponder my next move.

My mind was still with my Bavarian people. My heart was still on the tour I took after the war. I remained involved, but from a distance, ruling in distant isolation, in the safety of my beloved hills. At Hohenschwangau, I hiked to the ruins of Brunhilde's castle, on the peak of the Jugend Mountain, across from my childhood home. It was one of my favorite places to escape and think. Each step reminded me of The Ancient One's stories. Before I knew it, I was sitting among the ruins, lost in dreamy memories of the past. When I snapped myself to consciousness, it came to me. Brunhilde's castle was built to protect and hide her. If I could rule Bavaria in distant isolation, could he not rule his kingdom in the safety of this castle? I stood quickly and scanned the old mountain top, visualizing the castle that once stood there. It would be perfect — all of it. I would rebuild the castle and bring The Ancient One there. He could rule from there, through messengers, much as I rule Bavaria. We could be together, always. I could hardly contain my happiness and excitement as I considered the possibilities. My eager heart was torn between wanting to sit in the old ruins imagining the grand reproduction of Brunhilde's castle and wanting to rush to my study to draw up the plans.

I worked with stage designer, Christian Jank, who had rebuilt the wonderful and legendary scenes of old for Wagner's operas. I wanted it to be perfect, both a testament to The Ancient One's eminence and to my love and gratitude for him. I worked with Jank to recreate much of the original design. The swan spoke so affectionately about his time there with his dear Brunhilde, and with Tannhäuser when he returned. I did not disregard the King's warnings. While demolition of the old ruins began, I started designs for securing the portal, once and for all. I decided to finally build a palace in the valley.

I formed an ingenious idea for sealing the portal from wandering Grail Blood, preventing the escape of anyone who might pass to this side when I opened the portal, while allowing the coming and going of The Ancient One and the valley guardians. I would construct an artificial cave around the portal point, with a lake inside, and with an entrance sealed with a stone door. From the outside, it would look like the hillside — from the inside, like a cave with no exit. I imagined a mural resting flush against the portal point, so that the painting itself opened with the portal, directly above the body of the Queen. Poetically, I decided that the mural would depict the legend of Tannhäuser, retreated into the realm of Venus. Those who knew of the real Tannhäuser and his flight through the portal and into the Brunnen homeland would know the significance. They would only have to "follow Tannhäuser" to get to the Sweeter Realm. I was quite delighted with the scheme and offered myself a great deal of self-congratulations.

My first priority was to build The Ancient One's castle and see him safely inside. The castle project consumed my resources. The palace at Linderhof and the secret portal cave would have to wait. I never finished the castle, but I finished the King's bedchamber. I wanted it to resemble his nest, just on the other side of the portal, but enriched to fit his position as King. This was not the nest of a teacher. Tall bedposts, intricately carved, were set to resemble the trees that held the nest, a broad canopy to resemble the canopy of the forest. I knew that he would consider it a ridiculous display of human vanity, but it was my gift to give and I would see it deserving him. I did all that I could for it to remind him of the days of old, of the early Swan Knighthood and his intimate connection to my family. I blended my own memories of his stories with the sets of the Wagner operas, *Lohengrin* and *Tannhäuser*. Throughout the castle, I have put images of my dear friend. It is a swan's castle. There is no mistaking that. I also sought to impress him with the latest wonders of Bavarian technology, from the kitchen to the centralized heating. I am calling it Neuschwanstein (New Swan Stone). As Neuschwanstein Castle neared completion, I shifted focus to the projects at Linderhof.

I was so focused on preparing my friend for his war and securing him from attack, I did not see the trouble brewing around me. France was the dominant power on the European continent. They did not like the growth of Prussian power. They also knew that the pending consolidation of German states under the warlike Prussians would threaten their position on the continent. Prussia knew that a war with France would pull the southern German states into an alliance in accordance with the treaties in place. Prussia provoked a war with France, and Bavaria, once again, stared down the barrel of war. As the war with France became unavoidable, I wept. I saw every face of every widow I visited on my tour of Bavaria. I also knew that the conflict would take me from my duties to The Ancient One. Should France win, what would become of my kingdom and my quiet little valley?

War with France came in July of 1870. I did all that I could to continue my efforts to save my friend and serve him as the Swan Knight. My ministers grew weary of my absence from Munich, my absence from the war. But the war with France would happen as it happens, without my contribution. What could I do for the Bavarian Army? The war ran its course. As king of Bavaria, I could do little to affect the outcome. As the Swan Knight, I could do much to affect the safety and eventual peace of the Sweeter Realm. So, I kept my attention there.

In less than a year, the war ended with our victory — well, a Prussian victory in every sense. An emperor of the united German kingdoms would be crowned at the Palace of Versailles. There was little question as to who would wear that crown. It was the Prussian king, my Uncle Wilhelm. I was expected to attend the crowning. There was entirely too much to occupy my time. I could not run off to France. I sent Otto in my place. He had still not recovered from my consultation with him after I closed the portal and left the valley empty. He had nightly dreams about slaughtered Wühlenvogels and hornless unicorn corpses. He awoke almost every night from a dream about the bulky, knobby-headed monster. In it, he saw me, my father and mother, The Ancient One, and everyone he ever loved, hanging dead from the teeth of the mindless brute. He went to Versailles a broken man. The attendees of the crowning noticed him staring into the distance, quaking in fear, amid the boisterous festivities. He was quite out of place, and quite noticed. I should not have sent him.

Uncle Wilhelm was crowned, and once again, Bavarian sovereignty submitted to the authority of an emperor. My country was significantly weakened that day. Fortunately, Uncle Wilhelm had no interest in directly controlling Bavaria. He had political control, but distant and disconnected. Bavarian policies continued as they had been. Bavarian life was little affected. The valley was safe and my plans continued. The Ancient One's castle, though not complete, was fit for occupation by a giant swan. I turned my attention to the plans for the Linderhof estate. I could not bring myself to destroy the historic lodge. I moved it and built my palace where it stood for all of those centuries. I wanted my bed to sit in the exact spot where Lohengrin and Nethe slept together.

I was the first Swan Knight since Albert V to intentionally bring outsiders into the valley. The projects needed laborers. I am not Cunrad — and even he could not build my palace in a lifetime. I extensively researched the history of each worker, each artist. This did not ensure that no Grail Blood entered the valley. I forbade wandering from the work sites and resting areas — until it was time to begin the secret cave that would house and hide the portal point. My Aunt Alexandra helped how she could. She spent much of her time at Linderhof during construction. But she died in September of 1875. She sadly did not witness the completion of the Linderhof plans.

To open the secret door to the cave, I built a latch on a stone slab that blended into the earth around it. In front of the portal point, I filled a small lake. I put a shell-shaped boat on the lake, so that I could easily get to the portal. I designed the boat after the one Lohengrin rode, pulled by The Ancient One, in the first staging of Wagner's opera that I saw as a teenager. Stalactites hang from the ceiling. It looks like a natural cave — a wonderful, majestic, but natural cave. The mural of Tannhäuser sits flush against the portal point, with a small stage between it and the edge of the lake.

When the palace and grotto were complete, I was comfortable that I had negated all of The Ancient One's concerns and could finally open the portal. As a final step to ensure his safety, I brought the largest swans in the region to the cave. If The Ancient One was followed through the portal by one of his enemies, he would be one of many swans floating on the artificial lake. I could finally summon him and invite him to live in his new, magnificent Neuschwanstein Castle that I had built for him. With the stone door closed, the cave was devoid of light — absolute darkness. I had to leave the door open to see what I was doing.

By the time I finished the cave, I had not seen the King of the Land of the Sweeter Realm in almost six years. I had prepared my kingdom for him, prepared myself to have him. In accordance to his wishes, the portal had remained sealed the entire time. Workers built the cave, while I directed from the precise distance from the portal point to keep the swan's directive. The painter of the mural wanted me to come closer, to take a closer look at his work. Of course, I could not. When all was complete, I cleared the valley of every artist and laboror. My flesh tingled with the expectation of my reunion with my dear old friend. He could not have imagined all that I accomplished in our years apart.

For six years, I wondered how he and my friends in the Sweeter Realm fared. It was finally time to open the portal, safely within the hidden cave, and commence the long overdue reunion. I invited Otto. But his mind was completely broken by then, haunted perpetually by the terrible images of Löwschock and his minions. So, I was alone. I spent the entire night before imagining the astonishment of my friends as they walked through the portal and fell into the lake in front of it. I laughed to myself. I held long, imaginary conversations, rehearsing my reunion with each old friend, each Scherier, each

Unicorn, and of course, The Ancient One. I rowed my shell boat across the water. I triggered the opening of the portal as the boat sailed past my trigger point. Each Swan Knight has had a unique opening trigger point. Each knew exactly which rock or root marked their spot. I was no different. But now, my spot was transformed and I did not know it exactly. I thrilled in the surprise as I drifted past my point and reunited my delighted ears with the crackling sound of the opening portal. The mural of Tannhäuser transformed into the sight and sound that had excited and comforted me since my ninth birthday.

I sat in my boat, floating near the open portal, staring and waiting for more than an hour. After the first several minutes, each second that passed brought me new images of death and destruction.

I spoke aloud, "Come through, my friends. Someone come through."

Finally, a Zweigwesen came through the portal. He must have run and leapt at great speed for a Zweigwesen, or been thrown through by a strong creature. He did not step from his realm to mine, at the bottom of the portal. He flew, head first, near the top. He landed in the little lake, with a splash, just to the right of my boat. I quickly pulled him out of the water and into the boat. He looked around the cave, frantic and frightened. He had passed through the portal hundreds of times and had no reason to expect such a drastic change in scenery. I calmed him as well as I could, explaining what I had built and why I built it. I went on and on about The Ancient One and my steps to ensure his safety, about the new castle of Neuschwanstein, on the peak where he lived with Brunhilde, about Linderhof and all that I accomplished, all that I spent, in order to be able to open the portal again and invite the swan and all of my friends back into Parsifal's valley, how I intended to rule my kingdom from Linderhof, always near the portal, while The Ancient One rules his from the safety of his new castle.

Zweigwesens do not shed tears. Instead, the rough flesh around their eyes swell and their eyes bulge. This Zweigwesen froze in attentiveness as I spoke of The Ancient One and my excitement to see him again. His eyes displayed, in full form, the Zweigwesen version of crying.

He allowed me to bring my delighted, self-congratulatory rambling to a close before taking my hand with one of his, touching my cheek with the other, and saying, "The King is dead."

I thought that my friends had finally defeated Löwschock. My heart and mind made the wildest and most drastic fall from the heights of exstacy to the very depths of despair as I considered that the referenced King might be my teacher. I focused fixedly at the Zweigwesen's swollen eyes, to read in them what I was afraid to ask. His sorrow told all.

I did not allow myself to believe it. I could not picture his beautiful white body lying lifeless.

I asked, "What king? Whose king?"

His eyes swelled nearly shut as he forced the words from his mouth, "Our King. The swan, The Ancient One — is dead."

I howled and screamed. I convulsed, pulled at my hair, and punched the side of the boat. The Zweigwesen sat beside me and released an occasional whimper. When the violence of my reaction ran its course, and my body lost the energy and will to mourn with such fits, I lifted the Zweigwesen to my chest and held him tightly. I held him and cried, without a word, while the portal remained dangerously open.

Perhaps half of an hour went by in this manner until the dear creature reminded me, "The portal, my King, you should not leave it open."

"Of course," I said as I gathered myself and replaced him on the seat beside me, "Of course, thank you."

The dangers of the enemy and the unknowns on the other side of the portal hit me suddenly. I rowed in a panic away from the portal. The crackle of the closing echoed in the artificial cave. Relieved of my fears from one side of the portal, my mind was free to realize how loud the portal sounded on the other. The crackle echoed off the walls of the cave. I could not risk opening and closing the portal with the stone door open. But with it closed, the cave was in darkness. In the following year, I used the latest in electric lighting to illuminate the cave. I powered the lights with an electricity generator, one of the first in the entire kingdom. But there was no more excitement, not more self-congratulations, no more happiness. The Ancient One was dead. He, who befriended Parsifal, who brought the Grail to the Queen, who taught every Swan Knight since Lohengrin, who led the flight to the Black Forest and defended the Wühlenvogel city, the only string of continuity sewn through the entire history of the Swan Knighthood was dead. Before I let the Zweigwesen home, I asked him to tell me all that he knew about The Ancient One's death.

He told me that the only creature who saw him die was a Scherier. The Ancient One flew to the Shallow Waters, despite the dangers that he knew awaited him there. He had heard of the great suffering of the kind creatures of the Shallow Waters under the cruel and despotic rule of Löwschock. Of all of the victims of the war, they fared the worse. Löwschock persecuted them for their centuries of loyalty to the Queen. He felt betrayed by them when they joined in unity with the Land — and his retribution was cruel and severe. The Ancient One could not hide away in the safety of the Brunnen and Unicorn wildernesses while such kind and loyal creatures suffered. He flew to the lake and paddled hesitatingly from the shore, poking his long neck into the water, trying to find signs of life. The darkness and cold of the Deep has entirely consumed the Shallow. The swan could not see beyond the edges of his own eyes. His feet must have ached severely from the cold. Yet, he continued to paddle — out toward the center of the Waters, looking downward and calling for the sweet creatures of the Shallow. He did not know that the Scherier had followed him. She stood hidden near the shore and watched closely for signs of danger. The Waters, though dark and cold, seemed placid.

The Scherier watched as her King paddled farther from the shore. Suddenly, the still water began to move. The Scherier, standing with her feet against the water, felt icy water lap against her low belly, as the waves from the Deep, which began low, silent, and subtle, grew larger and louder. She looked up to The Ancient One, whose head was still buried into the darkness of the water. She yelled a warning, but the swan did not hear. Her yells became screams and her screams became cries, as the waves from the Deep intensified. The Ancient One pulled his head from the water and noticed the Scherier on the shore. He looked around and noticed the motion of the water around him. He did not seem to fear for his life. He plunged his head back into the water, looking for his friends from the Shallow.

The Scherier continued to scream to him until silenced by a figure immerging from the Waters, within arm's reach of the swan. It was Löwschock. The beast had searched most of the Sweeter Realm for the King of the Land. And now, here he sat, floating at the gates of his enemy's home. Löwschock hollered something in his own language, with his blood-chilling voice. The Ancient One pulled his head from the water and saw his enemy. He spread his long wings to take flight, but Löwschock swiped one of his hard claws at the swan's head, knocking the life from him. The vile King of the Deep wrapped his powerful arms around the swan and dragged him down into the blackness of the Waters. The Scherier stood in agonizing horror, staring at the spot where The Ancient One disappeared, until the water returned to stillness, broken only by an occasional bubble to the surface, exactly where the King of the Land sank into darkness. She remained there, with her eyes on the surface of the Waters, silently begging her King to resurface. For hours she remained so. Each passing second drove the blade of her despair deeper into her small, flat body. When all hope had finally left her, she fled the Waters and returned to her homeland to spread the news that their good King was dead.

I was reminded of my father's death, when the realization of my ascension to the throne did not occur to me until a page referred to me as "Your Majesty". I rowed the Zweigwesen back to the portal.

Before he went through, he turned to me and said, "The Ancient One died almost three years ago. We have been lost without him. Now we await your leadership, Your Majesty. You inherit the kingship now, when the Sweeter Realm is at its most desperate."

I closed the portal with the weightiest possible thoughts on my mind. When I scanned the cave and saw the many swans that lived there, brought as decoys for The Ancient One's protection, the weight returned from my mind to my heart. The swans were beautiful, but nothing compared to the magnificence of my old friend and teacher, the father who gave me the love and attention that my real father could not. I rolled from the side of the boat, into the water of the cave lake. I exhaled all of the air in my lungs and sank to the bottom, lying face down against the floor of the shallow lake. I tried to convince myself to inhale and fill my lungs with the water. I did not think I could breathe another gasp of air while my dear, sweet, noble friend sat among the corpses at the bottom of the Deep, or after his angelic form was devoured by the angry, mindless creatures of Löwschock's army. Each attempt to draw the water into my body was halted by the echoing in my mind of the Zweigwesen's words, "Now we await your leadership". My Swan Knight's oath to the Queen passed to The Ancient One when the Queen died. My dismay at his lost grew into zealous and devout loyalty to my oath — to my friend. I stood from the water just as my lungs took that desperate, involuntary breath that simply could not be held another second. I filled myself with the air of the cave. I waded to the edge of the water, climbed out, and walked to my palace, where I fell asleep without a moment of considering the future.

CHAPTER 28

The Wheels in Motion

I AWOKE IN SUCH A LOST STATE of confusion. To whom could I turn? Otto had lost his mind. The fact was well-known, not just in Munich and Bavaria, but in Europe. I could not speak to him of the Sweeter Realm without throwing him into fits. My Aunt Alexandra was dead. Until she died, she was the only other living person who had trained under The Ancient One. Her counsel would have been priceless to me. But she was gone, my grandfather was gone, my brother was gone in mind and spirit, and the wisest voice to ever guide me was killed by a monster whose eyes must surely have turned toward me. How do I serve as King of the Land of the Sweeter Realm? How do I, from my castles and palaces, restore peace and safety to the Land and Shallow Waters and find and secure the Holy Grail? My passage through the portal is forbidden by the Laws of Ermenrich. How do I serve as King of Bavaria while my heart is elsewhere? The people of Bavaria, and my own ministers, already call me "The Absent King" or "The Fairy Tale King". How ignorantly unjustly they judge me. They see my constructions as the expensive hobbies of a dreamy, childish king. They cannot possibly fathom the burdens I carry. And I cannot tell them. I cannot share my burdens with anyone. I am completely alone.

My isolation affected my mind. But my recent decision, forced by the circumstances before me, and some gifts from the Sweeter Realm, have brought me clarity of mind like I have not known in eight years. Back then, I slipped into paranoia. My construction projects at Linderhof, designed to ease the mind of The Ancient One, failed to ease my mind after his death. I felt myself slipping down my brother's road. I could not sleep at night. Terrors of the dark kept me up. I felt much safer sleeping during the day. So, I reversed my schedule. I awoke at 18.00 to begin my day. I stayed up all night, trying to accomplish what I used to accomplish during daylight hours. The world around me slept. Once the sun was up, and I felt safer, I went to bed. The schedule destroyed my health. It further isolated me. And it made coordination with my ministers of state impossible.

The whispers about my madness grew to loud conversations. The night hours were long and grueling. The isolation that I sought as a young man stabbed at me. I went for long rides at night, but not the solitary rides of my youth, through secluded wilderness, in search of serene solitude. I rode under cover of a carriage, with guards and coachmen who I had aroused from their sleep. I rode through the rural towns. I was often so nightmarishly frightened that I would stop at a household, wake them in the night, and ask to be admitted into their homes. I ate, drank, and conversed with simple country-folk, with strangers, just to relieve my ominous sense of dread. I let them talk about themselves, about their lives. It pulled me from the depths of my waking nightmares. It sponged, for the moment, the thought that Löwschuck hunted me, and that the creatures of the Sweeter Realm waited for me to return them to the tranquility and happiness they enjoyed under the Queen. The people did not mind my late-night intrusions. They welcomed their king, and I always left them with gifts.

When I built the artificial cave at Linderhof, I was constructing my ideal setting. Before I reopened the long-sealed portal, I spent hours there, imagining the lives of the Swan Knights of old. The setting united the best parts of my childhood dreams. After hearing of The Ancient One's death, I could not bear the sight of it. The lovely painting of Tannhäuser, draped at the feet of Venus, charged my flesh and raised my hairs with admiration before I opened the portal and received the Zweigwesen and his terrible news. Afterward, I saw the mural merely as a thin, painted drop, behind which awaited more danger and despair. It took more than a year for me to feel comfortable there, to see without anguish the swans I had placed there, and to allow the scenery to once again elicit sensations softer and kinder than terror and anger.

For the first year, I was afraid to open the portal, expecting the clawed hand of Löwschock to seize me from the other side and drag me to the floor of the Deep. Otto's descriptions of his fears, for which I had long pitied him, were exact descriptions of my fears. From time to time, my desperate curiosity and concern for the welfare of the sweet creatures I had grown to love drew me into the cave and near the portal point. I spent much time on the boat, but too far to open the portal. A few times, I paddled slowly toward the painting until I heard the first crackle of the opening portal. Then I paddled frantically away before the passage appeared. I wanted to fill the cave with as many Bavarian soldiers as could fit, then open the portal and invite the foul monsters to attack. But I obviously could not do that. So, I sat alone in the cave, feeding the swans and volleying my thoughts between opening the portal and leaving the cave and burying the portal point under a mountain of stones, never to be opened again.

I spent most of my time at Linderhof. When I was not there, I was usually at Berg Castle or one of the two castles at Hohenschwangau. When I was at Hohenschwangau, I was usually in my childhood home. I did not spend much time at Neuschwanstein, the castle I built for The Ancient One. It was not designed for me and I never quite felt at home there. I spent little time in Munich. My time there was monopolized by busy hordes of ministers and officials, all pulling at me from different angles. I hated being there. As tormented as my mind was, I preferred to keep it in agony over what I loved than distracted by what I did not. My relationship with my government strained to a near rupture. I was too absent to be a good king and too frightened to be a good Swan Knight. I spent my entire childhood wanting to be Lohengrin. Now I shudder to imagine what Lohengrin would think of me. I went on like this for months — and then years.

Finally, I went to Linderhof and opened the portal. I did not have to wait this time. The Unicorns had posted guards near the portal point, both to protect it and to await my return. A Unicorn jumped through and landed in the water, clearly prepared for his surroundings by the description of the Zweigwesen who came to me. He wasted no time with words, no time with greetings. Angrily and impatiently, he pinned me between the side of the boat and the point of his horn, pressing it uncomfortably against my chest. Through it, I saw his memories over the last few years.

Löwschock had tripled his efforts to find the Grail and the portal point. He captured, tortured, and killed creatures of all breeds, trying to gain from them any hint of where to find what he sought. The dead were only outnumbered by the wounded. The Unicorns who survived the attack on Albert V were dead, their bodies dragged into the Deep before their memories could be extracted from the horn. The Scheriers and Wühlenvogels abandoned their homelands and united into nomadic groups of both breeds. They staged counter-attacks all over the Sweeter Realm, even attacking into the Shallow Waters. The Brunnens abandoned their cities and fled into their wilderness, living as their distant ancestors lived. The keenest of eyes could walk slowly through the Brunnen wilderness and not see a sign of the fair creatures, though the Brunnen woods were well inhabited. They did not fight. They hid. And they hid masterfully. Swarms of Löwschock's legions stormed through the Brunnen wilderness. Löwschock seemed certain that his answers were there. His army neither saw, heard, nor smelled anything. They walked over, under, and around the Brunnen population without knowing. The Zweigwesens fought for their cities. They fought and died. The only Zweigwesens to survive were the ones that Löwschock left for dead. Their medicines are truly miraculous, especially on their own kind. Those who lived, quickly restored to full strength and abandoned the cities in favor of the thick woods.

The Unicorns held their capital city. But all surrounding settlements were destroyed, along with the Unicorns who fought for them. Many of the shy, peaceful creatures of the Land, not known to the Swan Knights, were brought to near extinction. The nomadic breeds fared the best, especially those who lived mostly near the Waters. Löwschock's eyes went deep into the Land. He ignored many of the small breeds near the Waters. He knew that they did not hold the Grail or have access to me and to the portal. The only breed completely spared Löwschock's ambition and wrath was the Eulesängers. Their homeland was safe behind what was left of the Unicorn lands. When Löwschock did encounter them, he thought little of them. He viewed them as insects, of too little intelligence to waste the effort of capturing and killing them. They are small and fast, and they fly too high for the foul creatures of the Deep to catch. Löwschock left them alone. They were the perfect spies and they reported the movements of the evil army to the good breeds who still fight.

I sat in the boat receiving the images of the war through the Unicorn's horn. I grabbed the horn and lifted it from my chest.

"Stop! Stop!" I yelled. "It is too much at once. I cannot see clearly. I cannot think clearly."

As I said the words, "think clearly", an idea came to mind.

"The nectar," I whispered to myself. Then looking directly into the Unicorn's eyes, I said, "The nectar, I need the Unicorn nectar. Then I will think clearly and I will know what to do."

The Unicorn answered, "The nectar does not put any thought into your mind. It only sharpens the thoughts already there."

"I know what it does." I sharply retorted. "Bring me the nectar and I will know what to do."

The Unicorn's stern expression melted into a satisfied smile. He seemed pleased by the eager energy of his long-absent Swan Knight. In a long and graceful leap, he flew from the water of the cave, through the portal, and into the Sweeter Realm. I wanted the nectar more than I feared Löwschock. I waited in the boat, with the portal wide open, crackling and echoing. The colors of my electric lights flickered with the energy of the portal. I sat like that for at least four hours before a Unicorn came through. It was a different Unicorn, taller, thinner, older, pitch black, and magnificently beautiful, despite the many scars that ornamented her body like the stripes of a tiger. Wrapped around the base of her horn was a circular, wooden stopper, plugging the opening of a ceramic vile, no larger than my clinched fist. She lowered her head and the vile slid the length of her long horn and landed on my lap. I pulled the wooden stopper and drank every drop of the thick, bitter liquid within. A solution to our most immediate problem came to mind — a way to tend to the wounded and return them strong and healthy to their own kind.

A few years earlier, I had bought an island in the Chiemsee, Bavaria's largest lake. The island is called Herreninsel. Developers planned to destroy the forests of the island. I bought it to prevent development and save the forest. I imagined that, with its isolation, it could serve as a Swan Knight training site someday. Now, I had to destroy the forest and develop the island myself. I began immediately with the construction of a new palace, just as the final touches of the Linderhof palace completed. I called it Herrenchiemsee. The palace housed the wounded creatures. Within two years of the start of construction, the palace was fit enough to employ. I only found sixteen fit Zweigwesen to serve as nurses to the wounded. I supplied them with pots and gardens for growing their medicines. I built pools with fountains so that the creatures of the Waters could be treated there. The palace has secret rooms and chambers. The creatures hid in them until nightfall. After the servants lit the palace candles, I sent all of them from the island. They thought it strange that I remained on the island alone. But I was not alone. When the servants left, the palace came to life with the convalescing creatures and the Zweigwesens who treated them. I never finished construction on the palace. If I survive the battle to come, I would really like to see it completed and perhaps someday fulfill my original intentions for the island. If I do survive, it is unlikely I will be seeing much of my own country again.

Each night, after the servants left the island, small caravans of the recovered made their way back to Linderhof. They hid in the surrounding woods, as they had for centuries, until I joined them there and opened the door to their home to let them back and receive the next wave of wounded. This was my life, my duty as the Swan Knight. What else could I do? I am forbidden to enter the portal. I cannot grab a sword and join the fight. I cannot raise an army and march them through the portal. I used my resources to save lives and return brave warriors to the fight. Many Swan Knights passed their years with much slighter contributions. Many of the wounded did not return when they recovered. They remained at Herrenchiemsee or in the woods surrounding Linderhof. A few even took up residence in Neuschwanstein Castle and in the lakes and forests near Hohenschwangau. They were alive and safe because of me. But I still felt desperate and incomplete. I needed to do more. I asked for more Unicorn nectar, and I got it.

When I drank the nectar, I could feel my scattered thoughts gather and unify. Every piece of knowledge, every word of advice I had ever been given, every experience I suffered or enjoyed came together to bring one clear idea to the front of my mind. I would abdicate the throne of Bavaria, like my grandfather did. It is

542

something I had considered for many years, something I had threatened several times. The nectar gave me a clear vision of my deficiencies as the King of Bavaria. Bavaria would benefit and the Swan Knighthood would have the full commitment of a passionate knight. But to whom would I pass my kingdom?

The Unicorn who brought me the nectar this time stayed by my side. She is light brown, almost yellow, with bright gold, course and shaggy hair on her head and face. Her beard is longer than most, giving her a look of wisdom. We left the cave and walked the empty valley together. The sun set and the moon rose. We continued our slow circles of the valley perimeter, walking mostly in silence, but conversing as enough thoughts swelled in our minds to overflow to our mouths. We discussed the future of the Bavarian throne. I did not want to leave it to chance. I love my country and I want it to prosper — under a king who both loves it and can devote a lifetime to it. The wisdom of King Rupert's amendment to the laws needs no further justification than the example of my reign.

"I think I need more nectar." I told my companion. "I do not know to whom I should pass the throne of Bavaria."

She reminded me, "The nectar only focuses the knowledge already possessed. It does not introduce new knowledge."

"Then how can I know who — ", I interrupted myself. "No, not the nectar. I need the Queen's weed, the weed that makes those who love me most glow in my eyes."

"But the Queen is dead," she responded. "And so is the great swan who brought the weed here last time. Even if they were not, they could not come to you now. And the weed grows in the Shallow Waters. They belong to Löwschock. None of us go there. None of us can retieve the weed."

I closed my eyes and licked the last remnants of the sticky Unicorn nectar that clung to my upper lip. I forced my eyelids tightly together and gathered my memories into one clear picture before me.

"The jailor," I said, "I need the Queen's jailor. He should know where the weed grows. He has powerful legs. Can he run?"

"In a foot race, he is a worthy challenger for any creature on the Land."

"Find him. Tell him to bring the weed to me."

"He lived in the Shallow Waters, when Löwschock took control. He was always loyal to the Queen. It is unlikely that he still lives."

"You must try." I pleaded.

"Do you realize what you ask of me? To find him, I must enter the Waters. I am not safe within my *own* homeland. You ask me to dive into the cold, dark Waters and search for the Queen's jailor — to help you decide to whom you will pass your Bavarian crown."

"I understand what I ask of you. I pass the crown so that I can be your Swan Knight and commit what is left of my life to restoring peace to the Sweeter Realm, defeating Löwschock, and securing the Holy Grail and the portal."

"You are the King of the Land. I will obey you. I only wish you to understand what you ask of me. If Löwschock captures me alive, he may learn how to use the horns of Unicorns to locate the portal. Also, the jailor is a creature of the Waters. If he is seen running on the Land, he will surely arouse suspicion. He may be followed. He could lead the enemy to the portal and to you. Löwschock wants you dead, almost as badly as he wants the Grail. He will not stop at the Sweeter Realm. If he comes here, he will want the crown of Bavaria and your whole world. He will expose the Sweeter Realm to the human world. He —"

Each word of warning pulled my heart from my patience.

"Alright," I sharply interrupted, "I understand. But I have taken the nectar. My thoughts are clear. The years of learning from The Ancient One convene into a single thought, in the center of my head. I know what I ask. I ask it because it must be done. Find the jailor. Tell him to bring the weed to me."

She simply nodded as we continued our walk around Linderhof. Without a break in pace or pattern, we worked our way silently back to the portal side of the valley. We went into the artificial cave. She waded through the water as I climbed into the boat and paddled toward the portal point. She jumped at the center of the painting. Just as her horn touched the face of a cherub in the mural, I crossed the trigger threshold. The portal cracked open and the Unicorn disappeared into it. I knew that she would not find the jailor quickly, if he still lived. But I could not allow the jailor to come to the portal point and wait for me to open it. The open portal had to wait for him. I went to bed in the palace, slept at night for the first time in years, woke early, opened the portal and waited all day and night. I remained in the boat, before the open portal, catching sleep by the minutes, for six days. Finally, the jailor came through the portal.

He was a spectacular sight, with so much more depth and life, color, and expression than Gessner's sketch revealed. He held several leaves of the Queen's weed.

"I thought that only a few of them grew at a time." I commented.

"That was certainly true. But there is no need for its special properties these days, not in the Waters of the Sweeter Realm. They have grown untouched for many years. I bring them all to Your Majesty."

I thanked him heartily, to which he responded, "I serve you as I served the Queen, as I served the swan."

"Hurry," I ordered, "return before you are noticed. Be quick and silent."

He bowed low to me, dropping the point of his coned head to my face. I grabbed his cone with both hands and rubbed it, partly out of gratitude and affection, partly out of curiosity. The scales of his head are firm but remarkably soft. I sense his loyalty through that touch, his loyalty to the Queen, to the swan, to his world, and to me. He pulled his head from my grasp, climbed to the edge of the painting, and jumped through the portal.

With plenty of the Queen's weed, I rode from Linderhof, eager to witness its effects. I confess that I used the weed to satisfy my vanity. I nibbled on it as I rode through the villages and farms between Linderhof and Hohenschwangau. My concerns and my schedule had taken its toll on my health. By now, I have gained weight.

My joints ache. I do not ride as well, as majestically as I did. Nevertheless, as I greeted the locals, they glowed with love for me. This was exactly what I needed to see before abdicating and leaving them. Their glowing faces smiled at me, as their glowing hands waved. They still love their king. I rode to Hohenschwangau and greeted my mother. I did not expect to be blinded by a radiant glow from her. She always judged me harshly and favored Otto. Even with my low expectations, I was deeply hurt when I looked at my mother. At most, she appeared slightly paler than normal. She did not glow. Otto's love for me lit the room. I had to explain to him why I could not look directly at him. When I told him that I had the Queen's weed, he insisted on trying it. He cried as he squinted his eyes, trying to make out my figure through the shining light appearing to come from me. With tightly closed, defensive eyelids, we embraced lovingly and at length.

When I released him, I stared into his shining face. The darkness of his troubled eyes pierced the glow of his love for me. I thought that Otto must surely love me more than any human. But he could not be king. He had already been declared insane. His condition is well known. He cannot govern Bavarian officials or be taken seriously by the European leadership. Unlike the rumors of my insanity, there was much truth behind Otto's diagnosis. Still, I love him and I wanted to see him get what should be rightfully his.

I took the weed to Munich, where relatives who could assume the throne resided, both in and out of government. I met with my Uncle Luitpold, my father's younger brother and fifth child of my grandfather. My grandfather upheld the Laws of Ermenrich, albiet loosely, so Uncle Luitpold never learned the history, never trained with The Ancient One. He was entirely ignorant of the portal and the family connection to the Holy Grail and the Germanic legends. Luitpold is a steady-minded man, austere and responsible. He never displayed affection for me. His only expression of emotion toward me was frustration with my childhood immaturity and my reluctance to embrace the affairs of state. I stumbled in delightful surprise when I saw him. He glowed with love for me. It was a subtle glow, but I had not taken the weed since arriving in Munich. I pulled a piece from my pocket and chewed on it. Uncle Luitpold shone warmly. It was not the resplendent glow of a brother, raw and intimate. It was the softer glow of an uncle who cared deeply for my welfare, suffered through my misfortunes, and felt the pang of each stumble of my life, from a scraped knee to suspicions of insanity.

I calmly and gratefully thanked my uncle for his love. He was surprised at the sudden emotional authenticity of a man he always viewed as detached from reality. I told him that I would be leaving the throne of Bavaria, that he must take his clear mind and political steadiness to the throne. He is a prince of Bavaria. He has a legitimate claim to the throne, especially with Otto's diagnosis.

But I begged him, "Let Otto be King. Rule Bavaria as Prince Regent."

Uncle Luitpold is not a vain man. He cares little for titles and notations in the history books. He cares for Bavaria. I know he will rule wisely — much better than I have. He agreed to see the crown on Otto's head and rule Bavaria as Prince Regent. My brother would be Otto I, King of Bavaria. That pleasurable thought has erased many of the doubts I have had and fears I still have.

I left Nymphenberg Palace and visited my old friend and court psychiatrist, Dr. Bernhard von Gudden. I asked Gudden to publish a report officially declaring me insane and unfit to rule. Gudden was taken aback by the request and stuttered and stumbled for a reply. He asked several times, why and how would he do such a thing. I assured him that the story would not be difficult to sell. Gudden reminded me that there is nothing in Bavarian law that allows such a course of action. I assured him that the ministers would accept the claim. They have long desired a present and active king — and they are correct. They and Bavaria deserve one.

He asked me, "What has brought you to this decision? You will lose your throne. You will probably be taken into custody and locked behind the walls of the Royal Residence."

I answered, "I know. It is for the best. It must be done."

I had no intention of being taken into custody. Once the wheels of my abdication were set in motion, I was to disappear from the lives of ministers and doctors, of composers and soldiers. I would slip through the portal and live the rest of my days as the King of the Land of the Sweeter Realm, perhaps even reunite the Land with the Shallow Waters someday.

Gudden saw in my expression that I was both aware of the weight of my request and utterly determined to see it through. As I stood beside him, Gudden wrote his declaration, finding me insane, incurable, and incapable of exercising government. He promised that he would publish the report in the morning, which he did.

With the succession of Bavaria firmly settled, I returned to Linderhof. I confess that I felt relieved. The crown was always a heavy burden on my brow. As I rode from Munich, I felt like a Swan Knight — only a Swan Knight. My old, overweight, failing body felt lighter than it had in decades.

During the ride, every time a whisper of regret entered my head, I reminded myself, "Lohengrin was no king, no duke. He was a Swan Knight, like me."

As I rode into the valley, the sky, the surrounding mountains, the grass and the trees, were brighter and crisper than they had ever appeared to me.

I thought of a verse from Goethe, "I saw you, and a gentle pleasure flowed from that sweet moment onto me."

My lungs sipped the valley air and savored it in long held breaths, like the mouth holds a sweet sip of wine before swallowing. In the steady gallop from the valley edge to the palace, the truth of my situation overcame my boyish thoughts of Lohengrin. I was about to enter great uncertainty. I had no idea what awaited on the other side of the portal. I did not know if I could return, if the portal would open from the other side. That is a point that has been fiercely speculated for centuries. Parsifal opened it, entered, and returned. But then, he drank from the Holy Grail. I do not know if I would ever be able to return. At the time, I did not care. I was warmed and comforted by the sudden descending upon me of faith in God. I believed that I would find the Grail, that the Grail and the guidance of Divine Providence would lead me to victory. Everything that I had decided, everything that I had set in motion, seemed right.

I spent the night in the palace. I did not want to close my eyes on the valley. I knew that it was probably the last of the many nights I spent there. Perhaps I would be closing the door on the Swan Knighthood in Linderhof forever. But I wanted to sleep, so I could get an early start. My intention was to go through the portal soon after sunrise. With no idea of what or who I would find, or how long it would take me to find it, I wanted to give myself as much daylight as possible. I also hoped to arrive in the Sweeter Realm while it still slept. Perhaps my entrance could go unnoticed. I thought about the Zweigwesen medicine book, with the drawings of the plants. It would have done me little good. I do not read Zweigwesen. But I desperately wanted it nevertheless. I thought about the map that Rudolf drew of the Sweeter Realm, from the descriptions given to him by his Eulesänger friends. I had not thought about the old map in years. I had never seen it. I did not even know if it still existed. Suddenly, in the midst of my deepest desire to have it, I remembered a pile of books and papers in a corner of the lodge's study, where I remember seeing my grandfather retire for hours at a time, collecting dust along with the forest of books and papers that filled the room. When I had the lodge moved, I ordered the study to be reproduced exactly as my grandfather left it. It sat as a shrine to the most influential architect of my character.

In a rush of excitement, I ran to the old lodge and rummaged through the study. The books and papers that were meticulously replaced, the shrine to my grandfather that was painstakingly recreated, flew across the room in a feverish ransacking. But there, in the middle of a stack of yellowed old papers and parchment, I found Rudolf's map. I have included it at the front of this journal. Perhaps you will put it to use — you, the Swan Knight that I pray will find this and restore the line and the traditions. May your reign be brighter, more peaceful, more blissful than mine. For that, dear brother or sister, I pray whole-heartedly.

The map was in remarkable condition, with none of the weathering and tattering that its years should have inflicted. Instinctively, I held it to my nose and inhaled deeply, trying to gain the smell of Rudolf's hand, the smell of a younger, less troubled Linderhof, as if the parchment hoarded such a treasure in its dusty folds. It held no such treasure, but my sentimental nose did excavate the slight scent of my grandfather in the old map. He must have handled it thoroughly. The slight scent went directly to my store of childhood memories, unlocking the gates and sending images of my grandfather rampaging through the halls of my mind. I handled the map as gingerly as possible, afraid of destroying the last remnants of my grandfather, which held precariously to the old parchment. As I walked back to the palace, my circumstances evicted all such sentiments from my refocused mind. Before settling into bed, I rolled the map tightly and stored it in the small bag along with the few items I intended to take with me into the Sweeter Realm. The map was still a treasure to me, but a practical, not a sentimental one. Its discovery seemed Providential to me and it gave me faith in my mission.

Through the night, my faith slowly gave way to fear. The images from Gessner's book haunted my thoughts and half-conscious dreams. The sounds of the Queen's burial echoed in the silence of my imagination. I thought about the Swan Knights who died senselessly — Duke Ludwig I, assassinated on the bridge in Kelheim, the promising young Ludwig, murdered at the tournament in Nürnberg, Adolf, shot in the mouth with an arrow. I did not want to die. I did not really expect to die. But if I do die, I want it to mean something. I want my final heroics to be praised and perhaps set to stage in an opera. I realized that, live or die, I would be gone from this world, having taken with me all knowledge of the beautiful history of the Swan Knighthood, those sacred moments from the life of the Grail Blood — Gütel's rescue of Parsifal, Nethe's Christmas song, the giggle of baby Elsa as the toy Unicorn, gifted by the Zweigwesens, ran down the hill toward the old house, The Ancient One, wearing a dress on stage at the hundredth anniversary celebration, Brunhilde's laughter as she hung from a tree, the defeat of the Welf knights, the "Hurah" of Adolf when the Wühlenvogel pulled him into Einigkeitstadt, the "Swan Day" celebration, in honor of the noblest being to ever draw breath, Milli's long hours of study, learning the Zweigwesen language, my own great-grandfather's accidental introduction to the valley. I mourned deeply the death of these stories as the last holder of them planned to exit the valley for the last time. It was in those mournful musings that I first drew the inspiration to write them all down before I depart. But I did not have time to do so. I was to step through the portal at sunrise.

These and other thoughts kept me awake until I saw the first rays of light in the valley. I had hardly slept a wink. I dressed myself in my finest military tunic, strapped on the sword that I hardly know how to use, and walked up the hill to the cave. I pulled the latch, lit the cave with the electric lights, mounted my boat, and rowed to toward the painting of Tannhäuser. I sailed past my trigger point and opened the portal. I stood in the boat as it continued to drift toward the painting. The boat bumped against the small stage, directly under the mural. The mural was gone. In its place was the open portal, humming its low crackle. I closed my eyes and savored the sound. Under the crackle, I thought I heard a voice.

Sound had never penetrated the portal, so I assumed it to be my imagination. I enjoyed it anyway.

With my eyes still closed, I focused on the voice. It was high pitched, but soft and melodic. As I focused on it, it seemed to grow louder, immerging from beneath the sound of the portal. I suddenly opened my eyes with an inexplicable expectation to see something. A Brunnen came through the portal, screaming in pain and terror. Around her waist was the clamped claw of Löwschock, followed by his monstrous arm, then the rest of the beast. He stood on the small stage at the edge of the water, beneath the open portal. He held the Brunnen high over his head, nearly touching her against the ceiling of the cave. He squeezed his claw shut, cutting the Brunnen in half. Her lower half fell into the boat, hitting against my knees. Her upper half remained in Löwschock's grasp.

He stabbed at her lifeless upper half with his other claw, puncturing and slicing her until she was not recognizable as anything that had once lived. He threw what remained of her mutilated body through the portal and raised his eyes to me.

He spoke in clear German, "Letztendlich!" (at long last).

He lunged at me as I leapt from the boat and splashed my way through the water to the edge of the lake and out of the cave. Behind me, I heard him bump into the boat. I heard his angry scream, followed by the sound of violent splashing. I ran to the stable, mounted a horse, and rode from the valley toward Hohenschwangau. Behind me, at a distance, I heard the rustling of flora and the breaking of branches. But each time I looked behind, expecting by the sounds to see the monster closing upon me, I saw nothing.

When I arrived at Hohenschwangau, I headed toward the family castle. I thought about Otto and my mother. I did not want to lead Löwschock to them. So, I turned toward Neuschwanstein Castle. I entered the courtyard and barred myself behind the gate. I rushed to the right-side gate tower and watched Löwschock drag his long tail with his powerful arms quickly in circles at the base of Jugend Mountain. He paused, looked at me, and rushed into the thick woods behind the castle. I ran to the back of the castle and looked out from the large windows that face the Alpsee and Hohenschwangau Castle. I strained my eyes as I scanned from the base of Neuschwanstein, across the thick woods, to the castle where Otto and my mother sat innocently. I saw nothing. I ran from window to window, scanning the entire area around Neuschwanstein. There was no sign of Löwschock. He hid well, and he waited for me to exit the safety of the castle.

I could not wait long. The wheels of my dethroning were in motion. Government officials came to Neuschwanstein to serve my papers of deposition and take me into custody, just as Dr. Gudden said they would. I did not give up my throne to be locked away in a Munich palace, away from all that I love, surrounded by all that I despise. I had expected to be in the Sweeter Realm, delighted by the thought of what mysterious explanations and rumors arose around my sudden disappearance. I ordered local police to send the officials away. The locals are still loyal to me. They sent the officials away empty handed. But what could I do from there? This was not what I had planned. If I tried to leave Neuschwanstein, I had government officials wanting to lock me away and Löwschock wanting to kill me. I held up in the castle, waiting for the officials to return.

I remembered my regrets for the lost Grail Blood history. I began this journal, deciding that my fate was either death or incarceration. I imangined that my destiny as the Swan Knight was to face Löwschock and either kill him or die trying. In either case, death or incarceration, I would not fulfill my duties as Swan Knight. In fact, the Swan Knighthood would likely end with me — that long, rich, and beautiful history would end with my failure. I began this journal with the hopes that it could link this Swan Knight with the next. There is no longer a beautiful, ancient teacher to perpetuate the family history. Every tradition of the Swan Knighthood survives only in this account. I devised an ingenious plan to hide it until a Swan Knight discovers it, until Grail Blood can continue what I could not finish. To that end, I employed the assistance of a Brunnen who had convalesced at Herrenchiemsee and remained near Neuschwanstein.

Two days later, the officials returned. I placed myself in God's hands. I allowed myself to be taken into custody. They rushed me into a carriage and rode toward Munich. Dr. Gudden came with them and accompanied me in the carriage. I held this journal in my lap. The Brunnen I recruited followed swiftly on foot. We stopped at Berg Castle for the night. The approach to the castle loops from behind and circles between the castle and the Würmsee. As we approached the castle, I looked out of the carriage window and saw Löwschock slip into the lake. He followed me, as I knew he would. Now he waited to follow me to Munich. He could cause so much damage there — so much death. I prayed to God that the monster would attack the caravan on the way to Munich and either kill me or be killed by the soldiers accompanying me. But if he killed me, what next? He could not return through the portal. He is locked on this side. Bavaria, perhaps the world, faces its greatest danger. There is no way to know how the armies of men would fare against the King of the Deep. I wanted to die for a purpose. Perhaps I have found it. The only way that Löwschock goes back to his world is if I lead him there. I must escape. I must either kill the beast or lead him back to the portal. I have decided to try.

It is 13 June, 1886, likely the last day of my life. This will be the last I write in this account of the Swan Knights. I have decided to face Löwschock alone. I will try to lead him back to Linderhof, but I have no horse and no carriage to which I have access. Gudden says he will not leave my side. He means well, but he has no idea of what I face and I do not wish to risk his life. If he must accompany me, he must. Frankly, I am scared and do not want to be alone. But no attendants may follow. I will not place them into my danger.

I stayed up all of last night and well into this day, furiously finishing this account. Now, I must be content with the efforts of my pen and rest myself for the fight ahead of me. The keeper of our history is dead and soon I probably will be too. It is time for me to hide this book so that it will be found someday by a Swan Knight. Otto, Luitpold, or perhaps some distant cousin will have to assume the Knighthood and protect the portal. I pray that when that hero arrives, the fight is not already lost and there is still a Swan Knight legacy to continue. After dinner, around 18:00, I will give this book to the Brunnen. I will go to the lake and confront my enemy, the enemy of everything I have always loved, the murderer of the Queen and of the dearest friend I have ever known. I have no sound reason to expect success. But I am the Swan Knight. I will fight the enemy of the Sweeter Realm, the enemy of the Grail, the enemy of the portal. God help me. God help Bavaria. God help the Sweeter Realm.

That was the end of *The Journal of Ludwig II.*

CHAPTER 29

The Line Continues

I CLOSED THE BOOK SLOWLY — very slowly, as if trying to give it one last chance to produce more words. It didn't. It sat mutely on my lap, the pages compressed between covers squeezed tightly by my clinched fists, leaving me only to digest what I had just consumed — Ludwig, Löwschock, The Ancient One, the amazing creatures, the Queen, the Wittelsbach, Elsa, Lohengrin, Parsifal, the portal, the Holy Grail. And there, tied loosely to the end of this long chain of thoughts, was my missing family. I had forgotten that I entered the grotto in a frantic search for them. The remembrance jolted me abruptly to my feet, entirely forgetting the book. I had one foot on the edge of the boat, ready to leap into the water and continue the search for my father, mother, and Karl, when I found myself flat on my butt again, still in the boat. I had fallen, but why?

As I struggled to get back to my feet, I realized that the boat was moving, off of its support legs, in the water, carrying me backward in a jerking, tugging motion. I held tightly to the side of the boat. The jerking tugs slowly smoothed into a steady draw toward the mural. Only, when I looked over my shoulder, there was no mural. The mural was gone, except for the very edges. In the center was a void. It had no color, no describable shape. It was nothingness. A sound came from this void, unlike anything I had ever heard. It was a cross between bubbles — like when you blow through a straw, into a full glass of milk — and the sound of slowly cracking glass. The nothingness did not frighten me. The sound that came from it chilled my blood.

Somewhere in the back of my head, I knew it was the portal. It was exactly where Ludwig described it. It was exactly how Ludwig described it. But it was so foreign to my own senses. And the fear of my senses was stronger at first than the understanding of my mind. My initial instinct was to fling myself into the water and leave the grotto as quickly as I could. But that instinct had no control over my body. It screamed inside of me with violent terror, but my body remained frozen as I stared at the approaching circle of nothing. I suddenly realized that the portal is opened by Grail Blood. I quickly and nervously scanned the entire cavern. My eyes came back with no explanation for the opening of the portal. I doubted them and scanned the grotto again. I was alone.

Curiosity and a sense of destiny seized all control from fear and my natural instincts of self-preservation. The intimacy I gained with my surroundings from the story I had just read calmed my fears into intruiged apprehension. By the time I was within arm's reach of the portal, the fear screaming silently inside of me had turned to resolution. This was the portal, and I opened it. I opened it with the Grail Blood that must be flowing inside of me. The thought that I had Grail Blood surged into my head. I evicted it quickly. But it forced itelf back in. Not only did the portal open when I was the only person in the grotto, it pulled me. Yes, the boat moved toward the portal. There was a physical pull. But much stronger was the spiritual pull. In fact, the drift of the boat toward the opening struggled to keep up with the yanking, clawing, pulling sense of destiny that drew my spirit to the portal.

As I felt myself pulled from the boat, lifted from my feet into the portal, I wanted to close my eyes and cover my face. But like lumber on a river, I just floated toward the portal, that piercing crackling sound getting louder and louder. It ceased with a strange snap, like a slightly muted and lower pitched crack of a whip — then silence and darkness. The silence gave way to a slow return to sound, the normal sounds of breeze through trees. My eyes, having never closed, began to perceive light and shapes. I began to smell the air. All of these senses came together, from nothing to normal in a few seconds, like an old television, warming up and slowly revealing the picture.

What a beautiful picture it was. There was no grotto. I was outdoors, sitting on the ground, inclined by my arms, which were posted behind me. The land and the hills, as far as I could see, were identical to those surrounding Linderhof. Only the trees were different. There was nothing peculiar about the trees, except that they were a different breed of tree. I am no botanist, but they looked more tropical, with large, thick, and wide leaves. The air was warmer and more humid. The air felt thicker, almost like I could climb it, but it did not weigh on me. The ground beneath me was densely grassed. The blades were broader than any grass I had ever seen.

There were holes in the ground, hundreds of apple-sized holes, strewn haphazardly, without pattern, as far as I could see. What is a hole, if not a mystery? I was simultaneously charmed and frightened by what they might be, and what might be inside of them. There was no gurgling, crackling void, and no portal to walk through. I marched a long zig-zagging pattern of steps, being sure to have stepped on every inch of ground, trying to trigger an opening of the portal. I did not want to immediately leave this place. I just wanted the option. I began walking the area around me, trying to reopen the portal.

After covering a large area, in an ever increasing radius, I was slapped with the sensation of being trapped. I could not trigger the portal to open. Was there more to it — something I failed to learn from the rapid scribblings of Ludwig, or was Ludwig right? Is the portal unopenable from this side? Next, I was consumed by a sudden wave of gratitude that I had read the book, and had not been pulled through without any preface to the experience. How confusing and terrifying that would have been. I thought that perhaps someone might know how I can open the portal, if only I could find someone. The idea of encountering anything or anyone shot ice down my spine, but it quickly turned to wonder. My thoughts went from a fear of the horrible monsters of the Deep to a strong desire to see the wonderful creatures of the Land and Shallow Waters, those creatures who felt like family to me, from the narrative left to me by Ludwig. Gratitude to fear to curiosity, my mind took the full trip in the briefest of moments. All of the things I had just read about stood perhaps just out of my sight. My mind started growling with hunger for answers, to see, touch, and hear what I had just read — the touch of a Brunnen, the spiritual connection with a Unicorn's horn, the song of an Eulesänger. My yearning to have those things overcame my terror of Löwschock's monsters.

I thought, "Ludwig died more than a century ago. God knows what has happened since. Who won the war?

Is it still being fought? Are any of the sweet creatures still alive?"

My memory began to franticly reach for details of the journal, to root them to my poor eyes, which were darting in all directions, too fast to make much sense of anything they perceived. Just as I collected myself enough to wish I still held the journal, I squeezed my left fingertips against the book. I looked down to my hand laying flatly at my side, and saw there, still clinging to my palm, the journal, as if my hand had secretly anticipated my needs and took it upon itself to bring the book with it through the portal. I immediately squeezed it against my chest with both hands, pushing it forcefully against me, as if trying to place it inside of me.

Once I felt that the journal was securely in my possession, my eyes, which had been defensively scouting the area, returned to a mode of surveying and exploring. They became captivated by the swirling off of the ground of some fallen leaves. As I watched the leaves swish and stir in random patterns across the ground, into the air, and back across the ground, I was vividly recalled back to seeing Ludwig's lips move on the portrait in my classroom. I had a brief but deep reflection over Birgit. It was startled from my mental grip by a rustling sound. Perhaps I would have remembered Rudolf's map, still wedged tightly against the binding in the front of the book, if not for the disruption of the sound. It came in concert from all sides of me, accompanied by a soft and distant whistling. Except for the lingering minuet of the few twirling leaves, there was a visual stillness to the entire area that was eerily incongruent with the rustling and whistling I was hearing.

My left brain, unable to make any sense of the incongruences, yielded navigation of my mental faculties to my imagination, which seized the helm without hesitation and sent me several rapid steps forward before I realized I was moving. Even the mysterious holes in the ground became less ominous and more curious. I strode over them without fear, eagerly inviting their mysteries to approach. As I continued to walk forward, I gradually picked up my pace. At first, I walked in search of something, of anything. By the time I reached my top speed, I was walking for the sake of walking, no longer looking around me, no longer scanning the scenery. I kept a consistent cadence in a march without a purpose. My mind *and* my body were very loosely in my grip.

I began to question myself. What was I doing? Where was I going? Why such a fast and determined march to nowhere in particular? The forest got thicker and darker, though the sun was still high in the sky. I continued the line of questions to myself, as if interrogating a stranger whose thoughts were unknown to me, until the questions evaporated at the sight of a clearing in the woods at the banks of a lake. The lake was large. I could barely see the dim outline of trees on the far side.

I spoke aloud, but under my breath, "Is this *the* lake? The Queen's lake? Löwschock's lake?"

I suddenly remembered the map. I opened the book and pulled the map from within, unfolded it, and rotated it ninety degrees, several times, until the map must have made five or six complete rotations. I could not get my bearings. I could not tell where on the shore of the great lake I stood. The portal point was not marked on the map. I have since amended it. Unable to determine where on the map I stood, I randomly picked a point on the old parchment and declared it my location. From there, I plotted a course to the Zweigwesen homeland and began walking. I could not have given a good reason for determining my location on the map. Yet, within a few steps, I was certain I was walking to the Zweigwesens. Between the water and the edge of the thick woods was a strip of sand no more than six feet wide. I walked along it, feeling equal apprehension toward both sides of me. My mind drifted uncontrollably from meticulous focus on each step to imagining Conrad Gessner setting his sketch book against a tree and walking into the Shallow Waters — between painstaking evaluations of each sound my ears perceived and visualizing Tannhäuser wandering through the woods to my right, crying, "She is gone. I have lost her."

I walked along the sand, with the water to my left and the woods to my right, trying to keep an identical distance between the water and the woods. My eyes volleyed back and forth in some strange mixture of fearful anticipation and alluring curiosity. My thoughts projected far from the input of my physical senses, only to snap back abruptly. I glanced to my left and was suddenly captured by the beauty of the water and surrounding hills. I turned to face the lake, entirely forgetting the forest behind me, caring nothing for the fear *or* the curiosity it had elicited. I stood, staring out over the lake, imagining what creatures live beneath the surface.

"Is this the lake of the Queen?" I asked myself again. "Are the Deeper Waters below?"

As I stared out onto the water, I thought about Gessner being dragged toward the Deep. An intense chill encased me, as if I was suddenly embedded in ice, as I allowed thought of The Ancient One to enter my head.

Perhaps I stood where the Scherier stood and watched Löwschock pull the Swan Knights' teacher into the water. A wave of debilitating loss swept over me, not for my parents, or even for the life I knew, but for The Ancient One, for the creatures who adored him, for Ludwig. My imagination wandered to a frightening place. In my thoughts, I saw the water get darker as it went deeper. I saw a clear distinction as the Shallow Waters gave way to the Deeper Waters. I saw violent and angry creatures slashing about, fighting, killing, and asking for me by name. I imagined one large creature, darker, stronger, and angrier than the rest. He turned to me and caught my eyes directly. I was awakened from this wretched fantasy by the pulse of chills those eyes sent down my body.

Snapped back to the moment by fear, I quickly scanned the area. Just as I determined that nothing had changed, I heard the eerie whistling again, only much louder than before. I instinctively jumped behind a tree, hitting my heel on something and knocking it over with a crashing, clanging sound. I turned and caught a glimpse of shining, black metal poking out from a pile of leaves, twigs, and dirt. I cleared the debris and found there, right against me as I knelt behind the tree, a beautiful set of armor, there as if set ceremonially and reverently. The armor was small, sized and shaped for a woman. The helmet, with its long, unfolding metal feathers sloping ornately backwards, had topped the pile until I knocked it over. Mounted atop the shoulders of the breastplate were intricately designed swans, smaller than my hands. Each strand of each feather of the swans was set to perfection.

I recognized this armor immediately by its description in Ludwig's book. It was Elsa's armor, the very armor that The Ancient One brought into the portal so that Elsa would retire and bequeath her responsibilities to Bechtold, her son — the armor forged by Lohengrin. I hesitatingly and gingerly placed the helmet on my head, with a full understanding of who had worn it. I could not help it. My actions were controlled by the profound homage I paid to the artifacts before me. I stood up, tall and proud with the helmet on my head. Involuntarily, as if in a trance, I put on the rest of the armor. A profound sense of well-being overcame me, like nothing I had ever felt before. It was overcome suddenly by a lowly sense of shame. I dropped my head, cursing my vanity in defiling such sacred items.

But before I could take off a single accoutrement, I reminded myself, "*I* found Ludwig's hidden book. *I* opened the portal."

As I thought the words, the armor seemed to embrace me. I felt a sense of invitation, bolstered by a swell of confidence. I knew that the gift of the Scheriers to the infant Elsa was working its magic on me.

Then, in bold defiance of my earlier shame and timidity, I spoke aloud, "I am a child of Parsifal and Lohengrin, a daughter of Elsa. I am a cousin of my beloved Ludwig. I did not find this armor. It found me."

Only then did I allow myself to cherish the reality. My head was embraced by the very helmet that was worn by the greatest Swan Knight, so very long ago. The hands of Lohengrin sculpted the armor now cradling my body.

Then I shouted, "I am a Swan Knight!"

I could have sworn that I heard my words crash against the nearby trees, creating a swishing sound, then repeat back to me in the faintest and softest echo. This was followed by a low creaking sound and a rustle from within the woods. Startled, I backed away from the trees until my heels sank into the water of the lake behind me. Much more afraid of the lake than of anything coming out of the woods, I stood my ground. I ran my hands across the breastplate, from top to bottom, reminding myself of my recent proclamation and stiffening my posture with pride and resolve.

Five little creatures, not quite knee high to me, appeared out of the woods, as if they had been invisible until they broke the threshold of the trees, then appearing in clear, plain sight just a few feet in front of me. They had oversized, human looking feet, not much smaller than mine. Their bodies were stout and round, the size and shape of a large pineapple. They were covered from chin to foot with short, round, green feathers that looked more like scales. Behind them, they dragged a long, hard, grey tail that looked like it was made of bone. The feathers of their bodies blended seamlessly into the flesh of their bald heads. Their faces were of a slightly lighter green. Other than the fact that they had no noses or eyebrows, their faces appeared very human. Deep wrinkles sat above their eyes, allowing vivid facial expressions. They were like nothing detailed in Ludwig's book.

As they stood side-by-side facing me, I thought, "Perhaps this is one of the nomadic breeds."

One of them took an additional step ahead of the others and said to me in a voice astonishingly low for a being that size, in perfect but rather formal and antiquated German, "Madam, you have finally come."

"Tell us!" the creature said, "What happened to the King?"

At this, the others joined in, all with vastly different vocal ranges, creating a symphonic and harmonious concert, demanding, "What happened to the King? What happened to Ludwig?"

I told them about the book, showing it to them but not handing it over. I read to them excerpts from the last part, explaining Ludwig's plan to kill the monster or lead him back to the portal. I explained that Ludwig's body was found in Lake Starnberg, alongside his doctor's. Their confused looks reminded me that they would know the lake as "Würmsee". I told them that human history had no explanation for Ludwig's death, that the truth is only found between the covers of Ludwig's book, which remained hidden until I discovered it. They wept as I read more, growing louder with each word from the journal, and sounding even more musical, more beautiful in concerted sobs than they did when they all spoke together. The leader took another step ahead of the others and was standing directly in front of me, forcing me to remove the helmet in order to angle my head downward to him.

He asked me, "What is your name?"

"Verena," I told him.

He clicked his giant heels together, prompting the others to stiffen their postures, and he announced in a formal tone, "We put our lives in your hands, Verena, Queen of the Land and Shallow Waters."

The creatures all sat down with their large feet in front of them. They bent forward in unison until their faces nearly touched the ground. My attention was drawn from them when the trees in front of me all bent slightly downward, with a creaking noise that sounded painful. I looked at the trees for a moment, then turned my attention back to the creatures, who had not moved. I did not know what to say. My modesty wanted to denounce the honor, but my reason quickly compiled a list of what I knew to be true. Elsa's armor fit me like an old pair of jeans. Ludwig spoke to me through a copy of a photograph, all the way in Centennial, Colorado. He ordered me to the grotto. I found the book that his Brunnen must have placed there as I ran into the grotto. I opened the portal and came to them. Perhaps I *had* rightfully inherited this title from Ludwig. At any rate, I was prepared to help the dear creatures in any way I could, and under any title they wished to give me. I reached my hand downward toward them. They all rose to their feet and embraced my legs, humming in dulcet harmonies a tune that filled me with hope.

I thought about my family, Birgit, Herr Fischer, and I said silently to myself, "If I must lose them, if I must give up everything, let it be for a good cause. If this is my destiny, may I make the most of it."

GLOSSARY

Warning: Plot points revealed in definitions

Aachen, Germany [a: x ə n] – A city near the French border, between Luxembourg and Düsseldorf, Germany. It is where Emperor Friedrich II held his re-crowning as King of Germany. Duke Ludwig I of Bavaria, Swan Knight, gave an impassioned speech at the re-crowning. Afterward, Friedrich asked him to lead the Imperial Forces in the Fifth Crusade.

Achima [a x ı m a] – A Unicorn and Queen of the Land of the Sweeter Realm, before the Land and the Shallow Waters united.

Adolf of Wittelsbach, Count Palatine – Swan Knight and ruler of Einigkeitstadt during the Schism. He is the second son of Duke Rudolf I, the Rightful Swan Knight and Mechtild of Nassau. He married Irmengard of Öttingen, one of the most beloved and respected Swan Knight's spouses.

Adolf & Friedrich – Twin sons of Rightful Swan Knight Adolf and his wife Irmengard. They were killed as young children in the Battle of Einigkeitstadt.

Agnes of Loon – Swan Knight's wife who married Otto I. She is the mother of Heilika, Agnes, Richardis, and Ludwig I, Duke of Bavaria. Agnes became a countess when she married Otto, but became a duchess when Otto received the Duchy of Bavaria.

Agnes of the Palatinate on the Rhine – Swan Knight's wife who married Duke Otto II. The two enjoyed the closest, most tenderly romantic Swan Knight marriage since the first generations of Swan Knights. Agnes grew particularly close to Brunhilde, Tannhäuser's daughter, assuming a maternal role in her upbringing in the absence of her father.

Agnes of Wittelsbach – Swan Knight and third child of Duke Otto I. She came to the valley as Second-in-Training under her sister Heilika when her brother Otto died. When Heilika left for marriage, Agnes became the youngest Swan Knight ever. She married at sixteen years old to Count Henry of Plain. Count Henry died two years later, leaving Agnes with his responsibilities and forbidding her regular visits to the valley.

Agnes of Wittelsbach, daughter of Duke Ludwig II – She was the daughter of the Duke's third wife, Matilda of Hapsburg. She married Heinrich of Hesse, passing the position of Second-in-Training to her youngest sibling, Ludwig.

Albert IV, Duke of Bavaria – Swan Knight at Linderhof during the Schism. After years of civil war in Bavaria, Albert finally reunited the duchy under one Duke. He retired to Linderhof and became the first Duke of Bavaria in many generations to spend time near the portal. During the war, he abandoned his son Wilhelm in the Portal Valley with The Ancient One, who raised him to be a good man.

Albert V, Duke of Bavaria – The Swan Knight who sealed the schism. His mother is descendant from Duke

Rudolf I and his father from Emperor Ludwig. He is the first descendent of Rudolf I to serve as the Swan Knight in the portal valley. He exposed the portal to his friend, Conrad Gessner, who entered the Sweeter Realm and drew the attention of Löwschock.

Albert's Battle – A battle at Linderhof between Swan Knight Duke Albert V and hunters and prize seekers who had seen Gessner's book. Involved in the battle were The Ancient One, four Unicorns, six Scheriers, and seventy Zweigwesens.

Aldwin of Welf – A German noble, raised in the castle on the Alpsee. He married Hildemar, the daughter of the third Swan Knight Elsa. He is father to Ermenrich, fifth Swan Knight and framer of the Laws of Ermenrich.

Alexandra of Wittelsbach – Second-in-Training, sister of King Maximilian II of Bavaria and daughter of Swan Knight King Ludwig I. She is the very influential aunt of Swan Knight King Ludwig II.

Alpsee [a l p s e] – Lake in southern Bavaria. The old Welf castle was off of its northeastern shore. It was on that site that Maximilian II, King of Bavaria built Hohenscwangau Castle.

Amberg, Germany – A city in northeaster Bavaria where the Rightful Swan Knights maintained alliances. Adolf, son of Duke Rudolf I, sent his wife Irmengard to Amberg to safely give birth to their first child, Rupert II.

Anna of Austria – wife of Swan Knight Duke Albert V of Bavaria.

Anna of Carinthia – Swan Knight's wife. The Wife of Rightful co-Swan Knight Count Rudolf II of the Palatinate. Anna died young in an accident at Heidelberg

Castle. She and Rudolf had one child, a daughter named Anna. In accordance with the Laws of Ermenrich, Adolf's children were First and second-in-Training, so young Anna never joined the Swan Knight legacy.

Anna of Glogau – Swan Knight's wife and second wife of Duke Ludwig II. They had three children, Maria, Agnes, and Ludwig. Anna died when the children were young.

Anna of Wittelsbach – Youngest child of Rudolf I, the Rightful Swan Knight. She died suddenly as an infant, one hour before news of her father's death came.

Anna of Wittelsbach, daughter of Rudolf II & Anna of Carinthia – She was the only child of the Rightful Swan Knight, Rudolf II, but her cousins, the children of her Uncle Adolf were First and Second, so she remained ignorant of the Swan Knighthood. She married Charles IV, Holy Roman Emperor. Her political influence assisted the knighthood in ways she would never understand.

Anna of Wittelsbach, daughter of Rupert II and Beatrix of Sicily – First-in-Training in Einigkeitstadt during the Schism. She learned the languages of all creatures in the hidden city. She learned to use the Wühlenvogel holes to enter and exit the city. She married William, First Duke of Berg, passing the Swan Knight inheritance to her brother, Friedrich, who was greatly influenced by her goodness.

Augusta of Wittelsbach – Second-in-Training behind her brother, Ludwig I, King of Bavaria. She is the daughter of Swan Knight King Maximilian I.

Battle of Einigkeitstadt – An invasion of the underground city in the Black Forest by the forces of

Duke Ludwig IV of Bavaria against the children of his brother, Duke Rudolf, the Rightful Swan Knight. The invaders breached the underground city. Many creatures were killed, including the young twins of Adolf and Irmengard, Rupert and Friedrich. The battle saw the return of Brunhilde, who arrived just in time to save the line of Rudolf I.

Battle of Verona – A battle near Verona, Italy between the escort caravan of Holy Roman Emperor, Friedrich Barbarossa and an ambush of assassins. First-in-Training Otto I was in the caravan. He saved the Emperor and most of his army with his heroics. His battle-axe and flaming red hair became famous because of the battle. The Emperor eventually rewarded Otto with the Duchy of Bavaria.

Bavaria – A state within Germany. It was a duchy during the Holy Roman Empire and a kingdom when the empire dissolved.

Beatrix of Jülich-Berg [b ə a t r ɪ k oː f j ʏ l ɪ ç b ɛ r k] – Swan Knight's wife. The wife of Rightful Swan Knight Rupert II Count Palatine, the son of Duke Rudolf I. Beatrix and Rupert had no children.

Beatrix of Sicily – Rightful Swan Knight's wife of Rupert II, Count Palatine and son of Adolf, grandson of Duke Rudolf I. Rupert II and Beatrix had seven children.

Bechtold [b ɛ ç t oː l t] – Forth Swan Knight and son of Elsa and Cunrad. He died without children and passed the knighthood to Ermenrich, the son of his sister Hildemar.

Berthold of Wittelsbach [b ɛ r t ɔ l t f ɔ n v ɪ t ə l s b a x] – Swan Knight's husband. He married Swan Knight

Elika of Walbeck. Their son Heinrich was the first Wittelsbach Swan Knight.

Birgit [b ɪ r g ɪ t] – Daughter of Swan Knight Elsa and her husband Cunrad. She died in the house fire that killed Elsa's parents, Swan Knight Lohengrin and his wife Nethe.

Birgit (Hope) – Verena Kessler's best friend in middle school. She took German class with Verena and bonded with her over her obsession with Bavaria and King Ludwig II.

Bishop's mitre – A pointed hat worn by a bishop.

Brunhilde [b r ʊ n h ɪ l d ə] – The daughter of Tannhäuser and his Brunnen lover, born deep in the Brunnen wilderness and raised alone with her parents until her mother died and her father abandoned her. She was adopted by the Swan Knight family and raised by The Ancient One. Among her amazing talents is the ability to jump high into the air and float weightless, and to sense the nature of human hearts. Duke Ludwig I built the castle for her, over the ruins of which King Ludwig II built Neuschwanstein Castle. (See also Valkyrie).

Brunhilde's Castle – A castle commissioned by Duke Ludwig I to be a home and hiding place for Brunhilde. Later Wittelsbach referred to it as Vorderhohenschwangau, after a second, twin castle was built behind it.

Brunnens [b r ʊ n ə n s] – Creatures of the Sweeter Realm, with tall, feminine figures, and almost clear bodies that ripple like water when they move. They have two throats through which they speak in sweet melodic tones.

Charles Theodore – Count Palatine when Swan Knight Duke Maximilian III of Bavaria died without an heir. Charles inherited the dukedom but never went into the valley. Linderhof remained without a Swan Knight until Charles died and the duchy was inherited by the Count Zweibrücken, Maximilian IV. Maximilian IV rode into the valley and was surprised by The Ancient One and the creatures who had been trapped there since the death of the last swan Knight.

Chiemsee [k i: m z e:] – The largest lake in Bavaria, located to the southeast of Munich. Upon it is a large island. It was on this island that King Ludwig II built Herrenchiemsee Palace, which served as a Zweigwesen hospital during the war with Löwschock.

Conrad of Wittelsbach, Archbishop of Mainz – Brother and Second-in-Training behind Otto I, the Redhead. He was appointed Archbishop by Emperor Friedrich Barbarossa as a reward to Conrad's brother. Conrad was the first to take a Sweeter Realm creature from the valley. He kept a Brunnen as a personal friend when he left Linderhof.

Conrad IV of Hohenstaufen, King of Germany – Son of Emperor Friedrich II, friend of Swan Knight Duke Ludwig I. He married Elizabeth, the first child of Swan Knight Duke Otto II of Bavaria. It was a marriage of duty, cementing the connection between the Hohenstaufen and the Wittlesbach.

Cunrad – Swan Knight's husband. He is the husband of Elsa and the father of Bechtold, Diterich, Hildemar, and Birgit. He built the first lodge of Linderhof.

Deep Waters – A kingdom of the Sweeter Realm consisting of the deep parts of all bodies of water. It is ruled by Löwschock, whose throne is in the deep center of the Queen's Lake. There is a tangible border between the dark, cold waters of the Deep and the bright, warm waters of the Shallow.

Diterich [d i: t ə r ɪ ç] – The second son of Elsa and Cunrad. He fell out with his parents and left the Grail valley.

Donauwörth, Germany – A town in Bavaria where the Danube River and the Wörnitz River meet. It became the seat of Upper Bavaria when Duke Ludwig II split the Duchy of Bavaria with his brother, Duke Heinrich I

Einigkeitstadt [aɪ n ɪ ç k aɪ ts t a t] – Literally "Unity City", an underground city, beneath the northern part of the Black Forest, built during the Schism by the Wühlenvogels for Rudolf I, ruled by the Rightful Swan Knights until the schism sealed with Albert V.

Elika of Walbeck [eː l iː k a   f ɔ n   v a l b ɛ k] – Swan Knight who married into the Wittelsbach family, permanently attaching the knighthood to the Wittelsbach.

Elizabeth of the Palatinate – The daughter of Rightful Swan Knight Count Philip and sister of Ludwig V, Count Palatine. Like so many younger children of a Swan Knight, she married away from the family legacy. Her daughter is Marie Jakobäa, who married Duke Wilhelm IV, sealing the Schism. Maria and Wilhelm's child Albert was descended from both Duke Rudolf I and his brother Emperor Ludwig IV.

Elisabeth of Wittelsbach – First-in-Training and first child of Swan Knight Duke Otto II and his wife Agnes. Elizabeth was raised in the valley by The Ancient One, along with her childhood companion and dearest friend, Brunhilde, the child of Tannhäuser and a Brunnen.

Elizabeth married Conrad IV of Hohenstaufen, King of Germany and later Count Meinhard II of Tirol.

Elizabeth of Wittelsbach, daughter of Adolf & Irmengard – Youngest child of Rightful Swan Knight Adolf. During the celebration of her birth, her father was killed by one of Emperor Ludwig's assassins. She grew up as Second-in-Training behind her brother Rupert II. She married and left Einigkeitstadt, but remained close to her brother and kept her skills sharp and prepared to fill her brother's shoes as the Rightful Swan Knight, were she needed.

Elsa – The greatest Swan Knight. She was the third Swan Knight, the daughter of Lohengrin and Nethe. She is the only Swan Knight to fully control the behavior of the portal with her mind. She developed telepathic communication with the Unicorns without having to make contact with the horns.

Elsa of the North – The young woman rescued from a lynch mob by Lohengrin and The Ancient One. She was Lohengrin's first wife who sent Lohengrin away by asking his name. She was banished from her community and died in the forest.

Ermenrich [ɛ r m ə n r ɪ ç] – Fifth Swan Knight, the son of Hildemar and the Welf prince Aldwin. He was the grandson of Elsa. His royal obligations and his concern over the proliferation of Grail Blood led to the Laws of Ermenrich.

Eulesängers [ɔʏ l ə s ɛ ŋ ɐ s] – Creatures of the Sweeter Realm, brown, ankle-high birds, with awkwardly large wings, a bushy tail, and a hooked beak like an owl's. They communicate in high-pitched, high-spirited whistles. They are the favorite breed of Rudolf I.

Eulesänger Eggs – Stone replicas of the eggs of the Eulesängers, gifted to Nethe at Elsa's birth, with a hole on one end. When blowing through the hole, the eggs replicate the song of the Eulesängers.

Excalibur – The famed sword of King Arthur of Camelot. Parsifal knew the sword well. He fought beside it in battle. He spoke animatedly about the sword in his discussions with The Ancient One. In their weakest and most desperate time, during the Schism, when Rudolf I, the Rightful Swan Knight had lost his dukedom and the Palatinate, and was living in Einigkeitstadt, beneath the Black Forest, The Ancient One recalled thee stories. He told them to Rudolf who embarked immediately for England to find the sword. Rudolf died in England, having never fount it.

Exodus, the – The midnight flight of more than one hundred Sweeter Realm volunteers from Linderhof to the Black Forest to live with and train the children of Rudolf, the Rightful Swan Knight.

Falkenstein, Castle [f a l k ə n ʃ t aɪ n] – Originally called Castrum Pfronten, it was the castle and home of Former First-in-Training Elizabeth, daughter of Swan Knight Duke Otto II and her second husband, Count Meinhard of Tirol.

Fifth Crusade – An attempt by the powerful Pope Innocent III to take the Holy Land. When Innocent III died, the crusade was continued by his successor, Pope Honorius III. The crusade failed and resulted in the capture and imprisonment of the crusaders. In the Egyptian prison, Swan Knight Duke Ludwig I met the Teutonic Knight and descendant of Parsifal, Tannhäuser.

First-in-Training/Second-in-Training – The oldest and second oldest children of the reigning Swan Knight, the only two children who may know of the portal and train with The Ancient One, according to the Laws of Ermenrich.

Herr Fischer – Verena's German teacher. He is a young man of German Heritage. He has a powerful passion for Germany, the German language, and the culture.

Friedrich I of Hohenstaufen, Emperor [f r i: d r ɪ ç f ɔ n h o: ə n ʃ t aʊ f ə n] – Known as Friedrich Barbarossa, Holy Roman Emperor saved at the Battle of Verona by Otto of Wittelsbach. He rewarded Otto the Duchy of Bavaria.

Friedrich II, Duke of Austria – Austrian Duke who gave shelter to Tannhäuser.

Friedrich II of Hohenstaufen – Holy Roman Emperor and King of the German, friend of Duke Ludwig I of Bavaria, Swan Knight.

Friedrich II (Friedrich the Wise), Count Palatine of the Rhine – Rightful Swan Knight and last of the direct line of Swan Knights from Rudolf I. His sister Elisabeth is the maternal grandmother of Duke Albert V, Swan Knight. Before he died, without an heir to the knighthood, he united the two Swan Knighthoods in Albert V.

Friedrich & Johann Sons of Rightful Swan Knight Rupert II and Beatrix of Sicily. They were First and Second-in-Training after the marriage of their older sister Anna, during the Schism. They died in battle before their father and neither inherited the knighthood. After their deaths, their brother Rupert III assumed the Knighthood-in-Training and eventually the knighthood.

Füssen [f y: s ə n] – Town in southern Bavaria, Germany, on the banks of the Lech River, near the Forggensee. The Romans called it Foetes, a name that evolved over time into its current name.

Gefängniswärter, Der [g ə f ɛ ŋ n ɪ s v ɛ r t ɐ] – The Jailor.

German unification – Although unification sentiments had been popular for a long time, the official unification of Germany into a political state occurred on 18 January, 1871 in the palace of Versailles in France, following the Franco-Prussian War.

Gessner, Conrad – Friend of Duke Albert V, Swan Knight. He is a biologist and naturalist. Albert V opened the portal for him and he ran through it. He published *Historia Animalium* in 1551, with sketches and descriptions of Sweeter Realm creatures.

Goethe and Schiller - Johann Wolfgang von Goethe and Johann Christoph Friedrich von Schiller were eighteenth century German poets.

Graswang Valley [g r a s v a ŋ] – A long valley in southern Bavaria. It runs near the Austrian border. Its western end in just south of the southern tip of the Portal Valley.

Gregory IX, Pope – The Pope who refused Tannhäuser's request to be reinstated into the Teutonic Order.

von Gudden, Bernhard, Doctor [b ɛ r n h a r t f ɔ n g ʊ d ə n] – Psychiatrist and friend of King Ludwig II.

Ludwig asked him to make the case for his disposition. Gudden regretfully obeyed with no idea of the King's motivations.

Gütel [g y: t ə l] – First Swan Knight spouse. She rescued Parsifal from the enchanted flowermaiden. She is the mother of Lohengrin.

Heidelberg, Germany [h aɪ d ə l b ɛ r k] – German city on the Neckar River, eas of the Rhine. Its castle is the residence of the Counts Palatine on the Rhine.

Heilika of Wittelsbach – Daughter and second child of Otto I. She served as Second-in-Training behind her older brother, Otto. When her brother and father died, she became the youngest Swan Knight to that point. She was dreamy and irresponsible. She married young and left the knighthood to her much more capable younger sister, Agnes.

Heinrich of Hesse – Husband of Agnes of Wittelsbach, daughter of Swan Knight Duke Ludwig II and sister of Rudolf I, the Rightful Swan Knight and Emperor Ludwif IV.

Heinrich of Hohenstaufen [h aɪ n r ɪ ç f ɔ n h o: ə n ʃ t aʊ f ə n] – Holy Roman Emperor and son of Emperor Friedrich Barbarossa.

Heinrich of Wittelsbach, Duke of Lower Bavaria – The third child of Swan Knight Duke Otto II. He became Second-in-Training behind his brother Ludwig when his sister Elizabeth married Conrad IV, King of Germany. When Otto II died, Heinrich and Ludwig split the Duchy of Bavaria into Upper and Lower Bavaria. They also shared the Swan Knighthood until The Ancient One finally insisted upon adhering to the Laws of Ermenrich.

Henry of Plain, Count – Noble who married Swan Knight Agnes, daughter of Otto I. He is not a Swan Knight's husband. Agnes passed the knighthood to her brother Ludwig I before her wedding. Count Henry died two years after the wedding, burdening Agnes, at only eighteen years old, with the responsibility of the Count's lands.

Hermann of Wittelsbach – First-in-Training, son of Count Otto IV and brother of Duke Otto I. He left the valley in defiance of his father, yielding the First-in-Training to his brother.

Herrenchiemsee Palace [h ɛ r ə ʃ i: m z e:] – Royal Palace on the Chiemsee, built by King Ludwig II to serve as a Zweigwesen hospital during the war with Löwschock.

Herreninsel [h ɛ r e: n ɪ n z ə l] – The island on the Chiemsee on which King Ludwig II built Herrenchiemsee Palace.

Hildemar [h ɪ l d ə m a: r] – Daughter of Swan Knight Elsa and her husband Cunrad. She married Aldwin of Welf and moved to the castle on the Alpsee, near Füssen. She is the mother of Swan Knight Ermenrich. She is the first descendant of Parsifal to marry into nobility.

Historia Animalium [h ɪ s t ɔ: r ɪə æ n ɪ m ə ɪ ɪə m] – 1551 publication by Conrad Gessner, in which he demonstrates with illustration and description many of the Sweeter Realm creatures he encountered when he entered the portal.

Hohenschwangau [h o: ə n ʃ v a ŋ aʊ] – The region surrounding the Alpsee and the original Welf castle where Hildemar lived with Aldwin. The area includes Neuschwanstein Castle.

Hohenschwangau Castle - The castle constructed by King Maximilian II over the ruins of the old Welf castle where Lohengrin first met the House of Welf. Hohenschwangau Castle was the primary country residence of Crown Prince Ludwig II and his brother Otto.

Hohenstaufen, House of [h o: ə n ʃ t aʊ f ə n] – Powerful German noble family who held the crown of the Holy Roman Empire for several generations. They were kin with the Wittelsbach and played key roles in the story of the Swan Knights.

Honorius III, Pope – Successor to Pope Innocent III. The Papacy enjoyed tremendous political and military power during his Papacy. Pope Honorius III oversaw the Fifth Crusade, where Swan Knight Duke Ludwig I and the Teutonic Knight Tannhäuser were captured and met in a prison in Egypt. Pope Honorius III negotiated the release of the prisoners.

Innocent III, Pope – Roman Catholic Pope who sided with Otto IV of Welf against Friedrich II of Hohenstaufen when the two families fought over the throne of the Holy Roman Empire. Otto sought land gains into Italy. This forced Pope Innocent III to switch his allegiance. Friedrich won the war. As repayment to the Pope for his support, Friedrich had to commit to the Pope's Fifth Crusade. Innocent III died before the crusade developed. The Fifth Crusade was continued by his successor, Pope Honorius III.

Irmengard of Öttingen [ɪ r m ə ŋ a r t o: f œ t ɪ ŋ ə n] – Swan Knight's wife of Adolf, the Rightful Swan Knight during the Schism. She had an instant connection with the Unicorns and was the first human to share in their collective connection ritual. It was often assumed that she had Grail Blood, but her husband's banishment from the Portal Valley forbade the truth from ever being known.

Johann III of Sponheim – Husband of Knight-in-Training Mathilde of Wittlesbach, daughter of Rightful Swan Knight Duke Rudolf I.

Kandake – The Queen of the Land and Shallow Waters. She followed the Unicorn Achima as Queen. She is a creature of the Shallow Waters.

Kelheim, Bavaria – The ancestral seat of the Wittelsbach dynasty. It became a hub of political power in the duchy of Bavaria when the Wittelsbach assumed the dukedom. It was abandoned as a ducal residence after Duke Ludwig I was assassinated on a bridge in Kelheim.

Klavierchens [k l a v i: r ç ə n s] – Sweeter Realm creatures, small insect-like creatures who speak in musical notes that sound like a piano. King Ludwig II's Aunt Alexandra accidentally swallowed one when she opened the portal and it flew from the Sweeter Realm into her mouth.

Knobby-headed Serpent – A creature of the Deep Waters. It has a large, knobby, scaled head. Each scale on its head is larger than a human hand. Its mouth is wide, with its lips wrapping around to nearly meet at the back of its enormous head. It has a bulky, rounded body with no arms or fins and a long, wrapping tail, which begins fat at the base of its bulky torso, and narrows as it winds and wraps, until it comes to a fine point at the tip of a crusty appendage that looks like an arrowhead. It is commanded by the King of the Deep Waters.

Königin, die [k ø: n ɪ g ɪ n] – The Queen

Land and Shallow Waters – The known region of the Sweeter Realm, excluding the Deep Waters. It is the jurisdiction of the Queen. It includes in its citizenry all breeds except for the creatures of the Deep.

Laws of Ermenrich – A set of laws set down by Ermenrich, the first Swan Knight born into royalty. The laws mandate the structure of the introduction of spouses and children to the Swan Knighthood. They were formed in response to the spreading of Grail Blood and to the secular demands of royal Swan Knights. Ermenrich was the son of Hildemar and the Welf prince Aldwin. He was the grandson of Elsa.

Linderhof [l ɪ n d ɐ h oː f] – The name of the portal valley, given by Duke Ludwig II when he was very young. He was trying to say that it was a soft and gentle courtyard compared to the palace at Landshut. The name stuck and it was called Linderhof ever since. By the swan Knight family and the Sweeter Realm creatures, it is also called the Portal Valley, the Grail Valley, Parsifal's Valley, or simply the Valley.

Linderhof Palace – The palace at Linderhof valley that King Ludwig II built where the old lodge stood. He built it so that he could rule Bavaria without leaving the portal valley.

Lohengrin [l oː ə n ŋ r ɪ n] – Second Swan Knight and only child of Parsifal and Gütel. He married Nethe and was father to Elsa, the greatest Swan Knight.

Löwschock [l œ v ʃ ɔ k]– King of the Deep Waters, a large, clawed, horned water creature with the face of a lion, muscular arms and shoulders, a scaled tail with short, knobby legs and webbed feet.

Ludmilla of Bohemia – Swan Knight's spouse, wife of Duke Ludwig I. They married for political alliance but developed an intense love over their years forced apart by war. Ludmilla oversaw the construction of Brunhilde's Castle.

Ludwig I (the Crusader), Duke of Bavaria – Swan Knight and youngest child of Swan Knight Otto I, Duke of Bavaria and his wife Agnes of Loon. Ludwig became Duke at ten years old, when his father died. His mother served as regent until Ludwig came of age. His sister Agnes yielded the Swan Knighthood to Ludwig when he grew strong enough. Ludwig served in the Fifth Crusade as Commander of Imperial Forces.

Ludwig I, King of Bavaria – Swan Knight and son of King Maximilian I, the first King of Bavaria. He is the grandfather of King Ludwig II.

Ludwig II, King of Bavaria – Swan Knight who faced Löwschock on the banks of Lake Starnberg. He was killed by Löwschock and his body was found in the lake the next day beside that of his friend and psychiatrist, Dr. Bernhard von Gudden. Ludwig constructed Castle Neuschwanstein to be a home and refuge for his friend and teacher, The Ancient One. He built Herrenchiemsee Palace to serve as a hospital for creatures wounded in the war with Löwschock. He recorded the Swan Knight history in a journal left for Verena Elizabeth Kessler, Swan Knight, to find.

Ludwig, son of Duke Ludwig II of Bavaria – First-in-Training murdered at twenty-two years old during a tournament in Nurnberg.

Ludwig, son of Duke Rudolf I of Bavaria – First-in-Training. As the Schism began, and tensions rose between Duke Rudolf and his brother Ludwig, Young Ludwig's uncle sent assassins into the valley to murder the sons of Rudolf, Ludwig and Adolf. Adolf was away with his parents and young Ludwig was alone in the valley. He was murdered in front of the open portal, trying to call creatures to his defense.

Ludwig IV, Holy Roman Emperor, Duke of Bavaria – Youngest son of Swan Knight Duke Ludwig II of Bavaria, the false Swan Knight who usurped his brother Rudolf and stole the dukedom and the Swan Knighthood. He initiated and maintained a long civil war with his brother. His assassins murdered Rudolf's sons Ludwig and Adolf. After becoming emperor, he reconciled with his nephews, Rudolf and Rupert, the surviving sons of his brother Rudolf.

Ludwig "Louis" V of Wittelsbach, Duke of Bavaria – False Swan Knight and oldest son of Emperor Ludwig IV. His sister Mathilde should have been the Swan Knight but her father doted only upon his sons.

Ludwig V, Count Palatine of the Rhine – Rightful Swan Knight and great-great-grandchild of King Rupert. He is the father of Friedrich II, Rightful Swan Knight, who befriended Duke Albert V. During the peasant uprisings, Ludwig invited the leaders to dine with him. They came to peaceful compromise, without the loss of a single drop of blood. More that a hundred thousand peasants were slaughtered across Germany in the uprisings. Albert V followed his cousins example, saving thousands of lives.

Luitpold of Wittelsbach – Son of Swan Knight King Ludwig I of Bavaria and uncle of King Ludwig II. With the deposition of Ludwig II, Luitpold ruled as Prince

Regent during the reign of King Otto I, Ludwig II's brother.

Main (river) – A river in northern Bavaria. It makes up a portion of Bavaria's northwestern border. It is a tributary or the Rhine River.

Maria of Brabant – Swan Knight's wife. She is the first wife of Duke Ludwig II. She was determined to spread the secret of the portal. To protect the Holy Grail and the Sweeter Realm, he accused her of adultery and had her put to death.

Marie Jakobäa – Daughter of Elizabeth, Count Palatine Ludwig V's sister. Maria married Duke Wilhelm IV of Bavaria, the Swan Knight at Linderhof. The marriage sealed the Schism that began when Duke Rudolf I lost his dukedom and the Swan Knghthood to his brother Ludwig IV.

Matilda of Habsburg [m a t ɪ l d a f ɔ n h a p s b ʊ r k] – Swan Knight's wife. She was the third wife of Duke Ludwig II and the mother of Duke Rudolf I and Emperor Ludwig IV. She sided with her youngest son against her oldest creating the Schism. (See also Schism, the).

Mathilde of Wittelsbach, daughter of Ludwig – The first child of Emperor Ludwig. Her father ignored her and passer off to The Ancient One to raise in the valley. The Ancient One used her Grail Blood to open the portal and commence his plan to train the children of Rudolf I in the city beneath the Black Forest.

Mathilde of Wittelsbach, daughter of Rudolf – Fifth child of Duke Rudolf I of Bavaria, the Rightful Swan Knight. She lived in Einigkeitstadt and trained as an equal with her brothers Rudolf and Rupert.

Maximiliana "Milli" Maria – Swan Knight and fifth child born to Albert V, Duke of Bavaria. She developed close relations with the Zweigwesens and worked with them on a manuscript of Zweigwesen medicines. The manuscript was acquired in 1912 by Wilfrid Voynich and is now known as the "Voynich Manuscript". With the break in the line of Swan Knights, after the death of King Ludwig II, the manuscript, written in Zweigwesen, has remained a mystery to the world.

Maximilian I, King of Bavaria – Swan Knight and first of the line of Counts Zweibrücken to assume the knighthood. He is the gained the Dukedom of Bavaria with the heirless death of Charles Theodore and the Kingdom of Bavaria with the dissolution of the Holy Roman Empire. He is the great-grandfather of Ludwig II, King of Bavaria, Swan Knight and builder of Neuschwanstein Castle.

Maximilian II, King of Bavaria – First-in-Training and son of Swan Knight, Ludwig I King of Bavaria. He died before his father and never held the knighthood. He renovated the old Welf ruins near the Alpsee, the castle of Hohenschwangau. He is the father of Ludwig II, King of Bavaria and his brother Otto I, King of Bavaria.

Maximilian III, Duke of Bavaria – Swan Knight who died without an heir, leaving the valley without a knight. His cousin Charles Theodore, Count Palatine, inherited the duchy but not the knighthood.

Mechtild of Nassau – Swan Knight's wife. She married Swan Knight Duke Rudolf I of Bavaria. She is the mother of Swan Knights Adolf, Rudolf, and Rupert. During the Schism, she was Countess Palatine and matriarch of Einigkeitstadt. She is the daughter of King Adolf of Germany.

Meinhard II of Tirol, Count – Second husband of Elizabeth of Wittelsbach, oldest child of Swan Knight Duke Otto II of Bavaria.

Minnesinger – A German poet and singer of love songs during the twelfth, thirteenth, and fourteenth centuries.

Neckar, River – Tributary of the Rhine. It runs east of the Rhine and holds Heidelberg, Germany on its banks. Heidelberg Castle is on the river, the residence of the Counts Palatine of the Rhine.

Nethe [n ɛ t ə] – Second wife of Lohengrin and mother of Elsa, the greatest Swan Knight. She died in the house fire with Lohenfrin and their grand-daughter, Birgit.

Neuschwanstein Castle [n ɔʏ ʃ v a n ʃ t aɪ n] – A castle built by King Ludwig II to be a home for The Ancient One after the Queen's murder and The Ancient One's ascension to the throne of the Land and Shallow Waters. Ludwig built the castle over the ruins of Brunhilde's castle, where The Ancient One spent some of his happiest days.

Neustadt am Main, Germany – A city on the Main River. Rightful Swan Knight Adolf, son of Duke Rudolf I, was brought there by his brothers, Rudolf and Rupert, after being shot with an arrow during the celebration of his daughter's birth. Adolf died in Neustadt.

Nomadic Belt/Der Nomadengürtel [d e: r n o: m a: d ə ŋ ʏ r t ə l] – A strip of land in the Sweeter Realm, which wraps around the Queen's Lake. It is where the Nomadic Breeds roam.

Otto I (The Redhead), Duke of Bavaria - Swan Knight, first Wittelsbach Duke of Bavaria, known as The Red-Head. He was the hero of the battle of Verona, where enemies attacked the caravan of Emperor Fredrich Barbarosa. He inherited his Grail Blood from his paternal great-great-great grandmother, Elika van Walbeck, who married Berthold of Wittelsbach and attached the Swan Knighthood to the Wittlesbach. Otto's brother was Conrad, who became the Archbishop of Mainz and later of Salzburg.

Otto II, Duke of Bavaria – Swan Knight and only child of Duke Ludwig I and Ludmilla of Bohemia. He married Agnes, daughter of Count Heinrich of the Palatinate on the Rhine. The marriage gave Otto's father, and later Otto, the electorship of the Count Palatine.

Otto IV, Count of Wittelsbach – Swan Knight and father of Otto I, Duke of Bavaria. He gave his son the famous axe that won the Battle of Verona.

Otto IV of Welf – Regional Welf noble who disputed the Hohenstaufen claim on the Holy Roman Empire. Otto won the throne in 1209, but lost it later to Friedrich of Hohenstaufen.

Ottokar I of Bohemia – Uncle of Ludmilla, wife of Duke Ludwig I, Swan Knight. He had been an enemy of Bavaria until his niece's marriage to the Bavarian Duke. The marriage secured Bavaria to the north.

Palatinate of the Rhine – An electorship of the Holy Roman Empire, governed by the Counts Palatine. Its seat of power is in Heidelberg. The Wittelsbach gained the Palatinate when Otto II married Agnes of the Palatinate of the Rhine.

Palatinate of Zweibrücken – An electorship of the Holy Roman Empire, governed by the Counts Palatine of Zweibrücken. Its seat of power is in Mainz. The Wittelsbach gained the title when Rupert II, Count Palatine of the Rhine, came to the financial rescue of the Count Zweibrücken, who had no heirs. Rupert III inherited Zweibrücken. He gave it to his son Stefan. It is from the line of Stefan that Maximilian I, King of Bavaria descended.

Parsifal [p a r z i: f a l] – The First Swan Knight and a keeper of the Holy Grail. His spilled blood created the portal after he drank from the Grail. He and his wife Gütel founded the portal valley. He was father to Lohengrin. He was the first person to enter the portal and the only one to open the portal from the Sweeter Realm and return to the portal valley. He was the first to meet The Ancient One.

Parsifal's Valley – The name The Ancient One called the portal valley, later called Linderhof. It is where Parsifal was attacked by an enchanted flowermaiden and spilled his blood to open the portal. Parsifal and Gütel built their home there.

Passau, Germany – A town in Southeastern Bavaria, on the Austrian border. The River Danube is met in Passau by the rivers Ilz and Inn. Tannhäuser spent a few weeks in Passau on his way to the court of Duke Friedrich II of Austria.

The portal – A passage into the Sweeter Realm, opened for the first time when Parsifal's Holy Grail enchanted blood fell to the earth. It opens at the approach of all with Grail Blood —all descendants of Parsifal.

Queen/King of the Land and Shallow Waters – the ruler elected by the creatures of the Sweeter Realm to rule the known region on the other side of the portal, excluding the Deep Waters. The Queen from the shallow waters, who ruled during the lives of the Swan Knights was named Kandake.

Queen's Jailor – A creature of the Shallow Waters in the Sweeter Realm. He controls the underwater cave that serves as a jail. He obeys the Queen. Conrad Gessner was held in that jail. He spent many long hours in the company of the jailor and sketched him into his book.

Queen's Weed – A weed that grows on the lake floor of the Shallow Waters, in the Queen's Lake. When eaten, it reveals love by making those who love the eater of the weed glow. The deeper and more committed the love, the brighter the glow. Different forms of love glow differently. An old, familiar love will glow softer and warmer, but no less bright. A fresh, passionate love will glow raw, in simpler hues. Only a few of the Queen's Weed grows at a time.

Rhine (river) – European river that forms borders for Germany, France, Switzerland, Austria, and Liechtenstein. It was a profitable trade route for German royalty whose lands it crossed.

Richardis of Wittelsbach [rɪçardɪs fɔn vɪtə l s b a x] – Second-in-Training behind Agnes, the daughter of Otto I. She and Agnes held the valley until their brother, Ludwig I came of age and took the Swan Knight oath. She married at thirteen, bringing Ludwig to the valley as Second.

Rightful Swan Knight – Swan Knights in the line of Rudolf I. During the schism, they governed and occupied Einigkeitstadt, an underground city beneath the Black Forest, built by the Wühlenvogels.

Rudolf I, Duke of Bavaria – Swan Knight known during the Schism as the Rightful Swan Knight. He was deposed of the knighthood and the dukedom by his younger brother, Ludwig. He maintained his other hereditary title, Count Palatine of the Rhine, until he yielded that to Ludwig. He was the first to rule Einigkeitstadt, the Wühlenvogel city beneath the Black Forest. He died in England, in a desperate search for the mythical sword Excalibur.

Rudolf II, Count Palatine – Rightful Swan Knight during the Schism, along with his brother Rupert. He is the son of Rightful Swan Knight Duke Rudolf I and Mechtild of Nassau. He inherited the knighthood from his older brother Adolf. He died without heirs and passed the knighthood to Adolf's son.

Rudolf's Map – A map of the Sweeter Realm drawn from the descriptions of his Eulesänger friends by Duke Rudolf I when he was a boy. King Ludwig II wedged it into his journal to be found by Verena.

Rupert I, Count Palatine - Rightful Swan Knight during the Schism, along with his brother Rudolf. He is the son of Rightful Swan Knight Duke Rudolf I and Mechtild of Nassau. He inherited the knighthood from his older brother Adolf. He died without heirs and passed the knighthood to Adolf's son.

Rupert II, Count Palatine – Rightful Swan Knight and son of Adolf and Irmengard.

Rupert III, King of Germany – Rightful Swan Knight during the Schism. Son of Rupert II and Beatrix of Sicily. He amended the Laws of Ermenrich to help focus the attention of the Swan Knight. He gave the Palatinate of Zweibrücken to his son, Stefan.

Scheriers [ʃ eː r iː r s] – Creatures of the Sweeter Realm, with white hair and short, flat bodies. They are social creatures who love to wrestle. After The Ancient One, they were the first breed to meet the Swan Knights. They gifted a boulder of ore from their homeland to Elsa. Lohengrin forged it into Elsa's armor.

Scherier Stone – A large, round boulder of ore that sat outside of the Sherier capital for countless centuries. Contact with it provides a magical sense of well-being. Lohengrin smelted the metal from it to make Elsa's armor.

Schism, the – The split in the Swan Knighthood after the children of Duke Ludwig II, Rudolf and Ludwig, fought over the dukedom and the knighthood. During the schism, the line of Ludwig remained in the portal valley as Swan Knights there, while the line of Rudolf maintained a simultaneous Swan Knighthood in Einigkeitstadt, a secret city beneath the Black Forest. For most of the Schism, the Rightful Swan Knights in the Black Forest held the title of Counts Palatine on the Rhine.

Schwansee [ʃ v a n z eː] – Literally "Swan Lake" is a small lake east of Füssen, Germany, near the Alpsee and Hohenschwangau.

Seligenthal Convent – A convent in Landshut, the primary ducal residence of Bavaria after the murder of Ludwig I in Kelheim. The convent is run by the nuns of the Cistercian Order. Ludmilla, Swan Knight wife of Ludwig I, died in the convent.

"Sisi" Elisabeth Amalie Eugenie – Cousin of King Ludwig II. Her casual manner and quirky mind brought Ludwig great comfort. She never knew of the portal but bore many traits of a Swan Knight. Ludwig II was engaged to her sister, Sophie, but the engagement was broken.

Sophie Charlotte Augustine – Cousin of King Ludwig II. She and Ludwig had a strained engagement while Ludwig's romanticized image of her gave way to reality. He realized that she would never make a good Swan Knight spouse, especially during his troubled reign. After several postponements, Ludwig finally cancelled the engagement.

Sophie of Wittelsbach – Forth child of Swan Knight Duke Otto II and his wife Agnes.

Spätzle [ʃ p ɛ ts l ə] – A German egg and flour noodle, served often with gravy or with a cheese sauce.

Stams Abbey – An abbey run by the monks of the Cistercian Order. It was established by Elizabeth of Wittelsbach, former First-in-Training and daughter of Swan Knight Duke Otto II. She built the abbey in Tirol, Austria after marrying Count Meinhard II of Tirol. She secretly dedicated it to prayers for the safety of the Swan Knights and the security of the Holy Grail.

Starnberg, Lake – A large lake southwest of Munich in Bavaria. King Ludwig II referred to it as Würmsee, as it was called during his lifetime. It was in Lake Starnberg that Ludwig's body was found alongside the body of Dr. Gudden, Ludwig's psychiatrist.

Stefan, Count Palatine of Zweibrücken [ts v aɪ b r ʏ k ə n] – Son of King Rupert of Germany, Rightful Swan Knight. He remained ignorant to the Swan Knight legacy. He perpetuated the Grail Blood down his line to Maximilian I, King of Bavaria and great-grandfather of King Ludwig II.

Stefan II, Duke of Bavaria – Son of Emperor Ludwig IV and brother of Duke Ludwig IV.

Swan Knights – The line of the descendants of Parsifal, knighted by The Ancient One, whose Grail enchanted blood opens the portal. They are sworn to the protection of the portal and to the service of the Queen of the Land and Shallow Waters.

Sweeter Realm – The known world on the other side of the portal. It consists of two kingdoms, the Land and Shallow Waters, ruled by the Queen, and the Deep Waters, ruled by Löwschock.

Tannhäuser [t a n h ɔʏ z ɐ] – A Teutonic Knight with Grail Blood. His name means that he comes from the house of the Lords of Tannhausen. He fought with Duke Ludwig I in the Fifth Crusade. He met Duke Ludwig in the Egyptian prison where the captured crusaders were held. He was unaware of his Grail Blood until he accidentally opened the portal.

Teutonic Knights – "The Order of Brothers of the German House of Saint Mary in Jerusalem". They were a holy Catholic military order of German knights, founded in 1190

The Ancient One – Creature of the Sweeter Realm, a giant swan, the first creature to meet Parsifal. He took the Grail from Parsifal and gave it to the Queen. He is the teacher of the Swan Knight children and the keeper of the Grail Blood history. He taught German to the Queen and the other creatures of the Land and Shallow Waters.

Topsell, Edward – An Englishman and man of the Church. He was a scientist of natural history. He published a book titled, *The History of Four-Footed Beasts and Serpents*, in 1658. The book included the

Knobby-headed Serpent that grabbed Conrad Gessner at Löwschock's command. Albert V's sketch of the creature must have made it into Topsell's hands.

Trausnitz Castle – Palace in Landshut, Bavaria. It is a royal residence of the Wittelsbach. Duke Ludwig I commissioned it in 1204 as a wedding present for Ludmilla.

Unicorns/ Die Einhörner [d i: aɪ n h œ r n ɐ] – Creatures of the Sweeter Realm, single-horned goat-like creatures, with shaggy, bearded faces, the height of a horse, but with a slightly sloping back and narrow hips. They can communicate with each other and others through a touch of their horns. For many hundreds of years, they were the primary sentries of the portal valley.

Unicorn Altar – A monument in the heart of the Unicorn capital in the Sweeter Realm. It is a tall obelisk, in the shape of the horn of the greatest hero in Unicorn history. Around it are several stones, each with a single hole facing outward from the altar. The Unicorns insert their horns into the holes to connect with each other and their ancestors. A replica was built in Einigkeitstadt, the hidden city beneath the Black Forest.

Unicorn Nectar - A thick nectar, the consistency of honey, but salty and bitter. It gives instant clarity of mind when eaten. It reveals no secrets that are not already known, but it clears away peripheral distractions from the subject at hand. The Unicorns consume it when important decisions need to be made.

Valkyrie [f a l k y: r i:] – A Norse myth that sprang from the actions of Brunhilde. She traveled north when she left her castle at Hohenschwangau. She descended upon battles, felt the character of the human hearts involved, and killed the soldiers with cruel and evil hearts, after which she disappeared high into the air. Her soft, pale skin reflected the sunlight like armor. Out of the direct sunlight, her bare skin appeared as soft and delicate as a Brunnen's. (See also Brunhilde).

Venus Grotto – An artificial cave built by King Ludwig II to hide and protect the portal. A mural depicting Tannhäuser and the goddess Venus sits precisely on the portal point. The grotto holds an artificial lake and a boat built to replicate Lohengrin's boat pulled by The Ancient One. The grotto was one of the first places in Bavaria to be lit with electric lights and powered by an electric generator.

Veronika of Welf [f ɛ r oː n ɪ k a   f ɔ n   v ɛ l f] – Swan Knight and great-granddaughter of Swan Knight Ermenrich. She had an adventurous youth before taking the Swan Knight oath. It was from her adventures that the legend of Tristan and Isolde was born.

Vogelkrötes [f oː g ɛ l k r øː t ə s] – Creatures of the Sweeter Realm, literally Bird Toad. They live in the Shallow Waters. They are the first wet creatures encountered by Conrad Gessner.

Vorderhohenschwangau [f ɔ r d ɐ h oː ə n ʃ v a ŋ aʊ] – The castle commissioned by Duke Ludwig I to be the home of Brunhilde. It was over the ruins of this castle and its twin, **Hinterhohenschwangau** (h ɪ n t ɐ h oː ə n ʃ v a ŋ aʊ), that King Ludwig II built Neuschwanstein Castle.

Wagner, Richard – Opera composer and friend of King Ludwig II. His operas *Lohengrin* and *Tannhäuser* reminded Ludwig of his connection to the Swan Knighthood and inspired the king to patronize Wagner, pulling the composer out of debt and lavishing him with riches far beyond his station. Wagner's expensive relationship with the king frustrated Bavarians, eventually resulting in his banishment.

Wiener schnitzel [v iː n ɐ   ʃ n ɪ ts ə l] – A thinly pounded, breaded and fried cutlet, usually of veal, pork, or chicken.

Wilhelm IV, Duke of Bavaria – Swan Knight at Linderhof during the Schism. His father abandoned him in the valley during a civil war with his cousin over the duchy of Bavaria. Wilhelm was the first from the line of Emperor Ludwig to be raised full-time under the schooling of The Ancient One. He maintained a long-running written correspondence with the Queen of the Land and Shallow Waters. He married Marie Jakobäa, the granddaughter of Count Palatine Philip, a descendant of Rudolf I. With the marriage, the Schism was sealed. Their children were descended from both sides of the Schism.

Wilhelm V, Duke of Bavaria – First-in-Training. He yielded his position as First to his much more capable sister, Maximiliana "Milli" Maria. Maria had no children and passed the knighthood upon her death to Wilhelm's children.

"Wir reisen zusammen" [v iː r   r aɪ z ə n   ts uː z a m ə n] – German for "We are traveling together". Birgit planned to shout the phrase to Verena while revealing her signed permission form for the eighth-grade trip to Germany.

Wühlenvogels [v yː l ə n f oː g ə l s] – Sweeter Realm creatures. They are birds, with long necks and the snouts of wolves and jaws just as powerful, teeth just as sharp. They stand just shorter than The Ancient One.

They have two hard, curled horns on their heads, which they use, with the powerful swing of their long necks, to smash the skulls of their enemies. They have large, clawed feet, which they use to burrow into the homes and hideaways they make underground. They have long powerful tails that can wrap and squeeze, with amazing dexterity and strength, whatever they choose to grab. They live in large underground cities, which they burrow with their collective efforts in a few days' time. They are hunters, predators. They built Einigkeitstadt, the city beneath the Black Forest.

Würmsee [v y r m z e:] – Now called Lake Starnberg, it is a lake southwest of Munich, between Munich and Linderhof. The Wittlesbach retreat, Berg Castle, is on the northeast coast. It was in this lake that King Ludwig II's body was found alongside that of his friend and psychiatrist, Dr. Gudden.

Zweigwesens [ts v aɪ g v e: z ə n s] – Creatures of the Sweeter Realm, branch-thin, chest-high, covered from head to toe in soft, almost glowing, coarse, brownish-orange hair. Their hair looks like tree bark on their thin bodies. They have the ability to seamlessly connect to one another and form balances in intricate geometric shapes. When many connect together, they can form into the shape of a tree that nobody could distinguish from a real tree.

The Zweigwesen Medical Manuscript – A book of Zweigwesen medicinal plants and recipes, written collaboratively with Swan Knight Maximiliana "Milli" Maria, daughter of Albert V. The plants are all native to the Sweeter Realm. The book is written in Zweigwesen. It has been passed through many owners throughout the centuries. The Swan Knights are the only humans who know the origin language. It has baffled linguists since it left the hands of the Swan Knights. The manuscript was acquired in 1912 by Wilfrid Voynich and is now known as the "Voynich Manuscript". The manuscript has illustrations and descriptions, with specific details, from the collection and storage of the plants to the preparing of the ingredients to the application and dosage of the medicines.